BEYOND ALL SENSE AND REASON

MIKE DICCICCO

MI-BET Press

Warrington, Pennsylvania

DEDICATION

To my incredibly supportive wife, Fran Jacob Diccicco, our daughter, Mariliz, and our son, Michael. You are my favorite people on the planet.

ACKNOWLEDGMENTS

First of all, enormous thanks to my first three beta readers: Fran Jacob Diccicco, Eileen Jacob, and Heather Luchak Kunkel. Without your thoughtful comments, questions and encouragement, *Beyond All Sense and Reason* might never have made it across the finish line.

Thanks to my brother Bob for being my fourth beta reader. The two of us—and eight other Diccicco kids—lived through historic days in Birmingham together.

Thanks to my fifth and sixth beta readers, Zenita Henderson and Sam Rumore, for saying yes to my late-in-the-game request and giving my story a read. Plus, a big thank you to Therese Jacob Gallagher for fighting through some tedious proofreading work and catching stuff I'd missed.

Thanks as well to Jennifer Sherlock of Jenna Communications for some valuable PR guidance and support.

A huge thank you to my editor (and author of several novels), Jon McGoran. Your insights and guidance improved the telling of this story immensely.

A special thank you to my excellent page designer, Adam Turner of Cherrymoon Media.

Particular and personal thanks to my former business partner and former creative director, Sean Donahue, for your exceptional cover design.

RECOGNITION

Throughout the writing of this novel, I drew inspiration and motivation from the true experiences and recollections published on a one-of-a-kind website, *kidsinbirmingham1963.org*. The website is one of several initiatives by a nonprofit organization of the same name, made up of many individuals, both black and white, who witnessed The Year in Birmingham. Their purpose is to foster dialogue on the truths about race in the United States as an essential first step toward racial reconciliation—in Birmingham, throughout the USA, and globally.

AUTHOR'S NOTE

For purposes of both historical accuracy and dramatic tension, there are four different words used in the novel to reference African Americans. Mickey and his family typically call all African Americans "colored people" or, formally, Negroes. This was the polite vernacular of the South during the 60s. In a few cases, an individual may be referred to as "black." A number of characters, including a principal antagonist, who is also a member of the Ku Klux Klan, call all African Americans "niggers." Sadly, the use of that abhorrent term was ubiquitous throughout the South of the 60s and later; it is used only where necessary in this novel.

CHAPTER 1
AUGUST 24, 2000

Who in the world would argue with the idea that Love is the most powerful of all human emotions? What have our great thinkers and writers told us for centuries? Love is always the answer. Love will set you free. All you need is Love. Love conquers all. Where there is Love, there is life. And the greatest of these is Love.

I was sixteen years old when I concluded that our great thinkers and writers had it all wrong.

From my vantage point, and I think it's a pretty solid one, Hate makes Love look like the skinny guy on the beach that gets sand kicked all over him. Let's face it: People fall in and out of love all the time. But hate—now that rascal has staying power. Once hate gets his claws into you, there is no dislodging. Hate plops himself down, takes off his boots, puts his smelly feet up on the ottoman, and settles in for infinity and a day.

As if to underscore my point, the hate in me starts waking up and stretching as I drag my overnight bag with the broken wheel up the jetway and into the airport terminal. I'm not surprised by this—but I am determined to push my hate and Jessup Rawlings and the dark events of August 1964 way down deep and out of my brain, for as long as I can anyway. I focus instead on my immediate surroundings: the large banner that reads Welcome to Birmingham, the Magic City; the familiar accents of Southern voices all around me; the unmistakable aroma of sausage gravy and biscuits that floats toward me from the food court.

It's been thirty-six years since I was last here in my hometown, the place they once called The Most Segregated City in America. Back in the 50s and early 60s, the state of Alabama took its segregation seriously, so much so that even water fountains were typically located in pairs, one for each race. As young kids who loved to think we were rebels, my twin sister Marti and I often drank from the fountain with the sign reading Colored, in full view of others, daring Fate or the Birmingham police to catch and punish us. It never happened, though we did receive a fair number of disapproving looks from white adults who witnessed our transgression.

Once, in the WT Grant store near our home in Roebuck, Marti noticed that the signs on the water fountains were attached with magnets. On an impulse that was so typical of her, she glanced around quickly and then switched the signs, forcing white folks to unknowingly drink from the water reserved for African Americans. I often wondered how long it took store management to discover the switch. Or if they ever did.

Walking through the terminal, and feeling a little cocky about how well I was keeping hate at bay, I wonder why I'd never come back to Birmingham sooner than this trip. A good friend from high school still lives here, in the western part of the city, and we'd stayed in touch to some extent, infrequent telephone conversations that always ended with suggestions for getting together. "Y'all come on down and I'll get us tickets for a football game, Roll Tide!" But I never did.

Turning down the corridor toward ground transportation, I open myself up to a ragtag assortment of memories—mostly good ones—from the years living here with my eight brothers and sisters. I recall the sensation of an ice-cold Mission grape soda bubbling on my tongue—Mission was the soda brand that my younger brother Tom and I used to buy for ten cents from the corner grocer at Rugby and 80th Street, and drink in our private "clubhouse," a tiny open area under a set of outdoor cement stairs that led to the second floor of our house on 80th Place. I also remember smoking cigarettes there with Tom, and then trying to get rid of the taste of the smoke by picking honeysuckle flowers from bushes that grew wild on the side yard. If you pulled the stamen ever so slowly from the flower, you could capture a single, sweet drop of nectar. Our mother, Mary McQuade, taught all nine of her kids the proper technique for honeysuckle consumption. She was good at stuff like that.

Would Mary McQuade have approved of this sudden, somewhat impulsive, visit to the city where she'd raised me? Maybe, maybe not. In a sense, I've come 1200 miles to accomplish the simplest of tasks, one that will consume less than 15 minutes of my four days in town. Is it really that important to honor a promise made and kept, decades after it has ceased to matter to anyone, except me, my twin sister, and Detective Martino?

I have the letter that drew me here, tucked safely among my travel documents. I've read it multiple times. I could burn it tonight and no one would miss its existence. No one would care. Yet, here I am.

The thing is: Everyone knows that you can't change the past. You can't undo what has been done. But maybe, sometimes, you can look yesterday right in the eye and tell it, "I am done with you. You can't hurt me anymore."

I have four days to see if I can pull that off.

CHAPTER 2
JULY 27, 1963

"Mickey—you are not gonna believe what I just discovered in the woods. You gotta come with me. C'mon, c'mon – let's go!"

My younger brother Tom lived in a state of over-excitement about all kinds of things, and I did not react positively to today's enthusiasm.

"I'm reading," I replied. "Go away."

"No—" he said, "you gotta come with me now. I just discovered a secret town. Right behind our house. Ten minutes through the woods. A secret town."

Tom grabbed the book I was holding and yanked. It flew from my hands into a pile of clothes that Mom had given me two days before, scattering socks one way and t-shirts another.

"What the heck, Tom!" I was annoyed, but I was also a little bit curious.

A secret town was not quite the same thing as an anthill . . . an almost new wiffle ball . . . a tree with branches low enough to swing up into—all of which were discoveries that Tom had, in the recent past, announced with high levels of excitement.

"This better be good," I said as I rolled out of my bed and searched underneath it for my sneakers.

It was a Saturday afternoon, and it was Free Time, my mother's official designation for periods free from chores or homework. We did not get nearly as much Free Time as we thought we deserved, especially since we'd moved from Birmingham's East Lake section into our "new" house in Roebuck in mid-June. After six weeks, Mom was still finding "getting situated" jobs for us big kids—Sheila, David, Marti, Tom and me—and her list seemed endless, though many times our tasks were simply to keep an eye on the little kids: Ricky, Brenda, Bobby and the baby, Carrie Ann.

Of course, Tom and I often created additional, unofficial Free Time for ourselves by simply putting off the chores or homework that we were supposed to be doing, and doing other things instead, relying on the fact that it was impossible for Mom to closely manage all nine of her kids.

The good thing about official Free Time was that we were not forced to sneak out of the house. So Tom and I walked openly through the kitchen, past Carrie Ann playing on the floor, past the cat napping on a dishtowel, past our mother opening a large can of crushed tomatoes to start her spaghetti sauce. Saturday typically meant spaghetti with a meat sauce, a couple pounds of ground beef plus leftovers (if we had any) from the previous week's dinners. Leftovers were a rarity: the McQuades were not a family that ended meals with food still on our plates.

"We're going exploring in the woods, Mom," said Tom.

She did not look up but responded quickly to this news. "Don't go too far. Your father will be home in a couple of hours. Watch out for poison ivy. Watch out for snakes. Don't get your feet wet. Don't get filthy."

Many of Mom's warnings were issued semi-automatically, though usually well-tailored to the circumstances. They were always issued with the expectation that some of her cautions would sink in. And even if they did not, Mom clearly believed it was part of her job to deliver them as often as possible to whomever was in hearing distance.

If I'd told her that I was going down the street to play in a house fire, I suspect she might have peppered me with, "Don't get burned. Keep low. Watch for flare-ups. Don't get filthy." Getting filthy was a sin that Tom and I frequently had trouble with.

At this point, however, our only thought was to keep on the move so that she did not have a chance to come up with a spur-of-the-moment task that would interrupt Free Time and our trip to the woods.

"We'll be careful, Mom," Tom and I yelled in unison as the screen door slammed behind us.

* * * * *

The woods behind our house were real woods, not just a little stand of trees that you often find in developments with the sole purpose of separating one backyard from another. We had no idea how far our woods stretched because we'd not had time for extended exploring since we'd moved in.

Tom plunged ahead, trampling through thick undergrowth. I followed. We maintained a pretty good pace for five or six minutes, and then came upon a rise in the topography. He turned toward me, "Up here. Wait 'til you see this." He clambered up the slope with me close behind. We reached a little crest and looked down on exactly what Tom had promised me . . . a secret town.

Scattered across a landscape of gently rolling hills, Tom and I gazed at maybe fifteen very small houses. The way they were placed, in relation to one another, was picturesque—nicely balanced against the surrounding fields and an occasional tree. At first glance, one might have been tempted to call it a storybook village.

However, storybook villages, at least in my storybooks, always had nice beds of flowers surrounding the cottages, and neatly thatched roofs, and freshly painted doors of bright blue, or red, or green. Also, ever since I'd read The Hobbit in 7th grade, I tended to imagine them populated by cute little dwarf-like people with beards and bare feet.

Here, there were no flower beds, and no freshly painted doors. Some of the roofs were made of tin. If there was a little fence, it was broken. If there was a porch, it was missing a railing. Windows were dirty and some had broken glass covered by cardboard.

We were looking at a shanty town.

There were only a few people in evidence. A couple of kids, maybe eight or nine years old, playing with a hula hoop in front of one of the houses. An old man sitting in a rocker on a porch. A younger man walking beside a mule up the "main street" of the town, which was nothing more than a dirt road leading crookedly between the houses, working its way toward who knows where. All the people were colored.

"It's a secret nigger town," Tom said.

I reacted to that observation by swatting him hard on the back of his head and knocking his baseball cap off.

"Hey," he yelled. "What's that for?"

"You know what that was for," I answered. "Don't say that word. We don't call them niggers. They're colored people."

"Mr. Rawlings calls them niggers. Right in our house, he did," Tom said. Mr. Rawlings was our new neighbor from across the street. We'd met him and the rest of the Rawlings family the day after we'd moved in.

"What, that guy is going to be your role model?" I asked him. None of the McQuades was impressed with Jessup Rawlings. "Don't be an idiot."

"I'm not an idiot. You're an idiot."

Ignoring Tom's comeback, I asked him straight out: "Did you ever hear Dad call them niggers? Or Mom? Ever?"

"No," Tom admitted, with the age-old reluctance of a younger brother conceding to his older sibling.

"Mr. Rawlings has probably been calling them niggers all his life," I said. "He doesn't even think about it—it's just habit. For some reason, he just hates colored people and . . ."

"Mrs. Rawlings calls them nigras," Tom interrupted. "What about that? Nigras?"

"I don't know about that," I said. "Nigras is not as bad as niggers— but it sounds to me like someone who wants to say niggers but maybe doesn't think they should. So it's probably not as bad but it's not good."

"We should just call them colored people," I said, "or Negroes. That's what we've been taught."

"Okay," said Tom. "It's a secret Negroes town. Let's go explore."

* * * * *

Based on my internal clock, we still had a comfortable amount of time before we needed to be home. You always wanted to be in the house before Dad arrived, so that you could gauge his mood coming in the door, and act accordingly. "Act accordingly" might mean anything from trying to stay out of sight to being noticeably helpful to Mom by setting the table, or holding Carrie Ann, or sweeping the floor. My father was not a mean person, but he could be grumpy, especially, according to Mom, when he hadn't eaten for a while.

Tom and I walked slowly down the hill toward the shanty town, watchful for any signs that we were noticed by anyone, stepping way around one house so that we did not cross what seemed to be its back yard. The kids with the hula hoop had disappeared, as had the man with the mule. The older man on the porch may have been looking at us, or he may have been napping.

We reached the dirt road, dusty from lack of rain, and turned our heads in both directions. To the right, the road twisted and curved and disappeared up a hill. Too far to explore today. To the left, the road went mostly straight for a quarter mile or so, ending at a lane that led to a house that was clearly different from the rest. We went left.

I guessed that the house we were headed toward was once the "big house" of a mid-sized farm. The structure itself was not large, but it was more permanent looking relative to the other, much smaller houses in the vicinity. It was made of stone, with a porch that extended across the front, and a solid-looking, recently painted wooden railing.

Tom and I stood on the road, gazing at the house, wondering who lived there, when the front screen door opened and a tall colored boy—about my age, I guessed—came out, looked over at us, stared for a moment or two, and then waved. He jumped down off the porch, skipping the steps, and started walking toward us. We waved back, that's what neighborly folk do, and waited until he crossed the yard to where we stood.

"You live here?" Tom asked, though the answer seemed obvious.

"I certainly shore do," the boy replied. "Who are y'all?"

"I'm Mickey," I said. "He's Tom. We're brothers. We live over on Lynn Acres Drive, up through the woods." I pointed.

"Mickey's fifteen," Tom said. "I'm eleven."

"Oh, y'all live in the houses on that hilly street with the big ditch," the boy said.

"That's it," said Tom. The colored kid was talking about an odd feature of our neighborhood, a drainage ditch that ran all the way up and down Lynn Acres Drive on the far side of the street from our house. I called it a drainage ditch because I heard Dad call it a drainage ditch, but I hadn't seen any water in it since we'd moved in. Maybe that meant it worked.

"I been over there," said the boy. "Couple of times. But my grandma said to stay out of that neighborhood so I wouldn't get in any trouble."

"What's your name?" I asked.

"Jackie. Jackie Thomas."

"Is Thomas your last name?" Tom asked, "or is that like your middle name or your confirmation name or something?" Down South, many people were called by two names, rather than one. Sarah Ann, Betty Sue, Carol Jean. Billy Joe, Bobby Joe, Tommy Joe. It was a reasonable question.

"I don't know what a confirming name is," said Jackie, "and I never had me a middle name. I'm just Jackie Thomas—that's it."

"We're McQuades," I said, "McQuade is our last name." I thought it was polite to let him know our last name since he told us his.

"We've got nine kids in our family," offered Tom, "and Mickey's got a twin."

"I've got a sister," said Jackie, "but she lives in Tupelo with my mom. They live in a big house with some rich white folks, but there's no room for me so I live here with my grandma. Just me and my grandma—that's it. But my mom and my sister might be coming up from Tupelo soon. She just needs to find a good paying job around here and she'll be back fast as lightning."

"Hey," I said, trying to figure out what time it was since neither Tom nor I had watches. "I don't mean to be rude since we just started talking and all but we probably better get going. Nice to meet you."

"Yeah," said Tom, "we need to get home before our dad gets home from work. Where's your daddy?"

"I don't have one," said Jackie, "least not one I ever did meet."

"Okay," I said, and pulled on Tom's arm, anxious because I thought he might ask Jackie why he never met his dad and that would be rude. "We gotta go. See ya."

We turned and started back up the road. After about a hundred feet or so, I turned back and saw Jackie watching us.

"Hey," I yelled. "Do you play baseball?"

"Certainly shore do," Jackie yelled back.

"Okay," I yelled. "We'll come back. We can have a catch."

And that settled the matter. Tom and I had ourselves a new friend. His name was Jackie Thomas.

* * * * *

Later that evening, I told Marti about our encounter with Jackie. We were sitting on the front stairs, one of two flights connecting the upper and lower floors of our house. In the short few weeks since we'd moved in, the McQuades had shown a definite preference for the stairs in the back; they were much more convenient to the kitchen and the bathrooms on both floors. That was fine with Marti and me. The front stairs gave us a place to sit and talk—twin to twin— with little chance of interruption. While the two of us had our fair share of brother vs. sister friction, we also enjoyed a level of communication that our parents thought remarkable. Mom often claimed that we started talking to each other in the womb, and hadn't shut up since.

"I want to meet him," she said. "I want to go see this special secret town that Tom discovered, and I want to meet this Jackie Thompson kid."

"Jackie Thomas," I said. "Like Danny Thomas from TV. Except he's colored and Danny Thomas is white." The Danny Thomas Show was my dad's favorite—everyone knew who Danny Thomas was.

"Oh, Jackie Thomas. I got it," Marti said.

"Fine," I said, "but why do you want to meet him? He's just another kid. You usually don't care all that much about my friends."

"He's a colored kid," said Marti. "How many other colored kids do we know? I think it's time that I knew one, found out what a colored kid is like. Specially with all the civil rights stuff that's been happening around here these days."

Marti was talking about the events of the past spring in downtown Birmingham. Protests and boycotts and Dr. Martin Luther King getting thrown in jail. The Children's March that was met with fire hoses and policemen with dogs that ended up with a lot of colored kids also getting thrown into the city jails. And, finally, the "truce" that desegregated lunch counters and fitting rooms and water coolers throughout the city. Racial tensions, despite the truce, were running high.

"I can tell you what he's like," I said to Marti. "He's just regular normal, like me. Maybe kind of quiet—not sure. But I'm going to go back to the secret town and go to his house and see if he's around. Maybe I'll take my baseball glove with me and we'll have a catch or something."

"Let me know. I want to go. Promise me you'll take me."

"Sure," I said. "I'll probably go next Saturday."

CHAPTER 3
JUNE 16, 1963

Several weeks before Tom and I met Jackie, I'd met someone else that made a big impression on me. Actually, a whole family of someone elses.

It was Sunday, the day after we'd moved in. The McQuades had just gotten back from mass at St. Barnabas, our parish church, when Tom noticed a family of four marching toward our house, led by a woman carrying a covered dish of some kind, followed closely by a tall, hulking sort of a man, and two kids. One of the kids, a girl who looked to be about my age, captured my attention immediately. She had long, tan legs, extra-long, dark, straight hair, and a face that could easily have graced any number of the teen magazines that my sister Sheila tossed aimlessly around her bedroom. Right away I began wondering if she had a boyfriend.

The doorbell rang, but since we'd seen them coming, Tom and I opened the door simultaneous with the chime.

"Hi, y'all," said the woman as she offered to Tom and me what proved to be a homemade apple pie. "We're the Rawlings family from across the way. And we just wanted to welcome y'all to the neighborhood."

My mother stepped forward right away. "Why, thank you," she said. "Please come in. The place is a mess but, of course, we just moved in." What

Mrs. Rawlings did not know is that the place would look much the same three weeks and three months from now. This was primarily a result of the living habits of nine children and a busy husband. It's worth noting that my mother was not uncomfortable with clutter.

The Rawlings marshalled themselves into our downstairs family room and surveyed the scene. Most of us McQuade kids had quickly gathered there, eager to check out the neighbors. Sheila held Carrie Ann on her hip—she always seemed to have Carrie Ann on her hip—and Mrs. Rawlings noticed her immediately. "Oh, you have a little one," she said. It was kind of a statement and kind of a gush, and I quickly figured out that Mrs. Rawlings, like so many women of that age group, loved babies and toddlers more than just about anything else in the world.

"She's almost 13 months," said Mom. "Her name is Caroline Ann, but we call her Carrie Ann."

"So nice to meet y'all" said Mrs. Rawlings, smiling at Carrie Ann, then turning her eyes to the rest of us. "I'm Martha, this here is my husband Jessup, that's Yvonne, and our son is named Traynor." She gestured loosely to each person as she mentioned a name, as if we might have trouble figuring out who was who.

"I'm Bill," said my father, striding forward to shake Mr. Rawlings hand. "This is my wife, Mary," he continued proudly taking over the job of introductions. One of the things in life that Dad loved to do was introduce his family to a stranger.

"That's Sheila holding the baby," he continued, "Mickey and Marti, our twins, Tom, Richard, Brenda and Bobby. We also have a son named David, but he's probably upstairs reading a book."

"So nice to meet y'all," said Mrs. Rawlings, repeating herself. "I hope y'all like apple pie, but I guess I should have baked two." She laughed at her little joke.

"Don't worry," said Mom. "I'm an expert at slicing pies into 11 equal pieces. It was so thoughtful of you to bake this for us."

"So, y'all got moved in okay?" said Mr. Rawlings, perhaps feeling like he needed to enter the conversation. "Got all your stuff in okay?"

"We did," answered my father. "The moving team worked hard—it actually went a lot faster and smoother than we expected."

"Well, that's surprising," said Mr. Rawlings. "I noticed that your moving crew was mostly niggers." He snickered. "They are NOT the hardest workers God ever put down on earth."

"We were very pleased," my mom said, probably to cut off my father from responding.

"I'm glad it went well, honey dear," said Mrs. Rawlings, adopting the familiarity common to the conversation of Southern women. "But," she warned, "it is best to make sure you aren't missing anything. Why, two years ago, when the Eldertons down the street moved into this neighborhood, there were lots of nigras in their crew. And after they left, Joanne Elderton had a twenty-dollar bill missing from her purse."

"Niggers," said Mr. Rawlings, half under his breath. "They can get theirselves a couple bottles of cheap whiskey for twenty dollars—and have some change left over for watermelon." He laughed.

I thought Marti was going to say something, but she didn't. Jessup Rawlings seized the dead air. "Niggers are nothing but niggers," he stated to the room. "Oh, sure—there are good ones. Every once in a while you meet one, but for the most part, niggers were born lazy and shiftless—it ain't even really their fault."

Rawlings hesitated just for a second, then provided a final comment to support his statements. "I've known niggers all my life." His voice trailed away as he repeated. "All my damn life."

No one responded to that comment. But looks shot around the room faster than a pinball bouncing off bonus bumpers. Dad looked at Mom, Marti looked at Dad, I looked at Marti, then Mom, Mom looked at Dad, then Sheila, Sheila looked at Mr. Rawlings and then down at her feet. Dad started to say something, but Mom got him to hold his tongue with an almost imperceptible motion of her head.

The Rawlings family just stood there. I'm not sure if they were oblivious, but they acted the part.

My mother apparently decided that the best way to keep this first social occasion in the neighborhood from deteriorating further was to fashion a graceful but hasty retreat.

"You know, I hate to be rude," she said, "but we still have so much unpacking and stuff to do. Maybe you and I can have coffee sometime this week, Martha?"

"Of course, of course," said Mrs. Rawlings. "Here we are, taking up your morning. C'mon, everyone—let's get back home. I've got a chicken to get in the oven."

And so the Rawlings family shuffled back out the door, traipsed back down our driveway and across the street to their house. I kept a close eye on Yvonne as they were leaving, trying to determine if she'd even noticed me. The rest of the McQuades watched the exodus as well, not saying anything.

Over the next couple of weeks, we met more people from up and down Lynn Acres Drive. We discovered that ours was a neighborly neighborhood in the extreme. Luckily, the McQuades were more than up to the pie consumption challenge that this environment spawned.

We got a cherry pie from Mrs. Timmons, who lived at the very bottom of the street with her husband, kids grown and moved away, one to Nashville, one to Mobile. We got a second apple pie from the Farleys, who had three kids but none older than six. We got a rhubarb pie from an older woman who introduced herself as Aunt Bertie, no last name. She lived alone because her husband had died a year ago of a heart attack while shoveling one of the rare snows that Birmingham experienced. I remembered that snowstorm from when we lived on 80th Place. It was a good three inches and shut down the schools, and the city, for two days.

We got a chocolate cake from our next-door neighbor to the left, the Barnums. The Barnums had two older daughters, neither of whom lived at home anymore, and a dog named Bear Bryant.

Bear Bryant was unquestionably the happiest living creature on the street, if not the planet, a friendly, mixed-breed salt-and-pepper bundle of dog hair—roughly the size of a cocker spaniel— who immediately fell in love with all of us McQuade kids. We returned his affection in full measure, often playing with him in the front yard while Mrs. Barnum and Mom sat together on the carport, drinking coffee (Mom) and cokes (Mrs. Barnum), and smoking cigarettes together.

There were other neighbors whom we met over time. Most families had kids, several of them had dogs or cats as pets.

But no one on the street had a dog as friendly as Bear Bryant. And no one had a teenage daughter quite as interesting as Yvonne Rawlings.

CHAPTER 4
AUGUST 3, 1963

Exactly a week after meeting Jackie for the first time, I went to visit him again.

Marti did not come with me. She'd gotten a call during the week to babysit for a family from church who had three kids and a weekend getaway cottage on a little lake not far from Birmingham called Pinedale Shores. I knew the lake because one of my friends from my grade school, St. Barnabas, sometimes invited me out there to spend the weekend with him and his parents.

It was easy work for Marti because the kids were good and they just played in the sand on the little beach they'd built at one end of the lake. Marti mostly sat in the sun on a chaise lounge and watched the kids splash around. And got paid $1.00 an hour. That was way too much money, maybe twice the standard rate, to even think about passing up just so she could go with me to meet my new friend Jackie.

So, when Saturday came, I went by myself. Tom was off visiting his best buddy from the old neighborhood with Mom and the little kids. Dad was working. David was at his part time job at the gas station over on Killough Springs Highway. Sheila was in her room with the door closed. I could understand that—nobody got much privacy in the McQuade family, so you grabbed it when you could.

I entered the woods—which Marti insisted on calling "the forest"—struck once again by the thickness of the vegetation all around me. Shrubs and vines and clumps of wild grass grew everywhere. I saw large patches of poison ivy, here and there a poison sumac tree. Tons of sticker bushes, too. One of those bushes produced ball-like stickers that Tom and I nicknamed blowfishes based on a picture of a spiny blowfish that Tom had seen in National Geographic. Depending on where you walked in the woods, and what time of year it was, you could return home with a dozen or more spiny blowfishes clinging to the legs of your pants.

Our woods were mostly made up of pine trees, which my mother referred to as Georgia pines. I knew a little about pine trees based on a school project I'd entered in the science fair entitled The Trees of Alabama. I took some time after dinner one night to inform my mother that there were more than 100 different types of pine trees, with names like the Longleaf, the Loblolly, and the Shortleaf Pine. There is even a tree called the Virginia Pine. But there is, I told her, no species known as the Georgia Pine.

This information was of little consequence to Mom. Her sole knowledge of pine trees came from a popular song by a local band called the James Gang. Their hit tune, Georgia Pines, was one of my mom's favorites, and all the authority she needed to ignore my scientifically-solid attempt at telling her she was in error. Our pines were Georgia Pines, end of discussion. Georgia Pines that surrounded me on all sides as I pushed farther into the woods.

There was no path—Tom and I had simply bulldozed our way through the underbrush on our trek the week before. I did the same today, but at least I'd had the sense to wear a lightweight, long-sleeved jacket over my t-shirt to cut down on the scratches and cuts from the sticker bushes.

When I came to the clearing, I looked first to where Jackie's house stood, then across the town. No one was around. It could have been a ghost town, no people or animals in sight. But I hoped that Jackie might be sitting inside his house, not doing anything, and he'd come out for a catch if I went up and knocked on his door. So I took off down the hill toward the dirt road, pounding my baseball into my glove as I walked, careful not to trip over the ruts and the gouges of the hillside.

I walked slowly, looking from side to side. It was actually a little scary, not seeing anyone around. No moms hanging out laundry. No dads out working in the yards. No old folks sitting on porches in rocking chairs, sipping cool drinks and talking about the weather.

My unease faded when I got closer to Jackie's house, saw the front door open up, and Jackie step outside.

"Hiya, Jackie," I called.

Jackie waved back and came down the porch steps into his front yard to greet me.

"Hey," he said. "I looked out my window and saw you coming down the road."

"Where is everybody around here?" I asked. "Sure is quiet. I didn't see a single person."

"Well," answered Jackie, "I don't rightly know about everyone. But a whole lot of folks went to Saturday afternoon church. I heard tell some special preacher from Memphis was coming to talk about Jesus and freedom and segregation and such stuff as that."

"Saturday afternoon church?" I said. "We only have that once a year, around Easter. We're Catholics."

"We're Baptists," Jackie said. "Some kinda something Negro Baptists. Lots of singing, lots of amens and alleluias. Except my grandma and I don't like church too much, so we don't always go. Actually, we hardly ever go. And specially not on a Saturday."

"I brought my glove," I said. "Wanna have a catch?"

"Sure—let me grab my glove."

Jackie disappeared inside the house, and I took the time to look around the yard. There was plenty of open area for us to toss a baseball around. A big oak tree grew off to the left, a stone well just behind it. The well had a bucket and a rope, just like you'd see in pictures, and I wondered if that's where they got their water—I'd never known any family that did not have running water in their house.

I turned back to the porch when I heard the door to Jackie's house open, expecting to see him. Instead, I saw what I think must have been the largest colored woman in the world. She was wearing a big, necessarily big, floral print dress that seemed to spread out from her hips like a massive decorative umbrella missing its handle. The dress fell down to just under her knees. She had stout calves, well-muscled, but feet that were almost dainty, encased inside well-worn, faded blue house slippers. Just above her feet you could see saggy, rolled-down beige stockings, a look common to some women in the South when they could not stand the summer heat and humidity. Why they put stockings on in the first place in those environmental conditions I did not understand.

I looked at her and she looked at me. "And y'all must be Mickey," she semi-bellowed in a warm and welcoming voice that had faint echoes of a carnival barker in it. "I'm Jackie's grandmom—everybody calls me Nammy. Come here to me and let me see you. Step on up and set yourself down right here." She pronounced "here" like "cheer" — "rye cheer" was a phrase I heard often from Southern whites and coloreds alike.

I did as I was told. Not that she was threatening in a way that commanded instant obedience — in fact, just the opposite. You immediately felt safe with her. I took a little jump up the three steps to the porch and sat down on a once-white wicker loveseat and looked up at her.

"You want some lemonade?" she asked.

I smiled and said "Yes ma'm. I mean, Jackie and I are going to have a catch, but I do like lemonade."

"Just hold on, I'll bring out a pitcher," she said, "and some cookies. Not homemade, store bought. I don't always have time to bake cookies these days. Too much washing, too much mending, too much ironing, too much chasing after Jackie. Hey, where is that boy? Jackie, you coming out? Your friend from over yonder is here to see you!"

"Coming, Nammy," I heard him yell from inside the house. "Just getting my cleats on."

She made a face at that and half-whispered to me, "That boy moves slower than thick molasses right out the icebox on a cold day in January. In Alaska."

I nodded my head, but then felt a little disloyal because it appeared that I was tacitly agreeing with her assessment. However, while I was wondering what to say to defend my new friend without challenging Nammy as a grown-up, she moved on. She saw my baseball glove and said, "Baseball player, huh? What position do you play?"

"Well, when I played on a team, I liked second base best," I said. "But the coach always wanted me to be the catcher cause I don't blink when kids swing the bat."

"Catcher, huh?" She looked me over with a discerning eye. "You are mebbe a little skinny to be a catcher. How's that throwing arm? You throw out a lot of runners at second base? You gotta have a good arm to be a catcher."

Actually, I had a pretty poor throwing arm, which is why I liked second base. But, in Dixie Youth League—which was the last bit of organized baseball I'd played, and that was three years ago—the runners could not advance until the pitch passed the batter at the plate. So not much stealing went on.

Before I could respond to her question, though, Jackie pushed the screen door open and came out on to the porch, glove in hand, ready for a catch. He wasn't lying, he had real cleats on, which I could tell he was proud of, even though they were pretty scuffed up and sorry-looking.

"Did I hear that you were getting us lemonade, Nammy?" Jackie asked.

"What?!" she said. "Look at me. Forgot all about the lemonade. And the cookies. Store bought, not homemade." I was not sure why this was such a point of emphasis. Either she was excessively honest or, maybe, did not think so highly of store-bought cookies and wanted to be sure I didn't think she'd made them herself.

She turned to go back in the house and called over her shoulder, "Y'all go play ball. I'll be back in a little bit."

Jackie and I watched her go. She did not have to turn sideways to get through the door, but I noticed there was not much clearance between her and the doorjamb.

"That's Nammy," said Jackie. "You ever live in the same house with your grandma?"

"Never met mine," I said. "Both of them died when I was just little."

Jackie nodded understanding. "C'mon, let's play," he said.

We started out throwing nice and easy, maybe ten yards between us, but then backed farther apart as our arms got warm. After a bit, we started throwing each other grounders and pop-ups, and fly balls that were almost out of reach so that you had to run and stretch to haul them in. I made a couple of pretty good over the head catches. Jackie was good at everything: hard grounders that took bad hops, grass skimmers that you had to stay down on to keep the ball from rolling under your glove, high fly balls that he caught using the Wille Mays basket catch approach, even bad throws from me that forced him to go quickly to his left or right and snare the ball above his head or down at his shoe tops. No question in my mind—Jackie was a better than decent ballplayer. At least as far as fielding went. Although he looked like he might be able to hit pretty well too.

Thirty minutes later we were both sweating profusely in the Alabama sun, heat and humidity. I could feel that the back of my t-shirt was soaked through. It didn't bother me though—damp and drippy was just a part of Birmingham summer weather. You got used to it.

The toughest part for me was that the sweat dripped off my forehead into my eyes. I kept pulling my shirt up from the waist and wiping my face with it. I was more than ready for a break when Jackie's grandmom re-appeared on the porch with the promised pitcher of ice-cold lemonade, and the store-bought cookies.

"Y'all c'mon now," she called. "You need to sit a bit afore this heat turns y'all both into dishrags. Git on up here."

We settled down on the porch steps, put our gloves down beside us, and gladly accepted the tall glasses of lemonade that were offered. Jackie's grandmom collapsed with a big sigh onto the wicker loveseat, took a long sip from her own lemonade glass, then picked up where she'd left off earlier.

"Jackie, this boy here sez he is a catcher. Now does he look big enough to be a catcher to you?"

Jackie looked at me and answered supportively, "Well, Nammy, he might not be too big, but maybe he's quick. Maybe he's strong."

"Mebbe," she said, "but I think catchers should be built like Josh Gibson. Y'all ever heard of Josh Gibson?"

Theoretically, the question was directed to both Jackie and me, but I had a feeling it was mostly meant for me.

"No, ma'm," I said. "I've heard of Yogi Berra . . . and Sherm Lollar . . . but I never heard of Josh Gibson." At the time, Yogi Berra was moving toward the end of his career with the New York Yankees, but I figured he was the most famous catcher ever in baseball. And Sherm Lollar was the catcher for the 1959 Chicago White Sox, which was my favorite baseball team of all time.

"Yogi and Sherm," said Jackie's grandmom, as if she knew them personally and always called them by their first names. "Now those are two pretty good ballplayers. But Josh Gibson was better than both of those boys. Josh Gibson was the . . ." She emphasized *the*, pronouncing it like thee. ". . . greatest catcher who ever lived. Might never be a catcher like Josh Gibson again. Ever."

"Who'd he play for?" I asked, confused. It wasn't like I knew everything about baseball but I'd never even heard of Josh Gibson. So I was guessing that he must have played for some team back in the old days with Babe Ruth and Ty Cobb and Tris Speaker.

"Josh Gibson never played one single day in the white majors," Jackie's grandmom said, "not one single day." I'd never heard the phrase "white majors" before, but I understood. "Josh Gibson," she continued, "played in the Negro Leagues. But he would have been MVP for absolute dead certain if he'd played for the Yankees or the Dodgers or the St. Louis Cardinals. Now that man could shore hit a baseball. Yes, indeed he could. Why, he hit 55 home runs in just 137 games one year . . . along with a batting average of four sixty-seven! Can you imagine that, can you just imagine that?"

Those were impressive numbers. It wasn't that long ago that Roger Maris had hit 61 home runs to break Babe Ruth's record of 60, but his batting average for that season, 1961, was only .267. Gibson's numbers were astonishing, no matter where he played.

I looked at Jackie and guessed that maybe he'd heard a lot about Josh Gibson from Nammy before. Actually, I guessed that he'd heard a lot about a lot of things from Nammy before.

"Who's your favorite player?" Jackie asked me, either curious to know or maybe just to move the conversation down the road and away from Josh Gibson.

"Now that's a good question," Nammy said. "Tell us who you like best, Mr. Mickey."

Discussion of favorite players was standard stuff when you were talking baseball. My brother Tom and I talked about favorite players a lot, though he tended to switch his around pretty often depending on which team was in first place and which player was having a really good season.

"I've got two favorites," I said. "Baseball has so many good players that I think everyone should be able to have two favorites. You know, in case one gets injured or something." The last I said with a little grin, wondering if Nammy would appreciate this modest bit of humor, even though I did have two favorite players.

"Now, listen to you," said Nammy, laughing. "What kind of talk is this—two favorites? That's not right—y'all gotta like one more than the other."

"Not me," I said, encouraged to speak confidently by Nammy's friendly manner. "I like my two favorites exactly the same—just like my mom and dad love me and my twin sister, just the same." I smiled my most charming smile at Nammy, who opened her eyes wide at me, like I was telling her the earth was flat and that pigs could fly. Then she shook her head, laughing to herself. "Okay, Mr. Mickey Two Favorites," she said. "Who are they?"

"Well, one is Luis Aparicio," I said. "Shortstop. Chicago White Sox and now the Baltimore Orioles. But I liked him best as a White Sox cause of the '59 team."

"That '59 team was a good one," said Nammy. "Too bad they ran into Sandy Koufax and my Dodgers in the World Series. But with Early Wynn as their ace, and Aparicio and Fox up the middle on defense . . ."

I guess my surprise showed. You just don't expect someone's grandma to know that much about baseball, but Nammy seemed to have more knowledge than any of the kids from school, even the know-it-alls like Dudley Courson, who used to quote a previous year's batting average every time you named a star player from either the American League or the National League. I was sure she knew a lot more than I did—and I was starting to think she might know more than Dudley.

Nammy laughed again, the kind of laugh that draws you in and makes you feel good all over yourself, like you just told the funniest joke in the world. She looked right at me with a big, gap-toothed smile on her face. "Why y'all being so shocked?" she said to me. "You figure there's no way a fat 'ol Negro mammy was going know anything about our national pastime?"

Jackie looked at me and smiled. "She surprises a lot of people," he said in his quiet voice, a voice so soft and mellow that you almost had to tip your ear toward him to make sure you heard what he was saying. "She surprises most everybody," he said, "and not just cause she knows her baseball."

"That's right, I shore do," said Nammy. "Including knowing right now that I am spending way too much time chewing the fat with you boys. I need to be in that kitchen and fixin' us up some supper. You want to stay to eat supper with us, Mr. Mickey?"

"I better not," I said, "but thank you for inviting me. I better head home."

"I'll walk with you up to the woods," said Jackie.

"Y'all come on back again," Nammy said looking right at me. "Y'all are welcome here anytime. Besides," she said, "we still need to hear who your other favorite player is . . ."

Nammy pushed herself out of the loveseat, breathing a little heavy from the effort, and kind of muttered to herself, "Two favorites! I never . . ."

"Thank you, ma'm," I said, remembering my manners. "Thanks for the lemonade and cookies."

"No ma'ms for me," she said quickly. "You call me Nammy, just like Jackie. Just like everybody do."

CHAPTER 5
SAME DAY

Jackie and I didn't talk much as we walked across the grass from his front porch onto the red dirt road. But then I remembered to ask him the question that had never come up.

"So who is your favorite ballplayer, Jackie?" I asked. "And it better not be Josh Gibson."

Jackie snickered at my comment but then answered seriously. "I have lots of players I like. More'n just two. Jackie Robinson is one of my favorite favorites. Jackie Robinson of the Brooklyn Dodgers." He said this as if there were another Jackie Robinson in baseball and I could get confused.

I nodded. "Sure, of course," I said. "Who else?"

It was a tiny reaction, but I sensed Jackie stiffen a little bit up at my remark. Suddenly I felt like I must have said something wrong, though I wasn't quite sure what. I turned my head to see his face. It had a different look, not anger, but maybe what my mother would have called "miffed."

Jackie looked at me. "Why did you say 'of course'?" he asked me.

I got a little flustered by the directness of his question; it caught me off guard. "Why, nothing, I guess. Of course. Like, good choice. Like you made a good pick, I guess." I felt myself getting red in the face.

Jackie looked at me without saying anything for just a second or two. Then he shrugged his shoulders.

"It's okay," he said, almost as if he was apologizing to me for his reaction. "Nammy's always telling me not to be so prickly."

I was still confused and Jackie could see it.

"It's like this," he said. "Jackie Robinson is the favorite baseball player of all time for lots of us colored kids. But that doesn't mean he's the only choice a Negro kid could have. I could have said Al Kaline. Or Rocky Colavito. You don't pick favorite ballplayers by color—at least, I don't. I pick mine by the way they play, how they hit, how good they can throw, that kind of stuff."

I nodded, feeling somehow foolish.

"Your favorite player is Luis Aparicio," he reminded me. "But you're not from South America. And I bet," he said, with a little bit of a smile in his voice, "I bet you don't speak Spanish either."

"No, senor," I said, understanding his comparison. "No, I don't."

"So, who is your other favorite player?" Jackie asked.

I appreciated the way he asked the question. I think he was telling me Okay, I made my point, it's no big deal, let's move on.

And I was more than ready to do so. But I hesitated a few seconds before responding to his question, not because I didn't have an answer, but because I wasn't sure how Jackie might react to my response. Finally, I spoke. "Willie Mays. Say Hey Willie Mays."

Jackie grinned at my answer but didn't say anything. I got concerned. I didn't want him to think I'd just made up an answer to smooth things over.

"And I'm not just saying that cause he's colored and all. He's just good. Really good. Best centerfielder in the game."

"Second best," said Jackie. "Cause one of my other favorites is an even better centerfielder than Willie Mays. And I'm not saying it cause he's white and all."

I thought a second, then looked at him. "Really?"

"Yup," Jackie said. "Mickey Mantle, New York Yankees. He is the best centerfielder in the game of baseball today."

"Well, ain't that something," I said, as Jackie and I stood together in the middle of road. "You know, Willie Mays was born and raised in Westfield, Alabama, did you know that?"

"Nope," said Jackie, "but I know that Mickey Mantle was born in Oklahoma, Did you know that?"

I shook my head, thought a second, then asked straight out.

"Do you really think Mickey Mantle is better than Willie Mays?"

"Pretty sure," Jackie answered. "But if we need a tie-breaker, we can always ask Nammy."

* * * *

A couple days went by before Marti and I found a chance to catch up with each other again on the stairs. I told her all about my playing catch with Jackie, meeting his grandmom, having store-bought cookies and lemonade, even the part where I got all tongue-tied with my comment about Jackie Robinson, and what Jackie Thomas said about that.

Marti listened to everything I had to say before commenting. "Seems to me," she said, "that your new friend Jackie Thomas is not your average, every day, fifteen-year-old colored kid. Could be he's a little bit different."

"What makes him so different?" I asked. "By the way, he told me he was sixteen."

"Just guessing on both counts," Marti said. "He certainly sounds a little bit more thoughtful than I would have expected from someone about the same age as you. Maybe more perceptive." She grinned. "He certainly sounds a lot smarter than you," she said.

"Hey, I'm smart." I replied. "I'm thoughtful. In fact, I'm full of thoughts. What are you talking about?"

I tried to sound injured, but I really wasn't—I knew Marti was just playing around.

"If you were so smart," she said, "you'd know that Mickey Mantle is a better centerfielder than Willie Mays."

"I'll think about it," I answered, but not because I actually intended to do so. What I wanted to do was change the subject to something literally closer to home, the Rawlings family—in particular, Yvonne Rawlings.

"Speaking of new friends," I said, "what about the Rawlings kids? Here it is August, and you haven't even called Yvonne up and asked her over to play games or listen to records or anything. And I don't think Tom has connected much with Traynor. And we ought to be neighborly, right, and anyway I would have thought you wanted a friend your age in the neighborhood. Don't you think?"

I'd read somewhere that the best way to get a conversation going is to end whatever you say with a question, because that forces the other party to address what you want to discuss—but I wasn't sure this would work with Marti. She might guess that what I really wanted to do was talk about Yvonne. Marti was pretty smart.

Actually, Marti was extremely smart. I was a little bit smart and got decent grades in school, a dependable B+ guy with what I liked to think of as flashes of brilliance. My older brother David was smarter than me and would probably go to college on a scholarship. But Marti was clearly the smartest of all the McQuades—and that included book smarts, people smarts, common-sense smarts—the whole range of smartness categories.

Marti got straight A's in every subject and 99th percentile in all the standardized tests. She knew what to say to make Brenda stop crying, and how to intervene to make Ricky and Bobby stop fighting. She beat Dad and David in chess, me in checkers most of the time, the whole family in Scrabble. On top of that, she usually won in Crazy Eights even though I always thought that game was mostly luck and wondered why she got so much of it.

I liked listening to Marti's opinions on things—and now what I really wanted was her opinion on our new neighbors, starting with Yvonne. Unfortunately for me, she started in a different place.

"I think Mr. Rawlings is a jerk," she said. "Actually, worse than that. He hates colored people—I mean, really hates them. How can you go around with that much hate in your soul?"

"I don't know, Marti—maybe he just learned to talk like that from when he was a kid. Maybe he doesn't really hate 'em. You remember Mr. Barns from our old neighborhood. He was always complaining about 'niggers this' and 'niggers that'—but then we'd see him chatting away on his front porch with the colored delivery guy from the grocery store, like they were best friends. Maybe Mr. Rawlings just likes to talk that way."

"Maybe," Marti said, "but it feels to me there's a mean, hateful streak in Mr. Rawlings that goes pretty deep. I don't like him, despite the fact that he's got a very pretty daughter that you'd like to get to know a lot better. Am I right?"

Marti's directness startled me. My mind scrambled to regain equilibrium. If I were stupid, or if I did not know that Marti knew me better than anyone, I might have tried to dodge the question with a cough and a simple "I dunno." No point in that—Marti would see right through me. So I just said, "Yeah, kind of."

"Kind of what?" Marti said, with a little half-smile on her face. "Yvonne's kind of pretty or you'd kind of like to get to know her?"

I gave up any pretense of hiding my inner thoughts. "Kind of both, I'd say. Kind of both. What do you think of her?"

"I've been thinking about Yvonne," said Marti. "I think she's close to our age so it would be nice to have a friend across the street. But I'm not sure that she'd like what I like, or vice versa. I'll just have to get to know her myself."

"I think you should get to know her," I said. "Invite her over to the house some time. Play records or a game of Monopoly or something." Music and a board game continued to be my two first and best ideas for Marti-Yvonne interaction. Of course, I really didn't care what they did. I just liked the idea of having Yvonne in our house, maybe near enough for me to talk with her myself without it being especially noticeable.

"Don't worry, big brother," said Marti, reminding me that I was born a full seven minutes before her. "I'll get to know her at least well enough to find out if she has a boyfriend. Or, maybe," she said, teasing me a little, "if she is looking for one."

I could feel myself getting a little red as I considered the thought of me and Yvonne as boyfriend-girlfriend. There was a lot to like about that idea. So, rather than any attempt at denial of interest, which Marti would have seen through as well, I expressed simple gratitude. "Thanks, little sister," I said. "That's all a big brother can ask."

CHAPTER 6
AUGUST 7, 1963

It was just over seven weeks since the McQuades had moved to Lynn Acres Drive, and almost all of the unpacking and move-in jobs had been completed. Dad occasionally talked about painting the heated porch that served as a bedroom for David, Tom and myself, but we weren't counting on it. Many of Dad's home improvement projects seemed to evaporate, over time, into the early morning air of the Birmingham suburbs.

Mom still had some things she wanted done, tasks that would finally, in her words, "put the house to rights." Our mother was a highly organized woman, intellectually at least, who understood quite well the philosophy of "a place for everything, and everything in its place." She and her family experienced significant breakdowns, however, in applying her conceptual thinking to everyday life.

Laundry—in various categories—was the most significant contributor to the state of perpetual disarray in which we lived. Everywhere you looked, in every bedroom and spilling into other areas of the house as well, there were mounds, stacks, and heaps of clothing: t-shirts and tops, jeans and shorts, pajamas and underwear sufficient to clothe a family of eleven. There were dozens upon dozens of clothing items crying to be sorted for the wash, howling to be folded, clamoring to be put away. There were wicker baskets of shirts and blouses and skirts to be ironed, jumbles of socks to be paired with lost mates, and always a box or two of clothing to be given away to needy families in the parish. Since many of us McQuade kids had also received clothing from the same parish, I found this mildly ironic.

The second biggest challenge to maintaining a state of orderliness, at least in our old home, was the sheer number of books that we owned as a family. For years, books had overrun the McQuade household in much the same way that rabbits had once taken over the Australian Outback.

Our father and mother were both great readers, and my father a true lover of books for the place they occupied in the universe. It was an unwritten but definitive household rule that once a book had been read, it was ours forever. It became part of what should have been known as our permanent collection. It was a member of the family.

Most rooms—bedrooms, our living and family rooms, bathroom, and laundry room—seemed to have amassed their own private and at least semi-permanent collections: books on tables, books on chairs, books stacked on the floor, books everywhere the eye might land.

We all read, except for Bobby, who was two and just starting to pick up books and leaf through them to mimic his older brothers and sisters, and Carrie Ann, who liked to open a book, then slam it shut loudly, after which she would look around for approval and applause.

Fair warning to authors everywhere: If the McQuades somehow came into possession of your book but it was not read by someone within three months of acquisition, it might never be opened. It would simply get lost amidst the dozens of other volumes that had entered the household since yours had arrived, everything from NY Times bestsellers to classics like Little Women and The Three Musketeers to paperback whodunits (a favorite genre of our mother) to odd-titled, odd-subject books found and purchased from local garage sales.

So now, as one of the last big jobs on Mom's list, Marti and I were charged with "unpacking the boxes and getting all those books onto shelves in an organized way." Like many Mickey-Marti team efforts, this one began with optimism, purpose, and a plan, thanks to Marti. Hard cover books would be organized by size since that would provide a symmetrical appearance on the floor-to-ceiling bookshelves that lined three of the four walls in Ricky and Bobby's room. Their bedroom, it seemed, had once been a library when fewer people lived in the house.

Shorter books would be placed to the outsides of the shelves, taller books in the middle. Our 20-volume set of The Book of Knowledge—including the one with the warped cover and the water-stained pages because it had once fallen out of my hands while I was reading it in the bathtub—would get its own special section on a lower shelf. Paperbacks would be sorted by author and kept together since their dimensions, except for width, were all roughly the same. Mom's Agatha Christies would also be given a special section all to themselves, which forced a mixture of hardcover and paperbacks, but was a fitting tribute to the prolific output of the author whom Mom revered above all others.

Odd-sized or oversized books—and we had more than a few of these—would be re-boxed for later decision-making, their futures dependent on whatever space remained on other free-standing or wall-mounted bookshelves throughout the house (each room had at least one) after the bulk of the unpacking/shelving was completed. More than a few cartons of books would, of necessity, end up in our attic, never to be seen or thought of again until the next McQuade migration.

We started to work right after breakfast, with the intention of finishing no later than noon.

I held up a well-worn hardback with a red cover and embossed lettering on the cover. "*And Then There Were None,*" I read the title aloud.

"That's an Agatha Christie," Marti said. "It's one of Mom's favorites—here, give it to me. I'm putting it in my book pile."

Each of us older McQuades had our "to be read" book piles, a collection of volumes which we'd individually decided to tackle sooner or later, and that were consequently kept together for review and retrieval once the individual had finished his or her current read.

David's book pile was the biggest and had the most "velocity." Sometimes it seemed like David read a book a week. Dad and Mom also had book piles, with Mom's consisting mostly of paperback detective novels and Dad's spanning an amazing breadth of fiction and non-fiction topics and types.

"How 'bout this one?" I asked Marti. I held a slim hardback with a faded yellow cover in my hands. It was titled *My Name Is Aram.*

"Dad's," Marti replied. "But maybe you should keep it for reading yourself. It's funny, you'd like it. David's read it at least twice."

I deposited the book into a box I'd re-labeled MICKEY'S TO BE READ.

The process continued, sometimes speeding up when we came to a group of books of a kind, like the unopened series of handy-man books that promised "EASY DIRECTIONS FOR EVERY HOUSEHOLD FIX-IT CHORE." We put those on the highest, most inaccessible shelf in the room, because we doubted anyone, especially Dad, would ever go looking for the information they contained.

It was getting close to noon, and substantial progress had been made. While we still had several cartons to open, the bookshelves were filling up fast. And they looked good, arranged pretty close to our original plan.

Then Marti opened up a box labeled BOOKS—MISCELLANEOUS. I remembered that one because I'd packed it myself. It consisted of paperbacks that seemed to appear on floors in every room as the moving men disassembled beds and moved dressers. There was no way of knowing which books came from which rooms—this was the last minute, any port in a storm carton.

"Dad's? Or David's?" asked Marti. She was holding a book called *Black Like Me* by John Howard Griffin.

"No idea. What's it about?" I asked.

Marti took a moment to read the notes on the back of the paperback. "Hmmmm," she mused. "Mickey, listen to this. It's about a white man who used chemicals to turn himself into a colored man so he could find out what it was like to be a Negro in the South."

"Well," I said, "if he came to Birmingham, Alabama that could not have been fun." It was supposed to be a joke, but I could see from the intense look on Marti's face that she had not really heard me.

"I think I need to read this, Mickey," she said. Then, looking up at me, she added, "Maybe you should read it too."

"No thanks," I said. "I've got plenty to read."

I liked choosing my own reading material. I liked the Hardy Boys, and Bronc Burnett sports books. I would not admit it to my friends, but I also liked Nancy Drew mysteries. However, I'd also read some classic literature—like Tom Sawyer and Huckleberry Finn and Alice in Wonderland. I'd read a couple of Mom's Hercule Poirot novels. And I'd recently read a book of my father's called *Yellowstone Kelly*. I don't think I would have been allowed to read it with his knowledge, primarily because of a graphic love scene in a snow-encased Wyoming cabin between the hero, Yellowstone Kelly, and an Indian maiden who'd fallen in love with him. It was one of my first experiences in bending the corner of a page so that I could easily find a specific passage for re-reading.

In any case, my current collection of books to read—including a few that I had added to my pile during our sorting process—was substantial. The one Marti was holding did not seem like it would be much fun.

Marti didn't respond to my comment—she was already reading the first couple of paragraphs. I watched her face, noticed the tiniest bit of her tongue curled in concentration. She looked up at me. "I wonder what it would be like to be colored?" she asked.

I stared at her, a little uneasy with the gravity that had crept into her voice.

"Why would you ask that?" I said.

My question seemed a little bit challenging when I heard it aloud, which wasn't my intent, so I provided some explanation.

"I've imagined being a major league baseball player," I said, "and I've thought about being rich. And I've wished I were about six inches taller so I could dunk a basketball. And maybe I've thought about how fun it would be if I were a rock and roll star like Elvis. But why would anyone spend time thinking about something you don't want to be?"

"Because," said Marti, continuing in her serious voice, "maybe that's the kind of thing that opens our eyes. Think about your new friend, Jackie. What is his life really like? How hard is it to be a colored kid, instead of a white kid? In Birmingham? Or anywhere down South? What's his school like? Hey—I wonder if Jackie was in the Children's March back in the Spring. Maybe you could ask him?"

"Whoa, whoa, Marti, slow down. Jackie and I didn't talk about any of this stuff. We talked about baseball. I dunno what his school is like. It's fine, I guess. Except he goes to school with all colored kids—and our school is all white kids. Different but maybe mostly the same. School's school, right?"

Marti gave me an odd look. "Different but maybe mostly the same? Sounds a lot like 'separate but equal,' doesn't it? Don't you know that's what the segregationists say. That's what Bull Connor says! That's what George

Wallace says! 'Segregation now, segregation tomorrow, segregation forever.' Is that what you're telling me?"

Marti's voice got a little louder and more forceful with each sentence.

"Stop, Marti, stop! Please. You're getting all worked up. Maybe we should just finish this job tomorrow."

She stared right back at me for a few long seconds. Her lips were pressed together tightly, and she slowly shook her head from side to side. Then she tossed the book she was holding onto a nearby chair. "Forget it, Mickey," she said. "I shouldn't have gotten so . . . carried away. You're right—let's finish this up tomorrow."

I stayed silent as she turned away from me and headed for the door. "Tell Mom I went for a walk," she said.

When Mom asked me later, I said that Marti had gone 'walkabout.' That's what the whole family called it when she disappeared for a walk.

* * * * *

Two days later, I found an invitation on my pillow. It wasn't elaborate, just a folded card with a bright blue peace symbol on the front panel. Inside, in Marti's award-winning cursive, the words were simple and direct:

You are invited to a meeting

of the McQuade twins

August 9, 1963

8:45 p.m.

Refreshments will be served.

Marti was already comfortably sitting on the stairs when I got there. She was resting her back against a couple of throw pillows, a plate of Oreos balanced on her lap. "Welcome, twin," she said.

"Oreos. Nice touch," I said. "You're not going to yell at me again, are you?"

"I wasn't yelling," she said. "Was I? Here, have a cookie."

I settled onto the stairs in my usual position, grabbed two cookies off the plate, and answered her question. "Maybe not actual yelling," I said, "but you were pretty loud. You sure seemed mad at me."

"Yeah, I'm sorry about that. And I really wasn't mad at you, Mickey. Not even sure who I was mad at."

"But why, Marti?" I asked. "What made you so upset?"

Marti looked up at the ceiling, then down at her hands. She didn't look at me. "I think, I guess, I'm probably mostly mad at myself, Mickey. Mad cause we're sitting right in the middle of maybe the biggest struggle for social change that will happen in our lifetimes—and I'm not doing a single thing to help. Nothing."

"You're talking about all this civil rights stuff, right?" I said. "Integrating the schools and maybe opening up the swimming pools again and better education for colored people and all that?"

Marti gave me a half-smile. "Yes, all that, Mickey. I'm talking about everything that we do—everything that white people do—to keep colored people down. I'm talking about all the reasons that so many thousands of colored people across the South have joined in protests, and marches, and sit-ins, and boycotts. Not just in Birmingham, either. Do we—I'm talking about you and me—even know all the stuff that's going on? Sure, you and I know about the Children's March, but did we have one discussion in school about it?

"I know what's been happening, Marti," I said. "I know all about Martin Luther King and the protests and the sit-ins and everything."

At best, my words were half true. Living where we did, especially now in the suburbs, the McQuade family was well insulated from all the turmoil going on throughout Birmingham for the last couple of years. I found a lot of that stuff kind of boring—and learned most of what I knew from overhearing my parents talk. But I didn't want Marti to think I was stupid, or didn't care.

"I do know what's going on, Marti, mostly. It's been pretty bad downtown. Scary."

"Knowing isn't doing," Marti said. "I just feel like I need to be doing something. Helping. Marching. Something."

The idea of Marti marching through Birmingham, and maybe getting attacked by dogs, or beaten up by police, gave me a sick feeling in my stomach. "Marti—please tell me you won't get involved with any of that."

"We gotta get involved, Mickey," she said. "I've been thinking about this non-stop since we were sorting those books. We gotta get involved—because it's partly our fault."

"Wait a minute! Our fault?" I protested. "I'm not doing anything to colored people. I hardly even know any colored people, except for Ida Pearl and Beatrice. And now Jackie and Nammy." Ida Pearl and Beatrice were colored ladies who'd come in to help Mom with household chores—cooking and cleaning and laundry—right after the last two babies were born.

"C'mon, Marti," I continued in my slightly wounded voice. "How could 'we' be responsible for all that stuff?"

"You and me are part of white society, Mickey, aren't we? So we're all at least a little bit responsible for whatever our society does."

"Sounds a lot like me getting blamed for what Tom does," I said, "like when he sneaks a Snickers bar into bed at night and then Mom finds his candy wrapper on the floor in our bedroom. And once we had all those ants that got in, remember?"

"But suppose," Marti said," that you knew that Tom was sneaking candy into bed. And you didn't try to stop him, or yell at him for breaking Mom's rules. And you didn't speak up to Mom and Dad. Suppose you didn't do anything at all? Wouldn't that make you at least a little bit responsible when the ants invaded?"

Another perfect example of why I never wanted to get into debates of any kind with Marti. She was always one step ahead of me.

"Maybe," I said, "but that would also make me a tattletale. Who wants to be that? This whole thing just doesn't seem very fair."

"Good point, Mickey," she said thoughtfully. "Maybe what we need is a few more tattletales. Anyway, I'm going to read this book. *Black Like Me*. I'll tell you when I'm done. And then," she looked at me to drive home her point, "I want you to read it. And somehow, some way, we gotta get involved."

CHAPTER 7
AUGUST 31, 1963

"**G**et your money ready," Tom said, "here it comes."

We were standing at the bus stop near the Roebuck Plaza Shopping Center—Marti and me, Tom, plus Yvonne and Traynor—excited by the prospect of the day ahead. Since school started for all of us the following Tuesday, the day after Labor Day, this was effectively our last big adventure of the summer of 1963. In the McQuade household, this day was known as Last Happy Saturday, and carried the significance of a religious holiday, except you didn't have to go to Mass.

The bus wheezed to a stop. As we stepped past the driver to find seats, I noticed a dozen or so colored people spread throughout the bus, instead of sitting together in the back the way they once did. However, even though bus desegregation had officially occurred a while ago, and the Colored to the Rear signs were long gone, many white people still refused to sit next to a colored person. Not an issue for us—the bus was two-thirds empty.

Tom and Traynor found seats together, as did Marti and Yvonne. I was the odd man out but it didn't matter. All I cared about was managing to sit next to Yvonne once we got inside the movie theater. Actually, I'd been working out how to make that happen ever since we decided on this particular Last Happy Saturday outing, and had invited Traynor and Yvonne to join us.

Sitting beside Yvonne in a dark movie theater for two Elvis Presley movies would make an already good day just about perfect.

Our plan was simple. Get to the College Theater on First Avenue by 10:55. See *Blue Hawaii*. Get a return pass, then head across the street to Queen of Catfish for lunch. Then back to the theater for a later showing of *GI Blues*. With the second movie featuring Juliette Prowse, and Yvonne Rawlings sitting beside me, I would certainly be the luckiest hormonally-overloaded 15-year-old in the world.

Standing in the theater lobby next to Yvonne, surrounded by a small mob of noisy Elvis fans and waiting for the rest of our group to buy movie snacks, I was beginning to feel both comfortable and confident about the day ahead. Yvonne chatted on and on about school starting next week, and cheerleading practice, and Friday night football games to come. She'd be going to Banks High School in East Lake; Marti and I would be starting our sophomore years at John Carroll, halfway across the city, and the only white Catholic high school in Birmingham.

I seized a moment of relative privacy. "Tough question, Yvonne," I began with what I hoped was a twinkle in my eye and voice, "but I hope that you can be completely honest with me."

My semi-serious tone got her attention, and actually seemed to make her a little nervous from the look on her face.

I hesitated, pretending that I did not know exactly how to phrase what I wanted to say. She waited, not sure what was coming.

"Okay," I finally said, "I'm just going to ask it: If you were marooned on a deserted island for the rest of your life—and could only take one record album with you—would it be an Elvis album . . . or any other album in the world?"

I grinned at the end of the question, just to make sure she knew that I was joking. My spontaneous delivery was perfect, exactly as I had practiced it in front of the mirror at home.

Yvonne caught on right away. I was rewarded with a smile—and a little teasing in return.

"Now that, sir, is a very serious question," she said, matching my tone, "and I am not sure I can answer it immediately. Could I call you next week, after I've had a chance to think?"

She giggled, then dropped her character voice, and said the two best words that could possibly be expressed to a teenage boy trying to impress a teenage girl. "You're funny."

As I basked in the glow of Yvonne's reaction, I happened to notice two kids about our age standing apart from the crowd against the wall of the theater lobby. They were also standing with ten or twelve feet between them, but they kept glancing at each other for a few seconds at a time, then looking down. The boy was a colored kid, with a rich brown skin tone, not the black-black of Jackie Thomas. The girl was white, with red hair and freckles, and a long pony tail.

I sensed a connection of some kind between them, but didn't pay them much attention, because Yvonne was infinitely more interesting. When the usher finally announced that we could enter the theater, they disappeared into the crowd of Elvis fans.

We trooped down the aisle into the theater just as the previews were coming on. Tom and Traynor, as expected, walked rapidly ahead of us, looking for a row that had five vacant seats together. Marti trailed them by a few steps, Yvonne and I followed Marti. The sequence was perfect. I would definitely end up sitting next to Yvonne.

About halfway down the aisle, Tom found a row with five vacant seats in the middle, and gestured to a couple sitting on the end of the row that we'd all have to move past them to sit down. No problem there—the couple, teenagers, pulled their legs in to let Tom and Traynor squeeze by. Marti started to follow them. But, just as she was going to enter the row, the box of Mike and Ike's she was carrying slipped out of her hand and slid a couple of rows forward down the aisle. She took a step or two forward, bent over and picked it up quickly, but in the intervening seconds, just to keep things moving, Yvonne entered the row of seats. It would have been too weird, since Yvonne was Marti's friend, for me to follow Yvonne—and it would have been ungentlemanly to boot. So, with sinking heart, I stood motionless in the aisle, resigned, waiting for Marti, with recovered Mike and Ike's in hand, to follow Yvonne and sit next to her, leaving me a lot farther away from Yvonne than I had planned.

Fate was clearly dealing me a bad hand, but Fate was no match for my sister.

As Marti turned back toward us, Yvonne was sliding past the couple on the end of the row, and I was standing awkwardly in the aisle. Suddenly she whispered loudly enough for everyone, including Yvonne, to hear, "Go ahead, Mickey—I have to go the bathroom," and then walked rapidly back up the aisle. It would have been stupid to wait, standing, for her to return, so I followed Yvonne in, sat next to her, and whispered, "I'll move when Marti comes back." Yvonne did not reply so I had no way of knowing whether my statement disappointed her.

When Marti came back about two minutes later, which seemed like an inordinately short bathroom trip, I moved to get up and give her my seat. But Marti quickly waved me back into it, whispering more quietly, "The show's starting in a minute." She sat down next to me, and I settled back with Yvonne comfortably on my left, and my quick-thinking sister on my right. Not much later, Elvis started to sing.

* * * * *

A few minutes into the movie, Yvonne shifted ever so slightly in her seat, crossing one leg over the other in an effort to get a little more comfortable. I saw her movement through the darkness, heard the faint sound of denim brushing denim, detected her perfume keenly. More importantly, I suddenly felt the delicate pressure of her shoulder as it came into glorious contact with mine.

I became paralyzed, focusing on the precise point of physical connection, wondering if she was feeling a similar surge of electricity throughout her body. I was afraid to move, fearful that she'd notice that our shoulders were touching.

After several minutes, Yvonne shifted again, ever so slightly, and our shoulders were no longer in contact. Dismayed, I shifted as well, positioning my feet toward Marti so that I was leaning, I hoped not too obviously, in Yvonne's direction. It was my invitation to her to sit closer. She may have missed it, because nothing happened.

A little later, however, Yvonne leaned slightly toward me, reached her hand out and touched my arm, and said, "Oh, I love this part, watch, Mickey."

Discovery One: Yvonne had seen the movie before but still joined us for Last Happy Saturday. Interesting.

Discovery Two: Yvonne seemed quite comfortable resting her hand on my arm, instead of simply touching me to get my attention and then moving her hand away.

Discovery Two was, by orders of magnitude, more important. Yvonne's hand remained lightly on my arm as the movie continued. I looked furtively to my left and right, wondering if either Marti or Tom noticed this unexpected show of . . . Of what, exactly?

Before my brain could fashion an answer to that internal question, Yvonne moved her hand to brush some hair from her face, then dropped it back into her lap.

Yes, I was sad to see Yvonne's hand leave. I missed its presence immediately. But, the fact that it had been there, and stayed so long, had me glowing inside and out, right through our first movie, our lunch break, and well into the start of the second feature.

Fried catfish, typically, would have been the highlight of my day. Especially since you could also order fried chicken at the very same meal— no extra charge—along with an unlimited number of hush puppies. These culinary treats, however, were pushed far away from my personal center of attention. I was fixated throughout the meal on Yvonne.

I tried not to stare at her, though I did manage to notice how delicately she bit into a rather large chicken thigh, and how expertly she dabbed her lips with a paper napkin. She sat directly across the table from me, which caused me some worry: I became very concerned about the possibility of catfish getting caught in my teeth. So I hardly spoke. Before we went back across the street to the theater, I ran into the men's room and brushed my teeth with water and my finger, then quickly chewed up four or five breath mints that I'd secreted in my pants pocket.

GI Blues, our second Elvis film of the day, should have merited more attention from me. It showcased Elvis, of course, a few good songs, sun and sand and girls in bikinis, but mostly the radiant and long-legged Juliet Prowse, gliding across the screen and over-energizing the libidos of every male teenager in the theater. I appreciated none of it. I was, instead, totally focused on Yvonne and whether there would be a repeat of the slight touches of the first movie. My focus was rewarded beyond my wildest dreams.

No more than 20 minutes into the show, without any action on my part, Yvonne reached over and placed her hand on mine. Seconds later, she deftly moved her wrist and interlocked fingers. There was no hesitation, no awkwardness. I glanced down without moving my head—for fear of disturbing the magic—and concluded that we were, in truth, holding hands. Emboldened, I gave her hand the slightest of squeezes—and got an equal pressure squeeze in return.

At that moment, I wanted every clock in the world to freeze. Sadly, they did not. Before I knew it, Elvis sang his last song, received his last kiss, and the credits began to roll.

The lights came on in the theater suddenly and harshly, abruptly changing the atmosphere. I looked toward Yvonne, eager to see on her face some recognition of our special connection. What I saw surprised me: Yvonne staring at two other moviegoers hastily standing from their seats and awkwardly creating distance between each other, as if they'd had a fight. It was the two kids that I'd noticed in the lobby earlier, the colored boy and the red-haired girl. It did not take much intuition to realize they were a couple, had taken advantage of the theater darkness to sit together, but now felt exposed to the eyes of the other movie-goers. Colored boys and white girls did not socialize in Birmingham society, not ever.

I glanced back to Yvonne's face and she looked me directly in the eye. "Do you see that, Mickey? Right here. Right out in public. No shame."

I was surprised by the hostility in her voice, as if she had been personally insulted somehow. I moved a little closer to Yvonne, and lowered my voice. "I don't think it's really our business," I said.

"Oh, yes, it is," she snapped. "Nigra boys and white girls do not belong together. It's wrong—and it's disgraceful. And I don't care about letting them sit at a lunch counter or drink our water—there is just no reason for them to touch our women. I can't, I simply cannot believe this. If my daddy were here. . ."

"You guys coming?" Marti's voice reached us from the other end of the row. She stood there waiting with Tom and Traynor, oblivious to the exchange between Yvonne and me.

"Yeah, yeah, here we come, Marti," I said.

Yvonne abruptly halted her outburst—she just grabbed her sweater and started maneuvering through the row in Marti's direction. I wasn't sure if Yvonne was mad at the other couple, or mad at me, or what. But the mood—and, for some reason, the connection between Yvonne and me—had suddenly and definitively evaporated. It was a lousy ending to what up until then had been one of the great days of my life.

* * * * *

Later that evening, sitting on the steps, I only half-listened as Marti chatted enthusiastically about the day. She thought it was one of our best Last Happy Saturdays ever. She talked about both movies, cited reasons why *GI Blues* was better than *Blue Hawaii*, then commented on just how yummy the fried catfish turned out to be. She talked about how well Tom and Traynor got along, and then patted herself on the back a little bit as she described the Mike and Ike incident from her point of view.

"I knew all along that you wanted to sit next to Yvonne," she said. "I really am the most clever and quick-thinking of twin sisters, am I right?"

"Smooth as a cue ball," I told her.

Marti responded with a self-satisfied smile, then pushed the topic further along. "It was a good day for you with Yvonne, wasn't it, Mickey?" she said. "You two seemed to be getting along quite well."

The memory of holding hands with Yvonne flooded over me, and I could feel myself getting red, though I'm not sure why. It wasn't like I did anything wrong.

"It was a mostly good day," I said to Marti. "98 percent good. Just got a little strange at the end." I was thinking about Yvonne's rapid change in mood when she saw the red-haired girl and the colored boy together at the end of the second movie. Actually, I'd been surprised to see them at that point; it meant they'd probably planned a double feature and lunch outing as well. But I was more surprised by the intensity of Yvonne's reaction.

"What do you mean?" Marti asked. "You didn't have a spat or anything, did you? I noticed she was a little bit quiet on the bus ride home."

"No, no, nothing like that," I said. "She just seemed a little moody. Maybe she got tired."

All of a sudden, I felt odd about the direction our conversation was taking. I did not want to describe the entire incident to Marti, especially Yvonne's reaction. What would she think of Yvonne? What would she have done? How would she have handled it?

I decided to keep everything to myself, for now at least. I was not going to let a little thing at the end of the day ruin my Last Happy Saturday.

CHAPTER 8
SEPTEMBER 3, 1963

Three days after our movie outing, I sat beside Marti on the yellow St. Barnabas school bus, heading across town to the south side of the city and John Carroll Catholic High School. I wore my freshly ironed white shirt, my brand new, charcoal grey uniform pants, my uniform tie, and the confident look of a 15-year-old entering the tenth grade, and looking forward to a fun school year ahead.

I lost myself in my own thoughts, juggling confused notions about Yvonne with studying my schedule of classes, double-checking my pocket to make sure I had my thirty cents for a hot lunch (a special treat for the first day of school—after that, we'd bring lunch bags), wondering about the year ahead. Before I knew it, we were pulling up behind a long line of buses from other parishes—St. Anthony's over in Ensley, St. Paul's downtown, Blessed Sacrament out in the West End, and Our Lady of Sorrows in Homewood.

I scanned the crowd of kids pouring onto the sidewalks in front of the school, looking for friends that I hadn't seen since the end of classes last May.

Marti and I walked together to a large open patio where a number of other kids were gathering. I asked her if we should go into the school to look for our homerooms—we were assigned to different ones—but she thought we were supposed to wait for a school bell or something.

I never heard a bell, but after a few minutes on the patio, the crowd began to move toward the school doors. There was a direct entrance from the patio to the bottom level of the school, or you could walk up the sidewalk and go through the main doors. I lost Marti in the throng as it pushed forward. Eventually I found my way to Room 113, my homeroom. It was three quarters full of other sophomores, most of whom I recognized. I took a seat, nodded in greeting to a couple of others who were milling about, and then turned to look up at Sister Mary Petronella, the largest, most intimidating nun the convent had ever produced. I knew about her from last year, but I'd never been in any of her classes.

Sister Pete—that was the nickname the whole school used for her, though not to her face—was easily more than six feet tall. She was a Benedictine, the order of nuns that taught at the high school, but I could not help but imagine how much taller and scarier she would look if she'd been a Daughter of Charity, the order of nuns that taught us at St. Barnabas. Daughters of Charity all wore highly starched, white linen headpieces—called cornettes—that would have added significantly to Sister Pete's height and dominating image.

"Silence, everyone, and take a seat," she intoned, in a deep, authoritative voice. The room hushed immediately.

"In my homeroom, we start the day with a prayer," she said. "Bow your head."

I was not sure, but I guessed that everyone bowed his or her head as quickly as I bowed mine. I would not have been surprised if Sister Pete had finished her statement with . . . "or I'll cut it off."

With our heads bowed, Sister Pete quickly spewed a Hail Mary and a Glory Be, but those formal prayers were merely the warm-up to a long, complicated and obviously impromptu invocation directed toward Jesus

Himself. She first thanked Him for the nice weather we had to begin the school year, and then delivered a series of highly specific requests, prayerful pleas that all John Carroll students—especially her homeroom—would take their work as Catholic scholars seriously, that they would respect their teachers, and study hard, and do all their homework on time, and treat each other as vessels of Christ, and on and on and on.

She probably prayed for two minutes—it felt like ten. When she concluded, we all said Amen and it was time for roll call.

"Before I begin," Sister Pete said, "I want all of you to look carefully at your printed schedules and make sure that you are in the right homeroom, 113. Is there anyone," she asked a little sarcastically, "who has not read his or her schedule correctly?"

I examined my schedule with trepidation, and was relieved to see Homeroom: 113. I looked up, feeling oddly good that I had passed this first test, and noticed the kid sitting to my left tentatively raising his hand. I didn't recognize him from last year—I guessed he was a transfer from one of the public high schools. I'd heard that some parents were moving kids to John Carroll because we were, at that point in time, still an all-white school.

"What is it?" Sister Pete snapped at him.

"Well, S'ster," came the answer, using the truncated pronunciation of "Sister" that most Catholic school boys, all over the world, adopted early in life. In the South, this occurred soon after they'd learned that all Southern women should be addressed as "Ma'am" and all Southern men addressed as "Sir."

"I th-think I'm supposed to be here," the voice continued, with a hint of a quiver, "but the ink is smudged a little bit on my schedule. It's a little hard to read. But I'm pretty sure it says 113."

"Bring it to me," Sister Pete ordered.

The schedule was promptly handed over, Sister Pete inspected it, looked up, looked back down to the paper, and finally, in a resigned voice, asked, "What's your name?"

"Davis Williams, S'ster," he answered.

"What parish?"

"Blessed Sacrament, S'ster."

I wondered why Sister Pete needed to know the parish information. Did the nuns have some secret knowledge of their students relating to their parishes of origin? Were we that different?

While I briefly considered this question, Sister Pete consulted a document on a clipboard. Then she lifted her head and said abruptly, "You don't belong here, Mr. Williams."

"I d-don't?" Davis said. "But wh-where do I belong?" he asked, in a voice so pathetically sorrowful that it set off a round of giggles among the girls in the room.

"Quiet," Sister Pete commanded. But then her voice softened, almost imperceptibly, though enough to indicate the possibility that she had a soul. "Take your belongings and go to the office," she said, "they'll tell you where your homeroom is."

Davis Williams turned in my direction as he gathered his books. He glanced at me, and I gave him a quick eye roll, and a slight shrug, as if to say, encouragingly, "Don't worry about it, she's nuts." Unfortunately, Davis was not the only one who witnessed my gesture of support.

Sister Pete took two steps down the aisle in my direction, and in a voice infused with authority and venom in equal measure, boomed a question at me. "Did I just see what I thought I saw, Mister?"

I looked up at her and felt every feature on my face freeze.

"Stand up. What's your name?" she said.

"Mickey McQuade, S'ster," I answered, my face on fire with shame at being called out in front of the entire class.

"What parish?" Again with the parish?

"St. Barnabas."

"You, Mister McQuade, are an arrogant and disrespectful young man, a bold article, and I will not have that repeated in my homeroom ever again. Do you understand?"

"Yes, S'ster," I answered, as a new, even more intense wave of mortification swept over me.

"The last thing this school needs is impertinence. I will root it out."

"Yes, S'ster."

"So there will be no repeats of this disrespect. Ever again."

"Yes, S'ster."

"Are you quite, quite sure that you understand me, Mr. McQuade?"

"Yes, S'ster."

"Sit."

I sat.

Sister Pete turned her back to me, walked to the chalkboard, and began writing something, but I was too afraid and too embarrassed to look up and see what it was. I sat with head down and eyes unwaveringly focused on my own folded hands, one part of me trying to tell myself that my eyeroll-shrug was probably not all that disrespectful or egregious. However, the other part of me, at the moment the dominant part, rejected my rationalizations out of hand. Filled with regret for my stupidity—no one had forced me to be proactively supportive of a kid I didn't even know—I wondered if I could possibly become the first sophomore in the history of John Carroll to be expelled for unbecoming and disrespectful conduct before attending his first academic class. Given my humiliation, I did not think expulsion would be all that bad a fate. I wondered what the first day of school was like at Banks High.

Finally, after a few minutes, though time moves slowly for the tortured, the bell rung. Still stunned by the scene that they'd all witnessed, thirty sophomores filed out of the room in total, deafening silence. I cleared the doorjamb and entered a hallway of milling fellow students, happily talking about the day and the school year ahead, not knowing that a pariah now existed in their midst. I felt dizzy, a little disoriented, and sucked air into my lungs the way a near-drowning victim might, which made me even dizzier. I tried to compose myself, half-walked, half-stumbled down the corridor, wondering just what it was that I had done.

* * * * *

It was after 7th period before I saw Marti. For some reason, she was scheduled to eat lunch with the juniors. And, because of her placement test scores, we were not in any classes together. We passed each other in the hall as I was heading to Algebra and she was going to Religion.

"Mickey, are you okay?" she asked, with a little more than normal sisterly curiosity in her voice.

"I'm sort of okay," I said. "Why did you ask me that like that?"

By then, I'd managed to compose myself, after a fashion. Since I'd not been called to the office, I no longer worried about Day One expulsion. Now I was more focused on the fate that awaited me once my parents found out what I'd done. I was certain that Sister Pete would be calling them to deliver a highly descriptive report on my first minutes in her class. In truth, however, as much as I hated the idea of facing my parents and discussing my behavior with them, I hated the idea of having to tell Marti about the whole incident even more.

For better or for worse, I didn't have to.

"Mickey," she whispered at me, "the whole school is talking about you. They say you are the kid who eye-rolled Sister Pete. You! Mickey, what did you do?"

I closed my eyes. I didn't feel like looking at Marti just then.

"Kind of complicated, Marti," I said. "Can we talk about it later, like next year or so?"

Before she could answer, I was literally saved by the bell. "Gotta run, sis! Eighth period!" And with that I flew in the opposite direction from where she was headed, knowing that all I'd done was buy myself a little more time before having to relive my humiliating morning by telling her all about it. I was not looking forward to the bus ride home, with Marti wanting to know what happened and the rest of the bus probably staring at the two of us.

With nothing but bad thoughts running through my head, I somehow located my 8th period classroom. Following the approach I'd been using all day, I walked quickly, head down, to the last row. I slid into the desk, shoved books under the chair, grabbed a notebook, and prepared to grit my teeth through 40 minutes of mathematical mumbo-jumbo until my first official day as a sophomore ne'er-do-well ended.

I did not notice the person who slipped quietly into the seat in front of me, did not even know if it was a boy or a girl, until a voice I recognized from a few hours before quietly said, "Hey, Mickey McQuade. Thanks for being on my side this morning."

I looked up into the earnest face of Davis Williams. "I'm Davis," he said, and extended his hand. "I just transferred here from West End."

I reached forward and shook it. "I'm Mickey," I responded. "I'm arrogant and disrespectful."

"And," Davis responded, " a bold article."

At that, we both laughed. Not long, not hard, just enough to seal a connection. That's how friendships start sometimes.

CHAPTER 9
SEPTEMBER 14, 1963

The street we lived on, Lynn Acres Drive, was a steep climb by anyone's standards. It starts at the bottom of a hill, a right turn off Killough Springs Road heading west. From that point, it climbs almost 200 feet in elevation to its peak, which is where our house, at 637 Lynn Acres Drive, stood "proudly and majestically" according to Marti. There may have been a touch of good-humored irony in her description.

From there, Lynn Acres bends to the left, resembling the top of a horseshoe, then straightens out and transforms itself into Rose Lynn Lane as it heads back down the hill to meet again with Killough Springs.

Interestingly, though the street itself is steep, the lot our house sat on was graded to be fairly level. Facing our front door from the street, the yard sloped down very gradually, north to south, left to right. The back yard was flat enough to play football or kickball or wiffle ball.

Best of all, the driveway was level and that made it easier for us bigger kids to teach the little kids how to ride their bikes.

It was a Saturday afternoon. Tom had decided that Brenda was old enough, at six, to ride her new bike without training wheels. It wasn't actually a brand new bike; a friend of Dad's from St. Barnabas had given it to him because his daughter had grown too big for it.

Brenda did not seem to mind or even notice that her bike was pre-owned. Since Dad brought it home, she'd spent hours riding it back and forth on our short 65-foot driveway, cycling up into the carport if all the cars were gone, navigating the narrow turnarounds in the driveway slowly and carefully, happily waving to all who might be watching. The training wheels worked just the way they should: when Brenda leaned a little too far in one direction or the other, the wheels stabilized the bike to keep her from falling. Brenda seemed quite content with that arrangement; unlike Tom and I when we were her age, she'd never pestered anyone to remove the training wheels and teach her to ride without them.

Tom, however, felt that a few weeks of riding with training wheels was more than sufficient basic education and told her, excitedly, that he was going to teach her to ride without them. I watched his progress from the front stoop, where I was reading a book and keeping one eye on Bobby who was playing on a blanket in the front yard. Dad was still at work; Mom was out at the grocery store with Carrie Ann in tow. I did not know where Ricky was at the time. I'm sure I was supposed to be keeping an eye on him as well, but he was 8, reasonably self-sufficient, and not the same kind of mischief-maker that Tom had been at that age.

Brenda looked a little dubious as Tom told her how easy it was to balance without the assistance of the training wheels. He rode her bike back and forth slowly to demonstrate, then hopped off and announced that it was her turn.

As usual, Brenda seemed on the verge of tears, asking Tom, "Do I have to?" and shying away from her bike like a skittish colt balking at the sight of a saddle. Tom either did not notice or just ignored her concerns. "Wait 'til Dad sees you, Bren!" he said. "He will be so proud."

The prospect of Dad's approval was a powerful motivator for all of us

McQuade kids; I think that's what finally got Brenda onto the seat of her bike and ready to pedal into uncharted territory.

Tom was patient, holding onto the back of the bicycle by the seat and guiding Brenda back and forth along the driveway to let her get the feel of the ride without the safety net of the training wheels.

Maybe it was ten minutes, maybe twenty. I was wondering how long this unusual level of tolerance on Tom's part would last; I was ready to step in if he gave out. But somehow, across that interval, Brenda's confidence went from low to high, she got the feel of what it took to balance herself on the bike, and she began to pedal herself forward without Tom's assistance.

Tom stood beside her the whole time, grabbing the bike to steady her as necessary, but clearly pleased as she went further and further without his touch. Turning at such slow speeds was too challenging, however, so Tom reached out and grabbed the bike each time Brenda reached the end of the driveway or the carport wall, and turned the bike with Brenda still on the seat so she could head in the other direction.

I'm guessing Tom thought it was time for a graduation ceremony of some sort, because I half heard him telling Brenda, "Now this is what we're gonna do for Dad!"

Maybe if I had not gotten preoccupied with Bobby starting to wander off his blanket, I would have cautioned Tom when I saw what he was up to. Because I learned later that what he wanted Brenda to do was to bicycle from the carport down the driveway and into the street, turning to the right, and pedaling all the way up to our neighbor's driveway. Dad, Tom told Brenda, would be "amazed!"

I'm guessing that Brenda was feeling confident about the route because I do not remember hearing any protests. Our street was a quiet one and there was plenty of visibility to see cars coming, either from down the street or from around the other side of the horseshoe. What Tom wanted her to do was neither dangerous nor foolhardy and I'm sure everything would have turned out fine if it were not for the unexpected entrance onto the scene of Bear Bryant, our neighbor's dog.

As luck (the bad kind) or fate would have it, Bear Bryant was released into the front yard simultaneous with Brenda pushing away from the carport for her dress rehearsal for Dad. Bear Bryant saw her moving and bounded toward her, barking happily. And Brenda, having just learned to balance herself without distractions, panicked as Bear Bryant came running up to her on the bike. She started to wobble, straightened out and regained her balance for a moment at the end of the drive. By now, Bear Bryant was close enough to bark playfully at her heels. In order not to hit him, Brenda had to turn left, not right. All of a sudden, she was heading down the street. A wail escaped her as she realized that the force of gravity would soon have her traveling much faster than she ever had before.

"Tom! Help! Tommmmmmmm!" she cried.

Tom, proudly leaning up against the carport post, did not grasp the consequences of Bear Bryant's entrance until too late. When realization struck, he ran forward, but was half a driveway behind our suddenly terrified sister.

"Hit the brakes, Brenda," he screamed.

I turned from picking Bobby up when I heard both of their shrieks. "Brenda!" I yelled helplessly in response to both their cries.

"Brakes, Brenda! Hit the brakes!" Tom yelled again.

In her sudden terror, Brenda had taken both feet off the pedals and extended them widely to either side, a kind of intuitive balancing maneuver that provided no value at all. The speed of the bike increased as it and Brenda began to wobble precariously.

With a final, frantic scream, Brenda wrenched the handlebars to her right, completely losing control. The bike slid out from under her, grating along the asphalt and pitching Brenda off of it and into the drainage ditch that ran between the street and the neighborhood front yards.

At this point, Tom was halfway to where Brenda had disappeared. I was on the driveway, half-running as best I could while carrying Bobby in my arms.

Jessup Rawlings beat us both to our sister.

From out of nowhere, he came running and leaped feet first into the ditch. Brenda was screaming and crying, and he probably should have taken some moments to see if she'd broken any bones. Instead, he scooped her up into his arms and ran toward his front door, hollering for his wife.

"Martha," he yelled, "First–aid kit. Hurry!"

Mr. Rawlings threw the screen back with one arm while holding the wailing Brenda in the other. He kicked wide the partially opened front door and disappeared into the house, with Tom now following close behind and me, carrying Bobby, bringing up the rear.

When I got to the Rawlings kitchen, Brenda was still crying semi-hysterically. Mr. Rawlings was holding her in both arms, trying to soothe her, while Mrs. Rawlings was fishing around in a first-aid kit.

"It's okay, honeypie, it's okay," Mr. Rawlings whispered, "You'll be fine, it's okay."

It took a minute or two, but Mr. Rawlings' manner had its intended effect and Brenda began to calm down. "We just need to look at you, child," he said. "Can I just set you down right here?"

Mr. Rawlings carefully placed Brenda on his kitchen countertop and pulled away from her a little. She released the stranglehold she'd had on him, her skinny arms dropping to her sides. The front of Mr. Rawlings shirt was covered in red splotches.

When I saw it, I almost fainted. I was not so good with the sight of blood.

Both Mr. Rawlings and Mrs. Rawlings were examining Brenda head to toe. There was a lot of blood but it seemed to be coming from a single source, a profusely bleeding wound across Brenda's knee. She had scrapes and scratches on arms and legs and her cheek, but those were not bleeding, just oozing.

Mrs. Rawlings started to put a cold washcloth to Brenda's knee, but Mr. Rawlings took it from her gently and pressed it to the cut himself. He continued to talk soothingly to Brenda.

"There we go, honeypie," he said, "there we go. Not so bad, is it? More scared than hurt, I'm betting. Y'all gonna be just fine, now, y'hear. Just fine."

By now, Brenda was wiping her nose with one arm and sniffling.

"I got scared," she said.

"Of course you did, honey pie," Mr. Rawlings answered. "I've never seen a girl your age go so fast on a bike. That might have been a world record! Do ya'll think we should call the newspapers right now?"

At this Brenda combined a giggle with the last of her sobs.

Mr. Rawlings used that moment to gently pull back the washcloth from where he'd been holding it up against her knee. It came away drenched red, but you could already see how the bleeding was beginning to stop.

Mr. Rawlings bent down a little to get a closer look at Brenda's knee. "Just a little surface cut," he said to her, oblivious to the rest of us in the room. He reached into the first-aid kit and held a bottle of Mercurochrome up to the light. "You'll be back on your bike in no time, y'hear me, honeypie."

"My name's Brenda," Brenda said quietly.

"Why, of course it is, honeypie," Mr. Rawlings answered, "I just forgot that in all the excitement. I will call you Miss Brenda from now on."

Brenda giggled again softly at the "Miss Brenda" remark. "I'm just Brenda," she said.

"Well," Mr. Rawlings continued as he unwrapped a bandage package while holding eye contact with his patient, "how about I call you Miss Just Brenda Honeypie and cover all the bases?"

This made Brenda laugh out loud, and a feeling of relief kind of swept over me. I began to realize how heavy Bobby was, and looked at him, amazed that he was not causing his own fuss. But he was focused on Mr. Rawlings, too, watching and listening intently.

"Now this will sting just a little, Miss Just Brenda Honeypie. Are you going to be brave for me?" Mr. Rawlings voice maintained its low, soothing tones.

Brenda nodded tentatively, flinched as the medicine was applied but did not cry out. She closed her eyes as Mr. Rawlings completed his first aid work, expertly wrapping a sterile white bandage around her knee, then taping it so that it would not slide.

"I was a medic in WW Two," he said aloud, I guess for Tom's benefit and mine. "Me and a nigger boy name of Washington Jones patched up a lot of shot-up soldiers. And Jones got hisself shot up once, and I patched him up like new. Seen a lot worse than this here."

Tom shot me a look but I ignored him.

Knee bandaging complete, Mr. Rawlings got a clean, warm washcloth and gently pressed it to every scrape on Brenda's body. He looked at her clothes to make sure there was no blood coming from underneath. Then he picked her up in his arms and said to all of us, "I think it's time to get Miss Just Brenda Honeypie home. Y'all coming?"

"What about my bike?" asked Brenda.

"Don't worry about that," said Mr. Rawlings, "I'll bring it back in a little bit. You didn't want to go riding again today, now did you?"

Brenda smiled and just shook her head slowly from side to side. Then she put both her skinny, scraped-up arms around Mr. Rawlings neck and hugged him.

He hugged her back, looked at all of us looking at the two of them, then said in a gruff grown-up voice, "Party's over, y'all. Come on now. Let's get her home."

Together we walked down the Rawlings driveway and turned up the street toward our house. We passed Brenda's battered bike and trudged in unison to our house across the street. We were almost at our front door when Mom's car lumbered up Lynn Acres Drive and turned into the driveway. I remember thinking to myself that this was going to take a little bit of explaining.

* * * * *

I described the entire incident to Marti that evening on the stairs, after she'd already heard Tom's version at dinner, and comments from Brenda about her new friend Mr. Rawlings. I included Rawlings' remark about Washington Jones.

"I just don't get it," I told her. "He called Washington Jones a 'nigger boy,' but it almost sounded as if he liked him, or at least respected him, for what they did together, helping wounded soldiers. So why would he call him a 'nigger boy' like that?"

"Maybe this isn't the best explanation," Marti answered, "but my guess is that Rawlings has been prejudiced against colored people for a long, long time, probably since he was a kid. Hating colored people, believing that they're all lazy, or all dishonest—it's what he was taught by his parents, or even teachers at school. So now, hating anyone and everyone with black or brown skin is as natural to him as breathing. And putting colored people down by calling them all niggers has just become part of his everyday language, even if the person he's calling a nigger boy is somebody he knows well or works with. Doesn't matter—still a nigger to him."

"But does he really hate all colored people, hate them down to his soul? How can you hate somebody you don't even know?"

Marti made a face before answering, curling her lip and scrunching her eyes almost like she was in pain. "You know what I think, Mickey?" she said. "I think it's a lot easier to hate people you don't know. Soldiers hate the enemy cause they believe they're the bad guys and the bad guys want to kill the good guys. No one thinks about whether a bad guy has a mom and dad, or a girlfriend, or maybe even kids who are waiting for their father to come home."

I thought about that for a minute. I thought about being taught to hate. And I wondered if Yvonne was being taught to hate Negroes by her father. But I didn't mention any of this to Marti. I didn't want Marti to know about that side of Yvonne. Frankly, I wish I didn't know about it either.

∗　∗　∗　∗　∗

The next day, while Marti and I were cleaning up from Sunday breakfast, we heard on the radio that a bomb had exploded at the Sixteenth Street Baptist Church in downtown Birmingham. Someone reported, and it was later confirmed, that four young girls were killed in the bomb blast. I looked at Marti when we first heard that news. She had tears in her eyes, but all she said was, "I bet you that bomber never knew who those young girls were. Never knew a single thing about them."

After dinner that evening, before we cleared the table or anything, Dad and Mom led the entire family in saying the rosary for the four young girls and their families. I looked around the table as we prayed. Tom looked bored—and the younger kids didn't really know what was going on, so they were fidgety. Carrie Ann had that sleepy look in her eyes but, thankfully, did not start fussing.

The four older kids—Sheila, David, Marti and I—all wore somber faces, and I wondered at the time what each of us was thinking. David spoke up first, immediately after we said the last Glory Be. "I hope they catch the guy that did this," he said to the table at large, "and fry him like bacon in the electric chair. He needs to die."

"David," Mom said, "not in front of the little kids. Please."

Dad reached out and placed his hand on David's arm. They exchanged glances. I think he was letting David know that he understood his feelings, and maybe even agreed with them.

Sheila's thoughts were on the young girls. "They'll never get to go on dates, never go to parties, never get all dressed up for their proms. It's just so unfair. And so terribly sad."

Marti, whose voice I could barely hear when we were praying the rosary, suddenly spoke up loudly and clearly. "I know what you're saying, David and Sheila, and of course you are both so right. And the family rosary was a super idea. But I keep thinking . . . it's just not enough. Right now, we're all mad and we're all very sad, but this time tomorrow, won't we all start going back to the thoughts and the conversations and the activities that happen every day? And the importance of what occurred today will just naturally drop to second or third place in our minds. And a couple days later, ninth or tenth place. And I'm not saying that makes us bad people, or people who don't care. But what would we say, and how would we feel, if some hate-filled maniac set off a bomb during Sunday mass at St. Barnabas, set off a bomb in our church, and killed four of our friends. Somehow, I wish there was a way to be more angry. More outraged. More . . ." I could see that Marti was running out of steam. She paused. "I just wish," she said.

No one spoke for several seconds. Then Dad said, "Amen." A few more seconds of silence. Then Mom said, "How about we get these dishes cleaned up?"

CHAPTER 10
SEPTEMBER 28, 1963

It was late September before I found myself with enough free time on a Saturday to go visit Jackie again. I went alone. Tom and Marti were both off doing something with other friends from St. Barnabas.

I walked down the hill into the shanty town, not paying much attention to any nearby activity. I didn't want to draw any attention to myself. As I turned onto the dirt road, I noticed Jackie on his porch with a few other colored kids, and that made me a little nervous. Jackie was the first colored kid I'd ever known or spoken to. I wasn't sure I knew how to act around a group of them.

Luckily, Jackie saw me coming and made me feel good with a big wave and a shout, "Hey, Mickey!" I waved back. The other kids just stared at me.

Jackie ran across the yard to meet me. "I see you've got your glove," he said. "We can have a catch. But first, come meet some of my friends."

"Okay," I answered. "Do you have a lot of . . ." I caught myself before I said "colored friends" and quickly substituted "other kids in the neighborhood?" It would have been a stupid question. Of course any other neighborhood kids would be colored. I didn't think Jackie noticed my hesitation.

"Some," Jackie answered. "Us older kids all go to Hayes High School, all the way over to Avondale. Where do you go to school?"

"John Carroll," I said. "Catholic school. I'm a sophomore."

Jackie nodded that he heard me but then got distracted with the job of introducing me to the other kids on the porch.

"Hey, y'all, this here's my friend Mickey from the neighborhood over yonder," he said, pointing vaguely in the direction of my house. I looked around at the three other kids, and kind of nodded hello. None of them said anything.

"This here's Scrambles," Jackie said, pointing to the tallest of the three. "And this is Elliot." He gestured to a shorter, stocky kid with glasses. "And last but not least, this here is my cousin, LP, who is also a pretty good baseball player."

LP was an athletic-looking kid, maybe a little older than the rest of us. He had an unusual scar on the left side of his face. I tried not to look at it.

I nodded again to everyone and said "I'm Mickey."

LP looked right at me and said, "Yeah, we know who you are." It was not the friendliest thing anyone ever said to me.

I felt pressure to respond somehow, so I asked him "LP? Like the record?"

"I ain't no record," LP said.

Thankfully, Jackie jumped in to the exchange. "Don't mind LP," he said. "He's just kinda cranky today. His real name is Lazarus Patrick, but that there's a mouthful, so we all just call him LP."

I nodded understanding, but couldn't think of anything to say.

"Mickey brought his glove," Jackie said. "Any y'all want to have a catch with us?"

"Not me," said Elliot. "I got chores. I gotta git."

Scrambles shook his head. "Not me. Gotta babysit my little sister."

I looked toward LP. "I'm going home," he said, without any explanation as to why. I felt relieved. LP made me uncomfortable.

"Okay," Jackie said. "Another day. Mickey's got a younger brother Tom so we might have enough for a pretty good game someday."

With that, the three kids jumped down off the porch and started walking toward the road. Jackie and I just stood there watching them go. After a little bit, Scrambles turned around and yelled, "Nice to meet y'all, Mickey." I appreciated that, so I waved back. LP and Elliot just kept walking.

* * * * *

Jackie and I played catch for about forty minutes or so, but the sun was hot, so we eventually headed for the shade of the porch. I sat in an old, creaky rocker. I didn't see Nammy, but there were two tall glasses of lemonade waiting for us on a little table near the door.

After sipping our lemonades in silence, I decided to ask Jackie about his friends. "Do all those guys live around here?" I said.

"Pretty close to here," Jackie said. "LP lives just up on the other side of the hill."

"Any other relatives nearby?" I asked.

"Well, there's my great uncle, that's Nammy's brother, and then his son, my Uncle Winston, who is married to LP's mom. They all live together in the same house. By the way, sorry about LP's attitude. He doesn't like white kids much. You saw his scar, right?"

"Yeah. I tried not to stare at it."

"LP's used to stares, I guess. But he got that scar when he was just ten. Ran into a nasty bunch of white kids in the woods one day. Somebody threw lighter fluid in his face and lit a match. Then they all ran away."

"What?" I was horrified, and angry. "That's terrible, that's nuts. Why would they do that? Did they catch the kids? Did they put them in jail?"

"Nah, Mickey. It don't work that way. I think they figured out who did it, maybe. But nobody went to jail. Nobody did nothing to anybody. Someone called it 'kid stuff' but it shore didn't feel that way to LP."

I didn't say anything to that. What could I say? Anyone who lives down South hears stories about bad things done to colored people by white people, physical assaults done for no other reason than that someone is colored. Colored people getting beat up. Colored people getting shot. Colored people getting hung. But this was the first time that I'd ever met someone, actually knew someone, who'd suffered a racial attack. I didn't particularly like LP, but I got mad for him. And I felt embarrassed. For being white. Like somehow this was partly my fault.

Shame made me want to change the subject so I thought I'd ask Jackie about his family.

"How old is your sister?" I said. "I've got four sisters, you know."

"That's a lot of sisters," Jackie said. "Carmella—she's gonna be twelve soon. She was born on Christmas Eve."

"Do you miss her?" I asked. "I mean, her and your mom too, of course. I would sure miss my mom, and any of my sisters, or my brothers, if they lived somewhere else. Especially my twin, Marti. Though sometimes she's a pain."

My last comment made Jackie laugh. "I know what you are talking about. Sisters being a pain. But right now my momma's job in Tupelo is just too good to quit and move back to Birmingham. She and Carmella live in a great big house with some rich white people. Just no room for me. But my momma sends money up to Nammy every month to help with food and stuff. So, it's all working out okay for now."

Jackie and I sat quietly for the next couple of minutes. It felt good, relaxing on his porch, almost like talking with Marti on the steps at our house.

Pretty soon though, I realized that I needed to get home.

"Please thank Nammy for the lemonade," I said, standing up. "Oh, and if you ever really, really, really miss your sister too much, I can lend you one or two of mine. No charge."

Jackie looked up at me and grinned. "Why, that's right generous, Mickey," he said, "I'll let you know."

CHAPTER 11
NOVEMBER 30, 1963

By the time October rolled around, I felt like I was hitting my stride in almost every aspect of my life. At school, I was getting decent grades (not Marti-level, but good). I had a wider circle of friends than my freshman year and enjoyed cheering and clowning around with them at our Friday night football games. I got involved in some after-school activities too—chess club, the Catholic Students Mission Crusade, the debate team. I didn't have a best friend, but I found myself spending a good bit of time at school with Davis Williams. I even spent a weekend at his house that included a visit to one of his public school friends in Pratt City. This kid, Marty Engels, had eleven brothers and sisters. The laundry piles in room after room made me feel right at home.

Other weekends flew by, usually with at least one trek through the woods to Jackie's house. We played catch with the baseball, kicked the football around, played board games on rainy days. Sometimes we just talked. Tom came along with me once in a while. Occasionally, LP was there, and he would join when we played outside, though he still seemed mad at me. Jackie said not to worry about it. Nammy continued to supply us all with cookies, sports trivia, and hugs, depending on her mood.

The only area of my life that was going poorly, which is to say going nowhere, was my relationship with the pretty girl across the street. Yvonne and I had barely seen each other since the Elvis movies outing. Going to different high schools meant zero casual interaction. On top of that, Yvonne seemed very busy with cheerleading practice two or three times a week, and some kind of volunteer work on Saturdays. And the Rawlings family always seemed to be off visiting relatives on Sunday.

The result, sadly, was that Yvonne and I had very little communication with each other, week after week. I tried phone calls but our conversations always seemed to stall after a couple of minutes. So I gave up on that tactic. Occasionally, sheer coincidence would give us a chance to wave at each other across the street, as if we were buddies on the same baseball team. I didn't even know if she remembered holding hands with me in the movies.

On top of that, I was still confused about Yvonne's reaction to the colored boy and his white girlfriend at the movies. I kept asking myself: Was Yvonne prejudiced? Did the girl that I wanted as my girlfriend have an intense dislike for all colored people, like her father did? I did not understand this side of Yvonne. But maybe I was wrong about her. I tried to remember exactly what Yvonne said and how she acted that day, but it was a little fuzzy in my mind.

And then, in November, without warning, the world seemed to blow apart. The only president I'd ever really paid any attention to, the first Catholic president ever, was gunned down in the streets of Dallas, Texas. John Fitzgerald Kennedy and his promises for a better tomorrow were ripped from our lives with the sudden violence of a bolt of Alabama lightning. The vice president, a Texas politician named Lyndon Johnson, became president. For several days in a row, it was all my friends, our school, in fact, the whole country, talked about.

And yet, a week later, because life continues, even when presidents get killed, the Saturday after Thanksgiving dawned and I was feeling good. I'd set my alarm for seven, eager to jump on a bus and head for Legion Field.

If you were a sports fan of the University of Alabama or Auburn University, Legion Field represented a place of legends, the site of countless football games between those teams and other Southeastern Conference rivals. Built in 1927, expanded many times over the years, Legion Field would host almost 55,000 fans this last Saturday of November for the annual Iron Bowl, pitting the two largest Alabama universities against each other.

However, despite my preference for the Alabama Crimson Tide, football rivalries were not the first thing on my mind. Instead, I was focused on Legion Field as a place of commerce. My business: Coke vendor.

I met Davis Williams on the corner of Graymont Ave. and 6th Street W, both of us layered for the cool November morning, knowing that we'd eventually peel off our jackets as the effort of carrying trays of Cokes up and down stadium steps would generate a healthy sweat.

Davis was smiling as I stepped off the bus.

"Ready to make some money?" I said.

"Maybe," he said, "but I'm thinking I'm gonna watch at least some of this game. Joe Namath. Tucker Frederickson. Both teams in the Top Ten. Some good football going on here today."

"I'll watch a play or two," I said, "but I bet I can make $25 if I hustle. I need cash." Truth was, I always needed cash. I didn't have a regular part-time job or babysitting work like Marti to put money in my pocket.

Davis and I walked side by side across the huge empty parking lot toward the stadium. It was still early; there was little visible activity. The crowds would arrive later.

Davis and I had each brought food from home and, despite the early hour, we decided to have lunch. Once the stands began to fill with people interested in pregame activities, we'd be entering prime selling period, and have no time to eat.

It was nice sitting on the bench in the sun, watching the stadium slowly come to life. We still had plenty of time before we needed to get to the vendor's gate. So we talked about high school, teachers and friends, and our own high school football team—which had just finished its season at 7-2 and was looking good for the future. And we talked about girls.

Mostly we discussed four specific girls, whom we'd nicknamed the Fabulous Four, only two of whom we knew well enough to talk to. The other two we admired from a distance.

The girl that we knew best came from Davis' parish, Blessed Sacrament. Davis had known her since first grade. Her name was Sharon Golden—and everything about her made you realize what a perfect last name she possessed. Her hair was blonde, her voice was honey, her smile was like sunshine. Almost every guy in our class was completely and hopelessly in love with her, at least as in love as guys our age could be.

Davis confided that he was actually thinking about asking Sharon to go with him to the Queen of Hearts Dance, though he was worried that she might be dating a senior from West End High School. The Queen of Hearts Dance was in February. Davis was a planner.

"Who do you like, Mickey?" he asked. "Who's your favorite?"

"I dunno," I responded. With Yvonne on my mind, the question was mostly academic. "Maybe Millie?" Millie Roberts, which we'd learned was short for Millicent Roberts because that's what Sister Gabriella called her in history class, was the diminutive, perky, freckle-faced, cuter-than-a-puppy member of the foursome. I'd talked to her a couple of times at the Burger-in-a-Hurry near the Vulcan statue after football games, and we typically nodded to each other in the hallways. Millie was cute enough to consume ketchup-smeared French fries from a small, greasy paper bag and make it look endearing.

Davis jumped on my answer and started talking about what he liked about Millie. In detail.

"Millie," he declared, "is the kind of girl that you'd like to sit on the beach with in Panama City. Except that you'd never sit. You'd jump the waves, you'd throw a football around, you'd go to the arcades together. She'd be perfect for that kind of date."

While he talked, I tried to picture me and Yvonne in Panama City on the beach. That was a nice image. Yvonne in a swim suit would outclass any of the Fabulous Four, no doubt about it.

However, since my relationship with Yvonne was still complicated, and mostly non-existent, I decided not to bring her into the conversation.

Luckily, Davis took little notice of my silence and had now moved on to rapturous remarks about the other two members of the Fabulous Four: Donna Campignola, Italian, olive-skinned, exotic, and Wanda Littleman, tall, thin, willowy, with eyes like a doe.

"Sometimes," he told me, in a this-is-confidential whisper, "I put on my brother's Johnny Mathis album, and just sit next to the stereo with my eyes closed, and imagine what it would be like to slow dance with each one of those girls, one after the other."

There was really only one answer to a statement like that. "You're a madman," I said, grinning at him, "but I like the way you think."

Davis smirked and nodded his head in agreement.

"But now, Romeo," I said, grabbing up my lunch trash and brushing breadcrumbs off my pants, "it's time for us to make some money. Let's go."

* * * * *

We walked quickly from our lunch spot to the chain link gate under the east wing of the stadium. This was where the men who ran the concessions business made their selection from dozens of kids like us who came from all over Birmingham for the privilege of selling Coca-Colas and boiled hot dogs to thousands of rowdy, often inebriated football fans.

Last year, when I'd first heard about this vendor job and showed up for an Alabama game, I had to stand amongst a crowd of almost 75 kids, trying to look ambitious and strong, hoping to get picked, afraid that I'd be turned away from the chance to make some money, not to mention the game itself.

The concessions managers came to the gate intermittently, each time selecting four or five kids who would be allowed through the gate to complete their paperwork as temporary employees of the concession company. That task completed, they'd be assigned a vendor number and be given two trays of freshly-poured Cokes with ice in 10-ounce paper cups, 24 Cokes to a tray.

A year ago, I was selected in the second to last group of four to get in. Probably two dozen or more kids got shut out that day, sent home with nothing to show for their time and trouble, not even getting inside to watch the game.

I remembered that the first quarter had already begun by the time I took my first hesitant steps up into the stands, tentatively yelling "Ice-cold Cokes! Cokes here!" Cokes were twenty-five cents each and sellers earned a nickel for each one sold. A full tray of Cokes earned you $1.20.

Lots of kids were content with selling five trays of Cokes, earning themselves $6. Once they'd hit that modest goal, they'd sit down and watch the rest of the football game from the stadium steps, especially if it was a big game, like Alabama-Tennessee, or Alabama-Ole Miss.

I stood out my first day, even though I got started late, because I sold 14 trays. I could tell that Pete, the guy who recorded the sales results from each of his "salesmen" inside a large copy book, was impressed. "Nice work, kid. Go get 'em" he said as I returned late in the fourth quarter and asked for still one more tray to sell.

The way the system worked, you were given your first tray of Cokes on "credit." When you sold out and returned to the kiosk under the stands for a refill, you had to turn in $6. That's when Pete put a slash next to your name in his book.

At the end of the game, you got $1.20 for each slash next to your name.

The best times to sell Cokes were before the game began and half-time. Before the game was also the time when hot dogs sold best—they stopped giving us hot dogs to sell after half time because it was a waste of product. Unsold hot dogs were eaten by staff or thrown away.

Pregame also seemed to be the time that generated the most tips. On a good tipping day, you could add $5 to your overall take just from tips.

My best tip ever came from a guy who ran down to me from his perch near the very top of Legion Field seating. I liked to sell in the higher up sections, even though it was hard on the legs climbing the cement stairs, because there was relatively little competition. Most kids were too lazy to go there.

"Hey, Ace, I need six Cokes up here," he said, "can you follow me?"

"Sure thing," I responded. Six Cokes cost a buck and half. Even though I'd offer two quarters as change if he gave me two dollars, he'd probably tell me to keep it. I was very good and very quick at tip math.

I followed him up the concrete stadium steps to his seat, five rows from the top and at the end of a row. He was probably 24 or 25, and was seated with three friends, another guy about his age and two absolutely stunning women who were chatting away about something that did not seem to be remotely related to Alabama football.

He crouched down, grabbed a program, then quickly spread it out on the concrete step to create a make-shift tablecloth. He gestured to me to place the Cokes in front of him.

As I put each one down, he quickly ripped off the lid, poured half the contents down the stadium steps, and then refilled it from a sizable pocket flask with what I guessed was bourbon. He gave a drink to each of the women, two to his buddy, and then put the last two down by his feet for himself.

"What do I owe you, Chief?" he asked.

"Buck and a half," I responded.

"Here, keep the change," he said, as he handed me a $10 bill.

"Really, sir?" I wanted to just pocket the cash and run, but honesty—a McQuade family trademark—made me make sure that it wasn't a mistake. "That's a big tip!"

One of the women looked at me and smiled. "He can afford it," she said. "His daddy owns racehorses."

The woman who spoke winked at me as I turned to go. I wanted to wink back, but I didn't.

The memory of both the tip and the wink resurfaced as Davis and I pushed into the throng of kids outside the gate. It was many more kids than usual. Most of them probably just wanted to see Alabama beat Auburn. Or vice versa.

I caught Pete's eye as we stood in the crowd, and he gestured to me and Davis. We had to work our way through the crowd. I could feel the envy from the other kids around me, many of them older and bigger. Being noticed by Pete made me a person of some significance. But I was a veteran at this point and had earned his respect.

We got to the gate and Pete pushed it open to let us through. A couple of other kids who did not understand the way things worked tried to squeeze in behind me, but Pete said firmly, "No, just these two for now." Frankly, since this was his first year as a Coke vendor, Davis did not have the reputation for selling that I did—he kind of rode on my coattails to get himself inside the gate. Pete didn't care, so long as he got one of his top sellers—me—into the stadium and loaded with inventory as soon as possible.

And that's just what happened. In less than five minutes, I had two trays of Cokes and two boxes of hot dogs and I was heading out into the stands a full 40 minutes before kick-off. The next hour was going to be crucial to my success for that day. I ran up the ramp, turned to the gathering crowd, loosened my vocal chords and immediately got to work.

"Hot dogs. Ice-cold Cokes. Get your Cokes and hot dogs!"

CHAPTER 12
SAME DAY

Three hours later, the stadium was rocking with jubilant Auburn fans, rejoicing in a hard-earned 10-8 victory over the Crimson Tide.

My celebratory mood matched theirs—even though my team lost—as I'd just completed my best day ever as a Coke vendor.

Sixteen trays plus four boxes of hot dogs meant better than $25 in sales commissions. And, while I'd had no $10-bill-keep-the-change customers that day, I had earned more than a few bucks in tips as well.

I turned to head back down and under the stands, then stopped to pick up a game program left behind by a forgetful fan. And at that moment, entrepreneurial inspiration struck. Even though they were always visible at the end of games, the number of programs left on seats by fans—by accident or on purpose—had gone relatively unnoticed by me until that exact moment in time. There were dozens and dozens of them, some thrown under seats, some stained with mustard dropped from hot dogs, or spilled coke, or spilled bourbon. But many were in what any bookseller would term excellent condition; lots of them looked like they had never been opened.

I glanced quickly at the crowd heading toward the wide open Exit Gates, both north and south of where I stood. There were still thousands in the stadium, but the majority were out of the stands, walking slowly along the cinder track, following the people in front of them like lemmings out for a Saturday stroll.

I knew I needed to move fast—very fast. I ran up, then down, then up, then down four long rows of seats, grabbing programs as fast as I could. There was no time for any kind of inspection or quality check; the only ones I ignored were programs thrown under the seats.

Both arms full, I took the steps down two at a time. I raced under the stadium, past where a long line of teenage Coke vendors stood patiently waiting to settle up with Pete. I looked for Davis as I ran but didn't see him. I slipped through the now open vendor gate, and ran, breathing hard, to a point about 30 yards away from the North Exit Gate. Fans heading for their cars had to pass right by me. And hundreds of them were.

"Programs here. Used programs. Get your souvenir from a huge Auburn win. Used souvenir programs. 50 cents! Programs here!"

The reaction was immediate. First one guy came up, then another, then a husband-wife, then two more. If I saw that the program I was selling was stained, I just said, "Hold on. Let me get you a better one!" I was handing out programs, making change, stuffing dollar bills in pockets and fishing for quarters, all the while continuing my sales pitch, somewhat shortened: "Used souvenir programs. Just 50 cents! Souvenir programs here!"

At one point, a guy asked me for a deal: "How 'bout two for seventy-five cents?" he yelled.

"Sorry, no specials today," I answered. "Fifty cents a program."

In less than 15 minutes, my inventory was gone. I had grabbed 42 programs, thrown away 6 that were stained or wrinkled, and sold the other three dozen at fifty cents each. That was $18 in pure profit. Figuring the time to collect programs, run out to the gate, and sell out my inventory, I'd worked less than half an hour. That meant I was earning money at a $36/hour rate

— not bad for a 15-year-old kid from a family of eleven, especially when you figure it took me three hours of selling hot dogs and Cokes to make thirty bucks or so, including tips.

* * * * *

When Davis and I finally found each other, over by the concession gate, I couldn't wait to tell him about the program selling. He was suitably impressed.

"Eighteen bucks for thirty minutes work!" he practically yelled. "Unbelievable!"

"How was your day?" I asked.

"I made fourteen bucks," he answered. "Ten trays plus some tips."

"Good day," I said, deciding not to tell him that my earnings from roughly the same amount of time working was close to thirty dollars. That would have felt too much like bragging, especially after all the extra money I'd just made selling programs.

"Yeah," he said, "not bad. Heck of a lot better than nigger wages. That's what my sister told me I'd be making today."

The statement, and its casual, offhand delivery, jarred me. I could not smack Davis in the back of the head like I once did with my brother Tom. I was sure that Davis did not know or care that my parents had spoken to all of the McQuade kids—at different times and in different ways—about the hate that was carried by that word. Davis, like many of the kids I knew from school and in our old neighborhood, seemingly used the word "nigger" with no sense or recognition of its impact.

"Huh?!" I reacted. "What are you talking about, Davis? There's no such thing as. . . " I hesitated, not wanting to repeat the word, but not wanting to make a big deal out of it either. "No such thing as that," I said, emphasizing the "that" to avoid the language problem.

Davis did not appear to notice anything in particular about my reaction. He just explained what he meant, as if he were simply providing a piece of knowledge to an under-informed classmate. "I know," he said, "there's no real thing as 'nigger' wages. It's just an expression. It means not much money."

"Nigger wages," he continued, "is like working all day in a restaurant, clearing tables and wiping up, for like,"—I could tell he was making things up at this point—"for like, two dollars. All day. Two dollars. That's nigger wages, you get it?"

"I get it," I said. "I get it. I'm just thinking maybe there's a better way to say it." I tried to take a kind of scholarly approach to the issue. "You know, so people really understand what you mean."

Davis dismissed that notion quickly. "Everybody knows 'nigger wages,' Mickey," he explained with just a touch of patience in his voice. "Whites, coloreds—everyone knows what nigger wages means."

I looked at Davis, and wondered if Jackie Thomas had ever heard that phrase before, and what he might think about it. But I didn't share my feelings with Davis. Frankly, I wasn't sure I'd be comfortable asking Jackie about it either. It was a touchy subject.

So, I did what I often did when I wanted to avoid a topic that might lead to a difficult discussion. I changed the subject entirely. "Well, we sure made more than two dollars today," I said, "and now I think it's time to get home for a huge turkey and hot gravy sandwich. We've still got leftovers from Thursday."

Davis' eyes lit up, and I could see that his attention had turned immediately to whatever he had waiting for him at home.

"Now you're talking, Mickey," he said. "Let's get outta here."

* * * * *

I probably looked smug as I got on the bus for the long ride from the west side of Birmingham to Roebuck, where my father would pick me up. Frankly, I felt smug.

I was tired but ecstatic—and I could not wait to share my business success with my dad. As the sales manager for a local mimeograph equipment and supply company, Bill McQuade was the smartest businessman I knew. I was sure he'd be proud of me.

I resisted the urge to count my money as the bus rumbled through the downtown section of the city, then climbed across the viaduct with the steel mills glowing red and orange beneath it to the south. I stared out the window as we rolled through Woodlawn and East Lake, alternately folding my arms, then unfolding them to rub my palm across the outside of the pocket of my jeans, feeling the contours of the coins as they pushed against the denim.

I knew I had close to $50 in my pockets, and I was eager to know the exact amount, but it would be more fun to dump everything out on my bed and get Tom to help me count it. In a year or two, Tom would be old enough to go to Legion Field games with me, and expand the reputation of McQuade Coke vendors that I was certainly creating.

My dad met me at the bus stop and I told him all about my day, especially how I thought to sell the programs and how well that turned out. He didn't say much, just congratulated me on having a good idea and then working hard and fast to realize it, but I could tell he was proud.

Then, later, I had to go over the whole story for Mom. She was a little more talkative, asking me questions about how I came up with the idea, how many programs I sold, and whether I was careful out in the parking lot with all that money in my pockets. Mom, as usual, was quick to point out the potential ills that could have befallen me.

An hour and a half later, I sat on the steps with Marti and went over my day for a third time. Except now my description of the day included both my chat with Davis about the Fabulous Four and the exchange we had about "nigger wages."

As I described our conversations, I could feel myself getting bothered by Davis' comment all over again. So I also told Marti about Tom's comment back in the summer, when he called his discovery a "secret nigger town."

"The thing is," I said to Marti, "I don't know why I get so upset when I hear someone call a colored person a nigger. It's just a word, isn't it? Why should a word get me upset?"

My dad, in one of the few really good father-to-son talks we'd had in my life, once spent a good ten minutes with me, explaining his belief that most words are just words, but some words—and "nigger" was one of them—are like weapons. And bigoted, prejudiced people—from the South, the North or anywhere else—used the word "nigger" as a weapon against Negroes.

"But Dad," I'd asked him, "How can it be a weapon if there are no colored people around to hear it? I can see how that works if you call a colored man a nigger when he is right there in front of you. But what about people who use the word nigger all day long, even when there are no colored people around."

My dad thought a minute before answering. "I believe, Mickey, that it's like a man with a gun," my father said. "He feels powerful, more in control when he has that weapon in his hands, even if there is no visible threat, or anything to shoot at. Maybe that's the way many people use the word 'nigger.' When they say it, it makes them feel more powerful. It makes them feel superior. It gives them a feeling of control even if there are no Negroes around to hear it."

"Listen, McGurk," he said, using his special name for me, the way Mom sometimes called my brother Tommyboy. "We're living in a city and a state where people have been calling colored people niggers for a couple hundred years or more. Lots of 'em don't even know why they say it. Lots of people will try to tell you it's not even a bad word . . . that they really like some niggers . . . that there are good niggers and bad niggers . . . that it's just like people calling someone from Ireland a Mick, or someone from Poland a Polack."

"I've heard people say those words sometimes," I said. "Those didn't seem so bad for some reason."

"Well, I don't want you using those words either," he said. "And maybe calling a Polish man a Polack was once as bad as calling a Negro a nigger. But remember this: that Polish man was never a slave. And that Polish man never lived through anything close to the treatment that so many Negroes have had to endure in their lifetimes, just for the color of their skins."

He shook his head. "I don't know if I can explain it any better, Mickey," he said. "But please . . . don't you ever, ever use the word 'nigger' like so many people around here do. We may not be able to do much to help all the people who are involved in this Civil Rights cause that newspapers are full of . . . but at least we can do that."

I remember promising myself that night to do what my father asked, to follow his example and try to make sure that my younger brothers and sisters did the same.

Marti and I had talked about this before. She knew about that conversation with our father. As we sat together on the stairs, she reminded me of one part of it.

"Remember how Dad said that lots of people don't really think when they use that word. Mickey? They're not trying to be especially mean or nasty to Negroes—they're just using a word they've always heard used around them.

"Like Davis," she continued. "When he said 'nigger wages,' he wasn't even talking about a person. He was just saying it like an adjective. Like 'poor man' wages, or something like that."

I looked at Marti and thought about what she said. "Well, you're probably right. He's not a bad kid or a hateful kid. He's actually a really good guy."

"People aren't perfect," she said. "Except for me and you, of course."

That made me laugh.

CHAPTER 13
DECEMBER 1, 1963

On the Sunday afternoon following Thanksgiving, I trudged through the woods to see Jackie. I was eager to tell him about my success as a Coke vendor and used program entrepreneur. The day was gray and rainy—way too wet to throw the football around—so we sat inside his house. I left my shoes, muddy with red clay from the road, on a mat just inside the front door. No way I was tracking mud through Nammy's house. I sat in my socks on the floor by Nammy's big old green sofa.

Nammy had given me a big welcome when I came in. She'd wrapped her massive arms around me, hugged me tight, and told me that she'd missed me, even though she saw me most weekends. "We need to see ya'll more often, Mickey! Ya'll are welcome in my home anytime, y'hear me?"

Maybe to emphasize her point about how welcome I was, Nammy immediately headed to the kitchen, promising to be back in a "lightning flash" with some of her famous hot chocolate and her world-famous pecan shortbread cookies. I remember thinking that, no matter what was coming out of Nammy's kitchen, it was sure to be some kind of famous.

Jackie listened intently as I took him through everything that had happened since last weekend, including my day at Legion Field, getting in the gate with my friend Davis, selling hot dogs and Cokes early as football fans settled into place, then later running out to the front gate to sell used programs to the departing crowd.

"Fifty dollars for one day's work!" Jackie exclaimed. "I never made more than five dollars for a day's work in my whole life." He was quiet for a moment, thinking, before adding, "Mebbe I never will. Fifty dollars is a lot."

"I just got lucky," I said, trying to sound modest even though I didn't feel particularly humble at the time. "It was such a big win for Auburn, people just wanted a souvenir."

"But if Alabama won," Jackie said, "you could have sold souvenir programs to their fans. You were covered either way."

"You're right," I said, looking Jackie right in the eye. "I'm kind of a genius."

That made Jackie laugh out loud, a laugh noisy enough for Nammy to holler from the kitchen, "Y'all boys might be having a little too much fun out there!"

"Sorry, Nammy," Jackie said, "we'll quiet down a bit."

And we did. For one or two minutes, Jackie and I just sat there, on the floor, not saying anything, content with ourselves, enjoying the sound of rain hitting the roof. I was re-remembering all of my money-making moments from the day before until my thoughts shoved me right up against Davis Williams and his comment about "nigger wages."

I looked over at Jackie, wondering what he'd think of that phrase, wondering if I could talk to him about it, but nervous that I would say something wrong and get him mad at me. We'd never really talked about whites and coloreds before, except for the time when we were talking baseball players. Jackie looked at me, and seemed to guess that there was something on my mind.

"What?" he asked.

I looked at him. "What what?" I said.

"I seen that look before, Mickey. You got something to say but you're not sure how to say it, or if you want to say it, or if you should say it, so you'll probably just not say anything. Right?"

"Yessir," I said.

"So, say it," he said. "Just go on with it."

I considered Jackie's prompt, and how comfortable I felt just sitting there in the house with him, and I guess I found some courage. But I lowered my voice so that Nammy couldn't overhear us. "Well," I said, "when I was at the game, I heard a person in the crowd yell something about . . ." I hesitated.

"C'mon, Mickey . . . "

"About colored people wages. Except they didn't say colored people. They said something else."

Jackie stared at me, but not in an angry way. "Nigger wages?" he asked in a voice so low I could barely hear him.

"Yeah." I whispered. "Exactly. And it made me think of you and made me wonder if anyone had ever called you that, I mean, right to your face."

Jackie looked away from me, up toward the ceiling, then out toward the kitchen where we could hear Nammy bustling about, then finally settling on my muddy, well-worn sneakers sitting over near the door.

I waited. I felt nervous and was wishing I'd kept my mouth shut. In my head, I was trying to decide how exactly to apologize for my question.

Finally Jackie spoke. "How many times you put those old shoes on?" he said.

I was confused. My face must have shown it.

"How many times," Jackie said, "did you actually put your feet into those shoes, and tighten up the laces, and tie a nice ol' double knot . . . ?"

"I dunno," I said, "but I . . ."

Jackie interrupted whatever foolish answer I was about to give him.

"Take that number, Mickey, and times it by five, no, times it by ten, no, make it a hundred, and that's how many times I've heard the word nigger said to my face, or behind my back, or once whispered in my ear . . . that's how many times . . . "

"What y'all boys talkin' bout so low in there?" Nammy called from the kitchen. "I can hear you talkin'. Must be up to some foolishness. Must be thinking ol' Nammy's ears done give out."

Nammy's comment, and her sudden appearance in the doorway, broke the mood. Jackie looked at me and said, "Nother time." I nodded.

Nammy looked from one of us to the other, then said "You boys looking guilty as a fox coming out of the hen house with feathers in his teeth. What kind of mischief you talking about?"

"No mischief, Nammy. Just talking," I said. "Well, we might have been saying about how I am kind of a financial genius."

Nammy gave me a long, silent look with a raised eyebrow. Then she turned and went back into the kitchen, shaking her head. But I could tell she wasn't mad.

Jackie picked up on my last remark. "If you were really a genius," he said, "you'd know how to invest that fifty dollars and turn it into two hundred dollars. That's what a true genius would do!"

"Good thinking," I admitted, "but I'm actually planning to spend a fair amount of that money for Christmas presents. I've got a few brothers and sisters, you know. And I've never had so much money for gift-giving at Christmas time before."

"That's a lot of presents," said Jackie.

"Hey," I said, inspiration striking me. "How would you like to come Christmas shopping with me? Help me pick out gifts, maybe do a little shopping for yourself?"

"Well," Jackie looked at me dubiously, "I don't have much gift-buying money." Then he whispered. "But I've got an idea for a gift for Nammy if I can find it for under two dollars."

"We'll find it, whatever it is," I said, warming quickly to my own idea. "Listen—we can go on a Saturday, and we'll hunt for bargains together, and because I am the richest man in the world, I'll even treat us both to lunch at Burger Bonanza." Burger Bonanza was one of those new burger places, but maybe a little more upscale than McDonald's, that seemed to be popping up all over Birmingham. You ordered your food at a window, and then ate it in your car, or sometimes, at picnic tables scattered around the outside of the restaurant. Or you could eat inside at a table.

"Wait. Can we do that?" asked Jackie. "I mean eat burgers together at a restaurant, a white boy and a colored kid? Nammy and me know all about that big ol' Truce statement from last spring but it didn't say nothing about Burger Bonanza."

Jackie was talking about a well-known accord between Birmingham city leaders and the Alabama Christian Movement for Civil Rights, led by Martin Luther King and others. They'd reached an agreement last May, though it was followed by two bombings and riots in the streets immediately thereafter. The agreement included the desegregation of lunch counters in department stores. I didn't know if it specified anything about burger establishments, which I guessed most people assumed were still segregated under a long time Birmingham ordinance.

"No problem," I told Jackie. "We'll eat outside. We just can't eat together inside the restaurant." I spoke with a confidence that I did not feel and certainly couldn't back up. But it was good enough for Jackie.

"Hold on," he said, then turned and shouted to Nammy in the kitchen. "Hey, Nammy, can me and Mickey go Christmas shopping together? We could go on a Saturday. Mickey's mom or dad or maybe his brother could take us and bring us home." I had not really mentioned transportation, but it was good to see that Jackie had the ability to ad lib in order to advance our cause.

Nammy appeared in the doorway. "Christmas shopping? So that's what y'all was whispering on about?"

I guess we looked a little guilty, because Nammy let out with one of her big chuckles. "Ha-ha, you should see the look on your face, Mr. Mickey. Like a big old weasel."

I didn't say anything but gave her my most innocent look.

"Christmas shopping—the two of you—on a Saturday? Well, I guess so, if it's okay with your mom, Mickey. Now get in here and have some hot chocolate. These delicious Nammy cookies ain't gonna eat themselves."

Later that evening, I off-handedly mentioned to my mother that I was going to need a Saturday free at some point to do some Christmas shopping and maybe I'd get a friend to go with me. She said, "Sure, Mickey, good idea," but I don't think she was really listening.

CHAPTER 14
DECEMBER 21, 1963

On the Saturday before Christmas, I awoke early, looking forward to the day. Earlier in the week, I'd gone to Jackie's house after school, and confirmed that today would be the day for our gift-shopping expedition. Now all I had to do was to remind my mother and make sure that someone would be available to drive us. I hadn't mentioned anything to Mom about this since our brief conversation after Thanksgiving—truthfully, I did not want to give her any time to think up reasons why I shouldn't go.

The only serious objection I could anticipate was the fact that lots of people did not like the idea of white teenagers and "coloreds" spending any time with each other, especially in public. You hardly ever saw white kids and black kids together, not on ball teams, or the playground, or even just walking around at the shopping center. Traynor Rawlings asked me once why I was always going to visit "with that nigger kid in the woods." I told him to shut up.

However, daily life throughout Birmingham had calmed down quite a bit since the bombings and the riots of the previous spring. I was banking on that to get past any misgivings from my mother.

Pulling on my jeans, I began to work through a mental list of goals for the day. There were gifts to buy for each member of the family. I needed to find something a little bit extra special for Marti. I thought it might be nice to get a present for Jackie and Nammy, like a box of candy or something. And I needed to address my single most important objective for the holidays, finding the absolutely perfect gift—meaning beautiful, thoughtful, romantically suggestive, yet still appropriate—to give to Yvonne for Christmas.

This holiday season was an opportunity that, in my mind, had to be seized. This was my chance to resurrect the Yvonne-Mickey relationship which was clearly stalled. A harsher analyst might call it non-existent.

Despite having met Yvonne more than six months ago, in June, the high point of our "romantic" connection was still our time holding hands in the movie theater. Months had passed since those magic moments.

Marti and Yvonne were friendly, but not friendly enough for the two of them to spend much time together at our house, where I could be a part of the scene. Once, Yvonne did come over with Traynor to play Crazy Eights. But since Marti and Tom also played, there was not much chance to engage Yvonne in one-on-one conversation. And we did not even sit next to each other during the game. I had tried to make meaningful eye contact with her a few times, while someone was dealing the cards, or after I'd made a particularly significant discard, but she never noticed.

All in all, if the Mickey-Yvonne relationship were one of the romance novels that my sister Sheila loved to read, it would probably be described by critics as "a story that never really got going."

I intended to change all that with the selection and purchase of one symbolically-rich and timeless gift. I needed a gift that said "Hey, remember watching the Elvis movies together?" I needed a gift that expressed my romantic feelings, and touched Yvonne's heart, and won her love. Or at least her significant like.

I figured five dollars and a trip to the Roebuck Shopping Center would get the job done.

So I hurriedly got dressed and went downstairs to discuss arrangements with my mother, and secure the needed transportation. I found her sipping coffee in her bathrobe, smoking a cigarette while making toast for the little kids who would be wandering downstairs soon.

"Hey, Mom," I said brightly, "do you know who'll be taking me and Jackie to Roebuck for Christmas shopping this morning?"

Mom looked at me curiously, seemingly confused by my question. "What, Mickey?" she asked. "What are you asking me?"

"Mo-om." I used my almost-ready-to-whine voice, a combination of surprise and disappointment, which I did not like to do, but which felt necessary to avoid the possibility of a pre-emptive no. "You said I could go Christmas shopping with Jackie. I told you about it weeks ago. And now it's the last Saturday before Christmas. And I promised Jackie we'd go."

I let the confusion grow on her face. I could see her trying to recall a conversation with me on this topic, and failing. I felt a little guilty.

"You and Jackie? Christmas shopping? Out by yourselves? Mickey, I don't remember any of this."

"Mom," I whined. "I told you about this. Weeks ago. Right after Thanksgiving. We're just going to the shopping center. Why . . ."

My mom raised a finger to shush me. I shushed.

"Look, Mickey, I don't want to keep you from enjoying some time with your friend. It's just . . . well, the two of you . . . I guess it's okay, maybe . . . have you talked with your father?"

I was pretty sure I knew why Mom was hesitating. If I'd asked for Marti and me, or even Tom and me, there would have been no problem. She was wrestling with the white and colored issue, but did not want to acknowledge it, because she knew it would go against her strong belief that segregation at every level was evil.

While she struggled, I decided to press my advantage. "Mom, I'm sure Dad would say yes. We'll be gone for three hours max. Just to the shopping center. Somebody takes us, somebody picks us up. I'm fifteen years old, almost sixteen."

Mom relented. "Okay, okay. Go ask David if he can drive you. But be careful. Stay out of trouble."

Once victory was achieved, there was no reason to stick around. "Definitely," I said. "Thanks, Mom. I'll go find David."

* * * * *

By the time we reached the shopping center, it was 11:45 and I was hungry. David dropped Jackie and me off near Burger Bonanza, a modestly upscale restaurant if you compared it to McDonald's, Burger in a Hurry, and Jack in the Box, just three of the window-service, eat-in-your-car hamburger spots that were popping up all over town.

At Burger Bonanza, a hamburger was 25 cents, 10 cents more than McDonald's. It was supposed to be "juicer, with more beefy flavor." What's more, Burger Bonanza had inside tables, an important feature for car-less patrons.

"How many burgers you want?" I asked Jackie as we walked. "I'm thinking three myself – with fries and a milkshake. Remember, this is my treat!"

I was afraid Jackie might be too polite and not order enough to eat, but he surprised me.

"Three sounds 'bout right," he answered. "I didn't eat breakfast cause I knew where we were headed." He grinned at me.

Since it was still before noon, the restaurant was practically empty. I stepped ahead of Jackie to the counter and was met with a blank stare by the only order taker on duty, a teenager, maybe a year or two older than me, with a pile of dirty brown hair awkwardly tucked underneath a much too small Burger Bonanza server's hat. He had a face full of ugly red pimples.

I looked up at the menu board displayed above his head and opened my mouth to give our order, but he interrupted me right away with a half-whisper and a shake of his head, as if we were sharing a secret, and said "This'll be take-out, right?"

"Pardon me," I said, even though I heard him clearly enough.

"Niggers," he said, continuing his whisper although Jackie was close enough to hear every word. "Niggers do take-out."

Then, in a normal voice, he asked "What can I get for y'all today?"

I could not see but rather felt Jackie begin to turn away. Without even looking, I reached out and grabbed his arm to hold him in place. I could feel myself turning red, and tensing up, and getting a horrible knot in my stomach. Confrontations, of any kind, usually made me want to throw up. Even if I wasn't directly involved. On the playground at St. Barnabas, I was always the peacemaker, the guy who settled the arguments and disagreements, who figured out the compromises and the do-overs and got everybody happy again.

Even though my first instinct was to do exactly what Jackie seemed inclined to do, which was to leave the store and find lunch elsewhere, I followed my second instinct. I got stubborn.

My voice quivered a little when I spoke. "W-wait, listen," I said, "I think, uh, that you ha-have to serve us. You can't ask us to leave."

Pimple-face looked at me. "I didn't," he said. "I just asked if y'all wanted take-out."

"Are y'all having any kind of a problem here?" a commanding disembodied voice interrupted us. I looked to my right and saw a burly, sour-faced man approaching the three of us. He was wearing a bright yellow Burger Bonanza apron with the word MANAGER stitched into it in bold navy blue block letters.

Pimple-face and I both started talking at once.

He said, "I was just telling them that they could order take-out and . . ."

I said "All we want to do is order some lunch . . . "

The angry-looking man raised his hand to silence both of us.

"Do you want lunch?" he asked me.

"Yessir, we do," I answered.

"Do you want take-out?"

I felt Jackie move slightly but I increased my pressure on his arm to hold him in place.

"No, we want to eat here," I said, hating the way he asked the question, but finding some inner conviction that made me hold my ground. "We want to eat inside." But I did not want to come across as defiant. So I added a reasonable explanation, as if the outside temperature was the issue at hand, which it wasn't. "It's kind of chilly outside and there's no place to sit down. So we'd prefer to eat here."

"That's fine," he said, even though I could see from his face that it wasn't. "Actually, we're not properly set up for this but I'm willing to make an exception. You can eat at that table . . ." he pointed to a nearby table by the window, "and your nigger friend can eat over there at that one." He pointed to another table all the way across the room from mine.

I stared at him, confused.

"What?" I said. "That makes no sense. We came in together. We're gonna eat together."

"Not in my restaurant," the manager said. "City ordinance. Posted on the wall." He pointed. "I can serve whites. And I have to serve niggers. But y'all can't eat together. It's the law." He paused for a split-second. "So what's it gonna be? Take-out?"

I had no idea where my apparent calm came from, but I ignored the question, turned away from the counter and stepped over to read the framed document on the wall of the restaurant.

SECTION 369. SEPARATION OF RACES.

It shall be unlawful to conduct a restaurant or other place for the serving of food in the city, at all which white and colored people are served in the same room, unless such white and colored persons are effectually separated by a solid partition extending from the floor upward to a distance of seven feet or higher, and unless a separate entrance from the street is provided for each compartment.

The restaurant had no separate entrance, and no partition, but it would have been ridiculous to point that out. My jaw was clenched, my hands balled up into fists. I turned abruptly toward the door.

"We're leaving, Jackie," I said, trying to keep my voice from shaking. "C'mon." I didn't look at him, or the Burger Bonanza manager. Anger seethed through me.

Jackie calmly and silently followed me out the door.

"Y'all have a nice day," called the store manager. I could hear pimple face laughing in the background.

CHAPTER 15
SAME DAY

I was halfway across the shopping center parking lot, walking fast, head down, when Jackie reached out and touched my arm. I stopped, breathing hard. I was furious for him, and mortified for both of us.

"Hey, Mickey, it's okay," he said. "It's okay."

"It's not okay, Jackie!" I shouted, unable even to look at him. "It's not one bit okay. It's . . . it's . . . it's shameful. That's what it is. Shameful."

I hadn't cried for a long time about anything, but I felt I was getting close.

"Hey—that's a good word," Jackie replied. His voice was strangely calm. "Shameful. I like that."

I didn't get it. Why wasn't Jackie as mad as me? Madder? It was as if those two ignorant . . . my mind searched for a word that was bad enough to describe them. Sons of bitches. Ignorant, bigoted sons of bitches!

I turned on Jackie, fuming. "Why aren't you screaming?" I yelled at him. "Why aren't you furious? Why aren't you throwing rocks through the windows of that stupid place right now? Don't you wanna just punch pimple face in the teeth? What's wrong with you?"

My words, and the anger I was directing at Jackie, were completely unfair. But I didn't care.

Of all the responses that I might have expected—if I were thinking straight, which I wasn't—the one least anticipated would have been laughter. Jackie stared at me as I ranted. Then his cheeks suddenly puffed up and his lips clamped together like he was trying to hold his breath. And then he exploded into a fit of hoots and cackles, loudly, joyfully, uncontrollably. Like I'd just told him the finest joke he'd ever heard in his life.

"Man oh man, Mickey," he said, finally forcing the words out between mini convulsions. "You are . . . the funniest angry white kid . . . I've ever seen. I wish Nammy was here to see this. You're insane. Completely nuts."

More laughter. He couldn't speak.

I wanted to stay mad. I wanted to keep my fury going. But seeing and hearing Jackie in a laughing fit took all the rage out of me. I couldn't help myself, I started laughing too. Maybe not as fully as Jackie, but honestly.

"I'm sorry, Mickey," Jackie said, mixing words and giggling. "Not trying to make fun of you. I'm just . . . being . . . shameful." And that started Jackie off on another round of hysterics.

I let him go for another half a minute, and then interrupted him. "Hey. Wise guy. Glad you're having fun—but what's going on? How come you are laughing? That was not funny."

Jackie had calmed himself down by this point, and saw that I was asking a serious question. He tried to explain.

"Mickey, Mickey. I've had all that happen to me, and more," he said, "sometimes even in ways that made me afraid. And I've gotten mad, madder even than you did just now. And probably acted worse, like screaming and yelling in people's faces worse. And throwing mud and breaking windows worse. But what was funny to me was your reaction, a white boy's reaction— your outrage, I guess you'd call it—cause you were getting treated today like us colored kids get treated every day. And you didn't like it, not one little bit.

And you steamed and you sputtered and you pretty much turned into a crazy man, right before my eyes. And I'm sorry, but to me, you were just . . . just . . . hilarious!"

I stared at Jackie, beginning to understand. I was a rookie in a "get treated like dirt by bigots with half a brain" world. It was clear to me that Jackie was a seasoned pro, a veteran of many episodes like this or worse, too many to count. He may have hated every second of what we just went through—but he'd taught himself how to handle them with the least amount of pain and risk and danger. I was pretty sure that I just learned something important from my friend.

Wanting to move on, I complained. "Problem is, Jackie, after all your laughter, I'm still hungry. Think we can figure out a new plan here?"

"Okay, okay," he said, though he couldn't seem to hold back from grinning.

"And no more burger places—I've lost my appetite for them," I said.

Looking around the shopping center from the middle of the parking lot, I wondered if our best bet would be the lunch counter at Woolworth's. Ever since the Birmingham Truce, an agreement between the Civil Rights movement and Birmingham civic leaders that was reached last spring, colored people could be served at lunch counters in department stores. I'd learned that from David.

"How 'bout this?" Jackie said, looking past me to the row of stores farthest from where we stood in the parking lot. "There's a barbeque place right over there," he pointed with his finger, "next to the Grant's store. It's called Johnny Ray's. And Nammy says they have the best barbecue around. How 'bout we go get ourselves some barbecue pork sandwiches with extra pickles?"

I looked where Jackie pointed and saw a neon sign: Johnny Ray's—Best BBQ In The South!

"Do they do take-out?" I asked Jackie, seriously. I did not want to go through another scene like we just experienced.

"Yeah—let's do take-out," he said immediately. "We can eat it sitting on the curb. I need me some fresh air, Mickey."

We walked into Johnny Ray's together—and our appetites spiked instantly with the wonderful aromas of wood-fired, slow-roasted meats. Right inside the front door, huge cuts of pork turned slowly on a spit, flames licking up at the roasts. Our timing was perfect. No sooner had we entered than one of the staff began spraying the meat and the fire, forcing small billows of hickory smoke into the air. Theologians might disagree, but I was pretty sure that this is what it smelled like in heaven.

We walked to the counter, together, a little warily. A pleasant-looking young woman smiled at the two of us. "How can I help y'all?" she asked.

"Two barbecue pork sandwiches, please" I said. "Extra pickles. Two orders of fries. Two cokes. Make that four cokes." This was going to cost a lot more than Burger Bonanza—but I didn't care. Jackie nudged me to give me his extra dollar, but I waved him off. I wanted to pay for his entire meal myself.

"Take-out?" she asked, as if there was a choice to me made, which there wasn't. I guessed that the city ordinance governed barbeque restaurants as well as burger places.

"Take-out works for us," I said.

* * * * *

After our Johnny Ray's lunch, the two of us were about as full as any two teenagers can get. The barbecue sandwiches were large and delicious. We ate all the fries. Devoured the extra pickles. Washed everything down with our two cokes.

Jackie kept trying to give me his dollar, but I was feeling good about paying for the whole meal myself. "After all those cookies from Nammy," I said, "least thing I can do is buy her grandson some lunch."

He finally stopped offering, and said thank you. "You're mighty welcome," I said, "but next time, we're gonna need a sponsor. You eat a lot for a skinny guy."

"Big talk from a beanpole," he answered.

Our moods, understandably, were a lot better than when we stormed out of Burger Bonanza. Now we were ready to do what we came to do— spend money on Christmas presents.

Our first stop was a local department store, Benjamins. My dad had actually worked with the small chain a few years before, until he got his job as sales manager at the duplicating equipment and supplies company. I knew the layout of this store and the kind of merchandise it carried pretty well.

I led the way to housewares, Jackie close behind me. I wanted to buy an omelet pan for my mother—and Jackie was looking to buy a new apron for Nammy. Her current apron, he said, had holes worn in it from being washed so many times, and the edges were all frayed. His problem, of course, was going to be finding an apron big enough to fit around his grandmother.

Luck seemed to have turned in our favor. I discovered a beautiful little silver-colored omelet pan, on sale, which brought the cost into my price range. Jackie found an entire table stacked with aprons, neatly arranged by color, though not by size. It took a while but he finally selected a red apron that satisfied his sizing concerns—unfolded, it approached the dimensions of a small tablecloth. I nodded approval and we moved on.

We strolled the aisles, a little bit aimlessly, though I did have my list of gift recipients in my head. The store was crowded with shoppers, and I was distracted thinking about what I might find for Yvonne, so it wasn't surprising that Jackie and I got separated. I wasn't worried. I knew we'd find each other, so I wandered over to the paperback book racks to focus on gifts for Dad and David and Tom. Marti too—if I could find something special. I hated the idea of giving her just any old book.

Fortunately, with most of the people in my family, book selection was not a problem. Dad and David read almost anything and practically everything. Any sports book would work for Tom. Marti was a different story. I kept scanning title after title, with no success, when I heard a man behind me ask, in a cold, flat voice, "Is this the friend you claim to be with?"

I turned to see a large man in a dark suit wearing a blue button down shirt and a solid black tie. He looked like he might have played Alabama or Auburn football at one time—he was that beefy. He had a face that a caricaturist would love—strongly defined features, bulging dark eyes, a jaw that looked like it could take a Cassius Clay right hook without even disturbing the tight line of his lips. Right beside him, looking at me with nervous eyes and the slightest little quiver around his mouth, stood Jackie.

"That's him, yessir," said Jackie. "That's my friend, Mickey. We came on in here together."

"Is that right?" the man asked me. I noticed right away that he spoke without a trace of the familiar Southern accent.

"Yessir," I answered politely. I was not sure who or what the man was, but he clearly held some position of importance within the store. My parents had taught us McQuade kids to always respect authority—teachers, priests and nuns, police, school crossing guards, hostesses at diners—the list was extensive. The principle was to do what you were asked or told first, and, on rare, rare occasions, and only if absolutely necessary, ask questions later.

For a few seconds, no one said anything. Then I asked, "Is something the matter?"

The man ignored my question. "You boys planning on paying for all this stuff?" He indicated with head nods the apron that Jackie still held tucked under his arm, and the omelet pan on the counter which now contained three paperback books.

At the time, I did not grasp how insulting his remark was. I answered, "Of course we are. Why wouldn't we?"

I probably could have left off the "why" question, though I truly asked it more out of surprise than any other reason. I was not trying to be difficult.

"Have you finished your shopping?" he asked, once again ignoring the question I asked him.

We weren't, not by a long shot, but with the Burger Bonanza situation still fresh in my mind, I made what might have been called a battlefield decision. "Yessir, we are, we're all done here."

"Good," he said. "Come with me. I'll show you where the cash registers are."

He motioned to us to follow, and we did, looking at each other as we walked behind him, but not speaking. I paid for my books and omelet pan, Jackie paid for Nammy's apron. Then, with the store guy and the cashier and other shoppers staring at our backs, we pushed through the glass doors and into the crowd on the shopping center sidewalk. We walked, not speaking. We were almost to F.W. Woolworth's—a good half-a-shopping center away from Benjamins—before I finally stopped and turned toward Jackie. By this point, realization about what had just happened had begun to sink in—and intimidation was giving way to indignation. We'd just been "hustled" out the door of a store that I'd shopped in at least half-a-dozen times with my parents. And for what? By whom? What the heck was going on?

"That," said Jackie, in the understatement of the day, "was a large man."

"He was a large jerk," I said loudly. "What did we do to get treated like that? Did he think we were going to shoplift an omelet pan and an apron? And three books? Shoplifters don't read! That was unfair."

The sound of my own words was getting me progressively angrier. I was mad at the man for what he did—and madder at myself for what I didn't do to protest. For the second time that day.

Jackie put his hand on my shoulder to calm me down. Again. "It wasn't you, Mickey—it was me. Colored boys by themselves in department stores make white men nervous." He paused. "C'mon now, you understand."

"No, I don't understand," I said. "But I know what you're saying." And then I topped Jackie's understatement with one of my own. "It's not so easy being colored, is it?"

Jackie half-smiled at my question.

"Nope," he said. "It's not. Not always. Not every day."

* * * * *

Thankfully, F. W. Woolworth's seemed to be fresh out of large, anti-Negro security people. We cruised the store without incident, found an odd-looking styling hairbrush for Sheila, a little bag of plastic WWII army men for Ricky, small stuffed poodles for Brenda and Carrie Ann, and a toy truck for Bobby. I decided to go over budget and bought a sweater for Marti. It was a deep, almost iridescent blue that I thought would look nice with her brown hair. That left only one person on my list: Yvonne.

I was beginning to despair. I'd covered almost every inch of the two biggest stores in the shopping center, and I hadn't yet seen anything that felt right for Yvonne. And now we were beginning to run out of time.

I'd spent some time at the jewelry case, but everything was either too expensive or too intimate. I thought about a sweater like the one I chose for Marti—but I had no idea what size I should buy, and I didn't want Yvonne thinking that I thought she was fat by purchasing something too big for her. And too small might make it look like I was thinking about her chest.

Jackie suggested a Timex, but I knew Yvonne already owned a watch

113

that her grandmom had given her. He then proposed—in rapid succession—perfume that was much too expensive, slippers, a belt. I knew he wanted to help. But as good a friend as he was, Jackie was clearly deficient in the "gift ideas for a potential girlfriend" department. I was beginning to wish that Marti had come along with us.

And then, just as I was preparing to advance from desperation to panic, a small Christmas miracle occurred in the form of barely audible but unmistakable musical notes lifting themselves above the din and commotion of the store, and reaching my ear. The music itself was tinny, artificial, but clearly recognizable as the melody from Moon River, a song made famous by the singer Andy Williams. A few years back, it had been Sheila's favorite song—she practically wore out the 45 rpm record that she had of it.

I turned completely around, trying to determine the origin of the sound, and discovered that it was coming from a table display of two dozen or more snow globes, some of which were also music boxes. I located the one that was playing the song. It featured two little figures of bears, with one pushing the other on a playground swing.

I held the snow globe in my hand gingerly, as if it were a rare coin, a precious jewel, Sir Galahad's Holy Grail. I examined it for any possible flaws, reflecting, considering, excitement growing inside me. This, I said to myself, this could be it. The scene within the snow globe was romantic, but not overly romantic. It was a gift that Yvonne could place on her dresser or night table and see every day to remind her of me. It showed a young couple—us! It had visual interest, motion, sound. And it was only two dollars and ninety-nine cents. Before sales tax, but still.

Ecstatic, all I required was the slightest bit of confirmation that I'd made a good choice. This is where I truly needed Marti at my side. Lacking that, I turned to my shopping companion. "I've got it, Jackie," I said. "At least, I think I've got it." I extended the snow globe proudly, let him examine it while

I watched nervously, eager to see his reaction, fearing what it might be. He seemed less enchanted than I was, but then, he was not the guy who needed to make the significant impression. Nor did he know the recipient.

Jackie continued to study the snow globe, turning it upside down, testing the wind-up mechanism, holding it up to the light. I was impatient, and had almost convinced myself that I had given this incredible important evaluation task to someone hopelessly underqualified for the job, when Jackie looked up at me and said, "It's perfect, Mickey. I think she's gonna love it."

Relief and appreciation flooded through me.

"Thanks," I said, and got a 'no big deal' shrug of the shoulders from Jackie.

Then I looked at my watch. "Let's get out of here," I said. "It's almost time to meet David."

We were slowed at the register because of the number of shoppers, but we finally made it outside Woolworth's with a few minutes to spare. We turned to the right, and headed toward our rendezvous point. I could see that David's car was not there yet, which was good, because I did not want to keep him waiting. At Penney's, we were delayed trying to cross the driving lane into the parking area—traffic was heavy. Finally, there was a break in the line of cars. We crossed at a trot, saw David's car heading toward us from the very far end of the parking lot, and then were startled by the harsh blast of a car horn immediately behind us. We whirled around to see the pimply-faced kid from Burger Bonanza at the wheel of an old, junky-looking Chevy. He'd stopped his car and stared straight at the two of us. We looked at him, he looked at us. Then he spat out the window, yelled "Nigger Lover," and hit the gas hard to "burn rubber" with his departure.

"You're a jerk!" I yelled at the back of his car. He probably did not hear me. The Chevy never slowed, sped past David's car coming toward us, then wheeled away into traffic. All the good feelings connected to finding the perfect gift for Yvonne were gone in an instant. I was, for the third time that day, consumed with anger. I wanted to punch that kid's face in.

* * * * *

"Do you think it's always like that for Jackie?" I asked Marti, after telling her all about my day from the incident at Burger Bonanza to the shout of "Nigger Lover." We were sitting on the steps in our usual positions but with one step between us for a small plate of brownies, most of which I intended to eat myself. "Do you think he gets treated badly, and accused of shoplifting, every time he goes out to a restaurant or the shopping center?"

"No. Not every time," Marti said. "And, from what you said, you didn't get accused of shoplifting. The two of you were just 'encouraged' to move along."

I started to protest her defense of the store security man but Marti interrupted me.

"I'm not saying that he was right in harassing you," she said, "and that's exactly what it sounds like he was doing. I'm just trying to be accurate with the facts."

"Which made you madder?" Marti asked me. "The kid who called you a nigger lover . . . or the security guard who treated you like shoplifters just because Jackie was colored?"

I just stared at her. Marti always seemed to throw a different perspective on things—and I tried to sort through my feelings because I didn't really know.

"Which would you rather take on in a fight?" she asked. "Blatant, naked hostility like you got from pimple-face . . . or sneaky, underhanded discrimination like the security guy? And, by the way, from what you told me, nobody broke any laws so you can't go to the police on those kind of things to complain."

"I don't know. Both made me madder than anything. Not sure which one was worse."

Now it was Marti's turn to stare at me while I turned her question inside out in my mind.

"You know what I'd really like to do is ask Jackie that question," I said. "After all, the bigotry, the meanness, the injustice were mostly aimed at him, or because of him. But he stayed pretty cool no matter what happened. It was me that was flying off the handle, or getting all indignant, even if I didn't react right away, like, right on the spot!"

"Good idea, Mickey. Ask him. Tell me what he says. But no matter what," she added, "seems to me you have a pretty unusual friend."

CHAPTER 16
CHRISTMAS DAY - DECEMBER 25, 1963

Christmas mornings at the McQuades were joyous, memorable, and chaotic. With nine children—some of whom still believed in Santa Claus—pandemonium was not merely accepted, it was encouraged.

Davis Williams told me that his family exchanged gifts and unwrapped presents one at a time, with each individual taking a turn at choosing a gift (No, no, open the green one first!), trading pleasantries with the giver (I love this bow! or What could it be?), and then expressing appropriate levels of surprise (Oh, you didn't!), appreciation (This is so perfect, I love it!), and gratitude (Thanks, Mom!). Depending on the nature and substance of the gift, photographs might be taken to immortalize the moment.

Our approach was less methodical. In the McQuade household, we all sat together on the floor and everyone opened everything all at once.

As was tradition, we started by gathering outside the room where all of the presents awaited, one pile for each of us, arranged in a loose semi-circle in the middle of the floor. Sometimes it would be my dad, but this year and most years it was my mom who proclaimed, "Merry Christmas to us all!" Then the frenzy began. We flew into the room and attacked the gift piles en masse, flinging wrapping paper and bows and product packaging around with abandon. Mom and Dad were ringleaders to the madness, sitting cross-legged on the floor among us, helping the little kids open presents, ooohing and aaahing as items were held up for admiration and envy, accepting thanks and kisses and hugs.

Naturally, everyone talked at once.

"Look it, look it, an Etch-a-Sketch . . . Mom, help me, I can't get this to work . . . This is just what I wanted . . . Does this need batteries? . . . Can somebody help me? . . . I love it! . . . Ricky! Stop! . . . How does this work? . . . Look, Carrie Ann, your very own dolly . . . The color is perfect, Mom! . . . Who wants to play this game with me? . . . Ricky! I mean it! . . . What is this? . . . What did you get, Brenda? . . . Show me . . . Look what I got . . . I saw this on TV! . . . I was hoping I'd get one of these . . . Well, you'll have to give her a name, sweetie.

The tumult wound down as all the presents were opened and as each of the nine kids began to concentrate on one item of particular interest. For Tom and myself, that was usually a new board game. No one in the family liked board games as much as Tom and I did—from old standards like checkers and chess to newer titles like The Game of Life and Sorry. Our all time, hands-down favorite was Monopoly. Tom and I played it so often that we'd long since memorized all the rents for every property on the board, from Mediterranean Avenue to Boardwalk, including the rents for one to four houses and a hotel. This was a significant time saver, especially when combined with the fact that we each operated as our own bankers, taking cash that was owed—Advance to Go! Collect $200—and paying debts— Luxury Tax! Pay $75—without requiring any action by the other player, who was therefore free to roll the dice and move the game forward. One thing we did not do was adopt the bastardized rule of placing payments to the bank in the middle of the board to be collected when one of us landed on Free Parking! We considered that convention an aberration, strictly for amateurs.

One thing I loved about Christmas morning with eight brothers and sisters was the fact that many presents were shareable, thus doubling and tripling my own personal take. Marti was always given a couple of books that I'd like to read, Tom typically received at least one sports item—a football, a basketball, wiffle ball and bat—that we'd enjoy together, Sheila or David typically got 45s of popular songs of the day that I was allowed to borrow and play on my own record player so long as each one was returned to the owner unscratched. Even the little kids' presents added to my day: I could join them in playing with toys that I'd outgrown but which I still enjoyed fooling around with.

For years, long past when I should have gotten bored with them, my favorite toys were molded plastic figures of men at war. Over various Christmases, I'd received platoons and regiments of both World War I and World War II army men, along with tanks and jeeps and cannon. I'd gotten enough cowboys and Indians to stage Custer's Last Stand, been given armored knights in quantities sufficient to wage the Crusades. On one of my birthdays, I'd even received a large set of Civil War army men, half in blue, half in gray, some marching, some running with rifles, some kneeling and firing, along with horses and field artillery and wagons and more. I used much of the set when I built a diorama for sixth grade history class depicting the Battle of Bull Run. I had originally planned to represent Pickett's Charge from the Battle of Gettysburg, but since that particular event was disastrous for the South, a classmate had quietly and smartly suggested Bull Run instead.

Some Christmases were particularly memorable because one of my brothers and sisters received a gift that captured the imagination and interest of everyone in the family. There was the Christmas of the hula hoops. There was the Christmas of the sled, a nostalgic purchase by my mother which was rewarded by an atypical snowfall in January that covered the city and made us and our sleds the envy of the neighborhood.

In 1963, it was the Christmas of Little Miss Echo.

A gift for six-year-old Brenda from Santa Claus, Little Miss Echo was equipped with a built-in tape recorder which enabled her to faithfully repeat whatever was said to her.

When Brenda said, "I love you, Mommy," little Miss Echo quickly told her "I love you, Mommy" in return. Even though the voice was still Brenda's, the words coming from the doll somehow generated a degree of sincerity that made Brenda swell with affection. Of course, once Brenda had several turns, all the rest of the family, even Sheila, wanted a chance to play with Little Miss Echo. David had her say, "I'm hungry. When do we eat?" Tom had her ask, "Who wants to challenge Tom in a game of Stratego?" She echoed Marti saying, "Hey, quiet. I'm trying to read, okay?" Ricky got in trouble when Little Miss Echo came out with "Brenda is a poopie!" Who knows how long this would have continued if it wasn't for Little Miss Echo finally proclaiming, courtesy of Mom, "I'm tired. I need a rest. Time for all McQuades to get ready for church."

* * * * *

Our big holiday feast had drawn to a close. The aroma of Mom's traditional baked ham lingered in the air. Dinner plates were empty—McQuade kids were famous for finishing everything that was served to them, especially at holiday dinners. Mom and Dad sat at either end of the table enjoying their coffees and cigarettes. The rest of us sat in our places, waiting to be officially excused from the table. I was trying to decide if I was too full for one more piece of Christmas ham, with yellow mustard smeared all over it.

I'd concluded that I wasn't really all that stuffed—and was just reaching for the ham—when we heard a knock on our back door, the one leading into the dining room from our back yard.

Marti opened it, blocking my view, then surprised me by saying, with some excitement in her voice, "Well, hello! You must be Jackie Thomas!"

"That's me," I heard him answer. "My grandmom sent me over with some cookies for Mickey and the rest of the family."

"That's so nice," Marti said, taking the tray from Jackie and stepping back so he could enter the room. "Come on in. I'm Mickey's sister Marti."

Jackie walked in and glanced around quickly, and seemed a little taken aback at the sight of eleven McQuades in the same room at once.

From the far end of the table, my father boomed, "Merry Christmas, come join us." I scrambled off the bench to greet my friend.

It felt a little awkward with everyone looking at us, but we sort of shook hands, Jackie and I, and wished Merry Christmas to each other. Then I waved at the room and said, "This is my family."

"Introduce us properly, Mickey," my mother interjected quickly. "Tell Jackie who is who."

"Okay," I replied, gallantly gesturing toward her with my hand and saying, "That's my mom," and then waving toward my father and saying, "And that's my dad." Both of my parents responded to my introduction at once.

"Merry Christmas, Jackie, so nice to see you. Are you hungry?" That was Mom.

"Merry Christmas again, Jackie, welcome to the madhouse." That, with a big teasing smile on his face, came from my dad.

Jackie looked from one to the other and nodded his head, not knowing exactly how to respond. He did not seem all that comfortable as the center of attention.

I moved quickly with the rest of the introductions. "That's Sheila, over there," I said, gesturing toward my older sister and then continuing to point out each individual.

"That's David—oh, you know him from when he drove us to Roebuck the other day."

"You just met Marti, my twin sister. And you know Tom."

"Hey, Jackie!" Tom waved from across the table.

"And these are the little kids," I continued, "Ricky, Brenda, Bobby, and, the youngest of the family, but not the quietest, Carrie Ann. She'll be two in May." Carrie Ann was sitting in her high chair, right next to where Jackie stood.

Jackie looked around at everyone and smiled. Ricky just stared back at him without much reaction. Brenda gave him a shy little wave. Bobby tried to be funny and stuck his tongue out, drawing an immediate and sharp "Bobby!" from my dad. Carrie Ann stared at him with wide eyes—I realized suddenly that she had probably never seen a colored person this close before. She was a newborn when Dad and Mom had hired our last colored maid, Winnie, to help Mom through the first few weeks after coming home from the hospital.

Jackie noticed the special level of attention he was receiving from Carrie Ann and bent down slightly to get closer to her. "Hi, Carrie Ann," he said softly, and then waited for her response. I jumped in to encourage her. "Carrie Ann, this is Jackie. Can you say his name? Jackie?"

Carrie-Ann looked at me, then back to Jackie, and then said, "Jeckie!" This was different—Carrie Ann was usually very shy when she first met people.

Jackie smiled at her but repeated his name to correct her pronunciation. "That's right," he said, "I'm Jackie."

Carrie Ann looked right back at him and said, "Jeckie."

Tom chimed in. "No, no, Carrie Ann—it's Jackie. Jaaaaaaaaaaaackeeeeeeeee."

"Jeckie."

I couldn't help it. I laughed out loud at my baby sister, I heard Dad and Mom laughing too. Her pronunciation was close but decidedly off, and it almost seemed that she was saying Jackie's name incorrectly on purpose.

Marti took a turn. "Carrie Ann, Carrie Ann," she called. "Say it like I do . . . Jaaaaaaacckkeeeeee. Jackee."

Carrie Ann never took her eyes off Jackie, but immediately responded to Marti's coaching.

"Jeckie. Jeckie. Jeckie," she said, then convulsed into giggles, eyes darting around the room to see how her performance was being received, then quickly reverting her gaze to Jackie.

The McQuade family howled.

As the laughter died down, I interrupted. "It seems," I announced, "that Carrie Ann now has a new friend. And his name is . . . Jeckie!"

More howling, and everyone in the family talking at once, to each other, to Jackie, to Carrie Ann, to the room at large. It was joyous chaos, one of those Christmas moments to be savored and remembered and recalled with pleasure in Christmases yet to come.

As we began to quiet down, except for occasional "Jeckie" refrains from Ricky, Mom stood up with empty plate in hand and asked, "Who's got kitchen duty?"

"I think it's David and Mickey," said Marti, who maintained that kind of critical information in her head. "But since Mickey's got company, I'll trade places with him."

I gave her a nod of thanks, though I wasn't surprised—Marti was always doing something nice for somebody. I gestured to Jackie, who followed me into our family room. Tom and Jackie and I decided to play a game of Sorry, an old favorite of Tom's, while the rest of the family spread around us doing different things, playing with new toys (the little kids), studying her new hair dryer and hair styling booklet (Sheila), sipping a brandy and reading the paper

(Dad). I was delighted to learn that Jackie had already played the game before—it was painful to have Tom explain the rules of a game to someone; his descriptions confused me, even when I already knew the rules.

Carrie Ann wandered the room, from Dad to Sheila to each of the little kids in turn, and then to the three of us playing Sorry at our "activity" table, a small card table with folding legs that Tom and I used most often for all the board games we played. Every few minutes, Carrie Ann would approach the three of us, not saying anything, but gravitating to Jackie, then wrapping her little arms around his legs and hugging. Jackie would look down at her and say "Hi," nothing else, but that was more than enough conversation for an almost two-year-old. Then she would wander away again. I could tell that Jackie loved the attention—he was obviously becoming as big a fan of Carrie Ann as she was of him.

Our game of Sorry was not working out so well—we were all frustrated because each of us kept sending the other two back to START, and no one was making any progress. Tom, ever competitive, was especially annoyed and soon started whining about the cards he was drawing. This prompted a mild reprimand from my mother, who'd just come into the room with a big plate of Christmas cookies, including several of those from the box that Nammy had given us.

The cookie plate was passed around, Jackie politely selecting two, one from the McQuade batch, and one from the Nammy collection. The little kids lined up and were also allowed two each. Ricky and Bobby were decisive in their selections; Brenda agonized over her choices but finally walked away with a chocolate cookie that had a raspberry jam center, and a vanilla sugar cookie with sprinkles.

Somehow, amidst the gathering around Mom for treats, and the normal confusion of all the McQuades in one room at the same time, no one paid attention to Carrie Ann who had wandered over to the Nativity Scene. Since the pieces were fragile, Carrie Ann had repeatedly been told to "Look, but don't touch," by all of us from Tom on up.

I was the first to notice her, extending her arm and little fingers toward one of the figurines. I called out, "No, no, don't touch, Carrie Ann!" but by then she'd already turned back toward the room and headed, figurine clutched tightly in her hand, directly toward Jackie.

I was confused at first—but then, in one of those lightning moments of clarity that happen sometimes when our subconscious minds work faster than our conscious brains, I understood.

Carrie Ann crossed the room to Jackie and offered him the figurine of Balthazar, the black-skinned member of the Three Kings. Jackie took it from her with a smile and said, "Thank you." And Carrie Ann, without laughing at herself this time, looked up at him and said, "Jeckie," then extended her arms so he could pick her up. Jackie placed Balthazar on the table, lifted Carrie Ann, and then sat with her on his lap while they both ate Christmas cookies.

"You have a big fan," said Marti, looking right at Jackie. "You'll have to come back again soon and visit. Or, perhaps, baby-sit?"

Jackie looked at Marti as she spoke but seemed to get disconcerted when she mentioned baby-sitting. He lowered his eyes and mumbled, "Don't know about that."

Marti let him off the hook with a casual comment. "You can talk it over with Mickey."

We didn't resume our Sorry game, and because his pieces were worse off than either Jackie's or mine, Tom did not complain. Marti joined us at the table, Mom went over to sit beside Dad, the little kids returned to their toys, Sheila continued to read her booklet, David sat off to the side, quietly engrossed in his latest novel. Marti nudged me with her elbow and cocked her head toward Jackie and Carrie Ann who were making silly faces at each other. "God bless us every one," she whispered, and I nodded so that she knew that I knew she was quoting Tiny Tim from the Dickens Christmas story.

After a while, Jackie told us he thought he should go because Nammy was home alone. Marti walked over to him and extended her arms to take Carrie Ann. "Say good-bye to Jeckie," Marti said. In response, Carrie Ann simply turned her face to Jackie, puckered up, and gave him a big kiss on the cheek. Jackie laughed, maybe a bit embarrassed again, but then gave Carrie Ann a little kiss on the forehead in return.

Out of the corner of my eye, I could see my parents watching. My dad was holding my mother's hand, released it to wave goodbye to Jackie and call out "Come by any time, Jackie! Merry Christmas," then took her hand in his again.

I walked Jackie to the back door and was just saying good-bye when Marti came up behind me with a tray of cookies. "For you and your grandmother," she said.

Jackie took the cookies, said thank you, smiled at Marti for a couple seconds longer than I thought was necessary, then headed across our back yard and into the woods. Marti and I stood together and watched him go. "So, that's the famous Jackie Thomas," she said.

"Yes, ma'am," I said. "That's him. But, 'round here, we like to call him Jeckie."

CHAPTER 17
SAME DAY

I usually experience a bit of melancholy as Christmas Day winds down. It's a holiday with more than a month of build-up, and then it's over in a flash. This Christmas was different. What I was hoping might be the high point of the day still lay ahead. I had a Christmas present to deliver to the girl across the street.

I pulled on a light jacket and headed out the door with Yvonne's snow globe under my arm. It was gorgeously wrapped—thanks to Sheila—shiny blue paper with a silver bow and silver ribbon. A little tag dangled off of one ribbon: To Yvonne, From Mickey.

In addition to the gift, I also had a wonderfully complementary Christmas card that I'd found, by dumb luck, in one of the dozens of boxes of cards that my mother had purchased in after Christmas sales the year before.

The outside of the card featured an illustration of two bears—not totally dissimilar to the ones within the snow globe. The bears sat on opposite sides of a Christmas tree. Above them were the words *I'm so glad* . . .

On the inside of the card, the two bears were pictured again, but now they were sitting close together, with affection on their faces, and hugging.

On the inside, the message from the front of the card was completed with the words *that we're friends! Merry Christmas!*

I took a long, long time—most of Christmas Eve—trying to decide what to write on the inside of the card to underscore the message that the card and the gift were meant to deliver to Yvonne. Finally, I decided on *Merry Christmas to the best across-the-street neighbor that a guy could ever have. Wherever you're going, I'm going your way . . . Mickey McQuade.*

I'd worried initially that my words were too presumptuous, but then I'd decided that some level of boldness was needed. I believed that my idea to use the lyric from Moon River, which Yvonne would not completely understand until she heard the song from the snow globe, was a poetic and romantic touch.

We'll see, I said to myself as I crossed the street and walked up her driveway to her front door.

The porch light came on as I reached the top of the steps. Yvonne must have seen me coming, I thought, smiling. Instead, it was her father who opened the door, which made me immediately tense. Jessup Rawlings stared at me for an instant through the screen door—but then broke into a big smile. "Merry Christmas, Mr. McQuade. How good to see you!"

"Merry Christmas, Mr. Rawlings," I said, a little confused by his effusive greeting, until I smelled a hint of whiskey on his breath. "I was hoping I might see Yvonne for just a minute or two." When he didn't respond right away, I showed him the wrapped gift and card. "I have something I wanted to give her."

"Of course, of course," he answered jovially, ushering me inside. "Y'all come in. Yvonne," he half-shouted, "come on down here. Y'all have a visitor, a gentleman caller I b'lieve." For some reason, Mr. Rawlings found his last remark very funny, because he began to laugh out loud, but in a friendly way, and repeated the phrase. "A gentleman caller, I b'lieve."

Mr. Rawlings' hearty demeanor, created or at least augmented by alcohol, made me uncomfortable, but it was better than the dour look that I usually saw on his face. However, as soon as I saw his daughter at the head of the stairs, whatever he was saying or doing or looking like was rendered inconsequential.

"Mickey," Yvonne said, with a warmth that immediately made me wish I'd come earlier so that I could have stayed longer. "Hi. Merry Christmas. This is a nice surprise."

I waited until she reached the landing and then extended my gift and card. "Merry Christmas. Here I got you something," I said.

"Why, aren't you the sweetest thing!" she said. "That is so, so sweet. Come on in, let's sit in the living room."

Mr. Rawlings wandered away, toward the kitchen, and Yvonne led me to their big living room sofa.

"Sit here, Mickey," she said. "It's so nice to see you on Christmas Day. We hardly ever see each other now these days. How have you been?"

"Okay, I guess," I said. It was not my finest moment as a conversationalist.

We sat, and Yvonne placed the card and gift on a coffee table in front of her. "Mickey, would you like some Christmas cookies?" she suddenly asked. "My mom made them—they're really good!"

"Okay," I answered, though I would just as soon have skipped another round of cookies—and kept Yvonne sitting with me in the living room.

"Stay right here," she said, patting my knee lightly. "I'll be right back."

Yvonne disappeared, and left me seated on her couch in the warm glow of a table lamp and lights from their Christmas tree, looking at my knee that she'd just touched, and wondering exactly how to position myself to make it easy for her to repeat that gesture when she returned.

I gazed around the room, struck by the neatness and order that was so unlike any place in the McQuade household. I saw doilies, and bric-a-brac, and throw pillows, and one artfully-placed homemaker magazine. It occurred to me that that we did not have a single throw pillow anywhere in our house.

Yvonne returned, and handed me a small wrapped package. I guessed that she might have just wrapped it while she was gone—but that did not bother me in the slightest. "Merry Christmas to you too, Mickey."

She sat beside me, knees almost touching but not, and asked, "Should we open our gifts together, or separately?"

"I'll watch you open yours," I said.

"Okay," she said, agreeably, perhaps not noticing the slightest bit of quiver in my voice. All of a sudden I felt very warm in her living room. And nervous that my gift—which I was so proud of just minutes before—was kind of silly.

Yvonne opened her card first, looked at the bears, and the printed words, and my own handwritten message. I thought I detected the slightest bit of hesitation and confusion at my Moon River quote, but she was much too well-mannered to ask me what I meant.

Yvonne took great care and time in opening the gift itself, gently untying the silver ribbon, and barely disturbing the blue wrapping paper as she slid it off the box. She slit the tape on the gift box inside with her fingernail, then gingerly lifted the snow globe, wrapped in tissue, and placed it on the coffee table. She pulled the tissue paper away, and I was rewarded with an almost inaudible gasp of pleasure as she saw what it was.

"Oh, Mickey, I love these," she sighed, picking up the snow globe, and turning it upside down, then upright, to start the snowfall.

"And it's a music box too," I said. "Here, let me show you." I reached out for the snow globe and felt the electricity of my hand brushing hers as I took it from her. I turned the wind-up mechanism and then held the snow globe up in the light. Moon River began to play and, in what may have been the most wonderful moment of my life to that point, Yvonne began to softly hum the melody to herself.

She turned toward me, eyes bright, and said, "Mickey, I love it. That's one of my favorite songs—just ask my mom. You are just the sweetest thing going."

I could feel my face getting red.

"Yvonne, Mickey," came a sudden, and decidedly unwelcome voice from across the room, accompanied by a harsh burst of illumination from an overhead light that Mrs. Rawlings turned on as she spoke. "Would y'all like some hot chocolate to go with those cookies?"

Yvonne looked up. Did I see a flash of disappointment that we were interrupted? But she answered politely, "Sure, momma, that would be so nice. I'll help you."

She got up from the sofa as I put the snow globe on the coffee table, the final notes of the chorus just beginning to fade away. "I'll be back, Mickey," she said. Sadly, she did not touch my knee before leaving.

I didn't stay too long after we drank our hot chocolate. Mostly because Mrs. Rawlings, then Mr. Rawlings, decided to join us. Mrs. Rawlings asked about Christmas doings at the McQuades "with all those little ones." I gave her a quick summary of the day, the Christmas morning chaos, the Little Miss Echo episode, and our surprise visit from Jackie. I laughed as I described Carrie Ann and her insistence on calling Jackie "Jeckie"—but none of the Rawlings seemed to get the humor of it. At one point in my story, I thought I heard Mr. Rawlings mutter "niggers" under his breath. Neither Yvonne nor her mom reacted to him, so I chose to ignore his comment as well. Maybe I'd misheard him.

Not long after, I decided it was time to go, and stood up. Yvonne showed me to the door, and surprisingly, took my hand in hers. "I love my snow globe, Mickey," she whispered. "And, please, I want to apologize for my daddy. He just doesn't like the idea of a close friend of mine spending so much time with nigger boys. You understand." Then, without waiting for a response from me, Yvonne gave me a longer than necessary hug and a quick kiss on the lips, then opened the door for me to leave. "Merry Christmas, Mickey," she said.

I managed a weak reply, "Merry Christmas," just as the door closed in my face. I walked home with "close friend" and the memory of Yvonne's soft kiss and extended hug competing for my full attention. I immediately pushed "spending time with nigger boys" to the very back of my brain.

CHAPTER 18
JANUARY 15, 1964

The social calendar of John Carroll High School during the mid 60s was anchored by three major events. In the Fall, we had Homecoming, supposedly a welcome back event for alumni, though I never noticed any real welcoming going on, nor many alumni either. There was a dance preceded by a football game, and the school crowned a Homecoming King and Queen.

Davis Williams and I did not have dates for the Homecoming celebrations, but we had decided to go to the dance anyway. We watched the fun and festivities from the third row of bleachers in the gym, seeing many of our friends dancing slow dances with pretty classmates. We managed to have a miserable time.

A second major social event, the Junior-Senior Prom, occurred just before graduation in May. This occasion was of much importance for juniors and seniors but a non-event for most underclassmen. Unless you were one of the select freshman or sophomore girls asked to the dance by a junior or senior.

Sandwiched between those two events, in February, was the Queen of Hearts Dance. Unlike the others dances, Queen of Hearts was a fundraiser, with proceeds donated to the Catholic Students Mission Crusade. Each homeroom nominated a "princess." Students were encouraged to "vote" for their favorite princesses by depositing coins—a penny a vote—into highly decorated collection jars. The amount of money raised was minimal, though it funded projects like the school's annual mission trip to Clarksdale, Mississippi where John Carroll students conducted Bible study classes and played games with colored kids from the area grade school.

Immediately after the fiasco of Homecoming, Davis and I swore a private vow that we would have dates for the Queen of Hearts Dance. However, it was now a Wednesday night in mid-January. My vow was in jeopardy.

The Queen of Hearts dance was only a few weeks away, the second Friday in February. Kids at school were starting to talk. Posters in the halls read Vote Early and Often. And I had yet to take the first concrete step toward securing a date for myself, unless one considered frequent to-the-mirror pep talks, encouraging me to ask Yvonne Rawlings.

There were many appealing things about Yvonne being my date for this special social occasion. First, an event of this magnitude—a dress-up thing—would automatically move the Mickey-Yvonne relationship forward to some kind of next level.

Second, I liked the idea of the looks of envy that would assuredly come my way from other John Carroll students, not just my friends, but juniors and seniors as well. Only one or two other John Carroll girls were in Yvonne's league appearance-wise—and they were both dating upper classmen.

Third, if I could get my brother David to drive us (instead of my father), it could mean some reasonably private time with Yvonne sitting in the back seat of our Rambler station wagon or David's mechanically sound but less than elegant '55 Bel Air Chevrolet.

Not that I was complaining about the Bel Air. David had gotten his driver's license right after his 16th birthday last February—and bought his first car right away with money he'd been saving up for years. The seats were uncomfortable, and the radio had a lot of static, but the heater worked. Mom and Dad gave him gas money every week and, in return, David ran a lot of errands and drove himself, Marti, and me to St. Barnabas every morning to catch the parish bus to school.

I was hoping David would agree to function as my silent chauffer. I had no specific ideas in mind but believed that much could occur, romantically speaking, in the fifty minutes it took to drive across town from Roebuck to Southside.

During a rare phone call that evening, I reminded Davis about our pact and asked him if he'd gotten a date yet. He said no but promised that he'd work on it soon, right after next week's history test. He did not sound confident—but I had my own situation to deal with.

The next evening, with four weeks and one day to go before the dance, I decided that things could be put off no longer. I went upstairs after dinner, took the phone from my mother's nightstand, untangled its extra-length cord, and headed for the hall closet right outside her bedroom. This, I'd learned from watching my older sister, was an acceptable household practice if your phone conversations were reasonably short. It was the only way to guarantee a little privacy. After Sheila graduated from high school and got her first job, she arranged to have her own phone installed in her bedroom. She allowed Marti to use it occasionally, but it was off limits to her brothers.

I dialed Yvonne's number in the dim glow of the closet's bare light bulb, fought the impulse to hang up before I finished dialing, and then panicked when she answered the phone herself on the first ring.

Even though I knew it was her voice, I stupidly stuck with the opening that I'd prepared. "Hello. This is Mickey McQuade. From across the street. May I please speak to Yvonne?"

"It's me, Mickey," she said. "Don't you recognize my voice?" It sounded like she was smiling, or maybe snickering.

"Oh, it's you, Yvonne," I could hear the quiver in my voice and suddenly felt like I needed to clear my throat. I held my hand over the mouthpiece and coughed before speaking further. "I um guess you just surprised me is all. I thought your mom or dad, you know, would answer the phone."

It suddenly felt very warm in the closet, like the steam room at the Jewish community center over in Mountain Brook. Dad had taken us there once on a guest pass after they'd closed down the swimming pools in Birmingham to keep colored kids from swimming with white kids. But it cost too much to join so we never did.

"They're watching TV," Yvonne said. "And the volume is so loud because of Dad's hearing, I don't think they always notice or pay attention to the phone."

"Oh, okay," I said.

Silence. One Mississippi, two Mississippis, three . . .

Then we both spoke at once. "I saw you yesterday," she said. "I wanted to ask you . . ." I began.

We stopped talking at the same time. Silence. One Mississippi. Then Yvonne, thankfully, gave me the opening I needed.

"What did you want to ask me, Mickey?"

"Well, uh, I was just wondering, you know, if you were doing anything in February, like February 14th, uh, it's a Friday, and if you weren't like doing anything then if you might want to go to the Queen of Hearts dance with me at my school is all."

It was not my most articulate moment. Fortunately, Yvonne was much smoother at social discourse.

"Why, that sounds really nice, Mickey. That's Valentine's Day, you know."

I murmured a scarcely intelligible, "Oh, yeah." I knew that but I was afraid to make a big deal about it. I didn't want to assume that Yvonne was my valentine.

Yvonne continued. "I'm so glad you thought of asking me. I'll have to check with my mom, of course. How about I talk to her and then call you back tomorrow?"

"Oh, sure," I said. By this point, beads of sweat had formed along my forehead and I was sure that I'd used up all of the available oxygen in the closet. "Okay, well, bye," I said quickly.

"Oh." Was that surprise in her voice? But what else was there to say? "Oh, okay. Bye, Mickey."

I hung up just as Tom opened the door to the closet. "Hey, whatcha doing in there? Talking to a girl?"

"Shut up, Tom," I said, with a threat in my voice that squelched any possibility of a reply. "It's none of your business."

* * * * *

Later that evening, I recounted to Marti my conversation, if you could call it that. I asked her what she thought of my chances.

"I'm pretty sure she'll go," Marti said. "If she did not want to go with you, I think she would already have made up some kind of excuse, right then on the phone."

"Maybe," I said, considering all the possibilities, most of them bad. If Yvonne said no, what then? Time was running short. Who could I ask, especially since I didn't want to ask anyone except Yvonne. "Why can't girls just say yes right away if they get asked out?"

"Why do boys take forever to ask a girl out?" Marti countered.

I looked at my sister and suddenly felt very stupid. "Holy smokes," I said, "I totally forgot about you, Marti. I'm an idiot. Sorry. But . . . but you haven't said anything about Queen of Hearts—and now it's just four weeks away. Don't you want to go to the dance?"

"Nobody's asked me yet," Marti said. "Although . . . I guess I could just ask someone myself."

"What are you talking about?" I said. "Girls don't ask guys. You know that."

"Well, I don't know, maybe they should," she said, loosely folding her arms and looking up to stare at the ceiling. "Think about it. What would be wrong with that? What's the big deal?"

"Because," I said, hoping that Marti was listening. "Because if a girl asks a guy, it's like telling the world she's desperate. But you're not. You're fine. Guys like you. They do."

I was trying to sound casually definitive, but I really wasn't sure Marti was buying it.

She shifted her position on the step. "Look," she said, "guys ask girls cause everyone says that's how things are done, right?"

Marti's question made me nervous, like a trick true or false on a history test.

"I guess so," I said.

"But who says that 'everyone' is right? Everyone can't be right just because everyone says they're right—that doesn't make any sense. So who makes the rules? Our parents? The Church? The nuns at school? Society?"

I shrugged my shoulders, prepared myself for a torrent of Marti opinion. Marti relented. Her voice softened.

"Just because society is loudest doesn't mean society is right," she said with a smile. She paused for a few seconds before continuing, then smiled again, as if she had a secret. "But it doesn't matter anyway—cause I think someone is going to ask me real soon."

"Who?" I asked. "Who are you talking about?"

Marti looked at me with a "Should I say or shouldn't I say?" expression on her face.

"C'mon, who?" I said.

She thought some more, but finally spoke. "I was thinking maybe Davis Williams might ask me," she said.

Astonishment. "What!" I responded. "You mean my Davis Williams? You like Davis? Davis likes you? Really?"

Marti studied me some more, trying to decide, it seemed, whether she should turn my questions into a full discussion. While we regularly talked about most everything else in the world, Marti was kind of private in terms of boys and her social life. Fair enough. I'd certainly been holding back on a number of Yvonne items, especially her remarks about colored people.

"Okay, Mickey, here's what I'm thinking. But you are not, I repeat not, to share any of this with Davis or I will tell Yvonne every bad thing I can think of about you, including your smelly feet."

My feet were, unfortunately, McQuade household legends.

"Never," I said immediately. "Swear to God. Davis will never hear a word. But, hold it . . . I didn't even know you liked him!"

"Well, I do like him," Marti admitted, "but I'm not sure that I like him like him. You know, like a boyfriend kind of like him."

"Does he like you? Has he said anything to you? How long has this been going on? Why haven't you said anything to me? Why hasn't he said anything to me?"

The questions exploded from me like soda foam from a bottle of coke that somebody shook up before popping the cap.

"You are way too far down the train tracks, Mickey McQuade," Marti answered with her hand held in the air to signal Stop. "Nothing's been said, nothing's going on, there's nothing to talk about. It's just I get a feeling that he likes me a little. So let's wait and see."

"But . . ." I said.

"No buts," she said. "Patience."

My face must have shown my less-than-happy reaction.

"Patience," she repeated.

Turned out that all my worries—for me and for Marti—were unnecessary. Davis asked Marti the next day at school. Yvonne called me to say yes late Friday afternoon. Both of the McQuade twins now had dates for the Queen of Hearts Dance. Sometimes things just work out.

* * * * *

It was mid-afternoon on Saturday before Marti and I were able to escape to the stairs and catch up.

"You are looking pretty happy with yourself," Marti told me, after I gave her a detailed description of my conversation with Yvonne—including the fact that Yvonne wanted to talk to Marti as soon as possible to discuss details of the dance.

"And you are looking pretty pleased with yourself," I said. "Y'know, that sneak Davis Williams never said a single word about asking you to Queen of Hearts."

"Our only problem is transportation." Marti said, moving immediately to practical issues. "Since he lives all the way out in West End, he's got to ask his dad to drive him all the way here, then back to school for the dance, then pick us up and bring me home, then go all the way back to West End."

"That's like a hundred miles," I said. "Maybe more."

"I know," Marti said. "Davis said not to worry about it—he'd figure things out. But I don't know." Her voice trailed off.

I thought for a few seconds, considering the problem, but then abandoned it as I embraced a hazy vision of me slow dancing with Yvonne. I did not consider myself a polished dancer—but I'd gotten a few slow dances under my belt at the monthly Catholic Youth Organization, or CYO, meetings at St. Barnabas. I knew what it was like to hold a girl in my arms, kind of, which was good, but not nearly as good as it would be to hold Yvonne in my arms.

I looked at Marti, saw her twisting her lip a little, realized that the unresolved transportation question was bugging her and touched her arm.

"Do not worry, little sister. It's all gonna work out just fine."

CHAPTER 19
FEBRUARY 8, 1964

With less than a week to go before Queen of Hearts, panic set in. Suddenly it hit me that the evening would not only include slow, romantic tunes—I'd been mildly obsessing about these— but also more than a few fast songs. And I'd be expected to dance.

Sure, there would be a few fast songs that the girls—Yvonne and Marti and some of Marti's school friends—would dance as girl-girl couples, leaving their dates on the sidelines to stand around, pretending to say smart and funny things to one another. But I was pretty sure that Yvonne would want me to do at least a few fast dances with her, and I had zero confidence in my ability to handle that challenge without making at least a modest fool of myself. Sunday night CYO dance parties had not prepared me for the big time.

With no hesitation, I did what I almost always did when I was grappling with a tough problem. I went looking for my twin.

Marti sympathized with my concern, and then, as usual, came up with a solution. "Look, Mickey, I've got to do a couple of chores for Mom," she said, "and I'm planning on taking a nice long walk today, but if you can set aside some time later this afternoon, I'll teach you a couple dances. Easy ones."

That was exactly what I needed to hear. I felt better immediately. "How 'bout around three o'clock?" I asked. "I'm going over to Jackie's for lunch—Nammy's making her famous grilled cheese sandwiches for us—but I'll be back by three, no problem."

"See you on the dance floor," she said, "and by that I mean the family room. We'll push the furniture out of the way."

I explained all this to Jackie as we each finished off two of Nammy's grilled cheese sandwiches. He was actually more interested in my problem than I expected he'd be.

"You're telling me," he said, "that Marti is going to teach you, clumsy ol' Mickey McQuade, how to be cool on the dance floor? In one lesson?"

"That's the plan," I answered.

"I dunno 'bout this. From what you always say, Marti is kind of a miraculous problem solver. But this sounds like too much even for her."

"I'm confident."

"You crazy."

Jackie's last remark made me laugh. And prompted a response. "Come see, wise guy," I said. "I'm quite sure Marti would not mind if she had a witness to her powers of transformation."

Actually, I wasn't at all sure that Marti would be comfortable with me asking Jackie to observe her dance lesson. But then, I didn't really expect that Jackie would accept my invitation. What could be more boring than a teenage girl trying to teach her teenage twin how to be remarkable at a high school social event?

I got surprised. Jackie said yes right away. Enthusiastically. Where did that come from?

After confirming the time, three o'clock, I said thanks to Nammy for my delicious grilled cheese with sautéed onions, and I headed for home.

* * * *

When I walked into our family room just before three, I saw that Marti had already set it up for my dance lesson. Furniture was pushed back against the walls, and a pile of 45 rpm records sat next to Sheila's portable record player on the little table typically used for board games.

I was a little uneasy because I had not yet told Marti that Jackie would probably be showing up. My second big surprise of the day was her positive reaction to the news.

"Jackie's coming? That's great, Mickey. I haven't seen him since Christmas."

Those words were barely out of her mouth when we heard a knock at the door. Marti quickly stepped around me to open it and greeted Jackie with a big smile. "Jackie! What a nice surprise. Mickey just told me you'd be stopping by. Come in, come in."

Jackie seemed nervous as he stepped inside the door. He hardly spoke, just a barely audible "Hello."

"Here, Jackie, you can sit right here," Marti said. "Do you want anything before we get started? Glass of ice tea?"

"No, ma'am," Jackie said, like he was talking to Nammy, or my mother. I'm pretty sure he realized this verbal slip, because the next words out of his mouth were "I mean, I mean, no thank you. I'm okay fine."

I was ready for Marti to chide him, in a good-natured, teasing kind of way, for calling her "ma'am." But she didn't. All she said was "That's fine, Jackie. Just holler if you change your mind."

She turned toward me. "Let's get to it, Mickey. In the next hour, I'm going to turn you into a fast dancing prodigy. Are you ready?"

I heard Jackie chuckle at that, but it didn't bother me. I simply called out, without even turning around, "You can join in any time, Mr. Thomas.

Any time the mood strikes you."

Then Marti took over. She put on a 45 titled Mashed Potato Time by Dee Dee Sharp. And my emergency, get-this-boy-ready-for-the-dance-floor lesson began.

The next hour, which I was afraid might be dull, flew by. I was dumbstruck at Marti's knowledge and apparent mastery of an entire series of dances, some of which were never in evidence at the CYO parties. She only spent a few minutes on the Twist, because everyone could do that, even me. Then she quickly demonstrated the Pony, the Loco-Motion, the Mashed Potato, the Monster Mash and the Swim. She swapped out records, encouraged all the stiffness and self-consciousness out of me, kept the music as well as my feet, arms and hips moving. Twenty minutes in, I was beginning to feel dish-rag limp. Marti gave me a couple of breaks, but they were short ones. Jackie, our observer, was rigid and reserved at first, but toward the end, he was tapping his feet and drumming his hands on the table, keeping time with the rhythms. Flushed with exertion, Marti was clearly enjoying her roles as both instructor and social coach.

"Last one," Marti called out, then smoothly dropped the record player needle to begin a tune called The Loco-motion by Little Eva. Of all the dances I'd been trying for the past hour, the Loco-Motion was the one that came most easily and naturally to me. I got into a groove with the music from the first notes of the song, and hit my stride with a sequence that required me to pump my arms like pistons on a steam engine.

"You got it, Mickey," Marti called out, matching her motions to mine so well that we looked like a rehearsed dance team. Just under her voice we both heard Jackie singing softly, "Do the locomotion, do the locomotion" and then, "C'mon, c'mon, do the locomotion with me."

When the music finally faded away, Jackie spontaneously began to applaud, then I started clapping, then Marti joined in. And then we heard even more applause as we looked up to see Tom, and the little kids, and even Mom watching our performance.

Jackie left shortly after our big finale. Before walking out the door, he looked me straight in the eye, and with mock gravity simply said, "You're ready." Then he walked over to Marti, took her hand, shook it and said, "Thank you for the best hour of my week, ma'am."

Marti responded with the biggest smile I'd seen from her in forever, and said, "Thank you for stopping by and joining in . . ." She paused, then added, with mischief in her voice, "my very good sir."

CHAPTER 20
FEBRUARY 14, 1964

Friday, the day of the dance, was one of the longest, slowest days of my academic life. Every class dragged on and on. Thankfully, the teachers knew that their students' minds were elsewhere so no one gave us any tests that day or too much homework for the weekend.

The nun who taught us religion—Sister Mary Bartholomew, whom a few called Sister Barty Farty, though not to her face—did not teach a lesson but instead provided some lengthy commentary about boys and girls and growing older and urges and the myriad evils that would unquestionably ensue if couples attending the Queen of Hearts Dance were not extremely careful in their behaviors. She told us to remember that Jesus died for our sins on the cross and not to make things worse by committing immoral acts during an evening that was devoted to raising money for the Catholic Students Mission Crusade. Since Jesus had died for our sins almost two thousand years ago, I was not sure how anything that happened in Birmingham, Alabama that evening could make things worse for Him, but I did not raise this issue in class.

When the dismissal bell rang at 2:45 p.m., the exodus from the school building was even more chaotic than normal. From the conversations I heard in the hallways, a large number of girls had appointments with hairdressers and were being picked up at school by parents instead of taking their buses back to their respective parishes. This caused any number of traffic foul-ups on the single, winding street in front of the school.

With all the confusion, our bus back to St. Barnabas pulled away almost twenty minutes later than normal. Marti and I rarely sat together on the bus, but she winked at me from her window seat as I walked to my usual spot in the back. The wink said, "Relax, Mickey, we have plenty of time." Marti did not have a hairdresser appointment—our big sister Sheila had volunteered to help her and would probably do a better job than 90 percent of the professional hair stylists in Birmingham. Nonetheless, though time was not an issue, I was eager to get home and begin the process of preparing for the biggest night of my life.

Later, after dinner and after showering and scenting myself with just the right amount of English Leather aftershave, which I'd borrowed from David, I sat down in my underwear to shine my shoes, a decent pair of black wingtips. It was perhaps the second time they'd be shined since I'd received them as hand-me-downs from David when his feet got too big.

The shining process went well: I used Dad's leather cleaning soap, then carefully rinsed the soap off and dried the shoes before applying the black polish. I used an old piece of nylon from one of Mom's stockings to get a perfect shine, spitting on the shoes twice in the process, and then shining the spit off, because I had seen that done in a movie once. Unfortunately, the shining process somehow left me with black marks on my hands, one arm and my underwear. I debated internally for a few seconds, but then decided that another shower was called for. I re-entered the bathroom with a towel wrapped around me just as Marti was exiting—but she was already dressed and ready to go.

This got me a little nervous; Marti was never ready before me. Realizing that I must have spent too much time on the shoe-shining effort, I asked her what time it was. When she said twenty minutes to six, I panicked. We'd told Yvonne that we would pick her up promptly at 6 p.m. because her mother wanted to take pictures before David drove us all across town to the dance.

I went into high gear. Three minutes in the shower was all I needed to get rid of the black polish marks. I practically ran from the bathroom to my room, pulled on fresh underwear, scrounged in my drawer for two dark socks that looked like they were mates, jumped into the pants from the hand-me-down suit I was wearing, pulled on the brand new shirt that Mom had bought for me last week, and then started knotting a tie that I'd borrowed from Dad. This was way too big an evening to rely on one of my three clip-on ties from school.

Just as I was pulling the tie up tight and congratulating myself on dressing with grace and style under pressure, I remembered that I had not re-applied deodorant after my second shower. Concerned with the risk involved in relying merely on residue left from the original deodorant, because most of it could have washed away in the shower, I quickly ripped off the tie, threw off my shirt and undershirt, put on fresh deodorant, then re-dressed myself with a speed that would have put comic superheroes—like Superman or the Flash—to shame.

At 5:57, having completed all the other necessary steps like putting on a belt and combing my hair, I ran downstairs to the family room to find David and Marti waiting for me. The transportation plan was to have David drive all three of us—Marti, Yvonne and me—both to and from the school. Davis would meet us there. Not ideal, but practical.

"Let's go," I said with a feigned air of calm.

"Breath mints?" David said.

"Where's your corsage for Yvonne?" asked Marti.

"Damn it," I said.

We left the house at 6:02—and I practically ran across the street to Yvonne's while David and Marti got in David's car. Luckily, it was warm for February—some Alabama days are like that—so I did not have to bother with an overcoat of any kind.

All turned out well. Mrs. Rawlings answered the door and immediately alleviated one worry by asking me if she could take the corsage to pin it on Yvonne's dress. Mr. Rawlings stood in the living room looking all awkward and father-like, clearly unsure of his role or if he had one. Traynor looked up from his comic book and waved, but did not say anything.

And then Yvonne appeared at the top of the stairs, and took my breath away. I looked at her, she smiled at me and said, "Hi, Mickey, I'm ready."

All I could do was nod.

Her dress was violet, without frills, and it shimmered. I thought she looked like a movie star. She wore her dark hair down, straight and long and shiny. It was all I could do to keep myself from shouting with joy as she descended the stairs like a goddess coming down from Mount Olympus to spend time on earth with us mere mortals. Instead, I simply said, based on directions that I'd received from Mom, "Why, you look very nice, Yvonne."

"Thanks, Mickey. You are quite dashing yourself."

The sound of her words gave me shivers. Angels in heaven would have traded golden harps and the finest sets of wings to have a voice that soft and musical.

I could not take my eyes off Yvonne while Mrs. Rawlings pinned on the corsage, white flowers of some kind with little purple splotches. "Look how perfectly this corsage goes with your dress, Yvonne," acting all surprised at the coincidence even though I found out later that she and my mom had spoken specifically about Yvonne's dress color a week before the dance.

"Pictures, pictures," said Mrs. Rawlings. "Where's the Brownie, Jessup?"

"Hold on," Mr. Rawlings said gruffly. "I got it here. Where do you want them to stand?"

"Over here, by the stairs," said Mrs. Rawlings. There was no question that she had already planned this shot in her mind. "Y'all stand here, Mickey," she positioned me, "and then you here, Yvonne."

I thought it would be one picture. It turned out to be ten. Three with Yvonne and me. Then one with Yvonne and me and Mr. and Mrs. Rawlings. Traynor had to take that shot and was not especially happy about the task.

Then two with Mrs. Rawlings and Yvonne, then two more with Yvonne and both her parents. Then one with Yvonne and Traynor, and a final shot of Yvonne holding their pet cat, Savannah.

By the time we got out the door and to the car, it was 6:30. David was getting impatient.

"Let's get going, Mickey," he called out from the driver's seat, as if I had any control over the situation whatsoever.

I opened the door for Yvonne and she slid across the back seat of David's car with the grace of a New York City ballerina. Marti turned to her right away and told her how nice she looked. David said hi but kept his eyes forward, though I am pretty sure he took notice as Yvonne and I came down the steps from her house. I settled in, closed the door, and said, "We're in— let's go."

I was a little nervous about things from the start. How much conversation was I supposed to contribute? What were we supposed to talk about, especially with Marti and David in the front seat, hearing every word? But mostly, what was the proper distance to sit in relation to Yvonne, especially since it was our first real date? There were lots of options: A foot or two apart, a chaste couple of inches of separation, right next to each other with shoulders touching—it was a bench seat with no arm rest so all of those were possibilities.

I chose about 18 inches of separation as the proper distance since I wanted to behave as a gentleman, even though I was much more inclined toward the shoulders touching position.

Luckily, wonderfully, Yvonne made all of my concerns irrelevant in less time than it took David to back out of the Rawlings driveway and head down the street. Once I was settled, and with Marti looking back at both of us while asking Yvonne about her dress, Yvonne scooched over closer to me, her shoulder almost touching. And then, as casually as if she were rearranging a pillow on a sofa, she reached over, put her arm through mine, and took my hand. She entwined her fingers in mine, and gave my hand a gentle squeeze, all the while explaining to Marti that Yvonne's mom had found the dress just last week at JC Penney's.

David was oblivious to all of this, of course. Marti noticed—a millisecond of eye contact between us established that—but she did not visibly react. Yvonne was as comfortable and nonchalant as her cat Savannah, curled up on Mrs. Rawlings lap. In contrast, I sat statue-like, concerned that even the slightest movement on my part might upset some mysterious delicate balance within the universe, and Yvonne's hand would disappear from mine. I closed my eyes for a moment, experimenting with the theory I'd read recently that blind people have a richer sense of touch than others.

The rest of the ride to the dance went by in a blur. I might have spoken, and I'm sure I pretended to listen to Marti and Yvonne's chatter, but mostly I just embraced the wonder of what was happening right before my very eyes. I even looked down occasionally to see her hand in mine, and burn the image into my brain.

I had a moment of terror when Yvonne needed both arms to explain something to Marti but, as soon as she finished her thought, she replaced her hand in mine. I probably exhaled loudly in relief but no one said anything.

I could not wait to get to the dance and find a moment alone with Davis to bring him up to speed on our car ride.

* * * * *

Davis met us as David pulled up to the curb outside the school. He had a corsage for Marti, which he handed to her when we were all out of the car and on the sidewalk. Yvonne immediately suggested that she would be happy to pin it on Marti's dress once we got inside. Davis looked relieved.

We walked toward the entrance to the building, Davis and Marti side by side, Yvonne and I trailing them slightly, with Yvonne's arm in mine. I could not help but notice the glances from several other guys, including some juniors and seniors, looking at Yvonne, looking at me, and wondering what circumstances of fate might have brought the two of us together.

Mild chaos reigned in the entranceway, with several hundred teenagers finding their friends, shouting, hugging, admiring themselves and each other, loudly, before gradually moving through the interior entry doors and into the gym.

Once inside, we became separated from Marti and Davis almost immediately, though I didn't care. I knew we'd find them later and I wanted some private time with Yvonne.

"I can't believe this day finally came," I said, as we both looked out on the crowd milling about. "It feels like a year since you called me up and said yes." I turned toward Yvonne. "I was so afraid you'd say no."

I flashed her my most adorable smile.

Yvonne smiled back and squeezed my hand. "I would have said yes the night you called," she said, "but I knew I'd have to clear it with Daddy. He is just so worried about me going anywhere these days with all this Civil Rights commotion, and the agitators, and the way the niggers are acting. I mean, I know things have calmed down some since last April and May—but there's still a lot of tension." She paused. "I just want things to be nice, the way they used to be."

I was taken aback by the directness, and the undercurrent of racial hostility in Yvonne's remarks, but I blamed it on her father. "I guess your dad doesn't like colored people much," I said, though what I wanted to say was, "Hey, let's talk about something else."

"Not all of them," Yvonne explained. "Daddy doesn't hate all niggers. He says there are good uns and bad uns, but the bad uns are the ones making all the noise. Acting like niggers. And the bad uns are out to change our whole way of life. Hard to disagree with that, don't you think?"

I was silent. The last thing I wanted to do was talk about colored people with Yvonne at the Queen of Hearts dance. I wondered what I could do to get us out of this conversation. I didn't like the way it was going, what I was hearing from Yvonne, but I wasn't all that surprised. Our whole family knew that Mr. Rawlings was very prejudiced against colored people. We knew his views. I suddenly realized, however, that what I didn't want to know any more about was Yvonne's opinion.

Fortunately, she quickly abandoned this topic. "Hey, let's go find Marti and her date," she said. "And I would love a coke."

I nodded agreement. We quickly found Davis and Marti and the evening was officially underway. It turned out to be the three shortest hours of my life. With Marti and Yvonne chatting away, I had no significant conversational responsibilities, though I joined in occasionally with little comments or questions. Davis played the same role with Marti.

From time to time, both girls turned their attentions to us, their dates, so it was never one of those guys-hanging-on-the-periphery kind of scenes. Most of the time the music was fast, pop tunes played badly but recognizably by a band made up of five older kids. Thanks to my dance lessons, I acquitted myself with honor. After my first Locomotion, Marti nodded her approval.

By the end of the evening, Yvonne and I had danced to several songs, and I'd danced one fast dance with Marti. There were many fewer slow dances than I would have liked, but Yvonne and I danced every one, each somehow a little bit better than the last.

At different times during the evening, when the four of us were just talking together, with Davis and I doing more listening than talking, guys from my classes, or even older guys, came by to say hello. I knew them all, but was astute enough to realize they were not stopping by to say hi to me. They wanted to get a closer look at Yvonne. I introduced them all to her— and she dazzled them with smiles and little comments. I could only imagine the envious remarks that certainly occurred after they were out of earshot of us. There was no question at all who was the belle of that ball.

And then, in a flash, the evening was over. The last slow dance ended and the four of us left through the front door of the school's gym, looking for David's car amidst a sea of cars lined up to drive the freshmen and sophomores home from the dance.

Yvonne and I reached David's car first, with Davis and Marti trailing behind. As we were settling into the backseat, I realized that Davis would be saying goodnight to Marti in public, outside the car, with other kids from the dance streaming past them. As pre-occupied as I was with my evening with Yvonne, I now felt guilty that I had not paid that much attention to Davis and Marti. At this point, I was wondering just how well their evening had gone, and what kind of a goodbye was about to occur.

Not much of one, from what I could observe. Marti had her back to the car but I could almost see Davis' face. It looked like he was asking Marti if she had a good time, and she was nodding, but as he leaned in for what I am sure he was thinking would be at least a little kiss good-night, Marti turned her head. He kissed her on the cheek, started to pulled away, but then Marti pulled him to her and gave him a slightly longer than necessary hug. What the heck did all that mean?

Then Marti was in the car, and rolling the window down, and waving to Davis, and saying, "Thanks again, Davis! I had fun!"

Davis called back, "Me too, Marti!" as we headed for home.

* * * * *

The ride back to Roebuck was a magnificent repeat of the ride over. It became quite clear to me that holding hands with Yvonne was all I really needed for complete and total happiness.

When we reached her driveway, David let us out but then pulled away immediately, either because he was tired and knew that I could walk across the street easily enough, or perhaps to give us some privacy. Yvonne's porch light was on, which made me a little wary of Mr. or Mrs. Rawlings coming out to greet us, but that didn't happen.

We walked to her door hand-in-hand and then Yvonne turned to me and said, "You are so sweet, Mickey McQuade. Thank you for a lovely evening."

I stammered something about having a good time too, and somehow realized that I was looking down at my feet, rather than at Yvonne. So I lifted my chin to smile at her and that's when she kissed me.

It wasn't my first kiss—there was Lillian Stark in seventh grade—but it was my first real kiss.

Our lips met, lingered together. My eyes were closed to focus on the softness of her lips on mine. I had my arms on her shoulders, she had her hands resting lightly on my chest. And then, just as I could sense that she was going to pull away from me, her little pink tongue darted out, found its way between my lips, and touched my tongue. And then disappeared.

"Mickey McQuade," she said softly, "I know the both of us are always busy with school stuff. But it seems to me, if we are going to be a good boyfriend-girlfriend couple, like we were tonight, we need to see each other a little more often. How about the two of us work on that?"

Thankfully, though her words hit me like a Ford pick-up truck at a hundred miles an hour—boyfriend-girlfriend?— I did not fall off her porch. My verbal response, however, could have been better.

"Sure, I mean, absolutely, Yvonne. That seems very doable to me."

Doable?

"Good. Then call me this week. I really like you, Mickey. And here's something to remember me by."

Another kiss. Her earlier one had graded out with an A+. Her follow-up was A+++.

And then, with a smile and a wave and a "Thanks again, Mickey," she opened her door and went inside. The door shut, firmly and definitively, and I stood there, staring at it. I waited a full ten seconds for no good reason. I hoped but did not expect that lightning would strike twice and that she would re-appear. Finally, I turned and walked slowly up the street to my house, thinking about Yvonne and every single word she'd just said to me. And those two incredible kisses.

CHAPTER 21
FEBRUARY 18, 1964

I awoke Wednesday morning, the fifth day after Queen of Hearts, with four words running through my head. Today is the day.

Ever since Monday, I'd been struggling with the precise meaning of Yvonne's request to call her "this week." How soon is too soon (if there is a too soon), and how late in the week is too late?

I'd finally decided that Wednesday was the best choice, though my heart kept screaming Tuesday, Tuesday to my brain.

I actually waited until after dinner Wednesday evening. I set myself up in the hall closet, tried to calm my rapid pulse, then congratulated myself as I dialed her number from memory.

When she answered, I was ready for her. "Hi, Yvonne – it's me, Mickey. Don't mean to bother you—just calling like you asked." Smooth.

"You are never a bother, Mickey," Yvonne said. "And thanks for calling. I really had a wonderful time at your dance last week."

"That is such a coincidence, Yvonne. Cause I went to that very same dance and—guess what—I had a wonderful time too. In fact, I had a double wonderful time. Especially saying good-night."

My comeback was certainly not the most original, most elegant or most humorous ever, but it did the trick. I'd worried a lot about the last three words, but decided to be brave.

Yvonne responded with a little laugh, enough to reassure me. And then spent the next couple of minutes recalling moments from the dance, and how nice Marti looked, and how much fun it was to meet Davis and some of my other friends. I murmured agreements as appropriate.

Then Yvonne's voice softened. "I want to ask you a question, Mickey," she said. "Can you be honest with me?"

The tone of her voice made me nervous, but I agreed quickly. "Sure, sure, Yvonne, of course."

"Am I . . . would I be your first girlfriend? I mean, like, the first real girlfriend you've ever had. Not like a second grade girlfriend or anything like that."

I felt relieved. That question was a lot easier than I thought it might be, though I had no idea what I thought it might be.

"Yes, yes, Yvonne. Except . . . well . . . I didn't really know that we were real boyfriend and girlfriend. But I sure do like thinking about us that way. I mean . . . I would love to have you as my girlfriend. But . . . but . . . does this mean we already are real boyfriend and girlfriend?"

I was excited by this surprising conversation, and a bit overwhelmed. Kind of like going to a church bingo game, maybe hoping to win ten dollars, and then having someone tell you that you'd won the lottery.

"That's so nice to hear," Yvonne said. "I want to be your first ever girlfriend. And, of course, you're only girlfriend. And you and I can start doing things together, seeing each other a lot more often, going to movies and parties and school basketball games, that's the kind of boyfriend relationship I want."

"Wow, that sounds terrific, Yvonne. I'd like that. I'd like that a lot."

"I'd like that too, Mickey," Yvonne said. "Now, we won't see each other every day. But I bet we can find at least one thing to do every weekend, and maybe see each other during the week once in a while, like on Thursdays, cause I don't ever have any after school stuff on Thursdays."

There was a lot to digest in what Yvonne just proposed—and it did sound like a proposal of some kind—but for the moment I just savored the sound of her voice and the idea of seeing her a lot more. And then, since things were going so well, I decided to push my luck. "Y'know, Yvonne, I just checked my calendar and—guess what—tomorrow is Thursday. How about that?"

"I think you're getting the idea, Mickey. Why don't you come over tomorrow when you get in from school? I'll teach you how to play gin rummy. Sometimes I play that with my dad."

"Sounds great. Though I already know how to play. And I have to warn you – I'm pretty good."

"We'll see about that," she said, with a twinkle in her voice. "Maybe I'll let you win."

* * * * *

The next afternoon it took me less than five minutes to get out of the car, rush through the house, throw all my stuff on my bed, run down the hall, brush my teeth, dab on a little English Leather, and get back downstairs ready to head over to Yvonne's. "Heading out for a bit," I called to my mother, without waiting to hear her response. I was hoping she thought I was heading to Jackie's. That would eliminate a lot of questions at the dinner table later.

Yvonne answered her door on the first knock. "Mickey, come on in. I told my mom that you might stop by and we might play some cards for a bit."

"I am completely prepared," I said, "but nervous. Word on the street is that you know how to handle yourself in a gin rummy game."

"We'll see," said Yvonne. "We can play in the kitchen."

For the first several hands, we sat alone, enjoying the game, chatting about this and that, drinking glasses of Coke and devouring oatmeal cookies, store-bought, not homemade. Later, to my dismay, because I liked being alone with Yvonne, Mrs. Rawlings appeared and started bustling around, making dinner for the family. Then Traynor came in, sat down and watched Yvonne and I play. It was kind of like being at home—I felt totally comfortable.

At one point, Mrs. Rawlings turned to me and said, "Would you like to stay for supper, Mickey? I'm making fried chicken."

Good as that sounded, I decided to pass. While I was definitely enjoying my time with Yvonne, Mrs. Rawlings and Traynor, I was concerned that the mood would change as soon as Mr. Rawlings walked into the kitchen. Much as I appreciated how he'd come to the rescue when Brenda had her bike accident, Mr. Rawlings still made me uncomfortable. I did not want to have to listen to any of his complaints about colored people.

Using the manners that my mother had taught me, I thanked Mrs. Rawlings for the invitation. "I'd like to, Mrs. Rawlings, because that fried chicken of yours is sure smelling good, but I think I better decline. I'd love a rain check, though."

"Of course, of course, Mickey dear," Mrs. Rawlings answered.

"How about Sunday, Mom?" Yvonne said. "Aunt Jolene will be here, and Uncle Franklin. The more, the merrier."

"Good idea, Yvonne, darling. We'd love to have you join us all, Mickey."

I knew better than to say no to a second invitation—that would seem rude. "I'll ask my mom tonight, Mrs. Rawlings," I said, "but I'm a pretty definite Yes."

"Wonderful, it'll be a real party," Mrs. Rawlings said. "But now I have to ask you kids to skedaddle. I need to set the table for supper."

"C'mon, Mickey, I'll walk you out," said Yvonne. "But first I want to show you a project I'm working on." She gestured. "Follow me."

I wasn't sure where we were going, or what kind of project Yvonne wanted to show me, but I followed her out the kitchen door willingly, down the hall, down some stairs, then out into the garage. At this point, I was getting confused. Yvonne did not seem like the kind of girl that worked on projects in her father's workspace.

She wasn't. The minute we were alone, she threw her arms around me, and gave me another one of her special kisses.

It lasted a while. Then I pulled away, just far enough so that I could really look at her face and into her eyes. Yvonne looked back at me without speaking, just smiling. I kissed her lightly on the nose. "Let's play gin rummy again some day soon," I said. "I think I need more practice."

My comment wasn't all that funny, but Yvonne rewarded the effort with one more kiss before I headed for home.

CHAPTER 22
APRIL 18, 1964

The temperature was in the mid-70s, with low humidity, bright sunshine, no wind. You could not have asked for a better Saturday in April. Any sports announcer worth his salt would have called it a perfect day for baseball. And baseball was exactly what my brother Tom had on his mind.

The major league season had already begun. Last year's World Series champs, the Los Angeles Dodgers, were set to defend their title after beating the much loved, much hated New York Yankees in last year's October classic.

In Birmingham, the hometown Barons had a new owner, Charles Finley, a freshly painted ballpark, and, for the first time ever, an integrated team. On top of that, the fans would be cheering from stands that were no longer segregated. Times were changing.

I liked baseball well enough, but my brother Tom was a fanatic. He'd been able to play one season of the southern version of Little League, called Dixie Youth, but the following year the logistics of getting him to practice and games became too much. Tom whined and complained, and Mom and Dad felt bad about it, I think, but there was not much that could be done.

Tom compensated by playing the multiple backyard/street versions of baseball whenever he could with whomever he could get to play. Wiffle ball, stickball, halfball, corkball—anything that could be thrown and hit. Sometimes he played with Traynor Rawlings, occasionally with a couple of kids from school who lived a few blocks away. But I was his principal opponent. We played a lot of one-on-one versions of those games together, which I did not mind at all.

Tom's favorite baseball derivative—because it involved a real baseball or softball, bats and gloves, and running bases—was a game called scrub. And scrub was what we were planning to play this Saturday over at Jackie's house.

I was by now a regular at Jackie's on the weekends—either Saturday or Sunday. The other day I usually spent doing something with Yvonne.

This time, Tom had gone over to Jackie's the week before and made a date for baseball—scrub—this particular Saturday at 1 p.m. We never made any arrangements by phone; Jackie and Nammy, like many of the families in their neighborhood, didn't even have a phone.

A good game of scrub might involve five or six players. You could do it with three, but four was the minimum number for a decent game. Four gave you a hitter, a pitcher, someone to play first base, and an infielder/outfielder. Jackie, Tom and I made three, so we needed to recruit a fourth player. Jackie was vague about whether he could get any kids from his neighborhood to play, even though we'd asked about LP. We figured finding a fourth player was up to Tom and me.

Originally, we were hoping David would play with us. But he had to work. Our second choice was Traynor Rawlings. Traynor had actually played with us once before at Jackie's. One thing I liked about him was he never made any racist remarks like the ones that came from his father, and sometimes from his sister.

Around noon or so, Tom saw Traynor outside with his dad in the

Rawlings front yard. Mr. Rawlings was raking out flower beds.

Tom ran across the street—I followed right behind. "Traynor, Traynor — wanna play baseball with us? Scrub! We need a fourth guy for a good game."

Traynor, much like Tom, was always up for some activity or another. He turned to look at his father. "Can I, Dad? And please," he put a little anticipatory pleading into his voice, "don't make me go ask Mom."

"It's almost time for lunch," his father said.

"I had a late breakfast. I'm stuffed," answered Traynor. He patted his middle to drive home his point.

"Make your bed?"

"Yup — and all my dirty clothes are in the downstairs hamper," Traynor added, voicing a little pride, I thought, with this evidence of how he was managing his life.

"All right, I guess y'all can go," said Mr. Rawlings. "Where y'all playing?"

Tom took that one. "Over at Jackie's house," he said, pointing. "He's got a huge front yard so you can hit the ball a mile and it'll never get lost. We're playing scrub," Tom added, "softball, not baseball."

Softball was better because Jackie's front yard was big, but not baseball big. You could not hit a softball as far as a baseball.

"Jackie Thomas?" The look on Mr. Rawlings face changed instantly, taking on a dark, mean appearance. "Y'all talking bout that niggerboy? Niggerboy that lives in those shacks over through the woods?"

"Jackie lives in a stone farmhouse," said Tom, kind of missing the point of what had changed Mr. Rawlings' mood in an instant.

"Don't care if he lives in the palace of the King of Siam," said Mr. Rawlings." A niggerboy is a niggerboy and my son don't play with niggers."

"He's nice," I intervened, "polite and respectful and everything, Mr. Rawlings." I jumped in quickly before Tom let loose with the information that Traynor had already played with Jackie, back in the fall when we were throwing a football around and all of us were pretending to be Joe Namath.

If Traynor wanted his father to know that bit of information, we should let him reveal that on his own.

"Glad to hear that," responded Mr. Rawlings. "Some niggers are good niggers, and some ain't. Some got a real handle on how to conduct themselves. But the point is—Jackie's a nigger, and Traynor's a white boy. They don't mix. My boy ain't playing with niggers, and your daddy shouldn't be letting you play with niggers neither."

Mr. Rawlings suddenly looked at Tom and me suspicious-like. "Does your daddy know that you are going over to that niggerboy's house to play?"

"My dad's at work," said Tom, getting defiant. You could always count on Tom to escalate a ticklish situation from bad to worse.

"Our mom knows," I said quickly, but quietly and respectful, not like Tom. "She knows where we're going, and she knows Jackie's colored, and she's fine with all that."

Mr. Rawlings looked at me hard. Maybe he thought I was lying. Maybe he thought Mom was crazy, or stupid, or worse. But he didn't say anything at all right away. Just kept staring at me.

Then he spat, turned his head, and said quite clearly with his back turned to Tom and me, "Traynor ain't going. Period."

And that was that.

* * * * *

Tom slammed the door and stomped through the living room.

"Don't slam the door," yelled Marti from the kitchen. But then she saw Tom's face as he came in, and she knew something was wrong.

"What's the matter, Tom?" she asked. Sometimes Marti was a little mom, like she was right then, standing by the kitchen sink drying glasses and silverware with a towel, the things I'd left to "air dry" when I washed the dishes from breakfast.

And since Mom was gone with all four of the little ones to visit her cousin over in Bessemer, Marti probably felt that she needed to fill a vacuum for her little brother.

"Stupid Mr. Rawlings," Tom said. "He won't let Traynor come with us to play baseball at Jackie's. So now we'll have to play scrub with three people and that's no fun at all. Stupid Mr. Rawlings." Tom paused, considering the unfairness of it all. "Oh, and he called Jackie a nigger."

Tom added the last part, I think, just to throw more dirt on Mr. Rawlings name. The bigger crime, for Tom, was the decision to not let Traynor play with us. Mr. Rawlings vocabulary was, at that moment anyway, a secondary offense.

"I thought that man was a jerk when I first met him," said Marti, "and he's still a jerk."

Looking for solutions, Marti asked the obvious, "Doesn't Jackie have any friends that can play with you? Is he the only kid around?"

"I asked him before before but he told me no," Tom said. His mood was dark and heading darker.

"So, how about I play," Marti suggested. "I can play scrub. That'll give you four."

"Would you, Marti? Yeah, yeah, that'll work." Tom looked at the clock with a big smile on his face—Tom's mood swings reminded me of the roller coaster at Kiddieland, up and down and up again, always at scary speeds. "We have to be at Jackie's at one o'clock, Marti."

"I'll be ready," she said, putting the last glass away in the cabinet. "Let me go find my glove."

All things considered, we probably should simply have asked Marti if she wanted to play with us in the first place. She'd shown herself to be a pretty good first baseman on the girls' softball team at St. Barnabas, she could hit almost as well as Tom, and she did not throw like a girl.

Marti came back downstairs around a quarter to one, now wearing her long-sleeved St. Barnabas softball shirt, jeans, and sneakers. She had her glove, she had her favorite softball, she had a baseball cap. She'd pulled her long, brown hair back into a ponytail so that it would not get in her way during the game.

"Scrub One," I announced as we cut through the trees toward Jackie's house, taking a little bit of a short cut that Tom and I had discovered last fall.

"Scrub Two," said Marti quickly.

"King Scrub," said Tom, and then looked at us defiantly to see if we were going to challenge this aberration to the classic rules of scrub. "That's how we play it at school," Tom said.

The purpose of declaring your scrub number was to determine who got to bat when. In scrub, every man was his own individual team. When one was the batter, the other three were all on defense. In this case, pitcher, first baseman, fielder.

With four-player scrub, we'd only have one base, and a relatively narrow field of play—two diagonal lines running from home plate at about a 45-degree angle—to give the defense a chance.

An inning consisted of all four hitters getting to bat, with one out allowed per hitter.

When a batter hit the ball, he ran to the one base just like in regular baseball. If he hit a fly and it was caught, he was out. Hit a grounder and you could be thrown out. Hit a ball far enough so that you could make it to first and then home, you had a home run.

If you got to first base safely but could not advance home, you simply declared "Imaginary Runner." This allowed you to go hit again with the result of your next at-bat affecting not just you as the hitter, but also the invisible runner. Hit a home run with an Imaginary Runner on first base and you scored two runs.

In four-player scrub, even with a narrow field, the advantage was to the hitter. That's why we always played with a ceiling of five runs per hitter per inning.

Fortunately, no one had to review the rules for scrub. If you were a kid, you knew them. All you had to do was agree on the batting order and the game began.

"We probably shouldn't be calling out scrub numbers without Jackie," I said. "It's not fair."

"He won't care," said Tom. "Nothing bothers Jackie." Tom was partially right—Jackie was the easiest-to-get-along-with friend I'd ever had. I wondered why that was.

* * * * *

We walked along the windy dirt road to Jackie's house, trying to keep the red clay mud from caking too heavily on our sneakers. Jackie was waiting for us, sitting on his porch steps. He was wearing a faded blue long-sleeve t-shirt, jeans, and a Birmingham Black Barons baseball cap.

"Marti's our fourth," I said, figuring that Jackie might be wondering why we brought a girl along to play baseball. He did not seem to mind. "Last I remember," Jackie said, "Miss Marti was out-dancing everyone in the room, Mickey. Maybe she'll out-baseball all three of us."

"Why, Mr. Thomas," Marti said, "how good of you to remember our last encounter. But from what I hear, you're the best ballplayer in this crowd."

I think Jackie appreciated the compliment but he seemed a little embarrassed. "Don't know about that," Jackie mumbled. "Just like to play." He returned Marti's gaze for a quick second, then quickly looked at me and

Tom.

"C'mon, let's play, "said Tom. "I'm King Scrub," he told Jackie, "Tom's Scrub One, Marti's Scrub Two, so that makes you Scrub Three. You okay with that?"

Tom wanted to get the scrub batting order established quickly, I think, before I had a chance to come up with some fair way to do it again so that Jackie could be included in the process.

"So I'm outfield first," said Jackie. "Okay."

I quickly showed Marti the layout of the field and where the foul lines were. Home plate was just a very flat river stone and first base was a thick old piece of a tree branch.

As Scrub Two, she would start out playing first base. I would be pitching to Tom.

"Tom likes to hit grounders," I said, "because we don't have enough fielders to cover. So be ready for lots of throws to first base."

"Batter up!" yelled Tom, making sure we knew he was ready to go. Jackie caught a final practice fly from Marti and fired the ball to me. I turned toward Tom, who was standing ready to hit, taking practice swings, and the first game of scrub for the season began.

Tom was eager, maybe too eager. He swung hard at my second pitch, which was actually a little high, and popped it up. Jackie caught it easily. Tom slammed the bat down in early frustration, grabbed his glove, headed to the spot where Jackie was positioned, to replace him as outfielder. Jackie went to first base and Marti came in to pitch to me.

I was determined to be more patient than Tom, so I let three pretty good pitches go by before swinging at anything. On the fourth, I hit a screamer, a line drive between Jackie and Marti. If anyone else had been playing first, it would have gone through to the outfield for a sure homer. Jackie took two quick steps and leaped, extended his arm as far as it could go, and caught it dead center of his glove.

Tom exploded with praise at the play. "Way to go, Jackie!" he screamed. "Great catch!" Marti just kind of stared at Jackie, then called out, "Hey there, All Star. Nice play."

"Nice catch, Jackie," I called out graciously. "You're up, Marti."

For some reason, this game proceeded with much less offense than usual. We all got some runs, but there were a lot of pop-ups and easy grounders, and some good defensive plays, though none as spectacular as Jackie's first inning catch.

After four innings the score stood Jackie, 8; Tom, 6; Me, 5; Marti, 3. No one had yet reached the five-run maximum score in a single inning.

"How many innings are we playing, Mickey?" asked Tom as he was ready to hit to start the fifth. I looked at the sky, tried to calculate what time it might be, since Marti had to be home to start dinner for everyone, and we all needed to be there when Mom came home from visiting her cousin and Dad came home from work. None of us had a watch.

"I think we better make it the standard six innings," I declared.

"Okay, Jackie," Tom yelled quickly. "Two more innings. I'm coming after you."

Jackie just smiled.

In his next at-bat, Tom made good on his threat, achieving the first five-run inning of the day. Marti and I scored a couple each, Jackie scored three. Tom's last at-bat resulted in another two runs, I got nothing, Marti got one. So, with Jackie coming up for the last bat of the game, the score stood Tom, 13; Jackie, 11; Me, 7; Marti, 5. Jackie needed two runs to tie (though there was no such thing as extra innings in scrub), and three to win.

Based on the rotation of positions, Tom was pitching to Jackie, I was playing first, Marti was in the outfield. On Tom's first pitch, Jackie smashed the ball. Easy homer.

On Tom's second pitch, Jackie hit a hard grounder to Tom's right. Tom blocked it, bobbled it, made a hurried throw. The ball took a crazy bounce in front of me and I could not come up with it. Jackie made it to first safely. I could see the frustration on Tom's face. If I'd caught that ball, he would have won the first scrub game of the year.

"C'mon, Mickey," he yelled.

"Sorry, Tom. Bad bounce." I felt a little guilty but not much. It was a tricky hop. The error was on the throw.

"Imaginary Runner," Jackie yelled out. Then he trotted back to the plate to hit again.

Tom decided to get cute and try to make Jackie swing at a tough pitch. He threw three hard ones, much harder than he'd thrown all day. Jackie didn't swing. Then he tried a couple in the dirt. Jackie retrieved each unhittable pitch as it bounced against a makeshift, cardboard backstop that we'd set up. Patiently, time and again, he threw the ball back to Tom.

"Let him hit it, Tom" I called. That was the pitcher's job in scrub.

Tom relented, hoping for the best, and threw a beautiful, incredibly hittable pitch, right down the middle, perfect height, perfect speed. Jackie swung and did not miss.

Jackie's previous hit was a sizzling line drive. This was a majestic, towering fly.

Tom's shoulders slumped at the crack of the bat.

Jackie started to run to first, I just turned to look. But Marti, playing way deeper than normal because of Jackie's last homer, took off running.

Marti really had no chance to catch this ball, but no one told her that. She ran hard. The ground and grass clumps at her feet were uneven but she did not stumble. Her baseball cap flew off, her ponytail bounced up and down the way Brenda's did when Dad was giving her a horsey ride on his knee.

And just like that, it happened. She stuck out her glove, and the ball landed dead center in the pocket. Maybe she was as surprised as the rest of us, but she didn't show it. She ran a couple more steps to slow her momentum, turned back to the three of us, and trotted on in.

Tom went wild. "What a catch, what a catch, I win, I win!" He was giddy with excitement, with both arms in the air, doing a victory dance.

I did not say anything. I just dropped my glove, stood still while Marti trotted by me, and clapped my hands loudly and kind of slowly.

Marti blushed a little, slowed to a walk, looked over at me, smiled.

Jackie had picked up the bat and stood stock still with it angled over his shoulder watching Marti approach. As she came nearer to us, he called out in his loudest voice of the day, "Nice catch, Marti McQuade!"

"Thank you, Jackie Thomas," she yelled back at him.

The two of them stared at each other for a few seconds, but didn't say anything. Then Tom yelled, "Let's play again next Saturday!"

It was one heck of a way to start the baseball season.

CHAPTER 23
MAY 14, 1964

My father often admitted that he was out of step with the world around him. He traveled to the beat of an entirely different percussion section. And liked that about himself.

A World War II veteran who fought in the African campaign and was sent home in late 1942 after being wounded in conflict, Dad was a military man who did not believe in Lyndon Johnson's approach to the Vietnam War. In the early 60s, in Birmingham, Dad's views placed him in a distinct minority.

My father was also in the minority on the topic of race. Dad passionately believed in equal rights for all Americans, despite their color, and in the goals and objectives—not always the methods—of the Civil Rights movement. He never marched or participated in any demonstrations, but we kids knew his views well from family chats, individual talks, or listening in—with one ear held to the heating grate—on adult conversations during the rare occasions when our parents had friends over for drinks and cards.

On a more mundane level, Dad did not accept the notion that mowing one's grass was a weekly chore of any importance whatsoever. It was certainly not the personal obligation of the man of the house, nor a social responsibility owed to the neighborhood. Wherever we'd lived, lawn care was a hit and miss affair, at least until David was old enough to operate our cantankerous lawnmower and bring some sense of order to the McQuade front yard. The back yard was kept under control by the trampling of nine kids. Actually, eight, since Sheila was not a backyard kind of girl.

Another oddity, seemingly out of character given some of Dad's other views, was my father's belief that every young man should learn to handle and fire a rifle when he turned seventeen. Dad talked about this idea more than a few times to the disappointment of my mother, who hated guns. Why he believed this, no one knew, least of all our mother. Perhaps Dad had been taught to shoot by his father, perhaps this was a carryover from Army boot camp. My guess was that it was a rite of passage with some emotional significance of unknown origin, and not dependent on future gun usage to make it meaningful. Maybe like learning to ride a bike even if the rider never intended to sit on a bicycle seat again.

Whatever the case, Dad chose a warm Thursday evening in May to extend an invitation to David, who had turned seventeen in February, to "go out shooting" on Saturday.

David told me later that he was not really interested in learning how to shoot a rifle, but he went along with the idea to please my father. I think Dad knew that David was not enthusiastic, but that did not alter his plan.

They left without eating at about 8 a.m. on Saturday morning. I heard Dad tell Mom they'd "grab breakfast at Nick's," a truck stop out on the highway. It sounded as if a manly breakfast at a greasy spoon surrounded by burly and unshaven truck drivers was part of the "going shooting" experience.

They were home by eleven, and I'm guessing that the activity achieved some kind of bonding, because they were animated and laughing as they came through the door. A little while later I was passing Mom and Dad's room on the way to the bathroom, and I saw my father on a stool, putting his rifle away in the very top of his closet. He must have sensed my presence because he turned toward me, still on the stool.

Misreading whatever look was on my face, he smiled and said, "Don't worry, Mickey, you'll get your chance soon enough. You'll be seventeen before you know it and we'll go out together, just like David and I did today."

I didn't know exactly how to respond to his statement. I didn't want to tell him that I didn't really care. Just like David, I didn't want to hurt his feelings because this was a big deal for him. So, I responded with the first thing that popped into my head.

"Marti too?" I asked.

Dad turned his head just a little, considering my question. I wondered if the idea had ever occurred to him before. But he did not take too long to answer.

"You know, Sheila never expressed any interest but then I never asked her. Maybe I should have. So, yes, when you and Marti turn seventeen, we'll all go out together. Fair enough?"

I nodded. It wasn't too often that grown-ups admitted to making a mistake, but it certainly seemed like Dad had done so just then. I liked him for that.

* * * * *

A few days later I told Marti about my conversation with Dad. She listened to me but seemed to be thinking about something else at the same time. When I finished, she nodded her head, and kind of muttered to both me and herself, "Well, that explains that."

"What do you mean?" I asked.

"It explains the conversation that Dad just had with Sheila. She told me about it last night when we were going to bed. Dad caught her completely by surprise after dinner on Sunday—she was downstairs by herself making her lunch for work—and he sort of apologized to her for not asking her if she wanted to learn to shoot his rifle when she turned seventeen."

I snorted. "Sheila couldn't shoot a marble," I said, "and I'm sure she'd never want to. What did she say to Dad?"

"Actually, it sounded nice," Marti said. "Sheila gave him a hug and said thank you but she didn't want to learn to shoot a rifle—his or anybody else's—and never felt bad that he did not ask her. So, I guess it all turned out all right." Marti paused for a second. "But, you know, that was nice of Dad to say something."

I nodded understanding and then we sat quietly, each with our own thoughts. Mine drifted quickly away from Dad and his rifle as I began to picture Yvonne in a reasonably tight blouse with blue jeans and roller skates. We had a plan to go roller skating the following Saturday morning if we could get someone to drive us and, while I was definitely looking forward to it, I was also a little nervous. I was not an experienced skater. In fact, I'd only been to a roller rink twice in my life, once with Cub Scouts and once just with Mom to pick up Sheila after a birthday party for one of her friends. I had some legitimate concerns.

I was startled, then felt a little guilty, like I'd gotten caught doing something I shouldn't, when Marti interrupted my imaginings with an unexpected compliment.

"You know, Mickey, I think that was a good thing you did," she said. "Your question got Dad thinking."

Much as I loved getting an "attaboy" from my twin, I did not feel it was deserved. "I didn't really intend anything," I replied. "I just said whatever came into my head because I felt pressured to say something."

"Do you want to learn to shoot a rifle?" I asked her.

"I don't know. Maybe," Marti said. "But the important thing is that Dad would ask me. That he would treat me the same as the boys. That's what I'd want."

"Well, I'm sure if you asked him, he would take you," I said. "And if Sheila had asked when he said he was taking David, I think he would have taken her too."

"Probably," Marti admitted. "But if I was really being treated equally, I wouldn't have to ask. It would just . . . happen."

Marti's voice trailed off and she got that far-off look on her face, a look I knew well. It meant that something had occurred to her that she needed or wanted to think about—and maybe she was thinking about it right then and there—or maybe she was just mentally tucking it away for thinking about later.

In this case, she must have thought it through sufficiently, because she turned toward me with a wide-eyed, animated expression on her face, like she had just discovered electricity or something, and said, "Mickey—what I'm talking about is EXACTLY what Martin Luther King has been talking about."

I looked at her dubiously. "Huh?" It wasn't like Marti to give herself airs, but it sounded like she was comparing herself to the famous minister who'd been thrown in jail in Birmingham last year for causing all the riots. By this time, of course, I'd figured out that it was white people who called them "riots"—colored people called them "demonstrations."

"Mickey, don't you see," Marti said, her voice rising in pitch. "If things are really equal, then you don't have to ask. But when they are not, you have to stand up and say something or they might just go on being unequal forever. And that's what the Civil Rights Movement has been all about right from the beginning. It's been all about asking—or maybe, demanding—that things be equal because that's what they are supposed to be."

Another faraway look. But only for a few seconds. Then she came back again.

"But," she continued, focusing on me intensely and speaking faster than usual, "inequality between white people and colored people is just part of the whole picture. Think about it. There's also inequality because of religion— there are places where Jews, or even Catholics, can't get jobs because of where they go to church. And what's just as bad— there's also inequality between men and women. Women can't get certain jobs, or sometimes maybe they can, but then they get paid less than men for doing the same things that the men do."

"Whoa, whoa," I said, "you're going way too quick. How do you know all this stuff? Where do you get these ideas? We don't even know any Jewish people."

Even as I said it, I knew that my last comment made no sense. But it was hard for me to keep my thoughts together when Marti got this way—she was making my head spin with her passion. I reminded myself that she was, after all, a lot smarter than me and really understood what was going on in the world. And that made me feel kind of dumb and uninformed and not quite up to the role of being her older twin.

So I just shook my head side to side, like I was thinking hard about what she said.

"There's a whole lot of stuff that needs fixing, Mickey," she said, in a voice so low I could barely hear her.

But then she stretched both arms over her head, shaking off her somber mood and turning to what she probably thought was a much lighter topic. "Tell me how things are going with Yvonne, big brother. Seems like you two are seeing a lot of each other."

Almost perfect was the answer that immediately came to mind, though I did not say it aloud. It was true. Yvonne and I saw each other, somehow or another, at least once a week. We played cards, watched movies together at her house, occasionally took walks, managed to find private time fairly frequently, though our physical interaction had not progressed beyond an awful lot of kissing. The "almost" qualifier had to do with my continuing dismay and unhappiness about Yvonne's racial prejudices, how she expressed them, and how they made me feel. Which, in a word, was lousy. It didn't make sense for me to have a friend like Jackie and a girlfriend like Yvonne. But I was the only one who knew that. And I thought of myself as one huge coward because I never challenged Yvonne on any of her racial comments, and I never revealed the issue to Marti. But I did like kissing Yvonne.

Something sure needed fixing in this part of my life.

CHAPTER 24
MAY 23, 1964

A Saturday morning roller skating date might not seem all that romantic to most people. I had high hopes for mine, however. It had been almost two weeks since Yvonne and I had our last real date.

David dropped us off at Skate-A-Round, a rink near Trussville. I helped Yvonne out of David's car and carried her bag—she had her own pair of skates—to the entranceway. She wore her hair tied back in a ponytail, and I'm sure that Marti and Sheila would both have declared that she looked "just adorable." She wore lime-colored Wrangler jeans and a contrasting yellow top that could have been a little bit more snug, but I was not in a complaining mood.

Walking in the door, I felt the eyes of every other teenage male in the place all over us. Well, all over Yvonne.

Yvonne excused herself immediately to go to the Ladies' Room. I decided to go to the Men's Room. It was not the cleanest of all facilities—there were hand towels scattered across an un-mopped floor—but that didn't bother me much. What did catch my attention was a crude, hand-lettered cardboard sign, taped to the mirror over one of the sinks. In large letters it proclaimed NO NIGGERS ALOUD!

I had no idea who posted the sign, of course, or why someone felt a need to do so that morning. I'd seen no colored faces at all when we entered the rink—I wasn't even sure if there were any valid segregation laws to prevent colored kids from skating here. But I remembered my experience at Burger Bonanza with Jackie, and that got me mad. Mad enough to ignore Yvonne's history of anti-colored remarks, and try to get her to share my outrage.

I tore the sign off the mirror and stormed out to show it to Yvonne. "Look at this," I said, "I found this taped to the mirror. Look at it!" I didn't know what else to say.

Yvonne read the sign and put her arm on my shoulder. "Mickey," she said, "you're all mad. Don't be. We came here to have a nice time. You and me. Don't let some stupid sign get you upset."

Then she hugged me and whispered in my ear. "People are stupid—they can't even spell. And there's no niggers here. Forget it." Then she kissed me on the cheek.

I was still mad, but I could see that Yvonne wasn't, not even a little bit. I felt like she'd totally missed my point and that I needed to explain to her better why I was so angry. But I didn't even try. Instead, I simply let myself enjoy the sound of Yvonne's voice, and the way she hugged me, and her kiss.

"Let's get me rolling," I said, with a weak grin, then let Yvonne take my hand and lead the way.

Once I'd laced on my skates, we headed toward one of the openings into the skating rink. I moved slowly. Carefully. I'd already confessed to Yvonne that I "wasn't much of a skater." She'd laughed and said she'd teach me.

And that's what she did. She took me out on the beautifully polished and torturously slippery skating floor, and showed me how to push off by shifting my weight, and how to gather some momentum, and how to turn, and how to stop.

So I did what she did, and promptly ended up on my tailbone, surprised because it had happened so quickly that I'd barely realized I was going down, and then I was looking up.

I should have been mortified, but Yvonne giggled so sweetly, not in a "laughing at me" way, that I got past the indignity and laughed, too. She helped me regain my footing by pulling me with one hand and helping me get steady with her other, which meant that both hands were touching me, and I realized that there were some advantages to being inept.

Before long, we were actually skating around the rink, although I was visibly less smooth than most of the other skaters on the rink, many of whom were as young as seven or eight. There were also lots of ten- to twelve-year-old girls, and more than a few teenagers, some couples, some in groups of three or four.

And then there was Mr. Hotshot, a slim, athletic-looking teenager whom many girls, like my sister Sheila, for instance, would have declared quite handsome. He had dark eyes and high cheekbones, and a rich head of brown hair that was styled a little like Elvis. He was probably seventeen or eighteen years old.

During one trip around the rink by Yvonne and me, Mr. Hotshot must have passed us four times, swooshing by with long, confident strides, lifting a foot occasionally and gliding effortlessly on the other, sometimes crossing one leg over the other in a move with no discernible purpose other than to grandstand in front of the twelve-year-olds. And parade for Yvonne. At least, that was my opinion.

Ignore him, Mickey, I told myself. He's the big show-off, but you're the guy with the most beautiful girl in the rink at your side.

At least, I was that guy, until he suddenly appeared before Yvonne and me, flashing toward us out of the crowd and then stopping on a dime—a real hotdog move—and said, "Hey, Yvonne, want to do a 'couples skate' with me?"

What's this, I thought. They know each other? Now I wasn't just annoyed by him, I'd moved on to dislike.

"Ben," Yvonne said with a laugh, though why she laughed I didn't know, because he hadn't said anything remotely funny. "Meet Mickey. Mickey, this is Ben."

Ben and I shook hands in the awkward manner of teenagers acting like men, but not really pulling it off. The whole situation was made even more awkward, of course, because my initial dislike for Ben had transformed rather quickly into loathing.

"Mickey," Yvonne turned to me, "would you mind if I did one quick skate with Ben?" I noticed that she'd omitted the word "couples" from her question. I hoped that she did it on purpose.

"No problem," I muttered, trying to be nonchalant and failing miserably.

As if on cue, the house lights dimmed, and the glitter ball in the middle of the rink started to spin, and all of a sudden there were flashing lights all around me, and the music changed to some lovey-dovey kind of thing, and the two of them were gone.

For the next three, agonizingly slow minutes, my eyes never left the skating rink. I did not follow Yvonne and Ben's journey around the rink. Instead, I stared straight ahead as if I were terribly interested in the emergency exit sign directly across the rink from me.

Yvonne and Hotshot—my mind refused to acknowledge him as Ben— passed in and out of my vision every twenty seconds or so. I could see them approaching out of the corner of my eye, though I refused to move my head from its fixed position to watch them.

The first time by, Yvonne looked over at me and waved. Startled, I did nothing at first, then managed a limp wave, but too late for her to see it. I was ready to wave the next time they came around, but she didn't wave this time. The two of them were laughing, probably at some dumb remark that Hotshot made, and did not look over toward me at all.

The third time by, Hotshot pulled some fancy dance move—I was sure he'd waited until the two of them were directly in front of me—and switched smoothly from skating beside Yvonne to skating backwards in front of her, holding both her hands and staring into her eyes. I began to hope, at this point, that he might push himself beyond his own limits, and try something too fancy, and fall on his stupid face. It never happened.

Finally, after many more revolutions around the rink, the music ended, the lights came on, and Couples Skate was over. As Yvonne and Ben skated toward me, still leaning forward and gazing fixedly at the exit sign, I realized that the inside of my shirt was more than a little damp from perspiration.

"Hey, Mickey," Yvonne said gaily, "did you see us out there? Did you see me wave?"

"Oh, hey," I turned toward them, trying desperately to pull off the acting performance of my life. "Yeah, I saw you. Really good."

I could see that my interpretation of Cool Teenager, Unconcerned While Watching Girlfriend Flirt With Big Jerk was less than convincing because Yvonne gave me a sharp, questioning look before turning back toward Ben.

"Thanks, Ben, that was fun. You're really good out there."

"You too, Yvonne. See you again sometime?" he asked, pointedly ignoring me.

"Not for a while," she said, "maybe end of summer."

What? What was that supposed to mean?

Ben waved, ostensibly at both of us, but really just at Yvonne, and skated off.

Yvonne turned to me and made me instantly feel like an even bigger idiot than I'd felt so far by taking my hand, and squeezing it, and whispering to me, "Don't be jealous, Mickey. He's a good skater, but he is just so full of himself. So conceited!"

I looked up at her, and I could feel my whole face on fire, and somehow managed to say, "It's just that I wish I could skate that good, and do the Couples Skate with you, and all. And I can't. I stink."

I don't know how I came up with it, but it seemed that my pathetic, feel-sorry-for-myself approach—totally genuine—struck the perfect emotional chord with Yvonne.

"Silly goose," she said, squeezing my hand a little tighter, and entwining her fingers in mine. "Look, how about we go get some cokes and sit down for a little bit. I have something I want to tell you about."

"I'd like that," I replied, excited with the idea of getting away from the rink and Mr. Hotshot-on-skates for some period of time, eternity if possible.

"Let me freshen up," she said. "I'll meet you in the snack bar."

Yvonne skated off, leaving me to wind my way toward the men's room. It was almost as tough for me to walk on skates as it was to skate on them. I felt like a plough horse amidst a herd of thoroughbreds.

I needed "freshening up" as well. Luckily, the air conditioner inside the lavatory was blasting frigid air across the room—the intense cold felt wonderful. I splashed water all over my face, dried it slowly with a paper towel, then looked directly at my image in the mirror.

The words of my seventh-grade softball coach came to mind, and I silently mouthed them to myself. "You have to imagine victory before you can achieve it." For some reason, even though I wasn't sure whether his words applied directly to the situation at hand, recalling his pre-game motto made me feel better. I gave myself a little approving nod—a confidence builder—and went out to find Yvonne.

I saw her the moment I entered the crowded snack bar, sitting, as they say, "all by her lonesome," holding a little table for the two us, a pair of large cokes placed invitingly in front of her.

"I would have bought the cokes," I said, as I sat down beside her.

Yvonne smiled. "It's okay," she said. "Maybe you can buy us hot dogs—it's getting close to lunch time."

"Sure," I replied, and started to get up.

"Wait," she touched my arm. "I want to talk to you about something first."

I tensed up immediately. Something about what she said sounded ominous.

"You know," she began, 'how I've talked about my cousins from Chicago, Jillian and Katie, and how much fun they are, and how they're always asking me to come up and visit and stuff."

I nodded, slowly.

"Well, " she continued, "my parents told me last night that my aunt—Jillian and Katie's mom— invited me to visit them in Chicago for the whole summer. And my mom said yes. So I'll be leaving right after school's out next Thursday."

First Hotshot, now this?

"The whole, entire, beginning-to-end summer?" I asked, trying to keep my voice calm. "Why the whole summer? Couldn't you just go for a couple of weeks or so?"

"I don't know," she said, and reached again for my hand under the table. I let her hold it, but I did not respond to her squeeze. I was not about to roll over and pretend that it was no big deal and that everything was just fine with me.

"Mickey," she said earnestly, her voice dropping to a whisper. "Listen to me."

"I'm listening," I said, with my head down, staring at the table instead of looking at her.

"First," she said, "I have no choice. And second, well, I know I'll miss you, but I'm kind of excited about going. I've never spent any summers away from Birmingham, ever."

I maintained my silence, once again finding myself in a situation that seemed to require me to feel good—or at least not bad—about whatever she was doing, when in truth I felt lousy about every bit of it.

"Mickey," she cooed at me, "Mickey, don't be mad. It's really only going to be ten weeks or so. And I'll write you a letter every week and send you postcards—I promise."

She reached out with her hand and touched my face to make me look at her. "And to make sure you don't forget me," she said, "I have a present for you."

With that, she handed me a small wrapped box. "Here," she said, "open it."

Inside the box, tucked behind a covering of pink tissue paper, I found a 5" x 7" color framed photograph of Yvonne. It must have been taken at Christmas time because a decorated tree was partially visible over her right shoulder. She was seated, one leg demurely crossed over the other, in a wing-backed chair; I recognized it from the Rawlings living room. She wore a red Christmas dress, and her hair was up, like she was going to a fancy party. She wore a soft smile on her face, and she showed just a hint of a dimple on her right cheek.

The photograph was arresting—Yvonne at her absolute loveliest. I could not take my eyes off it.

"Do you like it, Mickey?" I heard her ask. "Will it help you remember me? I wrote a little message on the back of the photo."

I took the photograph out of the frame and read her short message:

Mickey, thank you for being the best boyfriend ever! Thank you for being in my life. Luv ya! Yvonne.

"Do you like it?" she asked again.

It wasn't easy, but I lifted my eyes from the photograph and looked directly into Yvonne's.

She asked me for a third time, "Do you like it, Mickey?"

I decided that three questions deserved three answers. So, right there in the snack bar, in full view of gawking pre-teens, and horrified eight-year-olds, and perhaps a few envious teenage boys, I put both hands around the back of Yvonne's head, pulled her to me, kissed her, then responded with, "Yes, yes, yes!"

Take that, Mr. Hotshot!

Five days later, Yvonne was gone. But I was okay, sort of, still enjoying the memory of those moments in the snack bar and some very enthusiastic good-bye kisses that Yvonne and I managed to exchange in her father's garage. And now I had my framed picture of Yvonne, sitting on the windowsill above my bed. It was like she was keeping an eye on me while I slept.

CHAPTER 25
JUNE 3, 1964

As a family, the McQuades were not vacation-takers. It made me jealous of my many friends who seemed to go on family vacations every year, sometimes two family vacations in a year.

Gulf of Mexico destinations were by far the most popular amongst my peer group. I'd hear stories about beach trips to Pensacola or Panama City or sometimes Tampa.

Other kids would talk—or brag, depending on the personality of the individual—about vacations to more exotic destinations, like New York City or Washington, D.C. One friend of David's spent two weeks with his family driving up and down the coast of California, visiting San Diego and Los Angeles and San Francisco. Jimmy Shields, who was in the same grade as Marti and me because he was held back a year, once spent a week at a dude ranch in Colorado. In a report to the eighth grade class of St. Barnabas, he described in a rather patronizing way how he rode horses, herded cattle, and roped calves—while the rest of us were just twiddling our thumbs in Birmingham—though his sister told me that they did a lot more watching than actual riding, herding and roping. However, she added, they also ate some really good bar-b-q that was cooked over an open fire somewhere out in the desert, then they spent the night under the stars in sleeping bags. That sounded like a lot of fun to me.

If any of my friends asked me about vacations with my family, I typically replied, "Nah, McQuades never go anywhere. Too many kids." It was an honest, matter-of-fact answer—I never felt any resentment toward my parents for not taking us on trips. For me, it was merely one of those trade-offs for all the good things that came with having eight brothers and sisters. However, understanding why we never took vacations did not stop me from being envious of my friends for the experiences they enjoyed traveling with their families.

On an individual level, I had managed to acquire a few bona fide vacation experiences. When I was in second grade, I spent a week at a place called Camp Tekawitha. It was a Catholic camp on a lake, not too far from Birmingham. We played softball, went for canoe rides with our camp counselors, had a morning swim and an afternoon swim. Meals were especially enjoyable—we'd line up with metal trays that had compartments in them and walk down a line where a team of colored ladies would put food into each compartment, as much as would fit. My favorite meal was fried chicken, especially because one of the women—whose name was Miss Petunia—took a liking to me and gave me two pieces, two breasts. At home, I usually got a drumstick and maybe some white meat pulled from a breast. Getting two breasts all to myself was, for someone not yet in third grade, culinary nirvana.

I also spent a full week's vacation once with a friend of mine, Dudley Courson. He was an only child, so I became his companion for the week. We went to Tampa, Clearwater and St. Petersburg, Florida. I still remember it as one of the best weeks of my life. One reason was that Dudley liked to play board games, same as me. We would play Monopoly, of course, and Chinese checkers, and Sorry. But because his parents had a lot of extra money to spend on him, Dudley owned a whole closetful of board games that we did not have in the McQuade collection. Dudley and I would play games like Careers and Clue and Lie Detector for hours on end, in the car while driving, at the hotel, sometimes even on the beach, finishing one and starting another, with barely a breather in between. Dudley usually won at first, because he had to teach me the rules, but once I caught on to the basic strategies, we played pretty evenly.

However, Camp Tekawitha and Dudley Courson's vacations—while they were lots of fun for me—were not family vacations. Which is why I got so excited—and all the rest of my brothers and sisters got so excited—when my father announced one Wednesday night in June that he and Mom were taking us on our first ever family vacation to the Atlantic Ocean and a little beach town called Sea Isle City, New Jersey, in just a couple of weeks.

The minute he finished his pronouncement, delivered that evening at an impromptu family meeting, the room erupted.

Sheila jumped up out of the fold-up chair she was sitting on, screeched something unintelligible, and ran over to give Mom a hug. Tom leaped to his feet as well and began singing Beach Boys songs, mixing up Surfin' Safari with Surfin' USA, getting the lyrics wrong and the melodies hopelessly confused, but doing a decent job of imitating a professional surfer, knees bent, arms extended front and back, swaying slightly to stay balanced while riding out a big one.

Marti kept looking at Dad, asking in disbelief, "Really? Really? We're going on a family vacation? Really? All of us?"

The little kids—Brenda and Bobby and Ricky—started jumping up and down too, not totally sure of what was going on, since we'd never gone on a vacation before, but clearly understanding that good news had just been delivered. I picked Brenda up, swung her around and told her that we would make the biggest sandcastle in the history of the world, just her and me.

Even David, good old show-no-emotion David, who was holding Carrie Ann on his lap when Dad told us the news, got carried away with the moment. He started tickling Carrie Ann and telling her, "We're going to the beach! We're going to the beach!" over and over. At two, Carrie Ann also had no idea why her older brothers and sisters had just begun to act like maniacs, but she got into the spirit quickly enough and started saying "Beak, beak" to anyone who would listen to her. I think it was safe to say that Dad's declaration was an immediate hit with all the McQuade offspring.

He provided some details when the room settled down. "We're leaving very early in the morning, two weeks from this coming Saturday," he said. "We've got a long drive ahead of us, probably 15 hours or better, so we want to get a big jump the first day. But we'll stay overnight in a motel somewhere in Virginia and then hopefully make it to the Sea Isle beach by late Sunday afternoon. We're going to stay four full days, then head back to Birmingham on Friday morning."

"However," he said seriously, "your mom will have lots to do between now and then to get us all ready to go. You need to help her, okay?" He looked at me and Tom, and then at Richard, Brenda, and Bobby. "Let's knock off the squabbling and bickering for the next couple of weeks, you got it?"

We all nodded yes. Dad looked at Mom, who looked back at him, shrugged her shoulders, and smiled. It was her I'll-believe-it-when-I-see-it-but-thanks-for-trying look. But she was excited too. I could tell.

CHAPTER 26
JUNE 19, 1964

On the Friday night before our departure, the McQuade kids were way too excited to sleep, although our parents finally got us settled into our rooms by eleven. Our biggest family adventure ever was to begin the next morning, with a scheduled departure time of 4:30 a.m. Actual departure turned out to be roughly 5:15 but, as an indicator of how good everyone was feeling, none of the kids was whining or crying during the packing of the car, not even Brenda, who at one point sat in the rear cargo area for a good twenty minutes, hugging her teddy bear and chanting to herself, "We're going to the beach, we're going to the beach."

Chaos, McQuade-style, reigned all around her. Dad and David were struggling with tying six pieces of luggage securely to the top of the car. Tom and I were assigned to shut-down tasks, making sure windows were secured and bedroom fans unplugged. Mom and Sheila and Marti were working together trying to figure out placement for all of us, with pillows and toys and coloring books for the little ones, plus a big picnic basket of snacks so that we could avoid the time and expense of snack stops. Our 1957 Rambler Cross Country station wagon was designed to seat six adults; squeezing eleven into it for a 920-mile ride was a space and logistical challenge of some consequence.

Our route, carefully planned by Dad and David, who would be our primary drivers and navigators, would take us through Chattanooga, Tennessee, then northeast through Knoxville, using both US 11 or Interstate 81, depending on traffic and any road construction, then straight through to Kingsport and up to Roanoke, Virginia. Roanoke was a little more than 500 miles from Birmingham—which meant 10-12 hours of driving time—and looked good as a stopping point for the night.

It was still dark when we pulled out of the driveway. Mom and Dad got their wish: the little kids, plus Tom, immediately fell back to sleep. Dad, David, and I sat up front, me in the middle, but we did not talk. Dad drove, whistling softly to himself. David dozed. Mom and Sheila and Marti sat across the back bench seat of the car, and chatted from time to time in low, whispery voices to keep the kids from waking up.

My eyes were tired, but I was determined not to miss dawn coming up in front of us as we headed northeast. I watched the road with my father and thought about all the fun I'd have with my brothers and sisters, especially with the little kids, once we got to the beach. This would be their first time to see the ocean and play in the surf. Then I thought about Yvonne, wondering to myself how she was enjoying her visit with her cousins in Chicago and whether she was even thinking about me. Then I thought about the Saturday playing scrub with Jackie and after that I silently sang all the words to *Don't Let The Sun Catch You Crying*, a recent hit song by a group called Gerry and the Pacemakers. I was doing anything I could to keep from nodding off.

It seemed like we'd been riding awhile so I looked over at the speedometer. So far, we'd gone about 22 miles. It was then that I began to understand just how long and boring a 920-mile car ride might turn out to be.

A few minutes later, we passed a destination and mileage sign, Chattanooga, 125 miles. "125 miles to Chattanooga," I whispered to the back seat. "Shusshh" said Sheila. "Thanks, Mickey," said Marti. "Go to sleep, Mickey," said Mom.

I closed my eyes for ten seconds, opened them, looked over at the speedometer: 27 miles. I decided that it was time to start capturing observations in my journal, a small spiral-bound notebook I'd bought for the trip. Perhaps, if I did a lot of observing, and wrote very, very slowly, I might not notice the snail's pace of the car's odometer.

To be honest, up to this point in my life, I hadn't had a very consistent record as a keeper of journals or diaries of any kind. I'd started many, maintained none. My most ambitious effort was *Journal of the 1962 World Series: Perspective of Two Fans*. My idea for the journal was to listen to each game on the radio or watch on TV if it was a weekend game, and express myself from the perspective of two different people. I would pretend I was a New York fan when the Yankees were batting and write down my thoughts as each hitter came to the plate based on the situation and what he accomplished during his at bat, and then flip to writing as a San Francisco fan when the Giants were hitting. After three innings of Game One, I was exhausted by the process and stopped writing anything at all. But it might have made for exciting reading if I'd kept at it: the Yankees won the World Series that year by a score of 1-0 in a game-seven pitchers' duel.

I pulled my notebook from my back pocket, along with a red Bic pen. The sun still was not up, but there was enough gray light of dawn that I could see to write.

The night before we left, at the top of the first page, I'd written *McQuade Family Vacation, 1964: Observations of an Engaged Participant*. I liked putting titles to things. I think I enjoyed creating titles for my journals much more than the journal-keeping itself.

Then I realized that I'd already neglected an important journal entry, so I quickly scribbled . . .

June 19, 5:15. It's dark and kind of muggy. The adventure begins.

Now what?

6:24. Looks likes it could be a beautiful day ahead. Sun not up yet. Dad is driving. David keeps dozing, then waking with a start, then falling back to sleep. The little kids are all sleeping, I think. I'm writing.

Not exactly Hemingway, I said to myself, as I considered what I'd written so far. However, I'd read once that the most important element of journal keeping was getting words onto paper, as they came to you, without a lot of mental composition and rewriting. Editing could come later. It was the thought—however captured—that counted most. So I sat quietly, waiting to see if I had any other thoughts.

After a bit, I turned slightly in my seat and looked over my shoulder, with the hope that the change in focus might provoke some insights worth capturing. By now, everyone seemed to be sleeping except Marti. She was looking out the window, eyes wide open, staring at nothing really, with a little half-smile on her face. As if she knew something amusing and was turning it over in her mind.

I raised my arm and waved at her. She noticed the motion, turned her head toward me, and waved back. Just at the moment, the sun broke through the early morning clouds and the tiniest, thinnest ray of sunlight struck the car window and shone directly on Marti's face. It was lighting the way portrait photographers prefer it: half of her face illuminated, half in shadow, giving her face depth and drama that I'd never seen before. And for the first time in my life, I realized that my twin sister was kind of pretty.

She wasn't strikingly gorgeous in a Yvonne kind of way. Yvonne was dramatically beautiful, with a look older than her years, one that turned every guy's head, including guys much older than me. Marti's attractiveness—for some reason, I was uncomfortable calling it anything else— was different somehow. There was a softness to it, and a warmth, something that radiated from inside and just spread itself to the outside, lighting up her eyes and entire face. Funny that it took me sixteen years and a car ride at dawn to really notice what my sister looked like.

6:37. I just discovered that my twin sister is pretty cute. I can't believe I never saw this before. And now I am wondering if she has always been this way and I was simply unaware, or if maybe she has been slowly turning pretty over the past year or so. I guess you see things a lot differently depending upon the circumstances.

After writing that, and reading it over a few times, I decided that this was exactly the kind of discerning commentary that a good journal needed. Perhaps I had finally discovered the type of observations I should be making. I quickly added to my comment:

I noticed this as the sun was coming up on the way to Chattanooga.

Satisfied with myself, I closed my journal for the time being and put it and my pen in the pocket of my jeans.

I looked over again at the odometer. We'd gone 85 miles so far, which meant Chattanooga was only another hour or so away. I looked out the window and my estimate was immediately confirmed with a sign that read "Chattanooga 62 miles."

I adjusted myself in my seat and closed my eyes. And returned my thoughts to Yvonne.

* * * * *

We took a short break somewhere past Chattanooga. The little kids were all awake by then and needed to go to the bathroom. We found a rest stop— bathrooms only. Mom helped Carrie Ann who was still getting the hang of big girl pants. Marti went in with Brenda. Tom and I shepherded Ricky and

Bobby. Dad and David rechecked the bindings that were keeping the luggage in place. Sheila went to the bathroom and then just stood around. Then we all hustled back into the car. David wanted to drive but Dad said later because of the morning traffic we might hit.

Back on the road, Mom passed out some breakfast rolls and muffins and orange juice. Surprisingly, everyone—even Brenda—was happy. No whining, no crying, no fighting. I wondered silently how long that might last.

Our first real break came somewhere on the north side of Knoxville. Dad pulled over and announced that we'd take forty minutes for a lunch break and to stretch our legs. The good news, he told us, was that we'd already travelled 316 miles and only had another 200 miles to go before stopping for the night.

I grabbed my notebook.

11:55 a.m. Lunch break. Chicken spread sandwiches, I bet.

We piled out of the car and gathered round an old wooden picnic table that looked like it had been there since Davy Crockett and his coonskin-capped buddies had roamed these very same Tennessee woods.

Mom opened a bag of potato chips that we all dove into while she fished in a brown grocery bag for the sandwiches she and Sheila had made the night before.

Marti and Mom made sure the little kids all got a sandwich, then Marti extended a paper plate, and a question, to me. "Peanut butter and grape jelly," she said, "or chicken spread?"

"Chicken spread, with extra ham and cheese," I replied, grimacing.

"Dad's having his favorite . . . sardines," she said, smiling. "Maybe he'll share."

"No, thanks, I'd rather eat grass," I said.

My father and his mystifying taste in sandwiches was an occasional topic of discussion among the older McQuade kids, mostly centered around which of his varied creations was the most disgusting. I always voted for the sardines with mustard on white toast, with roasted red peppers layered on top of the little wet and slimy fishes. To me, it smelled like a sandwich of old, wet socks with just a hint of rotting vegetation. Marti disagreed and made a good case for his fried egg and green pepper sandwiches, which actually would not have been so bad had he not "improved" them with slices of olive loaf and raw onion. Sometimes Dad would fry up bacon and then make himself two or three bacon and peanut butter sandwiches on rye bread. I never admitted it to Marti, but I did try that concoction once. If you could get past the visual of greasy slices of bacon atop chunky brown peanut butter, the sandwich itself was pretty good.

Fact is, my father had a big appetite and would eat most anything within the sandwich category, as long as it did not have butter or mayonnaise. I never knew why he hated those two condiments so intensely, but he'd have a fit if an open mayonnaise jar was accidentally placed too close to his sandwich plate. He said it made him sick. I found this a little ironic.

I'll say this, though: Dad was not a stingy chef. If any of us kids wandered by during the sandwich preparation process, you could be sure you'd get an invitation to join him. Acceptances were rare.

Perhaps, by this point, Dad had given up completely on the possibility that any of his kids would develop a liking for sardines on bread. He sat contentedly on the ground, up against a tree, a little way away from us so that the smell of sardines would not generate complaints from the crowd. I watched him eat his lunch, saw him look up from time to time to take in what one or another of us might be doing or saying. It occurred to me, at that moment, that my father was a happy man. I hadn't realized it before but taking his whole family on a vacation must have been a big, exciting adventure for him.

* * * * *

We reached Sea Isle City, New Jersey around 2 p.m. on Sunday. It was a quiet arrival, with Dad announcing to a car full of nodding, dozing McQuades that, "the ocean is exactly three miles away, dead ahead."

"Wake up everybody, we're here," said Mom. "Roll the windows all the way down! Smell that salt air. This is the world-famous Jersey Shore."

Born in Trenton, New Jersey, my mother had visited the seashore often as a child. I could hear both pride and nostalgia in her voice. I tried to imagine her as a little girl, playing on the beach. I couldn't. I don't know if anyone can truly imagine their parents as kids. Maybe as teenagers, or young adults. But there was just no way that I could picture my mother at Brenda's age, smiling one minute, crying the next, digging in the sand with a toy shovel and matching pail.

The car climbed to the apex of the causeway bridge and Sea Isle City spread before us, with houses to both left and right, and people in the distance walking in shorts and sandals along the main street, Landis Avenue. David, wide awake by now, resumed his role as navigator for my father. "We have to turn right at the end, Dad," he said. "The rooming house is on 69th Street."

By this point, everyone in the car was wide awake, staring out the windows, craning necks and squinting eyes against the bright sunshine to catch a glimpse of the ocean in the distance. We could feel the holiday atmosphere all around us. The next four days stretched ahead, filled with the promise of vacation adventures and memorable family moments.

We drove slowly south, down Landis Avenue, and finally arrived at our destination, a large and wind-weathered boarding house called Matilda's Rooming House. It might have been an impressive, imposing structure at one time, when it was first built, but the impression it made on me that day was closer to mildly dilapidated.

Matilda's had a large front porch with a wooden railing that had once been painted white, but not recently. There were several tired-looking beach-style rocking chairs available for McQuade lounging and relaxing, if we had been a lounging and relaxing family, which we weren't. The front door was wide open; a slightly rusty screen door kept out the flies. It would have worked better if the screen did not have a tear in the bottom left-hand corner. It might as well have had a sign saying Flies, Please Enter Here.

The foyer—which led to a living room and reception area featuring a lumpy sofa and four straight-back chairs—was clean, but dimly lit. And even though we were well into the season at mid-June, the whole place smelled musty, as if it had just been opened up that very morning and had not yet fully aired itself out.

All in all, the feel of the place was less than luxurious. But to us McQuades, on our first ever family vacation, it was wonderful.

Dad had checked in with our owlish innkeeper, a white-haired lady who introduced herself as Miss Simmons and whom Tom promptly nicknamed Persimmons, but not in hearing distance of Mom and Dad. Afterward, we were escorted to the topmost floor of the house by a freckle-faced girl whom I suspected was about the same age as Marti and me.

She unlocked the door at the top of the stairs and opened it wide. The whole family trooped past her, single file. I was the last one in line. Just before I crossed the threshold, she stuck out her hand, awkwardly, and introduced herself. "I'm Susan," she said. I was surprised but automatically extended my hand when she offered hers. I shook it, feeling a little self-conscious, thankful that the rest of the family was ignoring me as they investigated our living quarters for the next five days. "I'm Mickey," I answered. "Nice to meet you."

"You too," she said quickly, before disappearing down the stairs.

I watched her go, then turned my attention to our space.

The room was large, taking up the entire top floor of the house, and bright, with a high, raftered ceiling and windows on three sides. It was furnished simply and functionally: twelve single beds, arranged in two neat rows of six, and assorted other furniture pieces positioned against the walls and under windows. There was an open area to the left that contained a dining room table and chairs that could be pulled up to it for meals, even though the room had no stove, no sink, and no refrigerator. I heard David say "Army barracks" under his breath. But I thought it felt more like a cabin at Camp Tekawitha, without the bunk beds. It was very hot and still in the room as we entered, but Mom quickly opened up windows at either end and we immediately felt a refreshing cross-breeze.

Tom claimed the bed nearest the window at the far end of the room for his own. He established ownership by taking off his baseball cap and placing it squarely on the pillow, then turning to face the rest of us. "This one's mine," he said.

"Hold your horses, Tom," Dad said. "Let your mother think for a minute."

Mom surveyed the room and told Tom, "Okay, you can have a bed near the window, but it has to be at the other end." Then she went about assigning beds to each of us, pulling two twin beds together for her and Dad, and directing us kids to stow our belongings under each bed to keep things neat.

We'd been in the room for less than ten minutes before Tom started asking when we were going to the beach. I could see that Mom still had some arranging and "homemaking" to do. She told Dad that she needed him to go to a store nearby to get milk for our cooler. Then she sent David to ask Miss Simmons if they had an icemaker for the guests, so that we could put fresh ice in the cooler to keep the milk cold.

While she was discussing that, Marti and Sheila helped Brenda and Ricky and Bobby find their bathing suits packed away in their three little matching suitcases—which Mom had purchased a few weeks ago at a secondhand store. Carrie Ann just wandered the room on her own, content to drift from bed to bed and sibling to sibling, giving out hugs and laughs all along her route.

I unpacked my duffel bag, taking out my swimsuit, the three books that I'd packed to read on the beach, a pair of flip flops, and my beach towel. It wasn't really a beach towel because we did not own any beach towels—it was an old bath towel that I'd found in Mom's ragbag and rescued for my personal use because it only had one hole in it. I left the rest of my clothes in the bag, then shoved it under my bed. It was then that I realized we were all sharing living quarters in a room that offered no privacy whatsoever.

"Hey," I asked of no one in particular, "where are we going to change? There's no bathroom or anything." There was a bathroom for the family to use, of course, with sink, toilet, and an indoor shower to complement the outdoor shower that most of us would use coming up from the beach. But it was down on the second floor.

It seemed like I was the first person to realize that this was a problem because Dad, Mom and David all started looking around the room with a "Never thought about that" expression on their faces.

"I have an idea," David said. "Does anybody have any thumbtacks?"

He might as well have asked if we had drywall and carpentry tools. I was pretty sure that thumbtacks—or anything similar—were not items carried by any of the McQuades, not even our ever-resourceful mother.

I almost fell over when Sheila announced that she had some in her purse.

She handed a full, unopened pack to David with a whisper of a smile. "Let me know if you need anything else, little brother." She surveyed the room full of stares and open mouths, shook her head, then arched her eyebrows. "Really, y'all. I'm more than just a hairdresser, y'know."

While the rest of us stared in wonder at the McQuade version of Mary Poppins, David had gone back to work. He turned one bed over on its side, took the sheets off, tucked them into the upper section of the bed frame, then stood on a chair to stretch the sheet toward the ceiling. In minutes, he had thumbtacked the upper ends of the sheet to a wooden rafter, creating an on-the-spot changing room, large enough even for Dad to change comfortably.

"What do you think?" he asked us all.

"Perfect," said Tom, as he headed toward the tent to be its first user. "I don't know about you guys," he said over his shoulder as he ducked inside, "but I'm getting ready for the beach."

CHAPTER 27
JUNE 22, 1964

The Sea Isle City beach was three blocks from our boardinghouse—due east. At the start of our vacation week, none of us kids could believe how close we were. Five days later, the distance seemed impossibly far, especially heading back in the late afternoon, when we were all tired, and either hot and sweaty from beach-playing, or wet and salty from a last dip in the ocean.

Despite the trek, which Tom naturally complained about more than any of us, our beach days were an unqualified success. We typically had everything set up, including beach chairs, umbrellas, blankets, and coolers, by 10:00 a.m. We always stayed on the beach long after the lifeguards quit work at 5:00, although Mom took the little kids back to the boardinghouse every day after lunch for some quiet time. It kept them from getting over-tired—and saved them from the worst of the sun.

The weather was fabulous throughout our stay—rain-free, hotter than normal for June, but always with a cooling ocean breeze. Tom and I took the greatest advantage of the warm weather by riding the waves atop an old rubber raft that Miss Simmons lent to her guests, and that no one else ever borrowed. We also made sandcastles and dug for sand crabs with the little kids and competed at home run derby and horseshoes with each other—all of this for hours on end. I brought three books to read that week, and never opened one of them.

Neither Tom nor I could understand Sheila, who specialized in stretching out on an over-sized beach towel for hours at a time, moving only to apply generous amounts of baby oil to her body, and carefully turning from front to back to front again to ensure even tanning. David was a little better, he joined Tom and me for some games, and he built the most magnificent sandcastle of the week with the little kids—but he also spent a lot of time sitting in a beach chair, reading.

Marti seemed to be a goodwill ambassador to all: she'd sunbathe with Sheila from time to time, sit beside David to read, jump waves with Tom and me, and entertain the little kids with stories and spontaneous activities, like her "Let's Collect 100 Seashells" game, which ended with a beauty contest to determine the ten most beautiful shells on the beach.

One of the things I liked a lot was lunch by the ocean every day, including two days when we had hot dogs served from thermoses filled that morning with boiling water. The dogs were still hot by noon—ready for the hungry crowd of McQuade kids who quickly slapped mustard and ketchup on their dogs, sat in the sand to consume them, then jumped in the surf to wash off leftover crumbs and condiment stains. Lunchtimes were a little chaotic, one of the little kids always seemed to have a problem of some kind, with the most memorable being a sea gull that swooped in and grabbed part of a hot dog right out of Bobby's hand. Bobby spent much of the rest of the week chasing gulls across the sand, perhaps in an effort to exact revenge. He didn't seem to mind that he never caught one.

In between games or time in the water with Tom, I did fit in a couple of beach walks with Marti. It wasn't quite the same as sitting on the steps— you were always getting distracted by one thing or another—but it did give us a chance to catch up a little. We didn't discuss much of significance, mostly just observations about the little kids and how much they were enjoying the vacation, and how happy both Mom and Dad seemed to be with how everything was working out.

On our Monday walk, as we headed north along the shore line, we passed a family of colored people, parents and two very young kids, one of them—maybe a two-year-old like Carrie Ann—running about without any shorts or swim trunks on, just a bare baby bottom. Marti laughed at the scene, then commented about how you'd never see this in Birmingham, a Negro family out enjoying the day, in a public recreation area, surrounded by white families, and nobody bothering anybody else, and nobody much noticing.

I nodded in agreement. "Doesn't feel like Birmingham, that's for sure."

It occurred to me then that our walk was a perfect time to talk with Marti about Yvonne's views on colored people, which had not gotten any kinder over the past several months. I didn't like to admit this, even to myself, but my girlfriend was a racist, certainly not as vocal as her father, but a racist nonetheless. On the other hand, since I was calling people names, I was a coward. My relationship with Yvonne had gone on for several months, but I still had not found the courage to discuss this issue with Marti.

The two of us walked on for several more blocks, then turned to head back. When we passed the colored family again, both of the kids were running around half-naked, and dripping wet. It looked like the mom had just dipped them both in the surf to get the sand off of them.

I could hear a soft chuckle from Marti—I'm sure the kids reminded her of Bobby and Carrie Ann. Her mood changed in an instant, though, when she overheard an under-the-breath comment of "Filthy niggers—what's this town coming to?" It came from an elderly man who was walking along the beach with an older woman. The two had just passed us going in the other direction.

I stiffened but kept walking. Marti did not.

"What did you say?" I heard her call after the man, stopping in her tracks to turn around and stare at him. He disregarded Marti's question, kept walking as if he hadn't heard, but I knew that he had.

Maybe it was the ignoring of her comment, the total lack of acknowledgement, that got Marti really mad. Nervous, because I didn't know what might happen, I watched her run several steps to catch up to the couple.

"You're an ignorant man," she said, right to his face. "Ignorant and hateful and . . . and . . . and pathetic."

The man stopped at that, turned toward my sister. I ran up to stand beside her, not sure if she was going to need protection. I didn't think the man would hit her . . . but I wasn't 100 percent positive of that.

The man looked at Marti straight in the eye, not flinching at all, not embarrassed by his words, but pretty angry at being confronted, I could tell. I reached the two of them just as he spoke.

"Just what we need," he said, "another nigger lover." The woman put her hand on the man's arm. He shook it off, turned away, and continued his walk on the beach.

Marti was livid, I could tell. And probably had a lot more to say. But for some reason, maybe because she was so mad she couldn't even think, she allowed me to pull her in the opposite direction. The man and the woman walked on. The colored family did not seem to notice what had just happened.

I prepared myself for a blistering rant from Marti, but she was silent. "Let's just walk," she said.

And we did, wordless, until we were only a few blocks away from the McQuade family gathered on the beach.

"You know, Marti," I said, breaking our silence and trying to make her smile, "I don't think that man liked colored people all that much."

"I noticed that," she said.

We walked another block without speaking.

Then I said, "Guess you don't have to be from Alabama to hate colored people."

"Nope," she answered. "No, you don't."

Another half block.

"Don't tell Mom and Dad," she said. "I shouldn't have lost my composure."

"Okay," I replied. And I didn't. Though I sure was proud of her for speaking her mind.

* * * * *

On Tuesday, I came back from the beach a little earlier than the others. I felt tired, had a little sunburn, and I wanted to spend some time in the lukewarm, outdoor shower without getting rushed by my brothers and sisters.

I'd just reached the front porch at Matilda's and was headed upstairs to grab a clean t-shirt and shorts, when the girl that I'd first met on Sunday said, "Looks like you're a little red there, Mickey." She was sitting on the porch railing, in the shade of the house, and looked sort of cute in a bright blue top and white shorts. She'd remembered my name.

"Not too bad," I answered, "doesn't sting at all." I was lying about that—it did sting—but I saw no reason to share that information. I didn't want this girl I didn't even know to think I was a big baby.

"I'm going sunset watching tonight," she said. "You wanna come?"

I had no idea what sunset watching entailed, or where you went to do it, or what time you needed to leave for it, or any other details that my parents might ask me. I knew nothing about this girl.

"Sure," I answered without hesitation.

"Great," she said. "Meet me here on the porch at 7:15. I'll bring snacks."

It took a little cajoling, and some vocal support from Sheila, David, and Marti, but Mom and Dad finally said okay to my "date." I was told to behave like a gentleman, by Dad, and to be home no later than 10:30, by Mom.

Susan was waiting for me on the porch. She handed me a picnic basket to carry, motioned to follow her, and we took off, down 68th Street, across Landis, heading straight for the bay. We turned left at some point, then right, and finally ended up at a spot near the edge of the water, with the bay stretching out in front of us, and the sun poised to put on a show.

Susan found a spot of grass, retrieved a thin blanket from the picnic basket, and plopped herself down, sitting cross-legged, with a look of utter contentment. "This is what summers are made for," she said, "and it looks like," motioning to the sun, "we might see a good one."

I continued to stand, turning my head left, then right, then across the bay, as if I were keenly observing our surroundings, perhaps assuring myself that we were not in danger from wild animals or pirates.

"So," she said with a smile in her voice, "What's your story, Mickey McQuade?"

Before I could speak, she added, "Talk as much as you like now. But it's tradition to be silent during the actual sunset, which is scheduled for exactly 8:29 p.m."

"I see," I responded. "Please know that I am not a man to buck tradition. The rules, after all, are the rules."

I think she liked my comment. It won me both a soft grin and a pat of her hand indicating that I should sit down on the blanket beside her. I complied with her unspoken request.

She continued as I settled myself beside her. "Let's eat our snacks while you tell me what an interesting character you are."

My first instinct was to be cool, and give her a "Me? I'm not interesting.

I've got no story. What's yours?" response. Instead, I paused for a second, thought about the question, and said, "I think we have to start with the fact that I have eight brothers and sisters."

It was a straightforward remark, and carried no hint of what was to follow, a reasonably coherent but wide-ranging summary of the life and times of one Mickey McQuade. I talked about my family, of course, commented on my special relationship with Marti, then branched out to cover school, my interests, my buddies, my career as a Coke vendor, and my friendship with Jackie.

It may have been the most boring forty minutes of Susan's life, but she gave no sign of it. She sat quietly beside me, listened intently, asked a question here and there, and made me feel that maybe I did have a story, and maybe it was worth telling, at least to her.

The only thing I left out was Yvonne and the Rawlings family.

"One thing I don't understand," she said, "is how this colored kid Jackie is such a good friend. I thought Southern white kids did not like Negroes at all, and don't even want to go to school with them. Is your school segregated or integrated?"

I started to respond, but Susan suddenly looked down at her watch, then at the sky, then lifted a finger and placed it over my lips. With her other hand, she pointed to the sun.

I was surprised by her gesture, it felt romantic, like a girlfriend-boyfriend kind of thing. I thought briefly about Yvonne as I reached up and clutched her finger with my hand while nodding that I understood. We leaned against each other to watch the last rays of the sun as it sank. Just before it disappeared entirely, Susan lifted her head and kissed me on the lips, then snuggled her head into my chest. I was surprised, and delighted, with a little feeling of guilt because of Yvonne. We both lay back on the blanket and watched the day grow darker, interrupting our vigil with a few additional kisses, but not much talking. I managed to put Yvonne out of mind.

As we walked back to Matilda's, holding hands every step, Susan said she wanted to hear more about my friend Jackie, and maybe we could meet again tomorrow or Thursday.

"Good idea," I said, "excellent idea."

CHAPTER 28
JUNE 24, 1964

In 1964, Wildwood and Ocean City were two of the best-known resort towns on the Jersey Shore. Both featured boardwalks, majestic wooden boulevards stretching north and south, parallel to the ocean, offering to excess all the things that summertime vacationers want and need most: carnival rides; sausage and pepper sandwiches; apparel shops with cheaply-made and bargain-priced t-shirts, beach towels, swim trunks, and two-piece bathing suits for daring girls; pizza; games of chance (at least, that's what the customers thought); cotton candy; games of skill; ice cream; fortune tellers; soda (which most Southern kids just called coke); miniature golf courses; hot dogs and hamburgers; arcades filled with pinball and skeeball machines; and French fries.

Mom preferred Wildwood. It was the place she remembered best from vacations as a young girl. She talked to Dad, and they decided to take the whole family there on Wednesday for dinner and rides and fun. Lucky for me, I was able to find Susan and make a date with her to get ice cream on Thursday. Everything was working out.

Tom and I were especially excited for the boardwalk—it sounded like heaven on earth to the two of us. We ran up the ramp from the street, a good half-block ahead of the rest of the family. The panorama in front of us was even bigger, even grander, even more magnificent than either of us imagined. Sights and sounds and smells assaulted our senses—and we embraced it all.

Visitors to the boardwalk, numbering in the thousands each evening, were part of the show, a steady stream of fun-seekers, many of whom had abandoned all manner of fashion-sense, as if they were auditioning for a place in the Wildwood Parade for the Garishly Attired. The scene was both wonderful and appalling. It made Tom and me, to use one of Nammy's favorite expressions, "happier than a couple of tornadoes in a trailer park."

Tom and I wanted to take off immediately and go exploring by ourselves, but Mom insisted that the family have dinner together first.

We all walked together a couple of blocks along the boardwalk, just to get the feel of the place, then started looking for a pizza restaurant that would meet Mom's standards of cleanliness. Once we'd found one, with a sign that read Wildwood's Best Pizza—Guaranteed, Dad ordered three large pies for the eleven of us. In less than 15 minutes, we'd devoured every slice.

After Dad paid the check, Tom and I asked again if we could go off on our own to explore. We both had a little spending money that we'd brought with us, and Dad gave us each a dollar more to add to our total. We promised to meet everyone back in front of the pizza parlor at 8:30 p.m. I asked Marti if she wanted to come, but she decided to stay with the little kids to enjoy their reactions to everything around them.

Tom and I walked very fast for a block or two in order to separate ourselves from the rest of the family, then slowed down to examine every store, every fast-food offering, and especially every carnival game we passed. Tom announced his intention: he wanted to win one of the impossibly large teddy bears on display everywhere. When I asked him why, his answer was typical Tom. "Just to show everybody that I can," he said.

There were certainly plenty of places to try. Almost every carnival game on the boardwalk showcased one or more super-large teddy bears as its top prize. At roughly four feet tall, the bears were larger than any of our younger brothers and sisters, from Ricky on down.

First, Tom tried shooting basketball. On the playground at St. Barnabas, Tom had established a record once by hitting 12 shots in a row from the free-throw line. He noticed that the rims were set a little higher here than normal, but felt confident because, standing behind the counter, he was still closer than free throw distance.

Tom spent seventy-five cents—it cost a quarter for three shots—and only hit one of nine. It won him a consolation prize teddy bear, maybe four inches tall.

"Something funny about those rims," I said, "I'm not sure they're regulation."

"Yeah," Tom groused, "and those basketballs can't be official either. They're way, way too bouncy."

Concluding that the basketball game was rigged, we moved on down the boardwalk, taking our time, looking for a game that we felt we could beat. I lost another seventy-five cents throwing darts at balloons. Then we each lost fifty cents trying to knock over metal "milk cans" with a softball.

Disappointed and disgusted with our lack of success, we decided to split a cup of Boardwalk Fries and assess our situation. We found a large, almost empty bench on the ocean side of the boardwalk, occupied at one end by a scruffy-looking guy who was maybe eighteen or nineteen years old. He was staring down at the ground, smoking a cigarette, and didn't look up when we sat down. Tom and I promptly forgot he was there while we whined about the games.

"So, what now?" I finally asked Tom.

"I dunno. I really want to win one of those big bears. But these games are a lot harder than they look."

"You guys don't understand, do you?" The voice from the end of the bench was derisive. "You guys can't beat a carny. Nobody beats a carny."

Taught to be polite, I responded to the comment calmly, though his demeanor made me nervous.

"Excuse me," I said. "Were you talking to us, mister?"

"Look, kid" he said, even though he was only a couple years older than me. "I heard you talking, wondering if some of those games were rigged. "

Tom and I stared at him without speaking.

"You're part right. About the games being rigged. Except it's not some, it's all of them. There's not a chance in hell of you winning any decent prize. No way. You're just throwing your money away."

"I knew it," said Tom.

The guy half-smiled at us, sympathetically. "I heard you talking about basketball," he said. "Thing is, the hoop is smaller than regulation. It's installed a foot higher than a normal basketball goal. And the balls are over-inflated too."

"What'd I tell you, Mickey!" Tom exclaimed.

"Sometimes," the guy added, "they even bend the hoop a little, make it more oval, so that it looks bigger in front. But because it's not round, that makes hitting a shot ten times harder. Maybe you'll hit one shot if you're really, really lucky—but there's no way you hit three out of three to win the big bear."

"What about the other games?" I asked.

"They're all gaffed," he said. "Rigged. Fixed. And the suckers—especially men with girlfriends—just keep coming, keep laying down their quarters and walking away empty-handed."

"What about the ring toss?" I asked.

"Ring is so small it barely fits over the neck of the bottle."

"Darts and balloons?"

"Balloons are under-inflated, and the points of the darts are dulled."

"The milk can game?"

The guy paused for several seconds, seemingly thinking over his response.

"Looks easy, doesn't it?" he said. "Except that one of the three milk cans has lead in the base. As long as the lead-filled milk can is one of the two on the bottom, there's no way you can knock it completely off the wooden platform." He spat. "Never seen it done," he said, " never will."

"Cheaters!" Tom said. "Cheaters! No way we'll win a big bear—ever!

"You wanna win a giant bear," the guy said. "How 'bout I help you?"

Tom was instantly interested, no questions asked. "Great," he said, "what do we have to do?"

I was a little suspicious. "Why would you want to help us?" I said.

"Cause," the guy answered. "I hate my boss. And tonight's my last night working for him. I'm heading up tomorrow to Long Beach Island to work in a pizza shop. Better pay and lots of free pizza."

The guy looked at us. "You in or out? No skin off my nose."

"In," said Tom. I nodded, even though I was nervous. I didn't think Marti would have said yes to this scheme.

"Okay, listen," the guy said. "Come to the Milk Bottle Pyramid game, a couple blocks up." He pointed. "I'll be working. Come to my station. You'll have to play a few times. The first two times, you'll lose. But then you'll win on the third try, if you make a decent throw."

"Really?" said Tom.

I was still skeptical. "How do we know this is not just another carny scam?" I asked him.

"You don't," said the teen. "You gotta trust me. But what do you have to lose 'cept another few quarters? Gotta go!"

With that, the teen turned around and started running back up the boardwalk. Twenty feet away, he suddenly stopped and turned back toward us again.

"It's time to cheat the cheaters!" he yelled. "See ya!"

And then he was truly gone. He ran pretty fast for someone who smoked.

"Let's do it, Mickey!" Tom almost shouted at me, as we watched him disappear into the crowd. "Let's cheat the cheaters!"

We found the game easily, then watched for a few minutes from the middle of the boardwalk as a number of people came up, tried their luck, and walked away failures.

"Who's doing this?" I finally asked Tom.

"Me," he said, without the slightest hesitation.

We drifted toward the game, feigning mild interest, not that anyone, including an older man who seemed to be the head carny, was paying any attention to us.

"C'mon, you two," yelled our supposed co-conspirator, working one of the milk can stations, and startling us with his direct communication. "C'mon and give it a try. Anybody can win."

He demonstrated the game, we hesitated as if unsure, which was the truth, but finally nodded okay.

"Remember," the teen called out loudly so that everyone, including the head carny could hear, "you have to knock all three milk cans completely off the wooden platform. Knock 'em all off—and you win our grand prize!"

"Step right up," he said to Tom, "aim for the middle between the two bottom cans."

Tom gave him a quarter and was handed a softball. He stepped back slightly to give himself more room, then flung the ball as hard as he could at the pyramid. It seemed like a perfect shot—and two of the milk cans went flying. The third kind of toppled over, oddly, but never came close to falling off the wooded stand.

"Nice try, kid," said the guy. "Almost did it. Wanna try again?"

Tom looked at me, then back toward the booth. "Okay," he said, cautiously.

Same result.

"Third time's the charm," said the guy, once again in a voice loud enough for all to hear, though the head carny was trying to coax someone else into playing and not paying any attention to the three of us.

Tom handed over one more quarter without saying a word. He rolled the softball back and forth in his hands. He focused intently on the milk cans in front of him. He stepped back, took a baseball pitcher's wind-up, then fired the ball even harder than his first two attempts. His throw struck the bottom milk cans right in the seam between the two, a few inches above the wooden platform they stood on. Both bottom cans flew off the platform immediately. The top can hit the wood below, started spinning wildly. We watched, mesmerized. I held my breath as it seemed to slow down, teetering on the edge of the little platform, then finally falling off.

"I did it!" Tom whooped. "I did it, I did it! We win the grand prize."

Suddenly we had the head carny's full attention. He looked sharply at the third milk can that was angled crazily against the edge of the platform but clearly and definitively off of it.

"What?" he yelled, staring first at us, then at his worker, then back at us. "No way!"

"I want that one," shouted Tom, pointing to one of the large teddy bears—brown and white—suspended by a wire high above our heads.

"Sorry, kid," the carny began, clearly ready to declare some kind of a renege, based on who knew what grounds.

"Sorry, nothing," a deep voice growled. Tom and I both turned our heads to see who spoke. The words came from a very large man, wearing one of those muscle t-shirts, biceps bulging. He wore tight blue jeans and a baseball cap that read USMC. "Give the kid his prize, Ace," he said to the carny. "He won it fair and square."

The head carny stared at the speaker. We did too. And then, without another word, the carny grabbed a broomstick with a hook on it and used it to retrieve Tom's bear from the wire.

"Get out of here," he snarled, though not too loudly, as he lifted the bear across the counter and gave it to Tom.

We shouted, "Thanks, y'all" to the sour-faced carny, to the guy who helped us beat the system, and to our marine corps supporter, then raced away to find the rest of the McQuades.

We saw them before they saw us, standing in a group eating ice cream cones outside the pizza parlor. Carrie Ann was asleep in her stroller. The rest of them looked exhausted.

David spied us first, saw me waving, saw Tom walking quickly but struggling with both the weight and dimensions of a four-foot-high, very chubby teddy bear.

"What the heck!" David yelled. "Lookit, everybody!" At that, every McQuade head, except Carrie Ann's, swung in our direction.

In seconds, we were surrounded, barraged with questions, drowned in congratulations. Everyone seemed to be talking at once. Except for Brenda. Her eyes took in Tom's companion—and you could almost hear her heart beating faster.

Amidst all the tumult, Tom noticed Brenda as well. He worked his way toward her, knelt down on one knee so that he and the bear were eye-level with Brenda, then introduced the two strangers to each other. "Teddy Bear," he said, "please meet my favorite six-year-old sister, Brenda. And Brenda, say hello to my new friend Teddy Bear, who needs a name."

"Hello," Brenda said shyly, then reached out both her arms to give the bear a hug.

My parents and all of us older kids—Sheila, David, Marti, and I—watched Brenda hug Tom's bear with a complete and unaffected tenderness, the way a mother might nuzzle a newborn, though in this case the "baby" was a good two inches bigger than the "mom."

Tom must have sensed Brenda's feelings as well. He let her hug his bear a little longer, then tapped her on the shoulder. "Brenda," he said, "I'm wondering if you could do me a favor."

"What?" Brenda asked, still more taken with the bear than with Tom's question.

"Well," said Tom, "this bear not only needs a name, I think he needs someone to take care of him. Could you do that for me? Could you maybe be this bear's mommy?"

Brenda never said a word. But her eyes got even bigger. And she nodded her head, yes.

"Thanks, Brenda," Tom said. He reached out his arms real wide and gave both Brenda and the bear a hug. Mom and Dad exchanged looks. I'm guessing they were pretty proud of Tom at that moment.

CHAPTER 29
JUNE 25, 1964

I sat myself down in a rocking chair on the front porch of Matilda's promptly at 6:45, fifteen minutes early to meet Susan at seven. I was eagerly looking forward to the evening ahead, though three hours seemed way too short. Curfew from Dad was a strict 10 p.m. because it was our last night in Sea Isle, and we had a long drive ahead of us on Friday.

Marti and Tom had already left to go exploring around town, starting with a trip to the Post Office so Marti could mail some postcards. I'd asked her who she was sending postcards to, but I didn't get an answer. Just a mysterious smile.

David and Sheila were off by themselves as well—Sheila had been invited to a party by some college kids she'd met on the beach, and David was sent with her as companion, watchdog and bodyguard.

Mom and Dad had decided to take Ricky, Brenda, Bobby, and Carrie Ann to a tiny boardwalk-like amusement park they'd discovered. It featured rides targeted to the six-year-old and under set. Almost eight years old, Ricky might get a little bored, but it was the price he had to pay—and paid frequently—for being the oldest of the little kids. It was much better to be Tom, the youngest of the big kids.

Beyond ice cream, Susan and I had no real plan for our date. I was hoping whatever we did would include some private time somewhere and a glorious repeat of the moments we spent on her blanket together.

Earlier that afternoon, while I sat on the beach, I kept asking myself whether I should tell Susan about Yvonne. On the one hand, there was no reason to tell her. Susan hadn't asked if I had a girlfriend. On the other hand, Yvonne was certainly my girlfriend, and that implied some kind of obligations of fidelity I assumed, though we weren't officially going steady. For all I knew, Yvonne could have a boyfriend in Chicago.

In any case, did I owe Susan information about Yvonne, unasked? And what did I owe Yvonne?

Marti would probably know, but to get her opinion, I'd have to disclose to her the nature of my one-date-going-on-two relationship with Susan. I decided to pass, even though it now made two things I was holding back from my twin.

My ethical quandary was interrupted by a "Hey, Mickey!" from Susan as she walked through the front door of Matilda's and out onto the porch. "Ready for a double scoop, hot fudge sundae with jimmies?" she asked.

Her attitude made me grin. "It's my last night in town," I replied, "I'm thinking I might get three scoops. If I'm man enough."

Susan smiled back, pretended to look me over critically. "Oh, you're man enough," she said. "I'm guessing this will not be the first triple scoop of your ice cream career."

That brief exchange set the tone for the next hour we spent together. It was wonderfully comfortable, as if we'd grown up together, on the same block, had gone to grade school together, attended each other's birthday parties and school events, and then, one day, just decided to become boyfriend and girlfriend. Which we weren't. We were just acting like we were. For a couple of days. At least that's what I thought.

We bought our sundaes. I got sensible at the last minute and settled for two scoops. We ate ice cream as we walked, up one street and down another, all the way to the bay, then back up toward the ocean, crisscrossing Landis and Central Avenues multiple times. Twice we spied an empty bench and sat on it for a few minutes, watching other vacationers stream past us in both directions, commenting to each other on the more outlandish outfits that people chose to wear.

Susan did much more of the talking as we walked. She described her non-summer life in a large public school in a town called Vineland, classes and teachers and school events and friends. She did not mention whether she had a boyfriend. I was thinking of asking her but decided not to. I did not want a similar question asked of me.

Susan also told me that she was born in Trenton—just like Mom—and that she had two older brothers. She confirmed that Miss Simmons was her grandmother but had adopted the prefix "Miss" after her husband had died years ago in a car accident. She told me that she always spent the entire summer in Sea Isle, and that working in the rooming house was not that bad, but she wished she got off more than one day a week. She told me pizza was her favorite food and explained why she thought Elvis was more important than the Beatles, and that she did not understand what was going on in Vietnam.

I did think of Yvonne from time to time as we walked and talked, but I was determined to keep Yvonne's pretty face from distracting me. I worked to keep my focus on the girl by my side.

At one point, as we sat on our second bench, Susan took my hand and said, "I knew this was your last night of vacation in Sea Isle, Mickey. I checked our guest book." She looked up at me. "I'm glad you decided to spend it with me."

"Fancy evening," I joked. "Ice cream and walking around aimlessly. I'm a charmer."

"Maybe you were aimless," Susan replied. "But . . . my goal was to get to know you better—and I have."

It seemed like an odd remark to make since she'd been doing most of the talking throughout our walk. "You learned that I'm the strong, silent type?" I said, with a little bit of tease in my voice.

"Tuesday was about hearing what you had to say," she said. "Tonight was finding out if you knew how to listen."

I had no response to that, but it was just as well. Susan leaned up and kissed me. I kissed her back. Then she broke away and said, "Let's go sit on the beach. I want to hear more about your friend Jackie."

We walked hand in hand to the 88th street entrance, took off our shoes and trudged barefoot through soft sand to the lifeguard chair. It had been pulled way back from the surf. I'm pretty sure we passed a sign that read BEACH CLOSED AFTER DARK, but Susan and I quickly agreed that it was still twilight, and we were not breaking the law.

I climbed up onto the lifeguard stand, then held a hand out to help Susan up. Once we got settled, we just sat there for a minute or two, my arm around Susan's shoulders, staring at the ocean. Then I began to tell her all about Jackie Thomas. I told her how we met, about baseball and football in Jackie's front yard, about Nammy, about rainy afternoons in Jackie's house, about Christmas shopping and Christmas Day and even our big game of scrub when Marti made her amazing catch.

"Do you guys—you and Jackie—go to the same school?" Susan asked.

"No, no," I said. "There aren't any colored kids in my school yet. But I think we're supposed to get integrated this coming Fall."

"What? All white? No colored kids?" she said.

"Alabama," I said. "An awful lot of people down there still believe in segregation. Each race to itself. Separate but equal. They love that phrase down South."

"And what do you think about that?" Susan asked. "I guess 'separate but equal' sounds fair but . . . "

"It's not," I interrupted. "It's just not. All the white people in power care about is separate—they don't give a darn about equal. They even closed the swimming pools rather than have colored kids and white kids swimming together. Instead of two equal pools, we have no swimming pools. If you're a colored kid in Birmingham, equal is a pipedream. It's a charade. It's a joke. And that's why there are demonstrations and marches and . . ." I ran out of breath.

Susan was quiet for a moment, just looking at me, letting me calm down. Then she switched gears. "So Jackie," she asked me, "he's your best friend?"

"I don't know," I said, "I guess it's him or Davis Williams. I never really thought about who might be best. Guys don't talk like that." I paused. "I do spend a lot more time with Jackie, cause of where we live."

Susan nodded her understanding, was silent for another moment, then surprised me with a personal revelation. "I once had a boyfriend who was colored," she said, "back in eighth grade. His name was Newton Fairbanks. His mom named him Newton because of Sir Isaac Newton. She wanted him to be very smart, and he was. But he was also the nicest, kindest boy in the whole world."

Susan looked directly at me, perhaps to gauge my reaction. Because, for several seconds, I was speechless. And then, crazily, jealous. I wanted to bury that feeling—it felt wrong to me.

"What?" I said. "Really? There's no way that would have even happened in Birmingham. Well, probably not." I remembered the couple I'd seen at the Elvis movies and told Susan about them. And about Yvonne's angry reaction.

"Who's Yvonne?" Susan asked.

I froze for a moment at the question. "Friend of Marti's," I finally said, "lives across the street." I felt guilty at the lie, but I also wanted to know more about Newton Fairbanks. "Tell me about you and Newton," I said, working hard to sound not jealous.

"We met in seventh grade," Susan said, "but I didn't really start liking him 'til eighth. And then he moved away in the summer before ninth grade. But we were boyfriend-girlfriend for a whole year, even though we didn't really go out on dates."

"What did your friends think?" I asked. "Having a colored boyfriend or girlfriend in Birmingham would have been really hard. Maybe even dangerous. Most people—whites and probably even coloreds—would be against it. Completely."

"My close friends all loved Newton," Susan said. "We did get some ugly, prejudiced comments from kids at school that I didn't know well, and grown-ups too. People called us names . . . they called me a nigger lover . . . right to my face, sometimes right in front of Newton. He would get mad—and once he almost got into a fight with some nasty kids, but a teacher saw what was happening and stepped in."

"I don't know what my school will be like next year," I said, "I don't know how many colored kids will be in my classes and how that will go. I just know that things are changing. Maybe tomorrow will be better for colored kids like Jackie. I hope so. He's a really good guy."

"You're a really good guy," Susan said. "I'm sad that you are going home so soon. If you lived near me, you could be my boyfriend. How would you like that?"

This was my chance, a perfect time to agree with Susan about her big IF, but also tell her that I already had a girlfriend. Except I didn't want to. Just talking with Susan about Jackie, and her boyfriend Newton Fairbanks— it made me remember clearly how Yvonne reacted to the couple in the movie theater, and her many prejudiced comments about colored people. I wanted

Yvonne to be more like Susan, and not to be so much like her father, but she wasn't.

Susan broke into my thoughts. "Do you have yourself a girlfriend, back in Birmingham, Mickey?"

I'll say this: Susan had no problem with direct questions.

"Yes, kind of," I said hesitantly, "at least I think I do." And I immediately started to consider what I might want and not want to tell Susan about Yvonne.

As it turned out, I had no reason to worry—at that moment, I don't think Susan really cared whether I had a girlfriend in Birmingham or not. She simply looked at me with a funny little smile, a teasing kind of smile, and asked, "And does she think that you are handsome?"

I could feel myself getting pleasantly red in the face. I was very, very curious about what Susan might say next.

I didn't have to wait long. Just as I started to mumble some fumbling response to her question about my handsomeness, Susan leaned toward me and asked a third: "And do you like it when she does this?"

She touched her lips to mine, and held them there, closed, pressing a little harder, then opened her lips the tiniest bit, snuck out her tongue, and touched my upper lip with it. As I responded, we seemed to find ourselves engaged in a kiss without any hesitation, without a time clock, without boundaries. If there were a competition, it was a kiss that would have put all the other kisses of my life to shame.

Susan leaned back away from me. Smiled without saying a word.

I looked at her and said, "Wow."

That made her laugh, a soft, golden kind of laugh, a laugh that made you want to hit the replay button again and again.

With that, she leaned up against me, cuddling, but turned her face to mine, clearly expecting that she'd done enough leading.

Kiss followed by another soft kiss. Moments of bliss laced with moments of wonder intertwined with just the briefest moments of guilt because, as had clearly been established, I did have a girlfriend.

"You can touch my boob if you want," Susan whispered.

Sensing my hesitation, Susan took my hand and slid it smoothly under her top. "Just a little," she said, "and gently."

I was gentle enough to have held a spider web in my hand without leaving a trace of human presence. But I also remember that my hand felt like it was on fire, and every nerve in my body was tingling.

My unmoving hand rested haphazardly on her impossibly soft breast. Seconds passed.

At that moment, in a lifeguard stand in the middle of a pitch-black beach in Sea Isle City, New Jersey, I was sure I'd discovered heaven on earth.

"Time to go, Mickey," Susan whispered, just as I was beginning to get the courage to move my hand even the tiniest bit.

I withdrew my hand immediately, with an awkward speed that concealed its reluctance to abandon such a warm and welcoming place. I looked at my watch—and my heart sank. 10:45.

"I am so late," I said, "I'm gonna get killed."

We clambered down and ran much of the way back to Matilda's together. We slowed a block away, shared one more delightful kiss in the middle of the street. Then she said good-bye, good luck, see you in the morning.

And I trudged up the stairs to pay the piper in the form of one certain to be very angry Bill McQuade.

* * * * *

We had planned to leave Sea Isle around 10 a.m. the next morning. It took us a while to pack the car, and to clean everything up, and get ice and supplies for our cooler. Sheila and Marti took the little kids and Tom down to the beach to wave good-bye to the ocean. Dad and Mom and David and I finished up the preparations for the long drive ahead.

I wasn't saying much since I was in the doghouse. All in all, though, my "Where the hell have you been?" talk with Dad hadn't been that bad. I could tell that he and Mom had been mostly worried. And I said I was sorry, that I'd lost track of time, and was just out walking and talking with my new friend Susan. I didn't mention going down to the beach, or making out with Susan, as that might have confused the issue.

For punishment, I was grounded the next two weekends after we got home, plus was assigned two straight weeks of dinner dishes. It could have been worse. The grounding was not a big deal since I rarely went anywhere anyway.

It was 10:30 in the morning before we were finally ready to go, the car now jam-packed, not simply with luggage, but with the vacation treasures of eleven people who'd just spent six days at the beach. We seemed to have much more stuff than when we came, including, of course, Brenda's bear which Dad tied to the top of the car. Brenda was worried about Jasper—her current name for him, though it kept changing—but Dad said he'd bring Jasper inside the car with the family if it started to rain. What we'd have to abandon to fit Jasper in, Dad didn't say. Maybe me.

We had almost finished loading ourselves into the car, with all the confusion that this involved, when I heard Susan's voice from the porch. "Goodbye, McQuades," she called out, "Hope you all had a nice vacation in Sea Isle."

"Thanks for everything," my father responded.

I looked up and saw Susan looking directly at me. "Bye, Mickey," she said. "Come back next summer!"

I waved back and yelled, "Hope so!" then got in the car.

Dad started the engine, Tom started singing, "Mickey's got a girlfriend, Mickey's got a girlfriend." I told him to shut up. And off we went, heading home to Birmingham. I didn't say a word until we reached Tennessee.

Six days later, on July 2, 1964, President Lyndon Johnson signed the Civil Rights Act into law. I read an article in the Birmingham News about what the new law would mean, how it would truly end segregation throughout the South. I wondered if Susan might have read a similar article. And I wished I could talk with her about it.

CHAPTER 30
JULY 11, 1964

I woke up Saturday morning elated. I was no longer a prisoner, no longer an object of pity among my brothers and sisters. I was free to rejoin McQuade society in the fullest possible way. I was, to put it succinctly, no longer grounded.

All things considered, I looked at two weeks of house arrest in exchange for thirty extra minutes of romance with Susan in a lifeguard chair on the beach as a reasonable transaction. Memories of that evening still floated at the very top of my mind. And it occurred to me, since I'd not shared the particulars of that night with anyone, including and especially Marti, that a visit to Jackie's might be in order. Jackie and I had never really talked about "girls" much, but with a story like mine, would there ever be a better time to start?

It was no problem at all securing permission from Mom. She was tired of the grounded Mickey McQuade, hanging around the house, shuffling listlessly from room to room, whining about his lot in life. "Just be back in time for dinner, well, maybe an hour before," Mom said. "And don't get filthy."

For once, it was just Jackie and me at his house. Nammy was up the street visiting with her brother. I liked that we had his place to ourselves.

We chatted about nothing in particular for a little while, discussed a game of catch, decided it was too hot, and finally settled down on Jackie's front porch, hoping for a breeze but never getting one.

"Tell me everything about y'all's vacation," Jackie said, "especially jumping the waves. I want to do that someday."

"Best vacation ever," I said, "for about a dozen different reasons. Do you want to hear all of them, or just the top five?"

"Every one," he said. "Except I want you to start with jumping the waves—wasn't that the best thing?"

"It was close," I said. "Tom and Marti and I loved playing in the surf, and riding the waves on an old blue rubber raft that we borrowed from the rooming house." I took a little time to explain to Jackie the finer points of wave riding, from catching the wave at exactly the right moment to lifting the nose of the raft during your ride.

"Who was the best wave rider — you or Tom or Marti?"

"Me, of course." I wasn't bragging. It was the truth.

"Really? I would have guessed Marti. How did she do?"

"Marti, what, no, not even close." Jackie's remark surprised me. Why ever would he think that Marti would have been best? "She was good," I said. "But she was girl good. I was man good. She and Tom were about equal, I'd say."

Jackie laughed aloud. "Man good?"

"Oh, yes," I said. "Man good."

Jackie laughed again and shook his head. "Keep going," he said. "What else did y'all do? I need me details."

So I provided them. I took him through our entire trip. Sand castles with Brenda. Bobby chasing sea gulls. The Wildwood boardwalk adventure. Everything. Except for Susan. I was saving the best for last.

"Oh," I finally said, in my most casual of voices, "and I met a girl."

Jackie didn't say anything in response but I could tell he was interested. He sat up straighter, waiting for me to continue.

So I told him about Susan, from the moment we met to our final wave good-bye on Friday morning. And, because Jackie was aware of Yvonne, and knew that she was my girlfriend, I felt like I also needed to provide some context, historic detail of the Yvonne-Mickey relationship. Which I did. The one thing I left out was that Yvonne was prejudiced against colored people.

All in all, I must have talked for twenty minutes straight, with no hesitations on my part, and no interruptions from Jackie. I think he was dumbstruck.

"What?" I asked him, after several seconds of total silence. "No comments? No questions?"

Jackie looked at me like a D minus algebra student confronting his first quadratic equation. "I'm not even sure where to start."

"Start at the beginning," I said. A teacher had suggested that to me once, but I didn't think it made much sense. Kind of obvious, really.

Perhaps it made sense to Jackie. "Okay," he said. "The first thing I'm thinking of is . . . well . . . I just can't believe you actually touched her boo . . . . her breast. And she's the one who suggested it. It's . . . it's . . . it's incredible."

I nodded. "Not just that," I reminded him, "but she took my hand and placed it there."

"Amazing."

"Yes it was."

"And you never did that with anyone else ever? Not even Yvonne?"

"Nope. Although now I would like to. I think."

Jackie and I just looked at each other. I could not tell what he was thinking. After a few seconds of staring, I shrugged my shoulders. "Next question," I said.

Jackie seemed to be wrestling with something inside his head. Finally he spoke. "So, what, now you have two girlfriends? At the same time? Is Yvonne still your girlfriend? Is Susan your new girlfriend, even though she lives all the way up north?"

Jackie's question caught me off guard. I didn't have a ready answer. For the last two weeks, while I was grounded, I'd been thinking a lot about Susan. And Yvonne. And me.

"I don't know," I said to Jackie, "I really don't know how to answer you. Truth is, I really like them both a lot. If I didn't know Yvonne, or I never met Susan, I'd be more than happy with the one I did know as my girlfriend. Of course, Susan lives a long way from here, and Yvonne's still gone to Chicago, and for longer than she originally said. So at the moment, I guess you could say I have zero girlfriends."

"That's your answer?"

"It's confusing," I said. "Yvonne is so, so pretty, beautiful really. Everyone loves her. She looks good, smells good, always knows the right thing to say. We have fun. We play games, watch movies, even roller-skate, though I really don't like that so much. But how could a guy not want Yvonne as his girlfriend?"

"And Susan . . ." Jackie said, prompting me.

"Well, Susan is different. She's cute and funny and self-confident but in a totally different way from Yvonne. And we had some great talks together, about all kinds of things."

I thought back to my conversations with Susan, and realized that they were a big part of why I liked her so much.

"Feels to me like your brain may be doing a whole bunch of wiggling back and forth at the moment," Jackie said. "Like a big ol' fat worm on a rusty fishhook. But I figure y'all be coming up with the right answer for yourself, sooner or later. Give it some time. That's what Nammy says. Give it some time and you'll study it out."

"Hope so," I said. By that point, I was more than ready to talk about something else. Anything else. "Time to change the subject," I said. A thought struck me. "How come we never talk about any girls you like? Aren't there any pretty girls at your school? Anybody special?"

For some reason, my question seemed to make Jackie uncomfortable. Like he was embarrassed. Or confused.

He answered in a voice that was so soft, I could barely hear him. "Nobody special at my school," he said. "Lots of girls, but nobody special. Jest friends. Jest ordinary."

It was a weak response—and I wanted to challenge my friend to provide some more details about the girls in his school, even if he did not like anyone the way I liked Yvonne and Susan. I wanted to tell him that it was okay not to have a girlfriend. Everyone couldn't be as lucky as me. But it was getting late—Mom had told me to be home an hour before dinner. I did not want to get grounded for being late again.

"I gotta get going," I said, as I stood up, "so I'm gonna accept your answer for now. Call it a temporary answer. We will address this subject again. Before we head back to school."

But we never did.

CHAPTER 31
AUGUST 22, 1964

August nights in Alabama can be torturously hot. Often they are unbearably humid as well. On Saturday night, it was both. I lay in bed with the lights out, wearing nothing but my underwear, tossing and turning and cranky.

The thing is—it is virtually impossible to sleep if you are lying in bed with beads of perspiration forming so fast on your face and neck that you can almost hear them bubbling into life. You can't even doze because every toss and turn makes you feel slimy from damp sheets and a drenched pillowcase.

Despite the conditions, David and Tom were sleeping. I could hear David snoring. The rest of the house was quiet, except for the sound of electric fans coming from a couple of the bedrooms. We had a fan for our room, but it was broken. Something was wrong with the electric cord. Dad said he'd fix it or take it somewhere to get fixed but that hadn't happened yet.

I looked at the little electric clock sitting on the metal fold-up chair that functioned as my nightstand. Twenty minutes to twelve. I thought it might be a tiny bit cooler outside so that's where I decided to go. At least there would be some air. I thought that I could sit on Mom's chaise lounge out in the backyard, and if the mosquitoes weren't too bad, I might get some sleep.

I did not turn on a light, just felt around for my shorts, a t-shirt, sneakers. I peeled the moist pillowcase off my pillow, threw it on the floor, tucked the pillow under my arm, and headed as quietly as I could downstairs and out the back door.

It was cooler outside—but not by a lot. The air was thick and heavy. This kind of humidity usually meant a storm was coming, or even one of those ferocious Alabama tornadoes. Frankly, I would have welcomed a tornado just for the fresh air it would have brought with it.

For a second, I considered turning on the hose and squirting myself down. But the heat made me lethargic. Instead, I headed to the solitary tree in our back yard and the cheap, metal-framed chaise that sat beneath it.

I took the pillow from under my arm, positioned it to serve as a comfortable headrest, and then held it in place with one hand while I eased into a reclining position.

I'd been outside a good sixty seconds with no mosquito bites yet. The skeeters were oddly away for the night.

As I lay there, hoping to fall asleep, I considered the summer so far— and concluded that it had been mostly good. Other than the fact that Yvonne was not around, I'd had a fun three months off from school. The whole family had enjoyed our getaway to the Jersey Shore—and I had particularly fond memories of Susan and our time together. Since we'd come home, I'd received four letters from her, and written back twice. But I was planning on writing again.

Sure, I'd been grounded for two weeks, but the only thing of consequence that the punishment prevented was going over to Jackie's house, because I rarely did anything else. Since then, except for the week when Jackie was off visiting his mom and sister in Tupelo, he and I had spent a lot of time together.

Another high point of the summer was swimming at Cascade Plunge. Although the Birmingham public swimming pools were still closed in support of segregation, Tom and I had managed to get to Cascade three times. It was a private pool that did not have to answer to city government. Tom had even jumped off the tower platform—I was too chicken for that.

The rest of the family seemed to be having good summers as well. Sheila liked her job at the hair salon and was learning to be a beautician. Tom called her a barber—but that was just to make her mad. Sheila was also quite involved with boyfriends, but since they seemed to change every few weeks, I didn't bother learning their names.

David spent the summer doing what he always did—working at the gas station and reading books. He also spent a lot of time and energy working on his own car—he must have been learning a few mechanic's tricks at work.

Marti was getting rich babysitting. And staying healthy by walking. It seemed like every other day someone in the house would call out, "Marti's gone walkabout." Each to her own.

Marti and I weren't getting together on the steps and talking quite as much, mostly because it was hotter there than anywhere else in the house. We did have a couple of after dinner chats out in the back yard. She asked me about Yvonne, which I liked, and we talked about where my relationship with Yvonne was, and where it might be headed as the three of us—Marti, Yvonne and I—all entered our junior years. I never did open up to Marti about Yvonne's feelings toward colored people. I also didn't tell her all that much about Susan, especially our time on the beach. That was private. I didn't like keeping things from Marti—it felt weird. But I tried not to dwell on it.

Despite the oppressive heat and humidity, I must have fallen asleep, fitfully. I woke up at one point, tried to doze off again. I kept closing my eyes, then opening them, then closing them again. And then I saw the flickers.

They were there, and then they were gone: a couple of clearly unnatural flashes of light that shone through the pine trees. They appeared and disappeared so quickly that I was not sure if they were real or if it was the by-product of my sleep-deprived imagination at work. Maybe my eyes were playing tricks.

I continued to stare. Nothing. Blackness through the trees broken only by shafts of bright moonlight as they snuck through a partly cloudy sky.

Maybe I stared at and through the trees for one minute, maybe three, straining my eyes to see if there was anything out there. And then, just as I was convincing myself that it was all my mind's invention, I saw another flash. Something or somebody was definitely out there in the woods, with a light.

Smugglers, bootlegging moonshiners, witches and warlocks? The problem with reading a lot is that your imagination was filled with source material. No matter that the notion of smugglers was absurd—what would they be smuggling to where?—and the possibility of witches was nonsensical. The mind goes where the mind wants to travel.

The good news was that I was awake and clear-thinking enough to reject my sillier conjectures as fast as my brain conceived them. The problem this left, however, was obvious: What was going on out there in the woods, our woods?

I eased myself from the chaise lounge, then stepped quickly across the yard to the tree line, keeping my eyes steadily fixed on the spot where I'd last seen a flash. I was a little bit nervous—what if there really were moonshiners?—and a whole lot curious.

I figured that the intermittent light was probably coming from some kind of lantern, maybe one that was being turned off and on, or shielded somehow to hide the light. And the only reason I could think of for that was that the person or people with the lantern wanted to reduce the possibility of being noticed, even though it was now the middle of the night, and the neighborhood was long asleep.

Curiosity won out over better judgment: I decided to investigate. Cautiously.

I looked up at the sky, then into the woods. I thought there was enough moonlight finding its way through the clouds for me to see where I was going, especially since I knew this part of our woods pretty well. Carefully and quietly, I started toward the flashes of light, stepping softly on the ground cover of pine needles, making as little noise as possible, trying to avoid sticker bushes since I was wearing shorts, not jeans.

A couple of times the lantern—if that's what it was—stayed off for so long that I thought whoever held it had left the area. A couple of times, I simply stopped and stood in place, quiet and immobile, eyes sweeping back and forth from left to right, looking for another flash of illumination that would point the way.

After ten minutes or so of walking, stopping, walking again—which took me a good quarter mile from our backyard—I saw the light off to the left through a thick grove of trees. I crept closer, vigilant for any sign that I had been detected. The closer I got, the more nervous I became, realizing that this was becoming one of my stupider ideas. Nonetheless, somewhere in my brain, curiosity continued to beat common sense into a pulp. I needed to know what was going on in our woods.

I was getting very close to the light source, heard a voice, and stopped dead still. I moved a couple of steps to my left, concealing myself behind a large tree, peeked around it into a little clearing. I have never been able to forget, or even dim, the scene that I witnessed.

Two people—I assumed they were men from the size of them—stood covered in white sheets and hoods. Klansmen. Everyone in the South knew about them, the famous Ku Klux Klan who were determined to preserve "our southern way of life," but I'd never seen a Klansman in person, just pictures in the newspaper from segregation rallies and sometimes, not very often, arrests.

In front of them, only partially visible based on where they were standing, someone was tied up to a tree.

From where I stood my vision of their captive was largely blocked by the body of the larger Klansman. He was holding the lantern for the other Klansman. I could not get a look at the face of the person tied to the tree, though I guessed it was a man. I heard soft moans, an animal in pain.

The smaller Klansman, who was still fairly large, was brandishing a baseball bat. He stood directly in front of his captive. He kept his voice low, a muffled, whispery voice that was still loud enough to hear, filled with an intense hate that sent chills throughout my body.

"What did y'all think, niggerboy? Did y'all think that you could do what you did—defiling a white girl—and get clean away with it? That jest ain't happening on my watch, niggerboy."

The smaller man swung the baseball bat, hard, a blow that was intended to deliver serious hurt, pummeled flesh and broken bones. I could not see the bat land, but I heard the thud, and the primal though scarcely audible moan from the trussed-up prisoner. His cry was muffled, as if he were gagged, which I learned later that he was.

I stood and watched, frozen with fear, scared to death for myself as well as for the poor man who was being beaten. I had no idea what to do—I certainly could not intervene and forcibly stop things—and I was petrified that somehow I'd be discovered if I moved even slightly.

"Ain't happening on my watch, niggerboy," repeated the man with the bat.

Then the larger man spoke, in a voice that sounded almost gleeful. "Thas right, niggerboy, thas right. Ya'll make shore y'all tell all your little nigger friends. Y'all tell 'em what done happened to you. Y'all tell 'em, niggerboy."

With every statement out of his mouth, the man holding the lantern seemed to grow more excited. Like he was watching a sporting event, and his team was winning.

It felt like I was standing there for a half-hour or more, but it was probably only a couple of minutes. The man tied up to the tree moaned after each blow, with each pitiful sound weaker than the one before it.

I was dizzy and disoriented. I felt like I was going to throw up. Fear and revulsion like I'd never experienced consumed me, paralyzed me, muted me. And then, in a horrifying instant, everything changed.

The Klansman who was swinging the bat shifted his position. The man with the lantern moved slightly to his left. Now I had a clear view of the person who was being beaten. His face was bloody—had he been struck in the head?—and he had an old, dirty rag stuffed in his mouth so that he could not make any noise. His clothes were torn and there was blood soaking into his white t-shirt from underneath.

But there was no question, no doubt. I was staring into the tortured, barely conscious face of Jackie Thomas.

The shock of that image, and the pain that I saw all over my friend's face, pushed away my fear. I heard myself screaming as loud as I could; "Stop it. STOP IT! Stop hurting him. You're killing him. I'm calling the police. I'M CALLING THE POLICE!"

And then I ran.

I tore through the woods, oblivious to roots or fallen tree limbs underfoot. I burst through the tree line, into our back yard, hollering, screaming for my father and help.

I did not really notice but I'm sure that lights came on in the house before I reached the back door.

"Dad, Dad! You gotta come!" I shouted and wailed as I rushed through the dining room and up the stairs three at a time. "They're hurting Jackie Thomas. They're killing him! We gotta help! Hurry! HURRY!"

I was crying and screaming and screeching, frightening my dad and my mom and the whole household.

My Dad met me in his underwear at the top of the stairs. He grabbed me by my shoulders and held me fast. He looked right into my eyes and shouted loudly to drown out my shouts and force his voice into my brain. "Calm down, Mickey, calm down. Stop screaming. What's happening? Where's Jackie? Calm down and tell me."

"In the woods," I blurted. "Two men. They have Jackie tied to a tree. They're beating him with a baseball bat. They're killing him. I saw them. They're out there right now. They're killing him!" Each short sentence came out in a burst of fear and agony. But my words were clear. And, thankfully, my father, my slow-moving, I'll-get-round-to-it father, did not waste more time trying to get a completely coherent story out of me.

He shouted instructions like a military commander to those of the family that had gathered downstairs by the time I burst in the door. "Mary—call the police and an ambulance. David—get my rifle. Sheila, Marti—calm the little ones. Mickey—we're going back to help Jackie. Right now. Let me get some shoes on so I can run."

Fighting fear of different kinds—fear for Jackie, fear for all of us— I waited impatiently in our dining room for my dad to reappear. I don't remember much from that frenzied 90 seconds or so, but I do recall my mother looking at my father as David handed him his rifle.

"A gun, Bill?" she asked. She was not admonishing, just asking.

Dad looked back at her with both resignation and conviction in his voice. "I gotta, Mary, I gotta. I have no idea what we're walking into."

And with that the three of us—me, Dad and David—flew out the back door and ran full tilt back into the woods.

I was still panicked—and not sure that I could find my way directly to the site of the two Klansmen and Jackie. But some sixth sense guided me, guided us, and within a few minutes we drew close to the clearing. David had our big flashlight and it lit up the whole area. Dad was hollering Jackie's name. With adrenalin coursing through our bodies, we plunged forward recklessly. We were not sneaking up on anyone.

We reached the clearing and I saw Jackie's body slumped on the ground. David and I rushed to him, while Dad flipped the safety off his rifle and pointed it at the silent woods around us, looking for any signs of movement or danger.

Jackie's eyes looked back at me dully as I lifted him up. As gently as I could, I removed the gag from his mouth. Blood ran between his lips as I pulled the dirty rag away.

I felt my father kneel beside me to help, convinced that the men who had beaten Jackie up were long gone. David grabbed Dad's rifle and kept it pointed toward the woods around us, just in case.

"Help's coming, Jackie," I said, "Ambulance and police are coming." I was looking at my friend's face, and rage rushed through me. "Those cowards," I said, "those goddamn cowards. Goddamn them to hell."

We did not use that kind of language in the McQuade house. Ever. But my dad said nothing in response to my curses. He was too busy trying to hold Jackie's head up off the hard ground and make him a little more comfortable.

That's when we heard Marti, screaming and crying, and running into the clearing. "Jackie, Jackie, oh my Jesus, oh my God. Oh my Jesus, what have they done to you?"

Marti, dressed in shorts and a lightweight pajama top, ran to Jackie's prone body and almost pushed my father away so that she could cradle Jackie's head in her arms. She looked down at him, bloodied and broken.

"Jackie, oh my Jesus—they've hurt you so bad. So, so bad." She sobbed uncontrollably, tears streaming down her face and falling onto Jackie's cheeks and forehead.

Marti held Jackie's head, wailing in pain. I hugged my twin sister and held her weeping, convulsing body as close to mine as I could, trying to comfort her. My brain was screaming at me to tell her, "It's okay, Marti. Help is coming. It's going to be all right. It's going to be okay." But I didn't. Somehow, I knew that would have been a lie.

CHAPTER 32
AUGUST 23, 1964

Marti and Dad and I stayed with Jackie for what seemed like forever, trying to comfort him, scared to move him, horrified by what had been done to him. Even the slightest movement brought forth whimpers of agony, though I could not fathom how Jackie was still conscious, if he was. Tears streamed down Marti's face without interruption. During that whole time, until police and emergency medical help arrived almost forty minutes later, Marti never took her eyes off Jackie's face, never looked at Dad or me, never looked around at our surroundings, the tree where he'd been bound, the rope which now lay loosely at the tree's roots. In some corner of my brain, I'm sure I realized that her reactions were extreme. But I pushed away any thoughts of asking her why for a later time.

David had gone off to get help. Dad, perhaps not totally convinced that the KKK were gone from the area, kept his rifle at the ready. His army training must have come back to him: I'd never seen him before in this hyper-alert and ready for whatever manner.

We didn't say much, each of us lost in our own private thoughts. Marti and I sat on the ground beside Jackie. Marti held his hand, spoke softly to him through her tears, but I could not understand what she was saying. At one point, I asked Dad who was going to tell Jackie's grandmom, Nammy. If she knew he was missing, she was probably worried. Dad said we'd take care of that as soon as we could, once we got Jackie some medical help.

The ambulance, we learned later, drove around our house at David's direction and parked in our back yard, close to the spot where I'd entered the woods. Luckily, with little recent rain, the red clay of our yard was hard enough to stand up to the weight of the emergency vehicle.

When we heard someone coming through the woods, Dad yelled out "Who's there?" and David responded with "Help's coming, Dad!" That's when my father laid down his rifle, several feet away from himself and where we sat with Jackie. He did not want the police to burst onto a scene with a man holding a gun.

Two police officers entered the clearing first, with handguns drawn, followed by David. Shortly thereafter, two EMTs arrived and went right to work, checking Jackie's vital signs and discussing how they were going to move him. Before we left the clearing in the woods, four other police officers had shown up. One had a roll of yellow crime scene tape which he used to connect trees around the clearing and define the area.

I'm not sure when it started to rain. At first, it was just a few sprinkles, warm and gentle, but I could tell from the way the wind was starting to pick up, and the humidity, that it was probably going to turn into an old-fashioned summertime Alabama thunderstorm. I was hoping it would hold off until we got Jackie out of there and on the way to the hospital.

The EMTs slowly and carefully placed Jackie on a stretcher. At this point, I think Jackie was fortunately unconscious. It was going to be a tough walk across uneven terrain from the clearing in the woods to the ambulance.

Marti wanted to go with the EMTs wherever they were taking Jackie, but Dad said no firmly. He hugged Marti close as the rear doors to the ambulance were closed and I could hear him whispering to her, "Let the professionals do their jobs, sweetie. That's what Jackie needs now. We'll go see him as soon as we can, I promise."

I asked one of the EMTs where they would take Jackie and he told me that East End Memorial Hospital was the closest place with an Emergency Ward. But he thought they might eventually transfer him to UAB Hospital. It had better facilities for treating Negroes, he said. I didn't know what that meant—but I knew that, like so much else in Birmingham, even after the passage of the Civil Rights bill, there was still a lot of unofficial segregation, even in matters of life or death. And, as much as I did not want to think about the worst possibility, in the back of my mind, with the unshakable vision of the baseball bat cracking against Jackie's ribs and glancing off his head, I knew his life was on the line.

Once Jackie was on his way in the ambulance, we turned to the man who seemed to be the ranking police officer. "We've got to tell his grandmom," I said. "He lives with her in the little town on the other side of the woods." The officer looked at me and then nodded. "We'll go in the patrol car," he said. We trudged through the woods to our back yard. He motioned to the street, where three separate patrol cars were parked at odd angles, all with emergency lights flashing.

"We'll go in my car," the police officer said.

"I'm coming with you," my Dad said immediately. "Me too," said Marti. The police officer looked at all three of us and nodded. "Fine, okay," he said, "but we'll need y'all to give us statements after we notify the victim's next of kin."

We walked across the back yard toward the cars. And suddenly, as if coming out of a hypnotic trance, I became aware of how the neighborhood was reacting to the drama. Lights were on in every house up and down the street. We could see little huddles of people staring through the darkness to where the ambulance had just pulled away. I'm sure they could all see the glow from the police officer's flashlight as we headed toward the street.

My mother met my father in the back yard. "What?" she asked. "Tell me what is happening." Fear was a mask that blanketed her face.

"Mickey's friend Jackie has been beaten up pretty bad," he said. "He's on his way to the hospital now. He's alive—but beat up pretty bad."

My mother said nothing in response, but looked at him, then me, then Marti.

"We have to go, Mary," my father said. "We have to go see Jackie's grandmom. We have to tell her what's happened."

"Of course," she said, "Go." She was not crying, my mother was made of stern stuff that took over in any crisis, but I could hear a catch in her voice. She turned back to the house where Sheila stood with Tom. The little kids had actually slept through all the chaos, thankfully.

We piled into the police car, even more the center of attention than before. I looked across the street. The Rawlings house was lit, but no one was outside. I thought about Yvonne, and wished she was with me. I wanted to be hugged.

Instead, I watched as Dad tried to comfort my still visibly anguished sister. She curled up against him like an infant, and he hugged her tightly to calm her, yet I could still hear little sobs coming from her while we rode down the street and onto Killough Springs Highway.

I had no idea how we got there but, after a few turns in the darkness, the high beams of the police car headlights—ours and one other car that followed—shone on the shacks of our secret, nameless town.

"Do you know which house, son?" the officer who was driving asked me.

"Yessir," I responded. "It's the old farmhouse at the end of this road. Straight ahead."

The road was bumpy, each jolt bouncing us hard, throwing us from side to side in the back of the patrol car. We were not driving more than 30 miles an hour, any faster was impossible over the ruts and gullies of the dirt road. The rain was coming down harder now, making it difficult to see.

The police cars did not have sirens on, but both were flashing their overhead lights, giving the yards and houses we passed a surreal red and blue glow.

We pulled up to Jackie's yard, climbed out of the car in the rainstorm, and headed quickly toward the shelter of the porch, with police flashlights illuminating the ground in front of us. I heard the screen door slam and then Nammy calling out in a fearful, shaking voice, "Who's there? Who's out there? Jackie. Jackie, wake up, someone's coming."

I realized then that she thought Jackie was asleep in his bed.

"It's the police, m'am," called the officer.

"It's me, Nammy," I cried out, wanting to reassure her. "It's me, Mickey McQuade. Jackie's friend, Mickey."

Perhaps Nammy responded to my voice. She came out on the porch. I could see her face.

All across it, fear and confusion fought for domination, but fear was winning.

"Mickey? What are y'all doing here? What's happening?" She turned her head back to the house and called for her grandson. "Jackie? Jackie—wake up and get out here! Oh, my!"

I ran ahead of the officer so that Nammy would feel safe. I took the steps in a single bound, and threw my arms around Nammy, at least as far as they could go. And I started to cry. "It's Jackie, Nammy, some men have hurt Jackie. They're getting him to the hospital right now but it's bad. It's really, really bad."

I remember Nammy swaying as my words, tumbling out of me, forced their way into her brain. At first, I felt like she was going to topple over on top of me, but instead she fell back onto the porch settee.

"Oh, my Lawd," she cried out from her slumped position. "I thought my Jackie was in his room, sleeping like a lamb. Oh, my dear Lawd! How could this happen? Who would hurt my Jackie?"

By then, the police officer in charge had reached the porch and took over in a calming, professional voice. "We're doing all we can, m'am," he said. Your son . . . "

"He's her grandson," I interrupted.

". . . your grandson," he continued, "is on his way to the hospital." He looked at his watch. "He should probably be there by now."

"I don't understand. What are y'all saying? I have to go see him," she said, pleading, looking around at all of us. "Can someone take me to see him? Which one of y'all will take me?"

"I'll take her, Officer," my dad said. "Go get dressed, Mrs. Thomas. I'll take you right away in my car."

"I'm going too," said Marti, with conviction. "I'm not staying home."

"Me too, Dad," I said. "Jackie is my friend."

My father looked from face to face, closed his eyes for a brief second, sighed, then nodded. "Okay, we'll all go."

"I'm sorry, sir," the police officer said. "I can't let you go. You are all material witnesses to a crime scene, and we need to take statements from you right away. One of our detectives is on his way right now."

"What?!" I started to protest, but my father looked at me sternly and motioned me to say nothing. It was a look that I'd never seen from him before, but I had no doubt about what it meant. I shut up and listened.

"I expect our detective will want to talk to you as soon as we can get you back to your house," said the police officer. "Officer Purcell will take you back in his patrol car while I take the victim's grandmother to the hospital."

My father looked at the officer for a moment, but then nodded his head. "Please let us know right away where Jackie's been taken," he said. "Here's our number." Dad handed him one of his business cards with both his office phone and our home phone number printed on it.

"Yessir," said the officer, who could not have been more than 25 years old. "We'll radio ahead and find out exactly where the victim was taken for medical care."

I thought about what he said as we walked toward the second patrol car for a ride back to our house. I didn't like that word, victim. It scared me.

CHAPTER 33
SAME DAY

We were not back at our house for more than fifteen minutes before there was a knock on the door. It was now about quarter to five.

My father answered the knock cautiously. "Who's there?" he called through the closed door.

"Detective Anthony Martino," came the answer, in an official-sounding voice. "Birmingham Police."

Dad opened the door.

I'm not sure what I was anticipating, probably some transformed image of a hard-boiled detective from a crime drama on TV. But I'm certain that Detective Martino's appearance was less than the four of us who were gathered at the front door—my parents, David and myself—would have hoped for.

For one thing, he was fat. A lot more overweight than I would have expected from a man who, at some point, had to have passed the physical conditioning challenges of the Police Academy. On top of that, even considering that he'd probably been awakened to take over this case, he was kind of a slob. His tie was loose around his neck, the top button of his damp and undersized dress shirt seemed to be missing, and the shirt itself was barely tucked in. Whatever hair he had left on his head was a mess.

Even cutting him some slack because of the hour, Detective Martino was not one to inspire confidence in the powers of investigative law enforcement.

He did have a strong voice though; I had to give him that.

"Sorry, sir and ma'am," he said right away, "this is a horrible hour to do this, I know. But the faster we can get statements from everyone concerned with this incident, the people actually involved, the more accurate the information tends to be."

Martino looked at my parents for some kind of sign that they understood.

My father nodded. "We appreciate the situation, Detective. We'll cooperate in any way we can."

I stepped forward, feeling inadequate to the task of giving any kind of worthwhile official statement to anybody. "I don't think I've got much to tell, Sir," I said. "Everything was a blur, the men had hoods on, it was pretty dark except for their lantern and a little light from the moon. The only person I recognized was Jackie." At that point, I started choked up again. "My friend Jackie," I managed to say, choking on the words, "tied to a tree."

My mom put her arms around me immediately, hugged me. Everyone else just stood there without knowing what to say.

Detective Martino's voice softened. "I know this is going to be tough, Son," he said, "but the more you can tell me, the better chance we have of catching the perpetrators . . . " He hesitated, perhaps not liking the sound of the word. ". . . the person or persons who hurt your friend." Then he looked at my parents. "Is there a place where I could talk with your son by myself? It's best if I take statements individually, without other people around, so that each person's memory of what happened isn't influenced by anyone else's recollections."

"How about right here?" my mother said, indicating the well-worn sofa in our family room. "We'll sit out in the dining room until you're done."

"Who else will you want to talk to?" my father asked.

"Whoever was there," answered the detective. "Whoever saw anything or knows anything."

"Where's Marti?" I interrupted. I'd lost track of her since we were dropped off by the police car.

"I'll find her," my mom said. "Sit down and talk with the detective. Your father will be in the dining room if you need him."

She turned, gestured to my father and David to precede her. "I'll put some coffee on," she said as she followed them out of the room.

* * * * *

Detective Martino looked at me with everyone gone. "So here's how it is," he said. "Our best shot to catch the people who did this comes in the next 48 hours. The more I can learn from you, right now, the better our chances."

I think he saw the doubt on my face and he tried to address it. "We're professionals, son," he said. "We'll get whoever did this."

Sadly, I did not share the detective's optimism, even if it was genuine. Besides the fact that I had very little helpful information to provide, I also had a low level of confidence, based on everything I knew or had heard, in the Birmingham Police Force and its ability to identify white men who beat up Negro teenagers.

I sat on the couch. Detective Martino sat on a folding chair with a little paper notebook, kind of like the one I used for my vacation journal, and a pen. The first thing I had to do was make sure he knew all of the people involved.

"No sir," I told him after he called me by the wrong name. "I'm Mickey.

My sister is Marti. My father's name is Bill. My older brother is David."

"And the victim's name . . ." There was that word again.

"It's Jackie," I said. "Jackie Thomas."

I did not mean to come across like a wise guy, but I was pretty cranky and angry and tired, and that surely affected my manners and my patience. Luckily, we were alone, which saved me from a reprimand from my father for my attitude. I am pretty sure Dad shared my feelings about the Birmingham Police Department—it wasn't that long ago when Detective Martino's colleagues were beating and fire-hosing peaceful colored demonstrators on the streets of Birmingham. Still in all, the law was the law and no son of Bill McQuade's was going to get away with disrespectful behavior.

However I came across, it did not seem to bother Detective Martino.

"Okay. I'm going to ask you to take me through the entire evening, step by step," he said. "Let's just keep it nice and simple—but please don't leave anything out. Even things that seem unimportant to you might be helpful to us." He paused. "And I know that sounds exactly like what you hear on TV or in the movies, but it's true. That's one aspect of my job that the TV people get right."

I told the story just as Detective Martino asked, leaning forward from my seat on the couch, staring down at my shoes, replaying the different scenes in my head like I was recalling a movie I'd just watched. "Just the facts, m'am" was a phrase drummed into our heads by the popular TV show Dragnet and I was determined to be a good recounter of exactly what happened. I tried to remember and describe everything from the moment I woke up until the police and EMTs arrived in the woods.

"Thank you, son. Good job, very complete," the detective said to me as I wrapped up my recall of events, which took about twenty minutes, interspersed with some questions from him to clarify his timeline. "But let me ask you just a little bit more about the two individuals who were attacking your friend—now you're sure it was two men?"

"Well, yes," I said, "I'm as positive as I can be without seeing their faces."

"Got it," said the detective. "Now the man with the bat—do you remember anything more about him? You said he was a big man. How big would you say again? Bigger than your dad?"

"I guess about the same," I said. My father was 6'2". "Maybe a little taller and I think heavier, but with the robe or sheet on, I really couldn't say."

"Was there anything distinctive about him—and sure, I know he was covered with the robe and the hood—but was there anything unusual about the way he stood, or moved, or the sound of his voice, anything?"

"No sir, nothing I can put my finger on," I replied. "He had a gruff voice, he had a Southern accent. Neither one of them said much. He called my friend Jackie a 'niggerboy' a few times."

Detective Martino looked his notes over, hesitated a minute before he spoke.

"Could you tell me again what you remember him saying about a 'white woman?'" the detective asked.

"He didn't say 'white woman,'" I said. "He said 'defiling a white girl,' not a white woman. That's what he said."

Detective Martino looked at his notebook. "Right, yes, that's right—wonder what he meant by that?"

I didn't think the question was directed at me, more like Detective Martino was talking to himself. So I didn't say anything. But I was wondering myself, wondering about Marti and her reaction when she came into the clearing, how she had acted with Jackie, how she held on to him until the medical team arrived. What was that Klansmen talking about? I knew I needed to talk to Marti about this as soon as possible.

Detective Martino patted me quickly on the shoulder. "You did good, son. But if you remember anything else, call me. I'm going to give your father my number down at the station."

I nodded. Detective Martino looked down at his notes and then looked up. "Do you think I could talk to your father now?" he asked. "Oh, and while I'm talking to him, would you mind not talking about this with your brother and sister? Just want to keep everyone's memories straight."

I nodded again and went to get my dad.

I wanted to talk to Marti, but I figured I had to wait until she had talked to the detective herself. I went upstairs intending to sit on my bed until she had finished giving her statement—but then I fell asleep.

* * * * *

My parents let me sleep for a few hours, then woke me up. Detective Martino was long gone by that time.

"Do you want to go to the hospital?" my father asked.

I nodded yes, went and splashed water on my face, changed t-shirts. I was still groggy but figured I could sleep a little more in the car. I did.

Dad had called ahead to make sure he knew where Jackie was being cared for. From what he was told, they had first taken Jackie to East End Memorial Hospital, right down the street from the bakery we used to visit for Sunday doughnuts. There, the doctors worked on stabilizing his vital signs before transferring him to UAB, over on the South Side. That's where we went.

At UAB, they'd run a large series of tests, trying to determine the extent and severity of the injuries he had sustained.

We never really visited Jackie, never stood by his bedside. We found Nammy standing by herself in a hallway, watching through a half-glass wall into something of an intensive care setting. It was located in the basement of the hospital in what seemed to be a section reserved for Negroes. I did not know enough to declare it inadequate, but it was assuredly a different standard of care from what white patients received. Jackie was bandaged almost head to toe, and had two different tubes running liquids from different-colored plastic bags into his body. It was a frightening picture.

Thankfully, Jackie was still unconscious. The pain, the doctors told us, would be almost overwhelming if he were awake. They were prepared for that, they said, with both sedatives and painkillers. They could not predict when consciousness might return.

"This was a nasty beating," the young doctor who seemed most in charge told us. "He has internal injuries that we are still trying to assess, internal bleeding in different places, not too severe from what we can tell, but internal bleeding is always a serious medical issue, of course. He has broken ribs, a broken elbow, a broken collarbone. Thankfully, there seem to be only minor blows to the head."

Nammy, by this point, was stone-faced. She listened to what was being said but did not ask a question. Perhaps she thought that we would ask all the questions that needed to be asked. I could not tell what she was feeling.

Marti, with eyes horribly red from tears and lack of sleep, was similarly affected. She leaned on my dad, listening intently I could tell, but unable or unwilling to give voice to any questions or thoughts running through her head. She'd been that way throughout the night, and in the car.

My father was the strong one of our group. He asked the young doctor what the next steps in medical care might be, when the doctors might know better about Jackie's condition, when Jackie might return to consciousness, when it would make sense for us to return to the hospital to see him. He did not ask—maybe he was afraid to ask—the question that was burning in my brain: Was Jackie going to die?

After several minutes of speaking with the doctor, my father turned to the rest of us. "I think it's time we all went home, everyone," he said. "Jackie is getting the best care possible, the doctors will alert us immediately if there is any change in his condition, and they'll call when he wakes up . . . and then we'll go from there."

"I'm staying," Nammy said. "Staying put with my Jackie."

My dad nodded understanding.

We started for the door and then I turned back to the young doctor and asked him directly, with a little bit of shaky in my voice, "Is my friend going to live?"

The doctor hesitated, seemed to be making up his mind what to say, and then gave me an honest answer. "I don't know, son," he told me, looking directly in my eyes, which were already filling with tears again at a response that I somehow knew was coming. "At this stage, we just don't know."

* * * * *

Pure exhaustion hit me on the ride back to Roebuck from UAB on the Southside. Whatever adrenalin had been able to provide had run its course. I fell into a deep sleep and never felt a minute of the ride across town. I woke up when Dad turned into the driveway. I stumbled into the house, saw my mom embrace my dad and hand him a hot cup of coffee, then I crawled up the stairs to my still sauna-like bedroom—the hard rain from the middle of the night had provided only a brief respite—and then fell asleep with my clothes on.

I woke up after about four hours, soaked in sweat, bleary-eyed, and sore all over, hoping even as I began to gain consciousness that last night was nothing more than the worst nightmare of my life. I wanted to scream out loud when I realized it was not, when it hit me that the woods and the

Klansmen and the police and the doctors and my badly beaten friend were all as real as the suffocating humidity that surrounded me on all sides, draining away the will to get up and to move and to think.

Hope was the force that got me moving. Hope that we might already have gotten good news from the hospital. Hope that the police might have apprehended Jackie's attackers. Hope that somehow life would slowly but surely return to where it was at this time yesterday, once Jackie got better, once we could get together for a game of catch in his front yard. Funny how I did not appreciate how carefree I had been just 24 hours before.

I stumbled downstairs to find my mom in the kitchen, puttering, her way of fighting back against the madness that had just invaded the McQuade world.

"Hi, Mickey," she said. "Are you hungry?"

I tried to respond but the "Sure, Mom" got caught in my throat. I crossed the kitchen to give her a hug, burst into tears as her arms wrapped around me. She held me to her for a minute, let the wave subside, then gave me an extra hug, and released me. "I don't think you slept enough, Mickey," she said. "Do you want to go upstairs and try to go back to sleep? Your father and Marti are still dead to the world, I think."

"Too hot," I said. "Too hot for anything." I looked around the room, not focusing on anything.

"You're right," she said. "When it gets like this, those fans don't do anything but push more hot air in your face. Why don't you go take a nice shower, get some clean clothes on? I think you'll feel better." She looked at the kitchen wall clock.

"But first," she said, "why don't you just sit here for a minute? Let me get you some iced tea."

I sat. I drank my tea. I thought about everything that had happened since I'd stumbled onto two men in the woods, in stupid white sheets, with a baseball bat in their hands and pure evil in their souls, and I felt a whole bunch of hate, searing and intense hate, entering my soul. The worst thing was, I welcomed it in.

265

CHAPTER 34
SAME DAY

Late that Sunday afternoon, I found myself standing alone in our back yard, staring at the woods. I'd walked outside, through our cement-floor dining room and past the opening to the kitchen without saying anything to my mother, who might not have noticed me. She was preparing our traditional Sunday dinner—we always called it dinner even though my friends and their families called it supper: A huge bowl of rigatoni with meat sauce, a fresh green salad, two loaves of toasted, heavily buttered garlic bread. For a woman with an Irish meat and potatoes background, Mary McQuade was no slouch when it came to Italian cooking.

What I could not understand, however, was how she was able to perform her usual Sunday activities after last night. It did not seem right; it did not seem possible. Last night changed everything, or it should have somehow. How could any of us—from Dad and Mom to Marti and me to Carrie Ann—do what we normally did on a Sunday afternoon after everything that happened in the last 24 hours? Something was badly wrong with that reality.

My brain, of course, told me that this was an unfair thought. I'd seen my mother's face as the details of last night were described to her. I saw she was horrified, frightened, angry. But somehow, I wanted everything to change because of it—I could not understand how, or what exactly I wanted to have happen, but I could not imagine doing normal things, not then, maybe not ever again.

I stared at the pine trees in front of me, thinking about the different times I'd gone into them with happy anticipation, exploring with Tom or heading over the little rise and down to Jackie's house. Somehow, I knew I would never look at those woods with similar feelings again, even when Jackie got better. It wasn't that the woods felt hostile—trees are just trees—but they no longer stood before me as a portal to fun, adventures, discoveries. What happened out there had robbed the woods of their character, their innocence.

"What . . . wh-what are you doing . . . out here?" I hadn't heard Marti come up behind me. Her voice cracked as she forced the question through her lips. Each syllable was heavy, weighted down with emotion that she could not control.

I turned around and she stumbled, crashed, into my arms. She buried her head against my neck, and the sobs came in waves. And all I could do was hold her tight. For once in my life, I felt like a real older brother to my twin sister. It was always Marti who took the lead in tough situations, who knew what to say and how to act. But this Marti, the one I kept hugging tighter because I did not know what else to do, this Marti was a creature I'd never encountered before. She was lost, wounded, tortured. Feeling her pain was worse than feeling my own. She was broken, like a vase knocked off a mantle, shattered into pieces on the floor.

It took minutes before the tears and the shaking slowly began to subside.

"I was just thinking," I whispered into her ear. "This time yesterday—yesterday—I looked out at these woods without a care in the world. Might have thought about going down to Jackie's for a catch—or maybe just to sit on his porch and talk to Nammy. And here we are now, our lives are absolutely blown apart, like we stepped on some kind of a booby trap bomb, like those ones you read about over in Vietnam—and we never saw it coming."

Marti didn't respond, but I could feel that she was listening to me.

"At least our soldiers know the danger, know to be careful where they step. We just never knew, never suspected. And I'm betting Jackie didn't either."

Every mention of Jackie's name brought more pain to my sister, I could feel it. But her body must have been getting tired. She wasn't bawling now. It was more like a whimper, like a badly injured kitten.

"I can't tell you it's going to be all right, Sis," I whispered to her. "I can't tell you that. But I'm hoping it might be. It will take some time, but I'm hoping and praying that Jackie will get better. And that the police catch the men who did this. And that they send them to the electric chair. I hate those men with all my heart. I wish I could pull the switch myself."

Finally, she spoke.

"They hurt him so bad, Mickey. Why did they have to hurt him like that? He was so good, so kind. He was—is— the sweetest boy I've ever known."

"I don't know, Marti. I don't know anything. It's like this terrible, scary bad dream but it's not a dream. It's real. And I just don't understand it. Why did this happen to Jackie?"

I felt Marti stiffen just a little bit. My brain whirred, remembering little things, like walkabouts and Marti mailing post cards from Sea Isle City.

She pulled back away from me. She hung her head, did not, would not look at me. I stared at the top of her head, a tangled mess of brown hair. And let her give voice to her pain, her remorse, and her guilt.

"I think ma-maybe because of me, Mickey. I did it. It's my fault, my fault."

"What!?" I said, suddenly angry with her at this preposterous statement, pushing her back and holding her by her shoulders. "What are you talking about? How could it be your fault?" I shouted my questions at her.

"Because," she said, "because . . . because we . . . we . . . liked each other."

And that's when I knew, knew exactly what she was hinting at but could not say. For some reason, I had continued the charade of not quite understanding. I pretended ignorance though I did not know why. Maybe I was giving her time to tell the story in her own way, without me interjecting, without me assuming that I understood when, of course, I really didn't know or understand.

In spite of the fact that I knew what she was saying, I continued the charade.

"You liked him. Of course, you liked him. We all like him. He's a good guy, he's my friend, he's your friend."

"He was my b-boyfriend."

And then, even though it was impossible that there were any tears left in her body, the sobbing began anew.

It took longer this time for Marti to control herself. Finally, she did. And then she began to explain everything to me—not in a clear, coherent, Marti-like way, but in a jumble of half-sentences and semi-completed thoughts, punctuated by periods of silence and quiet sobbing, moments when she seemed to go completely back inside herself to feel her pain more intensely.

She asked me if I remembered how I'd felt when I first met Yvonne, when I didn't even know her but liked her immediately. That was what happened to her with Jackie. She'd liked him instantly, the moment she met him on Christmas Day, when he visited our house, and developed his special relationship with Carrie Ann.

She didn't talk to Jackie much that day and didn't really see him much in person after that, except for the one afternoon in February when he showed up for my dance lesson, and then not again until our baseball game in the Spring. But everything she saw on Christmas—his smile, his voice, his manners with Mom and Dad, his comfortable, gentle way with the little kids—everything about him contributed to a feeling like she knew him, and that they would become good friends.

It was a feeling that stayed with her. She would think about him. And, as she described all this to me, I remembered one or two mild suggestions from her about bringing Jackie over to the house.

"So, after Christmas," I said, "you never saw Jackie again until my dance lesson? And then not again until our game of scrub?"

"That's right," she told me, smiling at the memories through still watery eyes. "And we hardly even spoke that day, cause when you're playing, you're not together. But I remember him congratulating me when I caught his fly ball," she said. "You know, if it was Tom who'd hit the fly, and if I'd robbed him of a sure homer, Tom would have been upset, mad at me! But I kind of think Jackie was happy for me, like he was proud of me."

"That was a great catch," I replied. "But," I asked, still a little confused, "that was not enough to make you boyfriend-girlfriend. How could it have been?"

"No, that wasn't it," Marti said. "It didn't happen just then. But, you know how I love my walks, Mickey, how everyone in the family teases me about going walkabout. Like sometimes I would walk down our street and out onto Killough Springs, and maybe walk up to the little grocery store, or sometimes the other way all the way up the big hill. "

I nodded.

"So one day, not long after our scrub game, I decided to take a walk in the woods. I realized that I hardly ever did that. And I kind of wandered over toward all the little houses where Jackie lives. And I just sat there on the hill for a while, looking down at the houses, and maybe hoping I might see him come out into the yard. But he didn't."

"Okay," I said.

"Well, I just sat there for a while, maybe ten minutes or so, wishing that I could just see him. I kept looking at this front porch, and I just kept thinking, 'Please God, let him come out on the porch for just a minute. I just want to see how he looks, that's all.'"

"I don't think it works that way," I said.

"No, no, don't interrupt," she said. She smiled as she said it, and I could see that she was wrapped up in remembering that day, and it was probably the first time since last night that she was feeling even a little bit good about anything, so I shut my mouth and let her talk.

"And then I saw him," she said. "He wasn't even in his house. He must have been at one of the other houses up the hill to the right—because all of a sudden, I just saw him walking on the dirt road, heading back down toward his house. I'd been watching his porch so closely I didn't even see where he came from. And I got so excited that I just stood up real quick and yelled, 'Jackie, Jackie, it's me, Marti!' But then I got a little bit embarrassed because I was making a silly fool of myself."

"Sorry, I'm interrupting," I said. "But that doesn't exactly sound like you."

"It's not!" Marti replied. "It's not like me at all. But I guess I was just so surprised and all to see him . . . I don't know."

I could see her mind drifting happily as she recalled the scene. I was seeing a side to my sister that was new to me. Her features softened as she thought about that day. There was even a little flush to her cheek, like when you remember an embarrassing moment and the recollection is so vivid that you re-feel the feelings all over again.

"So . . ." I said.

Marti came out of her momentary reverie and looked right at me.

"Mickey, he recognized me right away. And he waved. And then he kind of made a motion like to say, 'Stay right there.' And then he literally ran up the hill—you know how fast he can run—and he got to the top and he said, 'Hello, Marti McQuade.' And it felt so good to see him, up close, right there in front of me."

I couldn't help it. I started smiling with Marti because I could picture the scene so vividly.

"And we just stood there, talking," she continued. "Probably for five or ten minutes. About nothing. School stuff. A little baseball. He asked how you were doing, and I said fine. I asked about Nammy and he said she was doing okay, but her feet were bothering her a bit. And he asked me what I was doing there, and I told him all about my walks, and that I'd decided to go into the woods that day, and he said he was glad I did, and then I said I'd better get going even though I didn't really want to go, and he said okay, but then he asked me if I was going to take a walk in the woods again someday, and I said maybe Saturday and he asked me about what time and then, before you know it, we were deciding to meet there, right up on the top of the hill at the edge of the woods on a Saturday."

Marti paused to catch her breath. I just looked at her, waiting until she spoke again.

"And that's how it all started, Mickey. Just like that. All of a sudden, Jackie started to become as much my friend as yours. And I began to take all my walks in the woods, sometimes with plans to meet him, and sometimes just hoping I might see him, and sometimes I did, and sometimes I didn't, but it was just so nice whenever I did see him. And I thought about telling you—but there really wasn't that much to tell—and somehow it was more special if it was just something between Jackie and me. And he was just—is just," she corrected herself, "the sweetest, kindest, gentlest person I've ever known."

I didn't want to ask, but I had to. "Friends are friends, Marti," I said. "But friends are different than boyfriends and girlfriends. Right?"

She didn't answer my question directly, which was okay, because I wasn't even sure exactly what I was asking. She just talked some more about her and Jackie.

"I'd probably seen him maybe three or four times," she said, "and then one day, we were just standing by the really big pine up there . . . you know the one I'm talking about, right? . . . and he just looked so cute that I couldn't resist . . . and I kissed him. A real kiss, Mickey . . . a girlfriend-boyfriend kiss."

"And we never did more than that, but we sure did a lot of that. In the woods, looking down on Jackie's little town. And I never knew kissing could be so . . . so good."

And then, because it had to happen, Marti came back to the present. "And now . . . and now . . ." And the tears welled up in her eyes, and she began to cry again, but softer, exhaustedly. "Why, Mickey, why? Why did they have to hurt such a sweet, sweet boy?"

I hugged her, tightly. I knew her question was rhetorical—she wasn't expecting a real answer from me. But I gave her one anyway, whispering in her ear the words that kept running through my head, over and over. "No reason, Marti. None at all. Why? Why such hate? It just makes no sense. No sense."

Then I hugged her again, and gently, ever so gently, introduced the questions that I needed to ask.

"Marti," I said, "can I ask you just two questions? Just two."

She didn't say no, so I plunged ahead. "When you were with Jackie, up on the hill, did anyone ever see you? Anyone at all?"

"N-no, no, I didn't think so," Marti answered. "Who could have seen us—out in the woods? We never saw anyone. But now . . . now I think someone must have seen us . . . because . . . "

"And did you tell Detective Martino?" I interrupted her. "About all this? About you and Jackie, I mean?"

"He guessed, Mickey. Somehow, he guessed. He asked me if Jackie was my boyfriend—and I said yes. But I think he already knew."

I'd promised to ask only two questions, though now I had five more that popped into my brain.

But for now, we'd said enough. So, I walked her back to the house with my arm around her, and Marti kind of leaning against me for strength. I wanted to cry myself. But Marti was crying enough for the both of us.

CHAPTER 35
AUGUST 25, 1964

Yvonne and I sat on the couch in her living room, not too close together because her parents were around. It was Tuesday afternoon, two days since the attack on Jackie. This was our homecoming/reunion get-together; Yvonne had just arrived back in Birmingham late on Sunday from Chicago.

Over the course of the summer, we'd written letters to each other a few times—and I'd gotten half a dozen postcards from her with scenes of Lake Michigan or the Chicago skyline, including messages like, "Wish you were here," or "Do you miss me?" or, my favorite, "Luv ya!"

Yvonne had called me on Monday morning, all excited about being back home and wanting to tell me all about the people she'd met, the places she'd gone, and the parties she'd attended with her cousin who was a junior at some preppy girls high in a suburb of Chicago. When I told her the news about Jackie, she was shocked, and kept saying how horrible it must have been for me. It made for a very subdued reunion conversation.

By Tuesday, however, the impact of Jackie's abduction and assault seemed to have lessened significantly for Yvonne. She greeted me with a big smile and hug at the door, and a little whisper of "Kisses coming later." I'm sure I would have been more enthused about her return and hearing all her news except for the obvious: my friend was fighting for his life, the grandmother who cared for him was distraught with worry, my sister Marti blamed herself and just stayed in her room, crying. And I was not doing so well myself.

At first, as we sat together in her living room, Yvonne did not seem to notice that I wasn't talking much. She was chatting about this and that, how she loved the Midwest, how the people she'd met in Chicago were so much more sophisticated than any of the people we knew from our high schools, how good Chicago pizza was compared to pizzas from our local restaurant, Pasquale's. I tried to listen, tried to comment, even made a little joke about pizza and how much my brother Tom could eat of it no matter where it came from.

But then, as she picked up on the listlessness of my responses, Yvonne paused, looked at me, and said, "Mickey, are you all right? You're not usually this quiet."

I looked up at her with what I am sure came across as an uninspired half-smile. "Sorry, Yvonne," I said, "I've been kind of down since Saturday night. This whole thing is kind of hard for me to shake off."

Yvonne gave me a sympathetic nod. "Yes, oh, I get it. Saturday must have been so horrible for you. My mom told me you were up all night and there were police and everything. You're probably still exhausted."

Her words were supportive—Yvonne always knew the right thing to say—but I didn't think she really understood the situation. And it felt odd to have her expressing so much concern about me, and very little for Jackie. I was not sure she really grasped the enormity of things, or genuinely sympathized with the fact that my very good friend was beaten up, tortured, by two men wearing the hooded outfits of the Ku Klux Klan, and that he was still in a coma, and that I had witnessed it, and that it had all just happened a few days ago.

She smiled and said, "That must have really been bad, Mickey." If I were sitting closer, it would not have surprised me if she had reached out and patted me on the top of my head.

"Why don't I get us some cookies and cokes," Yvonne said. "You just sit right here for a little bit. I'll be right back."

She got up and went to the kitchen. I sat alone in the living room, staring at the clock on the wall. It was one of those decorative clocks that had prongs or spokes or something coming out of it to make it look like the sun or a star. As I looked it over, I realized for the first time how ugly it was.

The phone on the table beside me suddenly rang, startling me, but was picked up immediately by someone upstairs. Then I heard Mr. Rawlings voice. He must have left the door open to the room he was in, because his comments carried clearly down the stairs to the living room. Lost in my own thoughts, I didn't pay any attention to his conversation, even though I could hear everything he said quite clearly. He was talking about some problem or other down at the steel mill where he worked as a foreman.

"That's what I told him, straight out. Those are the rules, I said."

Silence while the person on the other end of the line spoke.

"No, no, he didn't sass me back. He knows who's the boss."

Again, a short period of silence.

"Never, I said, never, never. That jest ain't happening on my watch."

Suddenly, my body went cold. I felt dizzy. I felt nauseous. Somehow, somewhere in the back of my brain, sparks flew, connections were made. I heard seven words—That jest ain't happening on my watch —and I knew. Something about the inflection of the voice, the rhythm of the delivery, little bits and pieces of pronunciation—it was a myriad of tiny vocal and linguistic elements that came together and I knew. Without a question, beyond any doubt whatsoever, I knew that the man who had beaten my friend Jackie with a baseball bat in the woods last Saturday night was Jessup Rawlings.

Sweat broke out on my forehead and my body started to shake. Yvonne came back into the room, saw me and knew that something was wrong.

She quickly put the tray of cookies and cokes on the table and turned to me with real concern. "Mickey? What's wrong? You're white as a ghost!"

I looked at her and knew that I had to get out of that house. I stood up, shakily, and said, "Yvonne, I gotta go. I think I'm gonna be sick."

Then I ran out her front door and back across the street to my house.

* * * * *

I burst through the family room door, ran toward the kitchen to look for Mom. I found her in our dining room, leaning over Brenda and one of Brenda's big coloring books. Other books and crayons were spread out all over the ping pong table. Brenda was whimpering, as usual. "No, it's not ruined, honey," Mom told her. "You only went over the line a little bit. It's okay."

Mom glanced up as I entered the room and immediately reacted to whatever was showing on my face. "Mickey, what is it? What's the matter? What's happened?"

I could feel cold sweat on my forehead, could feel my arms shaking. Once again, I felt like I was going to vomit. I closed my eyes and leaned on the counter to steady myself, hoping the feeling of dizziness and nausea would pass.

My mother didn't know what was wrong but knew it was serious. "Brenda and Bobby," she said, looking at me, "you two stay right here and keep coloring. I'm going to go see if Carrie Ann is awake from her nap."

Mom motioned me with her hand to go back through the kitchen and into the next room ahead of her. Then she closed the door behind us and lightly reached out her hand to touch my arm. "Mickey, what is it? Tell me what happened."

I had to sit down, had to get control of myself. I wanted to run away, to another room, to another place, to another life. This life was hurting too bad, throwing too much at me. I didn't ask for any of it—it just wasn't fair. I looked up at my mom as she continued to ask me what the matter was.

I remember looking my mother right in the eye, fighting back tears that were just below the surface, steeling myself, and then telling her what I now knew with an unshakeable certainty. "I know who hurt Jackie, Mom!" I cried. "It was Mr. Rawlings. I know it, I know it. He did it. It was him that night in the woods, calling Jackie 'niggerboy' and beating him . . . " At that point, I lost what little control I had and, once again, found myself sobbing hysterically into my mother's shoulder. ". . . beating him with a baseball bat."

"Mickey? What are you saying? Calm down. Tell me what happened? Why do you think this? What happened?"

"I don't think, Mom," I said with equal parts anger and conviction, as I pulled away from her embrace. And that's when I felt it and knew what I was feeling. Hate. Pure, single-minded, overwhelming, and all-powerful hate. The incredible strength of the emotion did not scare me, I did not shrink from the force of it. I welcomed it, welcomed the coldness of it, and the intense fury, and the sudden unshakeable resolve that came with it, resolve to make Jessup Rawlings pay dearly for what he had done to my friend.

"I don't think, Mom. I know. It was Mr. Rawlings. He hurt Jackie. And I hate him." The words snarled their way through my teeth and lips, dripping with the venom of a South Alabama cottonmouth. And it felt good, felt so good to give in to it, to let the hate wash over me. There was hate and there was the desire for revenge, and they were linked inextricably. "I hate him," I said again, loving the sound and the feel of those three little words. "I hate him. I want to kill him."

"Mickey, shush. Don't talk like that, don't say such things. You're scaring me, Mickey. Calm down, tell me what happened."

"No," I said, looking directly in her eyes. "When Dad comes home, I'll tell you both what happened. Right now, I'm going to my room."

I left my mom standing there, wondering, afraid, too surprised to try and stop me, too shocked to ask me again what had happened.

I went to my room, threw myself onto my bed, buried my face in my pillow, and let my rage consume me. At one point, I heard someone come into the room, and stand by my bed. But Mom must have told all my brothers and sisters to leave me alone. Whoever it was only stayed for a few seconds, never said a word, then left.

* * * * *

I had calmed down, at least outwardly, by the time my father walked into the house. I heard voices, he and Mom talking softly, then heard Dad talking to David, and telling him to take everyone out to dinner at the hot dog place by the Roebuck Shopping Center. I heard the little kids laughing and yelling as they piled into the station wagon. I heard the car backing out of the driveway and heading down the street.

Silence for a little bit—and then Dad appeared in the doorway. "Mickey," he called softly, "are you awake?"

I didn't respond at first.

"Mickey," he said, "your mom says you have something important to tell us. We're ready when you are. I asked Marti to join us. I thought you might want her to be there."

I rolled over, squinted my eyes to see him. I realized then that I was wet with sweat. "Good," I said quietly, without emotion. "I'll be right down. Let me just put on a fresh t-shirt."

When I walked into our family room, all three of them—Dad, Mom and

Marti—looked up at me, but no one spoke. It would have been a perfect time for someone to have broken the tension with a little joke. No one did.

I sat down on a chair, folded my arms across my chest, and told them exactly what had happened from the moment I walked in the door to see Yvonne to the moment I burst back into our house, near hysterical.

And, if I do say so myself, I did a very good job of describing things. I told them where I sat, what Yvonne talked about, how and when she got up to go get us some snacks. I told them how I just waited for her on the sofa in the Rawlings living room. I told them about hearing the phone ring, and hearing Mr. Rawlings talk with someone, and then hearing him say the exact same words he used when he was beating Jackie.

I told them that's when I knew that he was the one who did it.

Then I told them about running home.

When I finished, they all just looked at me. Marti was crying, looking at me through her sobs.

"Well," Dad said, just to break the silence.

"Are you sure, Mickey?" asked Mom quietly. "Are you completely sure that it was Mr. Rawlings?"

If she'd asked me that question when I'd first come through the door that afternoon, I would have screamed my answer in her face. "Yes!!" I would have yelled. "Yes, I am totally, completely sure!" I would not have been able to handle questions of doubt, even coming from someone that I knew was totally and completely on my side.

But now, though there was still some seething and some anger going on deep inside me, and hate for Jessup Rawlings was boiling in my gut, on the outside I had gone completely flat. Monochromatic. Emotionless.

I sat without fidgeting. I spoke in a low but clear voice. I did not rush my words. I repeated my story in answer to Mom's question while all three of them sat in stunned, frightened silence.

"Okay, then," Dad said. "I think we need to call Detective Martino."

"Yes, let's do that," I agreed. "I need to tell him that I know who beat Jackie." I hesitated. "I want to be there when they arrest him."

No one said anything to that. Dad went to the kitchen to make the call.

* * * * *

Detective Martino asked us to come down to the station. We got there the next morning around nine. Dad had called his office and told them that he'd be late that day. Detective Martino agreed that it was okay for Dad to sit with me while we talked, since we'd already made our official statements about the night of the beating. All my dad had said on the phone was that I had something new and important to add to the investigation.

The same outwardly calm manner of the previous day stayed with me as I began. "I know the identity of one of the men who beat Jackie Thomas."

Detective Martino did not react visibly, just shifted slightly in the chair and leaned forward. He looked at me to continue.

"Our neighbor across the street, Jessup Rawlings, he did it," I said. "I don't know who the other man was, but Mr. Rawlings was the one with the baseball bat." I paused. "I'd like to be there when you arrest him, so that I can tell Jackie."

Based on a call I'd made to the hospital yesterday, Jackie had still not come out of his coma. But I thought he'd want to hear this news anyway. I wanted to tell him myself, before anyone else did.

"Let's not get all ahead of ourselves here," Detective Martino said. "I want to hear your whole story, every detail. I want to know how it is that you know who one of the assailants is today when you did not know that person's identity three days ago."

Detective Martino's reaction, I felt, was not uttered in shock or doubt or disbelief. I appreciated that. It was a reasonable question that I was fully prepared to answer.

First, I explained the circumstances of why I was in the Rawlings living room.

"You and this Rawlings girl," Detective Martino interrupted to ask, "is she your girlfriend?"

I did not expect that question—and kind of stumbled with my answer. "Well, kind of," I said. "We haven't seen each other much this summer. She's been away to see her cousin in Chicago. But we write postcards."

"Might be important, maybe not," he said, "just asking. Go ahead, son," he nodded his head in my direction, "please continue."

I told him about Yvonne leaving to get snacks. About me sitting in the quiet living room all by myself. About hearing the phone ring and one-half— the Jessup Rawlings half   of the conversation that followed.

And then I quoted the words, exactly, because I knew them exactly. "Mr. Rawlings said, 'That jest ain't happening on my watch.' And that's when I knew that he was the man who beat Jackie with a baseball bat."

Detective Martino considered my last statement for a few seconds before speaking. "I have to ask you this, son," he said, "and I won't be the last person to ask it. Are you sure, I mean absolutely sure, that this man, your neighbor, is the same man who attacked the victim in the woods?"

"Yessir," I replied. "One hundred percent sure." There was no doubt in my voice because there was no doubt in my mind.

"And tell me again how you can go from 'no idea' to '100 percent sure' in four days."

"It's just the way he said those words. When I heard him say the exact same thing on the phone that he said the other night in the woods, it just hit me. I swear it was him."

Detective Martino looked down at his notebook and shook his head ever so slightly. He didn't say anything for a long time.

Then my father spoke up. "What happens now, Detective?"

"Yessir," I chimed in. "What happens now? When will Mr. Rawlings be arrested?"

"That's not my call, and what happens next is not exactly my call either. I will report everything you told me today to my supervisor. I'll need a signed statement. We'll probably begin an investigation of Jessup Rawlings right away. But I would be shocked if we'd issue an arrest warrant without some corroborating evidence."

"But he did it," I said. "I identified him. I know it was him."

Detective Martino looked at me again, and once again shook his head slightly. "We'll keep in touch. But that's all I can tell you for now."

We left the police barracks. On the outside, I probably still seemed under control, tight-lipped perhaps, but calm. On the inside, anger and disbelief were coursing through my veins.

It began to dawn on me as I walked beside my father to our car that my identification of Jessup Rawlings—my no-doubt-whatsoever identification— might not be sufficient to get him arrested. The police might suspect that he might have done it, if they believed my story, and I knew that he did it. But, I was beginning to think that might not be good enough, definitive enough. I asked myself if Jessup Rawlings might be able to get away with this whole thing. And I had to answer yes.

It wasn't fair, I told myself. This might be how the world worked, how justice worked, but I did not like it, not one little bit. And I told myself one thing: I was not going to accept it without doing something.

CHAPTER 36
AUGUST 26, 1964

"I want to go see Jackie," I announced to my mother. "I need to go see him today."

My Dad had dropped me back at the house after our meeting with Detective Martino, and then gone on to work. My mom was busy in the kitchen making grilled cheese sandwiches for the little kids and Tom.

"You could call . . . " my mother began to say, but I rudely cut her off.

"I don't want to call," I said loudly. "We called Sunday and they said: 'No change.' We called Monday when they transferred him to Holy Family Hospital. We called yesterday morning—still no change. Still in a coma. I'm tired of people telling me about Jackie—I want to see him for myself."

My mom looked at me and I knew I'd hurt her feelings by yelling at her. But I just didn't care. All I wanted was to go see Jackie and I did not want to have to argue or plead my case or explain how I was going to do it—I just wanted to go.

I think my mom understood my agitated state of mind. She let me get away with my bad behavior without reprimand. "Maybe David could take you when he gets home from work," she suggested gently. "If he's not too tired."

"I'll take the bus," I said. "If you can take me over to Roebuck, I can catch the bus right up on First Avenue North. I know where to transfer. It'll take a while, but then I won't have to bother anyone."

I actually did not know where to transfer, but I didn't want to give my mother any reason to consider keeping me from going. Holy Family Hospital—which I had heard called the "nigger hospital" by some, because it was one of the few hospitals where colored doctors and nurses were allowed to practice—was all the way across town in Ensley, farther even than Legion Field, and maybe not so easy to get to by bus. But I didn't care—I was ready to walk all the way if I had to.

Mom thought for a moment. I was afraid she was going to say no. But then she simply nodded and said, "Okay, I'll take you right after lunch. Maybe I'll take the kids to East Lake Park for a couple of hours. They can run around and feed the ducks. You can catch the bus right across from St. Barnabas."

I was grateful that I did not have to argue. "Is Marti around?" I asked. "She might want to go too."

"Babysitting," Mom answered. "She'll be gone all day, until dinner."

"Okay, I'll go alone. Maybe Jackie will be awake today. It's been three days."

"I hope so, Mickey," Mom said. She looked up at me. "But at least we all know that Jackie's not in pain while his body is healing. That's what the doctor said."

"I know, I know," I said. "But still—it would be nice to see him open his eyes and know that he's safe in a hospital and people are there and taking care of him."

"Go get ready," Mom said. "We can leave as soon as I finish giving the kids their lunch. Do you want me to make a grilled cheese for you?"

"Not hungry," I said. "I'll eat a big dinner."

I went upstairs, pulled on a clean t-shirt, brushed my teeth, combed my hair. I did everything automatically, scarcely conscious of my actions. My mind raced from place to place, recalling the events of the past several days. I revisited the fear I felt standing in the woods on the edge of that clearing, and the pain of my conversation with Marti, and my exhaustion—how much of it was simply overwhelming pain and depression?—all day long on Sunday and Monday. I recalled my conversation that morning with Detective Martino—and my disbelief as I considered the possibility that Rawlings might not have to pay, might never even have to admit that he did what he did. I remembered walking across the street yesterday to see Yvonne, trying to be excited by our reunion, but just feeling flat and dull. I thought about sitting on her couch, and the shock of the realization that it was Jessup Rawlings, my girlfriend's father, who had taken a baseball bat to my good friend's body and beaten him so ferociously. I experienced once more my initial revulsion and outrage and nausea—and then the calm, cold anger that possessed me later. I did not think about any of these things logically, or even chronologically—my mind skipped from thought to thought without direction or progression. All I knew was the power of my feelings and the fact that I hated Jessup Rawlings as intensely as any human was capable of. "You will not get away with this," I kept repeating to myself. "I will not let you get away with this." I did not know what that meant, but it made me feel better to say it to myself.

Mom's voice interrupted the chaos in my head. "We're ready, Mickey. Let's go."

* * * * *

I finally got to Jackie's hospital about 2:30 p.m., after two bus rides and several blocks of walking in the Alabama heat and humidity. My shirt was soaked and sticking uncomfortably to my back by the time I arrived. I thought I'd be chilled by the air conditioning when I went through the hospital doors, but it either wasn't working or wasn't working very well.

Holy Family Hospital was a lot smaller than UAB, smaller even than East End Memorial. It was older. But here, at least, Jackie would be cared for by colored doctors and nurses. I was not in a mood to trust the white medical establishment, even though that thought might have been unfair. But the trusting side of my nature had been rattled of late, especially after my session with Detective Martino that morning. I was glad Jackie was here at this hospital. It felt safe to me.

I did not see any other white people in the lobby. But the colored lady at the front desk did not seem to take much notice of my appearance. She barely looked up when I approached her.

"I'd like to see Jackie Thomas, please," I said. "He's a patient here. I'm his best friend."

Of course, Jackie and I had never exactly declared each other best friends—that kind of statement is what girls did. However, I thought it might be helpful in getting to see him. It was kind of obvious that I was not a family member, and I was concerned that my "relationship to patient" could be a condition of admittance.

"Thomas, Thomas . . ." the woman said to herself as she looked on a typed list. "Just moved him out of intensive care. You might be able to see him." She gave me a room number, pointed vaguely to her left, and told me to follow the signs.

I went in the direction she pointed. After a little bit of wandering, and asking once for directions, I found the room. The door was open. I began to walk in and almost bumped into a young doctor coming out.

"Is this Jackie Thomas's room?" I asked.

The doctor looked down at a chart he was carrying, then looked up at me and said, "Yes. Who are you?"

Perhaps he did not mean in that way, but I felt challenged by the doctor's tone of voice. "Mickey McQuade," I said. "I'm his best friend. I'm the one who found him," I paused, then continued, ". . . that night."

The doctor's demeanor changed; his voice became kinder. "Oh, I'm sorry," he said. He looked at me, eye to eye, then pursed his lips slightly. "I'm sure you know that your friend was beaten pretty badly. It's good you are coming by to see him."

I mistakenly thought that the doctor's comment meant that Jackie had regained consciousness. "Oh, is he awake? That's great." I started to move past the doctor into the room.

"I'm sorry, no," the doctor said quickly. "Our patient—your friend—is still in a coma. We have him connected to a ventilator to help him breathe more easily, and we're feeding him intravenously. The nurses check his vital signs frequently and they move him to help avoid bedsores. But he still has not shown any signs of consciousness. We're waiting, and hoping, but nothing so far."

The disappointment must have shown on my face because the doctor spoke quickly to provide a little bit of encouragement. "You know," he said, "we're not really sure if patients in a coma are aware of anything, but I like to think they can hear what is being said, they just can't respond. Talking to your friend, letting him know that you came by to see him—those things could be very important in his healing process. So, please, go in, visit with him a while."

I nodded to the doctor to show I understood and went to sit down at Jackie's side. Seeing him lying there, with a tube through his nose, and noises coming from the ventilator, was a scary sight. His face was completely swathed in bandages. But the dressings looked clean and fresh. It made me feel like he was getting the right kind of medical care and attention.

"Hey, Jackie," I said in a low voice, pulling up a chair to sit close by the bedside. "How did you ever get yourself into a situation like this?"

I was trying to be light, and funny, but I felt bad as soon as I said it.

"Sorry, Jackie, just kidding," I said. "You're not the one that put you here—no way."

It was not Jackie's fault, nor was it my sister's fault, that he was lying here in this condition. It was Jessup Rawlings' fault—he was the guilty party. And whether Jackie could hear me or not, somehow, I felt the need to tell him what I now knew.

"Listen, Jackie," I said. "I don't know how they grabbed you—or how they got you out into the woods. I'm sure you fought them as hard as you could. But you need to know—they are not going to get away with what they did to you."

My voice got a little louder. "I know who did it." I wanted him to hear my words, wanted them to force their way through the barriers of his unconsciousness. "It was Jessup Rawlings. He did it. Him and some other guy, some other low-life coward."

I didn't speak the words, I spat them out of my mouth. It was like the name Jessup Rawlings and everything I knew about him was a vile-tasting poison that I could not expel quickly enough or forcefully enough.

"He did it, Jackie. He was the guy with the bat that kept hitting you. But he made one big mistake. Cause now I know it was him. And I told Detective Martino. And they need to do some legal police stuff, but they are gonna get him. He won't get away with this."

I wished in my heart that I believed my own words as much as I wanted Jackie to hear them and believe them. My meeting with Detective Martino a few hours ago was still bothering me. But I shook off the doubt, the uncertainty that I felt inside. I was not about to let Jackie hear it in my voice. So I reached forward, and grabbed his wrist, and held it tight, and spoke clearly and directly and with conviction. "Jessup Rawlings, Jackie. He's the guy. He's the guy and they're going to get him. I swear it."

"Mickey, what are y'all saying, chile?" said a voice behind me. "What is this talk—what are you telling my sweet Jackie?"

I whirled around in my seat, almost jumped out of my skin. I hadn't heard Nammy come into the room. I had no idea how long she'd been standing there.

"N-N-Nammy," I stammered, "what are you doing here? I didn't hear you. You surprised me. Have you been here very long?"

"I jest walked in a minute ago, Mickey. I'm sorry to interrupt you—I jest liked seeing you there, talking to Jackie. But what's all this you are telling him?"

"Oh," I said, "Nothing too much, Nammy. I was just filling him in on things."

I did not know what Nammy heard, but I wanted to change the subject. I didn't want to tell Nammy about Jessup Rawlings and what I knew. I thought it would hurt her too much—or get her very, very angry. And I didn't feel like my telling her would do any good. I looked back at my friend lying in the bed. "I just wish he'd wake up, Nammy. I want to see him open his eyes."

"Lawd, yes," said Nammy. "I'm praying every day that he opens up those big ol' brown eyes of his, and looks up at me, and says 'Hey there, Nammy, I'm hungry.' That's what I'm hoping for." Then she smiled at me. "Are you hungry, Mickey?"

I was thankful that she'd moved on from asking me questions about what I was saying to Jackie.

"I brought along some of my famous oatmeal cookies. Made 'em myself. Not store bought. Just baked them this morning. Here," she said, rummaging around in the big purple bag that she always carried with her everywhere, "have yourself a cookie, Mickey."

"It's okay, Nammy. I'm not so hungry at the moment." I knew my words would not matter to her.

"Y'all gotta try at least one," Nammy said. "Here, take it."

"How 'bout we just sit here a while, Nammy?" I said, as I accepted the cookie she offered me. "The doctor told me that Jackie might know we're here. We don't have to talk about him or anything—he can just listen in on our conversation."

"Why, that's sounds nice and fine, Mickey," said Nammy. "We'll just sit and have a little visit—just the three of us."

And that's what we did. We didn't talk much, Nammy and me. Just sat together, watching Jackie lying there, waiting and hoping and praying that he'd open up his eyes. But he didn't.

I left after about an hour. I gave Jackie's arm a little squeeze, and gave Nammy a big hug, and thanked her for the cookie. She gave me another one to eat on the way home.

I looked back as I was leaving the room and saw Nammy holding Jackie's hand. And I wished at that moment that somehow, he'd know she was there, and be able to give her hand a little squeeze. So, I hesitated, waiting for God to intervene and make that little miracle happen. But He didn't.

* * * * *

After dinner that evening, my father said he wanted to talk with me a minute. I said sure, cautiously, because every time anyone wanted to talk to me these days, it seemed like bad news followed. We went outside, stood looking at the woods. Dad lit a cigarette and took a couple of puffs before he said anything.

"We got a call from Detective Martino while you were visiting Jackie," he finally began.

"Good," I said immediately, as if by pretending to expect positive news,

I could make it happen.

"He wanted to let me know—and he asked me to tell you—that the District Attorney will not be bringing charges against Jessup Rawlings, at least not right now."

"What?! That's crazy! He did it!! He hurt Jackie!"

"I'm sorry, Mickey. And Detective Martino told me to assure you that this does not mean the investigation stops. But they simply do not have enough to arrest Rawlings yet. All they've got is your story. It's just not enough."

"It's not a story, Dad," I pleaded. "People make up stories. I'm not making this up. I heard him say those words. I recognized his voice. It's not a story—it's—it's an identification!"

"I know," my father replied. "But it's just not enough to arrest a man. Especially . . . "

"Don't say it!" I shouted. "Don't tell me that it doesn't count because I didn't realize it til I heard Rawlings on the phone. That's not fair! The truth is still the truth no matter when somebody recognizes it. This isn't fair! Not to me—and not to Jackie!"

My father didn't smack me for being disrespectful and yelling, though he certainly had done so for less in the past. He didn't yell back at me and drown me out. He didn't even speak. He just looked at me with big, sad eyes and held out his arms. And I fell into them, crying, sobbing like a baby, sobbing like Marti. He hugged me, held me tight. And though I did not look up to confirm it, I'm pretty sure he was crying too.

CHAPTER 37
AUGUST 27, 1964

Jackie died on Thursday, sometime in the early hours of the morning, five days after he was beaten in the woods. We learned later that the hospital had called Nammy's brother, because that was the only way they could reach Nammy. Nammy's brother called Jackie's mother in Tupelo. She'd been up to sit with Jackie for three days, and had just left for Tupelo on Wednesday to make arrangements for moving back to Birmingham for an extended period, and nursing Jackie back to health.

I wasn't there so I don't know how Nammy took the bad news. But I was grateful that she asked her brother to call the McQuades on Lynn Acres Drive and let us know that Jackie had passed away.

Marti and I were both upstairs in our rooms. Mom called up to us to come downstairs.

The three of us sat down on our fold-up card table chairs in the family room. Marti and I looked at Mom. We knew that something bad was coming from the tightness of her face.

"I just got a call from Jackie's great uncle," she said. "He told me that Jackie died early this morning." She hesitated, but only for a moment. "The family wanted us all to know—but I thought I should tell the two of you first." She looked at us—and we stared back at her. "And I am so, so sorry," she said, "sorry beyond words. I know Jackie was a very special friend to both of you."

Neither of us said anything. My mother tried to fill the silence with what little she knew. "They said he died peacefully," she said. "One of the nurses went to check on him—and he had just slipped away. I don't know more than that—Jackie's great uncle didn't say too much."

Each one of us handles bad news differently, they say, but in this case, from all outward appearances, Marti and I were reacting to it exactly the same. Marti looked at Mom, and then out the window. I looked at Mom, then Marti, then down at my feet. Neither of us spoke.

"Do you want to talk about this at all?" Mom asked. "Right now, I mean. Do you want to talk?"

I just shook my head, no. Marti answered with a simple "I don't think so." We all sat in silence for another minute or so, then Marti stood up. I stood up at that point as well, and so did Mom.

Marti opened her arms and gave Mom a hug. It looked and felt like some kind of role reversal, as if Marti were trying to comfort and console our mother. Then Marti turned to me. She looked composed as she stood in front of me. No one could have detected anything otherwise from a distance. But her eyes were watery. Tears formed, silently, and slipped down her cheek. She blinked. Then she wrapped her arms around me and gave me a long, intense embrace. I thought she might say something to me, but she didn't. I could not think of anything to say to her, either.

Then she released me, turned to Mom and said, "I think I'll go to my room for a bit."

Mom just nodded, looking back and forth from Marti to me to Marti.

Once Marti left the room, my mother asked me if I was okay. I told her no. I told her I was sad. And I told her I was angry. And, at that moment, I could not say which feeling was stronger than the other.

I trudged slowly upstairs, with a tremendous heaviness in my legs, like I was dragging weights behind me. I wondered if I should go to Marti's room to see how she was. But the door was closed, and I could hear her crying softly to herself, and I decided I needed to let her be for a while.

I walked past her door and through Ricky and Bobby's room toward the bathroom. I knocked on the closed door and received Tom's automatic response: "Just got in here."

I slipped into my parents' room and sat on the edge of their bed to wait, surveying the room, observing its contents critically, as if it were particularly important that I remember the condition and placement of every item in it. I noted lotion and perfume bottles on my mother's dresser and wondered how long it had been since they were dusted, or even touched. I noticed clothes draped over the back of a folding chair, and a plastic wicker basket of folded laundry that probably needed to go into Dad's drawers but hadn't quite made it there yet. I saw one stack of books and one stack of magazines, both on Dad's side of the room, sitting on the floor, neatly, order amidst chaos. I saw the half-open sliding door of their closet, glimpsed dresses and shirts and a couple of Dad's suits, all on hangers, but oddly arranged, not grouped as one might expect. I saw multiple boxes of shoes—or at least shoe boxes, I had no idea what they contained—on the lower shelf above the hanging garments. And on the upper shelf, partially visible underneath what seemed to be a folded tablecloth for a table we did not own, I saw the edge of the locked, brushed metal case that contained my father's rifle.

I'm not sure exactly how long I sat there. I never heard Tom come out of the bathroom.

Moments and events from the past year flashed across my mind like scenes from a newsreel, each image or memory appearing then disappearing to be replaced by another. I recalled so many times I'd spent with Jackie, just the two of us, playing ball, talking about school, eating Nammy's cookies on his porch. For some reason, I thought about our vacation at the Jersey Shore, which Jackie wasn't even a part of, other than what I now guessed were postcards from Marti, telling him what we were doing throughout the week. I thought about all the good things and fun things that I'd enjoyed over the past year of my life, never knowing, never suspecting, that the stuff of good memories—and the way they made you feel—could be ripped away from you in an instant.

Of all the Jackie memories that tumbled through my brain like clothes in the dryer, the clearest, the most vivid, was from Christmas Day, with Carrie Ann sitting happily on Jackie's lap. How would we tell my baby sister that her friend would not be coming over again next Christmas? Would she think about him, remember him, when we set up the Nativity scene, and one of us placed the figurine of Balthazar next to the donkey?

I continued to sit quietly, thinking about Susan from our vacation, about Yvonne. I thought about Jessup Rawlings. Cringing physically as if the blow were delivered to me, I recalled the sickening sight and sound of a baseball bat cracking against Jackie's body, and the hate and the rage that poured from Jessup Rawlings' mouth that night.

For what, Mr. Rawlings? For what?! Because a black kid you didn't know kissed a white girl you hardly knew who just happened to live across the street? That was what this was all about? That was your reason?

I sat there, staring at nothing, remembering, wallowing in hate and rage and a desire for revenge. And, knowing it was morally wrong, knowing it was unimaginable, I could not help but think about the contents of the hard metal case in the top of the closet.

CHAPTER 38
AUGUST 29, 1964

Some people say that, under conditions of extreme stress, ordinary human beings are capable of abnormal feats of strength. Mothers have been known to lift cars by their rear bumpers in order to save a child. If so, perhaps there is a mental strength phenomenon that operates in a similar fashion. It's my only explanation for whatever it was that propelled me to challenge Jessup Rawlings in person, face-to-ugly face, two days after Jackie died.

My plan—if you could call it that—was to confront the man when he was alone. For a time, I considered taking my father's rifle with me, unloaded. I thought I could use it as a threat, use it to force a confession. I would compel Jessup Rawlings to describe details of that night that I would then furnish to the police.

As much as the notion appealed to me, however, there was still some remnant of common sense operating in my brain, enough to make me realize a bunch of things that were wrong with that idea. Including the very real possibility that Jessup Rawlings might decide to defend himself with a gun of his own. And his would be loaded.

So, Dad's rifle stayed in its case. Instead, I decided to confront Jessup Rawlings with something more powerful than a gun: the truth of what I'd seen and heard.

I did not anticipate any melodramatic reaction from him, could not honestly expect a confession of his crimes in the face of a 16-year-old accuser. But maybe, with no one around to see his response, I might get the satisfaction of seeing him drop his facade of denial just a little bit. I wanted him to understand that it did not matter what the police currently thought, or what the newspapers reported, or what the world believed. I knew.

In my exhausted and overtaxed brain, I was convinced that I was taking a stand for Jackie. Perhaps our legal system would never hold Rawlings accountable for his actions, but I would.

My opportunity came midday on Saturday. Mom was in the kitchen preparing lunch for the little kids. I glanced across the street and noticed that the Rawlings station wagon was gone but saw Mr. Rawlings moving around inside his garage. Perhaps Mrs. Rawlings was out with the kids. Just seeing him there, by himself, gave me a horribly sick feeling in my stomach; I was not positive that I could actually carry out the plan I had in mind.

Inside our house, Tom asked me if I wanted to play some wiffle ball in the back yard. He suggested that maybe it would take my mind off things—and I appreciated the gesture. But I said no, that I was busy, and he looked at me funny but didn't say anything.

I kept an eye on Rawlings from our living room window, the living room that we hardly ever used. I was talking to myself, rehearsing what I wanted to say, trying to build up the nerve that I needed to walk out our door, head across the street, and tackle this thing that I told myself I had to do.

I'd told no one of my intentions—not even Marti, who would probably have understood best, but who would have definitely tried to talk me out of it, and maybe told Mom or Dad to keep me from doing it.

At one point, after I'd gone to the bathroom for the third time and come back to the window, I could no longer detect any movement in the garage.

My heart sank. Perhaps Rawlings had decided to go inside. I felt sure that I'd missed my chance. I knew that I didn't have the guts to confront Rawlings after knocking on his front door, then looking up at him from his undersized porch landing.

Luckily, none of that was necessary. Just as I was ready to give up on what was beginning to feel like a harebrained scheme, I saw Rawlings cross from one side of his garage to the other. It felt like a now or never moment.

Something propelled me. I walked out of our house and headed across the street without looking back. I stepped into the garage. Rawlings was still there.

His back was turned as I approached him. "Mr. Rawlings?" I began, in what I thought was a normal voice, hardly shaky at all.

Rawlings either did not hear me, or simply ignored me. He never turned around.

"Mr. Rawlings," I said, much louder, "I know what you did."

At that he spun around, stared at me with narrowed eyes, suspicion and malice showing in every feature of his face, from the furrows of his forehead to the thin, cruel line of his lip.

"What did you say, boy?" he asked, though it wasn't really a question because I was pretty sure he'd heard me. "What are you doing in my garage and what did you just say to me?" That was a question.

I took a step back, frightened at the nakedly hostile tone, but determined to give voice to the words that had been playing in my head for the last couple of days, ever since I'd learned that Jackie had died.

"You're a murderer, Mr. Rawlings." There, I'd said it. I was shaking—but I'd said it.

Perhaps no one else would have noticed, but I think I saw him flinch at those words, just a little. His slight reaction gave me the strength to keep going.

"You're a murderer," I repeated, startled by how calm I had suddenly become, once I'd gotten the initial accusation out of my mouth. "You tied my friend Jackie to a tree, and you smashed him with a baseball bat, and you killed him. And I know you did it, and the police know you did it, cause I told 'em. And sooner or later you are going to jail."

Relief flooded over me—in waves. I actually felt lighter having stared Jackie's killer in the eye and said to him exactly what needed to be said, no hesitancy, no equivocation. Words that no other person on earth would or could say.

I had no idea what was occurring in Rawlings' brain, but, though rage and hostility seemed to dominate his physical being, he never stopped me from speaking.

Silence hung in the air between us. Seconds passed. No longer able to maintain my calm, I felt my breathing quicken as fear of his reaction grew. And, as the silence extended, I felt like I needed to say something more, something to punctuate my accusation.

"Mr. Rawlings," I began.

"ENOUGH!!!" The word exploded from him like a volcanic eruption, hurtling toward my body. I instinctively took two steps back. I wanted to turn and run. Something held me in place.

And then he spoke, in a quiet voice that ironically forced me to lean slightly forward in order to distinguish the words that hissed from his lips.

"You got some nerve, boy. You come in here, onto my property, into my home, and you throw wild talk and accusations at me! Now you listen to me, and you listen real good. First thing y'all got to get into that stupid head of yours is that I don't know nothing—nothing—bout what happened out there in them woods. Do you hear me? Do you hear me, boy?"

I wanted to blunt the force of his denial, so I spoke up. "That's not true, Mr. Rawl—"

"Shut up!" he yelled, shocking me into silence.

"I done told the police," he continued, dropping back to his whispery hiss. "I done told 'em that I didn't know nothing 'bout nothing that might have gone on out there that night. Oh, yeah, the police told me all about your lies, they told me everything you said, you lying piece of horseshit. But all I know 'bout that night is what I read in the papers. Cause I was out playing gin rummy with my buddy that night. And he done confirmed that to the police. Now what do you think, boy—do you think that I'm just going to stand here and listen to your nigger-loving lies said right to my face and then say, 'Why, thank you very much for dropping by!' Is that what you're thinking? You need to understand something, boy! You need to understand that I don't care one bit that that nigger who got himself kilt was your friend, not one bit."

As I listened, absorbing every word, I was stunned by the loathing and the hostility in Rawlings' voice. It was beyond my ability to comprehend.

"Maybe," he continued, "maybe the police will catch whoever did this, and maybe they won't. I don't give a good goddamn. All I know is that I had nothing to do with it, don't know nothing about it. What I do know is there's one less nigger in the world to worry about . . ." Maybe Rawlings intended a sarcastic laugh. But it came out more like the snort of a pig in the mud. I think he was waiting for a reaction from me that I did not give him the satisfaction of seeing. "Do you hear me straight, boy?"

I stared back at him, determined not to flinch in the face of his verbal onslaught.

"You better have heard me," he said. "Cause now I'm going to give you about five seconds to get your nigger-loving ass out of my garage and off my property. Or else I might need to defend myself against a trespasser. And one more thing: I don't want to ever see you again. I don't want you coming round, I don't want you setting foot on my property, I don't want you talking to my daughter, I don't want you . . ."

I'd finally heard enough. I'm not sure what happened or when, but I wasn't frightened by Rawlings anymore. I was sickened by his venom, disgusted by his arrogance, and I wanted to hurt him, wanted to slam my fist into his sneering, hateful face. But I was not afraid.

So, with a dismissive shake of my head, I turned my back on Jessup Rawlings—and turned directly into the line of sight of Yvonne Rawlings, standing less than ten feet away from me at the edge of the garage. She was staring at the two of us, with a frightened and uncomprehending look spread across her features. She must have just stepped around the corner of the garage the moment I was turning away from her father. Rawlings would have seen her otherwise.

"Mickey! DADDY! Why are y'all fighting? What are you saying? What's going on?"

I did not know how much she heard. I didn't care. At that instant, filled to my emotional brim with extraordinary hatred for Jessup Rawlings, I had no room for any feelings about anything else.

She ran past me, and I turned back to see her throw her arms around her father. Jessup Rawlings embraced his daughter gently, bent his head toward hers to whisper something, pulled her to him in a protective fatherly hug.

Then I turned away. I did not look back, even though some little part of me wanted to be the person who was holding Yvonne, telling her that everything was going to be all right, even though I knew that it wouldn't, that it would never be all right again.

I listened, shoulders hunched, wondering if more threats would be hurled at my back. Nothing came. I heard Yvonne sobbing, that was all. I walked away, trying to maintain the appearance of steadiness, walked across the street and into our house. I went straight to the downstairs bathroom and immediately threw up.

* * * * *

When I left Rawlings garage, I was no longer afraid of him. But each hour that I spent in my home following our confrontation increased my fears about what I'd just done. I was scared about what would happen if my parents found out, if Rawlings called and told them about the whole incident.

Or maybe Detective Martino would somehow learn about this—and I would be accused of interfering in a police investigation.

What had Rawlings said to Yvonne after I left? Would he have spoken to his wife about the incident? And then would Mrs. Rawlings call my mother and tell her—woman to woman—to get her son under control? What would Mom do? What would Dad do after Mom told him?

I jumped every time I heard the phone ring.

By the time evening rolled around, with no phone calls and no other repercussions from my encounter with Rawlings, I did not know what to think. Tom, my parents, the whole family knew that something was going on with me—they just did not know what. Marti asked me flat-out what was going on—I gave her some vague answer that she knew was a lie. Then she asked me to meet her on the steps—but I told her I was tired and just went to bed early. I wasn't ready to talk to anybody.

Sunday passed and Monday morning arrived and things were not much better. I was still worried that we'd get a call from Detective Martino but, within the family, people seemed to have moved on a little bit from worrying about me. We all seemed pre-occupied with our own thoughts, especially since Jackie's funeral was scheduled for the next day. My father went to work early and told my mother that he'd probably work late so that he could take time off for the services on Tuesday.

Marti and I promised to keep an eye on the little kids all morning so that Mom could do some food shopping. But neither of us talked to each other much. We played with the kids in the back yard, brought them in about noon for peanut butter and jelly sandwiches, then took them back outside and squirted them down with the hose to beat the oppressive late August heat.

When Mom came home, she herded the little kids inside the house for quiet time. She never liked them playing outside when the heat and humidity were in full force. That gave Marti and me some time for ourselves. Marti wandered off somewhere and I sat alone in the family room, doing nothing. I felt flat, emotionless. I also felt guilty that I was not mourning Jackie properly, but I did not know what else I should have been doing.

The heat was probably getting to me, because I was half-dozing when I heard a knock on the family room door. I answered it groggily, but was instantly jolted to attention when I saw that it was Yvonne Rawlings standing there. It was clear that she'd been crying. A lot. She was looking away from me, down the street, but I could see her eyes. They were missing the soft violet luster that I'd come to know—instead, they were red and bloodshot and angry-looking. The rest of her was angry as well.

"My mom would k-kill me if she kn-knew I was here," she began, in a trembling voice, but one that that allowed no interruption, not even to invite her inside. She looked down as she spoke, staring at her hands and a small brown sack that she was holding. She did not want to look me in the eye, or look in my direction at all.

"I talked to my father, Mickey—and he told me what you did, told me the horrible things you said to him. Lies! Lies! How could you say these awful, awful things?"

I could not imagine what Jessup Rawlings said to his daughter, but whatever it was, it was clear that she believed him, totally, unquestionably. What teenage daughter would not believe what her father told her?

"I'm sorry," I said to her, and meant it, sorry that she had to suffer for what her father had done.

"Sorry for what?!" she yelled, sobbing, and looking up at me. "I thought you were nice, I thought you were sweet, but you're just . . . you're just . . . horrible!"

I wanted to explain. I wanted to tell her my side of the story. I wanted to tell her the truth about her father. I wanted her to know that this thing, this tragedy, was not her fault, had nothing at all to do with her, or the person that she was.

"Yvonne, listen," I began, not having any idea what I would say next, but trying to establish some kind of communication, recall some kind of connection.

But she wouldn't let me. Maybe because she now hated me too much. Maybe because—though there was no sign of this—she did not want to hear, or was afraid to hear, what I might say about her father.

"No, Mickey, don't even try! Some things you can't explain, some things you can't undo." She sounded even more frenzied, even more agitated. She took a step back away from me as I stood there in the doorway. "I hate you, Mickey McQuade! You've just ruined everything! And I never, ever, ever want to speak to you again."

With that, she reached into the sack she held, and withdrew the snow globe that I'd given her at Christmas. "I don't want your stupid snow globe anymore. This is what I think of you!"

And with that, Yvonne threw it hard to the concrete. I guess she expected it to shatter like glass, but it didn't. It hit the concrete, and bounced, landing up against the wall of our house. The impact cracked the plastic case, and snow globe liquid began to seep out, making a tiny blue puddle on the cement.

In spite of the fact that the snow globe's resilience had robbed her of a grander gesture, Yvonne must have felt that she'd made her statement. Without another word, she turned and walked back across the street to her house, the reverse of my walk home yesterday.

We never spoke to one another again.

CHAPTER 39
AUGUST 31, 1964

Monday night, Marti and I found our way to the stairs to talk. It was our first try at a real conversation since the one we'd had in the back yard the afternoon after Jackie was attacked. We hadn't been avoiding each other, exactly. More like just missing each other, but kind of on purpose.

Thinking about it later, I believe we were subconsciously distancing ourselves from each other as a way to make things hurt less.

The assault on Jackie—all by itself—bludgeoned me as well as him. I'd never experienced pain like I did when I first saw him tied up to that tree.

Then he died, alone in a hospital bed—with neither Marti nor myself ever having had a last chance to hear his voice or feel the warmth of his smile—and that was like a second beating, only much worse, more intense.

On top of that, we were subjected to the relentless daily incongruity of knowing that the man who killed Jackie was living in his pleasant, comfortable house, right across the street, seemingly undisturbed and unaffected by what he had done. I'd told the police and they did nothing.

But, for me, the final straw, the most unbearable pain, partly because it was piled on top of all the others, was seeing the sister that I loved so much— my twin—torn apart, ripped to pieces emotionally.

If Marti was feeling even a fraction of what I was living, it was no wonder that we'd been maintaining a healthy distance from each other. Now, it seemed, we needed to come together.

"I still can't quite believe it," she said, as we both settled our heads against the wall behind us, with our feet sticking out across the steps. "I simply cannot believe that Jackie is dead—and that I'll be putting on a dress and going to his funeral tomorrow. It just makes no sense, not one bit of sense to me."

"And you know what the worst thing is, Mickey?" she turned toward me, and I could see her face, backlit by the glow of the naked light bulb at the top of the stairs, which gave her a beatific appearance. "The worst thing is, as terrible as I feel, as much as I'm still sobbing inside, I can't cry anymore. It's like I don't have any tears left for Jackie. I won't have any tears left for his funeral. And I hate that—I hate it so much."

She closed her eyes, hung her head, and rubbed her temples with forefinger and thumb, as if she were trying to ease the throbbing of a migraine headache.

I tried to think of something to say in response, but I couldn't. It wasn't even a case of considering whether I should say this or wondering if I should say that. I literally had nothing to offer. I felt empty of words, and exhausted by the sadness—as huge as the anger and the hate—that had taken up residence in my own psyche since that night in the woods more than a week ago.

At sixteen, I had never experienced the death of anyone remotely close to me, not even a favorite dog or cat. Our one previous family pet, a motley cocker spaniel named Eclipse, ran away one day, and he had no dog collar, so he just disappeared. But I'd always imagined him being found by some elderly, childless couple and living out his days peacefully, chasing butterflies and ground squirrels on a peanut farm in South Alabama. The finality of death was, up until now, abstract. Celebrities died. Grandparents I did not know died. JFK was shot and killed. But everyone that I'd ever been close to in my entire life was still living. Except for Jackie.

Marti and I sat quietly for a while before either of us spoke again.

It wasn't awkward; in fact, it was comforting for me, just knowing she was there. After all, the first nine months of our existence was spent in close proximity with nary a word exchanged. We'd spent a lot of time together without talking. Plus, I felt confident that, if anything popped into our brains that was worth giving voice to, we would.

After an extended period of silence, I decided to tell her about my confrontation with Jessup Rawlings in his garage. Up until then, the only other person aware of the incident was Yvonne, unless Rawlings had told his wife, or his Klan buddy, or the police. The latter no longer seemed likely because I was sure that I would have received a phone call if he had.

"This is what's killing me," she said, after hearing the full story and giving me her solemn promise that she would not tell Mom or Dad. "I understand our legal system—innocent until proven guilty, blah, blah, blah— but I just cannot believe that we are living across the street from someone that you know—absolutely know—killed your best friend, and my first real boyfriend, and he just goes on about his stupid life, puttering around in his stupid garage, and Jackie will be buried in the ground tomorrow, and the rest of the world just ignores it and says, 'Well, sorry, but, you know, that is how things are done.'"

I smiled thanks at her for her support.

"I'm glad you did it, Mickey," she said. "I'm glad you went over there, and looked him in the eye, and told him that you knew right to his face." She paused for a moment, thinking, the way she often did. "Maybe," she said, "maybe that's important."

"Why important?" I asked. It didn't seem all that important as I looked back on things. It actually made me feel kind of foolish, like a cartoon boxing match I saw once between a real big guy and a tiny little guy, and the big guy holds the little guy at bay by extending his arm and putting his hand on the little guy's forehead, while the little guy just keeps swinging, rights and lefts and rights, but never connects with anything but air.

"It's important," said Marti slowly, turning her head back and forth the way she always did when she was working out a problem or trying to figure out how to say something. "The thing is, we're just kids. We're sixteen years old. We certainly can't stop evil from happening, and maybe we don't have the power to bring evil to justice on our own. But we can expose evil. We can confront it. We can shine a light on it so that it does not have any place to hide."

She turned toward me. "That's what you did, Mickey. You shone a light right in evil's ugly, monstrous face!"

"Maybe I'm watching too much TV," I answered, "but I'm kind of hoping Rawlings will get nervous, make some kind of mistake, blow his alibi, something."

Marti nodded. She liked that idea.

We sat silent for another long while, then she turned toward me. "Have you thought about this, Mickey? Have you wondered how are we going to live with ourselves if they never find any more evidence, if they never arrest that . . . that monster? He's . . . he's," Marti searched for a word, "he's mocking Jackie, laughing at him, every day he's not in jail, he's laughing!"

"I don't know," I answered. "I think about that possibility—the chance that Rawlings may never be held accountable, never brought to justice— every day and night. And it's like a gnawing pain in my stomach—one that just won't go away."

I turned to Marti and put my hand on her wrist. "But thanks for believing in me. I'm not sure if any other people do, even Mom and Dad. I think they want to believe me—and they are supporting me verbally—but do they really believe, or do they think that maybe it's something my mind made up, just because I wanted somebody to blame?"

"It's easy to be skeptical," Marti said, "but I'm not. I'm just not. I understand how this could happen, how just the way Rawlings said something triggered recognition in your brain. The problem is that I'm not sure anybody else believes you like I do. Certainly not the District Attorney."

Marti's face turned thoughtful, considering. "You know, maybe Detective Martino does. Maybe he believes. After all, he talked directly to Rawlings, and he told Dad that the investigation is continuing, so maybe something that Rawlings said or did made Martino think 'Hey— this McQuade kid could be right.'"

"Maybe, but they need more," I said. "I wish I'd seen him—then there'd be no question. Or even if I'd recognized his voice right away—it would be a whole different story. But now, as long as his KKK buddy is willing to lie for him, and if the police can't come up with any other evidence, then Rawlings will get clean away with it."

That comment was enough to keep us both quiet for several more minutes. I do not know what Marti was thinking during that time, but my mind leaped to imagining different scenarios that could cause Rawlings' death. A horrible car accident. An unexpected massive heart attack. A meteor from outer space falling on his head. I wanted him dead, and I wanted him gone. Since the legal system might not do it, I wanted God or Fate to mete out justice.

Marti broke the silence and my visions of Rawlings' dying. "How does all this make you feel about Yvonne?" she asked. "That's got to be a whole separate set of weird feelings."

I sighed. I didn't really feel like going into it, but I felt like I had to. Mostly because I was tired of holding things in. I gave her the details—and answered all her immediate follow-up questions—about Yvonne's "visit" on Sunday.

"She's blind, totally blind," Marti commented, once she'd gotten the full story. "But I guess I can't really blame her. It's her dad. If someone tells you that your dad's a murderer, your natural first instinct is to deny the accusation, defend him. You know that would be what we'd do if anyone ever said anything about our dad."

"I know," I said. "And even if she believed me, or somehow knew the truth, where would that leave me? You can't really have the daughter of someone who murdered your best friend as your girlfriend, now can you?"

Something struck me when those words came out of my mouth. I noticed that I did not have quite the same internal reaction to my use of the word "murder." I'd said it aloud and in my mind so many times by this point that the word was losing its punch, it no longer produced the same catch in my throat when I said the word out loud. Jackie was not even buried, and already I was beginning to develop a "matter-of-fact" approach to discussing what happened?

Marti took me away from that line of thought by switching to another topic and asking me about Nammy.

"I've gone over once," I told her. "But it's really, really sad and there's nothing you can say or do. The whole time I was there, Nammy just sat on her rocker out on the porch, kind of crying, and kind of talking to herself, and hardly even noticing that I was there. And it wasn't like I needed it or anything—but she didn't even offer any lemonade. She always brought Jackie and me lemonade whenever I came over before."

I shook my head in resignation.

"Jackie's mom will be coming back again from Tupelo for the funeral," I said. "I found that out at least. I hope I can meet her—I never saw her when she first came up the day after Jackie was assaulted."

"I want to meet her too," said Marti. "Let's make sure we do that tomorrow, okay? I want to introduce myself and give her a hug and tell her just how much I liked her grandson—and that she should be proud about the kind of boy he was because . . . " Marti's voice trailed away. I'd been staring straight at the wall, but now looked over to catch her profile. And I could see she was wrong—my sister still had plenty of tears left for Jackie.

"I just can't bear it, Mickey," she said, her chest heaving from the effort it took to speak through her new tears. "I keep telling myself to just hang on. That it will get easier somehow. But it's not. It's getting harder. And I can't stand it. It's like I've been dropped into some horrible, horrible nightmare except I'm beginning to realize that there's no waking up. I'm just 16 years old and now I can't even imagine a day for the rest of my life that I'll be happy. How could this happen? We didn't do anything wrong. We didn't do anything!"

I looked at my sister and listened to the despair and agony in her voice, and I understood what it meant to be totally, completely, undeniably helpless. A self-righteous bigot, with a heart full of hate, and a perverted sense of mission, had pushed her off a tall building—and all I could do was stand by and watch her plummet to the ground.

I learned that day that sometimes there is no answer to anguish. No response that can make sense of it. No gesture that brings comfort. All you can do is bear witness.

CHAPTER 40
SEPTEMBER 1, 1964

The day of Jackie's funeral dawned sunny and bright. My friend would be laid to rest under a deep blue, cloudless Alabama sky, perfect for tracking high fly balls in a back yard game of scrub.

Five McQuades attended. Marti and me, of course, plus Mom and Dad and Tom. Tom and I each wore black ties and white shirts. I wore my John Carroll blazer, even though it was going to be very hot standing in a cemetery with no shade.

Tom's reaction to Jackie's death was not easy to determine. He and I had not talked about it, even though we'd had more than a few opportunities at night when we were both heading to bed around the same time. In truth, we had not ever talked about the attack, and I was so mired in my own jumble of feelings that I hadn't noticed that day after day had passed without Tom and I connecting on the topic.

I do remember walking in on Mom and Tom at one point, surprising them in the kitchen. Mom was giving Tom one of her comforting hugs and I heard her say to him, "I know, Tommy, I know. Jackie was your friend too."

It occurred to me that maybe now, once the funeral was over, it might be easier for Tom and I to talk about what happened. I felt bad about not reaching out to him.

Marti wore a simple dark blue dress to the services; she did not own a black one. But she looked beautiful, like a young movie star, especially with sunglasses that she wore to combat the glare from the sun, and to hide the harsh redness of her eyes.

Out of 100 or more funeral-goers, we were the only white people who attended. Surprisingly, though, a number of people seemed to know who we were. Several adults came up and spoke to Mom or Dad, using those hushed, respectful funeral service whispers that prevented me from hearing exactly what was said. There were not that many kids our age in attendance; Jackie had never talked all that much about friends from school. But Scrambles was there. And Elliot. And LP.

I don't remember many details of the service itself, or much of what was said by whom. I just have images, a collection of mental snapshots, not arranged in any particular order, but clear and crisp and bright.

Colored people in groups of three or four, dressed in their finest, gathered around a plain coffin with metal handles on the sides that flashed brilliant reflections from the morning sun.

A tall, distinguished-looking colored preacher, with close-cropped graying hair, who prayed from an old, frayed black Bible. His eyes and face looked tired, like he had done too many of these services before.

Nammy in black, with a big navy blue handkerchief that she kept applying to her eyes to catch the tears before they ran down her face.

Five colored women in purple and gold choir robes, huddled, whispering to each other, standing to the left of the preacher.

A yellow-and-black butterfly, flitting around the crowd, and once settling down for a few brief seconds on the coffin, adding to the color of the day.

Two grave diggers in jeans and white t-shirts, well off to the side, leaning on their shovels, waiting patiently for us to leave so they could do their jobs.

A pretty middle-aged woman standing next to a girl of about ten, arms around each other, rarely interacting with any of the other mourners, though occasionally someone would come up to the two of them, say something briefly, place a hand on a shoulder or give a quick hug, then walk away.

My brother Tom, uncharacteristically leaning against my mother, trying hard not to cry, at least openly, but not entirely succeeding. My mother supplying tissues from her purse as needed.

Dad standing with Marti, holding hands, both staring straight ahead. They looked like pillars of strength—but I knew they were wobbly.

The preacher said some prayers, then read two passages from the Bible. Then the choir sang, softly, beautifully, "Amazing Grace" and "How Great Thou Art." After that, Jackie's uncle thanked everyone for coming and said a few words about what a good boy he was. He expressed his condolences to the middle-aged woman and her daughter, whom I now knew were Jackie's mom and sister. A couple of other people spoke as well, informally, just saying something nice that they remembered about Jackie. Then the preacher looked around the whole group of us, and asked if anyone else would like to step forward and help remember our "fallen and departed brother, Jackson Richard Thomas."

I raised my hand, like I was in school.

The preacher nodded at me to go ahead, then reminded me to speak up so that everyone could hear me.

"I just wanna . . . want to"—I corrected my diction—"say something about Jackie Thomas . . ."

I could feel Marti's eyes on me. I made sure to project my voice outward, as best I could.

"I did not know Jackie very long—we just met about a year ago when my family moved here from East Lake. We didn't see each other every day, and we didn't talk on the phone cause Jackie didn't have a phone, and sometimes we'd go a few weekends without getting together for a catch or to throw the football around."

For some reason, maybe to help me concentrate, I'd been looking up to the sky while I was talking. Now, gaining a little confidence, I looked more directly at the people around me.

"Over the past year, though, Jackie became my best friend. I never had one of those before. The thing is—and I don't know how he did it—but Jackie always made you feel good about yourself somehow.

"In all the time I knew him, Jackie and I only had one serious disagreement. I told him that Willie Mays was the best centerfielder in baseball, and he said it was Mickey Mantle." I paused for a second, remembering that conversation. "And I'm going to miss talking to him about stuff like that." I paused again. "I guess that's all I have to say."

I looked over at Marti, wondering if she wanted to speak herself, knowing that she would do a much better job than I just did. But she looked back at me and gave me a slight shake of her head, no, and so I looked at the preacher and said, "Thank you," then went to stand next to my twin.

The choir sang one more hymn, "Be Not Afraid," and then the preacher thanked everyone again for coming. People started to drift away, back across the grass, thick, but a little brown from the August heat. Out of the corner of my eye, I saw the two gravediggers straighten up. It was time for them to do their job.

Later that evening, on the steps, Marti asked me if I had spoken to Jackie's mother, because she had. And I said that I didn't because I did not know what to say. I always regretted not doing so.

* * * * *

My father called a surprise family meeting on Tuesday night after the funeral. He waited until after dinner, and then sent each of us older kids a note . . .

You are invited!
A Meeting of the McQuades:
Parents and Big Kids Only
9:30 p.m.
Family Room
Refreshments will be served.

Dad had done something similar—with written invitations—only a couple of times that I could remember. Once was when he felt like all of us older kids were being lazy, even Marti, and not helping Mom enough around the house and with the little kids. We had a short lecture, some discussion, a little bit of finger-pointing at Tom and me for being more lazy than the others. All in all, though, it was a good family come-together. We all promised Mom and Dad that we'd do better, and we did, for a while at least.

The other time was when he and Mom wanted to announce that another baby was coming, who turned out to be Carrie Ann. Tom and I liked that meeting better, especially when we factored in the hot fudge sundaes that Dad made us all as a post-meeting treat.

Tom told me that he thought this meeting might be about another brother or sister on the way, but that seemed unlikely to me. However, Tom actually seemed more interested in the refreshments than whatever news was going to be revealed.

"Apple pie a la mode," he said to me. "Wanna bet?" I passed on the wager, my dessert against his. Happening the same day as Jackie's funeral, I wasn't much in the mood for a big family thing, special treat or not. Plus, I was still a little worried about fall-out from my confrontation with Jessup

Rawlings. On top of that, I was generally exhausted. I had very little energy—and nothing much interested me.

After we were all gathered together and seated, Dad and Mom both stood up together, and held hands. Dad spoke clearly and quietly. It sounded to me like he wrote down what he wanted to say and memorized it.

"Thanks for coming, everyone," he began, as if he were starting one of his sales meetings at his company.

"This may come as a little bit of a shock to all of you, because we haven't been here that long, but the McQuade family will be moving again." He paused, then continued when he got no immediate reaction from any of us. "I've been talking with a company up in Hackensack, New Jersey, a much larger company than where I work now, and they've asked me to come up and take over as their new vice president of sales. So, your mom and I talked it over and decided this was a good thing for the family, and yesterday I told them 'Yes.'"

Total, stunned silence. I don't think we were as upset as we were surprised and shocked. I could tell by the looks on all our faces that not a one of us anticipated anything like this.

I don't think my father expected no response whatsoever—he actually looked a little befuddled, standing there with Mom. She took over.

"I think," she said, "we should start by congratulating your father. This is a very big promotion—"

Awkward responses from us kids, called out from where we sat:

"Way to go, Dad."

"Congratulations, Dad."

"Good job."

"That's fab, Dad." (That one came from Sheila.)

"Okay, Dad. Good job."

Silence returned to the room for a second, then David spoke up, talking to the rest of us kids as well as Mom and Dad. "I'm not digging this idea," he said, "cause I'm heading into my senior year at Carroll. But, where the family goes, I go. So let's hear the details."

"I hate this," said Tom. "Why do we have to move? We like it here. At least, we used to before . . . before what happened . . . to Jackie, I mean."

Marti and Sheila and I said nothing—but multiple thoughts were running through my head. One of them was *Heck, yeah, let's move! Jackie's gone, Yvonne hates me, I hate Rawlings and can't stand the sight of him—let's move to New Jersey!* Right after that came *Hackensack, what a dumb name.* And then . . . *Wait a minute. Where's Hackensack? Is it close to Vineland, where Susan lives? I need a map.*

Dad spoke again. "We know it's sudden, but my new job starts in two weeks. The company will help us find and rent a house until we can get settled up there. I'm going to go up this weekend and try to get some things organized. We need to figure out where we're going to live temporarily, and where all you kids will be going to school. But the way it looks right now, we'll be loading up the cars and heading north—just like we did on summer vacation—in just a couple of weeks."

"What about all our stuff?" asked Tom.

"Movers again," said Mom, "but this time they'll be doing almost all the packing. We'll each take one suitcase in the cars -- and the movers will pack everything else and deliver it to our rental house in New Jersey."

"Do I have to go?" asked Sheila.

What? I asked myself. *Of course you have to go, Sheila. We're a family. We stick together.*

"We'd like you to come with us, sweetie," Mom said, with just a little catch in her voice. "But you're twenty now, and working a full time job. Your Dad and I think it might be time to let you make your own decision about this."

Whoa! What's this?!?

"I don't want to move," said Tom, obstinate as always, perhaps hoping that his complaining might have an effect on the final decision. Which I was sure had already been made.

"We understand, Tommy," said Mom, her voice sympathetic. "The hardest part of this decision for your Dad and me was considering how this move would affect you kids."

"Yeah, but me the worst," said Tom. I loved my brother, but he always had a heightened sense of his pain compared to the rest of the world.

"I knew this news would be tough for you, Tom," said Dad.

"So, why?" asked Tom. "Why do we have to move?"

"Because, in the long run," my father said, "this move will make things better for all of us. We had to think of all eleven McQuades. Besides," he added, "there are some good things about moving. We'll be closer to the Jersey Shore for another vacation. And we'll probably be living within an hour or so of Yankee Stadium."

Tom didn't say anything to that. He clearly wasn't happy—but now at least he had a couple good things to balance out the bad things about the move.

Throughout the whole discussion, neither Marti nor I had spoken up, other than to congratulate Dad. Mom looked toward both of us and asked, "So, what about you two? What do you think? How do you feel about this?"

I kind of shrugged my shoulders in a six-of-one, half-dozen-of-another way and mumbled, "It's good." No one believed me, of course, though I wasn't really lying. Truth was, I was so tired of emotional ups and downs that I didn't know how I felt. Lukewarm positive was about the best I could muster. At least it was an authentic lukewarm positive.

I looked over at my twin, saw in her face a mental struggle with exactly how she wanted to respond, perhaps whether she wanted to respond at all. I could not guess what she was going to say.

But when she spoke, there was no hesitancy in her voice.

"I hate Birmingham," she began.

"Hey," Tom protested, before quickly being shushed by Mom.

"I didn't use to hate it," she said, and looked over at Tom, "but I was never proud of it. Never. And I know," she continued, with the rest of us falling totally silent and attentive, "I know that there are good people and bad people everywhere. In every town, in every city, all across the country. People who love and people who hate. But this place, this city, just has too many of the hating kind of people. Too many people—like Jessup Rawlings—that have been that way for a long, long time, and they teach hate to their children, and they hope that it will live in them, so that they will pass it on to their kids."

Marti looked over at me.

"And after what has happened here, to me and to all of us, I think I have to go live somewhere else, or I will start hating all of them with an intensity I will never be able to smother, and I will end up as bad as them, or worse."

She looked at me again. I nodded support.

"I'm ready to go," Marti said. "I want to leave this house, and this neighborhood, and this city. The sooner, the better."

Her last four words came out almost indistinguishable from the emotion that overwhelmed the room, like a tsunami. Mom stepped forward, and Marti let her wrap her arms around her, and Marti burrowed her head in Mom's neck.

There was no signal or anything, but we all stood at that point, and moved closer together, toward Mom and Marti in our center. Hands were extended, soft words were spoken. The herd gathered in a loose circle to protect its wounded member.

We stood there, each with our own thoughts. And Tom whispered to me, "I don't even feel like apple pie anymore."

CHAPTER 41
SEPTEMBER 19, 1964

Something about moving vans: Whether they have seen years of service, or they are brand spanking new, no matter the make and model, they all sound like old men getting out of bed in the morning. They groan, they wheeze, they grumble.

I know this because the van that lumbered up Lynn Acres Drive that Saturday morning in September looked much, much different—newer, shinier, sleeker—than the moving van that had transported all the family possessions from East Lake to Roebuck, just 455 days previously. Yet, the two sounded like twins.

I watched from our family room window as the driver hopped down from the cab and went to speak with my father and David, who were waiting on the carport.

The rest of the McQuades were gathered in the family room with me, oddly calm and totally prepared for the day ahead. Carrie Ann—sitting on Sheila's lap—was singing a song to herself; the rest of the little kids were sitting on their suitcases, packed with enough clothing to last them the trip from Birmingham to Fair Lawn, New Jersey, where we'd all live in a motel for a couple of days until the van with our stuff caught up with us. Both station wagons were already packed for the trip, except for the little kids' suitcases that Mom kept out because she wanted to take a picture. Marti and I had helped Dad pack the cars with everything else the night before.

Dad and David were talking to the movers. Dad was providing last minute instructions before we left, and explaining that David would be at the house with them until the house was empty, the truck was fully loaded and it was on its way. In the end, Sheila decided to move with the family to New Jersey. But Mom and Dad had arranged for David to stay in Birmingham for his senior year, and live with another family, the Andrews.

I sat on a folding chair and surveyed the scene around me. Another big family adventure was about to begin, but nobody seemed particularly enthused. I felt dried-up, the way an orange peel gets when it sits on a counter too long after it's been pulled away from the fruit.

I was hoping that, once we got going, we'd get a little spark. Mom and Dad had actually planned a nice trip for all of us, starting with a visit in a few hours to Rock City in Chattanooga, a rock garden tourist destination famous throughout the South for its ubiquitous advertising campaign—white lettering painted on the roofs of barns, and on little birdhouses, everywhere.

For now, though, we seemed a bit somber—though much of that may have been simple physical exhaustion from all the preparation activity of the past several days.

Mentally, I was ready to go. I'd done all my good-byes, received all my good wishes from teachers, exchanged all my promises to write and visit with friends. Marti and I had attended the first two days of school at John Carroll—after that, we'd stayed home to help Mom. All of us kids would be a little more than a month late starting at new schools up in New Jersey, but Mom and Dad felt confident we'd catch up quickly. We were, after all, McQuades.

A week previous, I'd wrangled some free time and managed to meet

Davis Williams for a big lunch at Queen of Catfish in East Lake. He insisted on treating me. "You can pay for me sometime when I come up and visit you in New Jersey," he said. "Not sure what we'll have—but I guarantee you it won't be fried catfish as good as we get right here. You know," he added reflectively, "they might not even have catfish in New Jersey."

I'd also had a good-bye meeting, of a sort, with Detective Martino. Dad had informed him that the family would be moving. He wanted to be sure the detective knew that we were leaving the area, but that any or all of us would be available if needed, if they caught Jackie's attackers. For some reason, though, Detective Martino felt it necessary to talk to me personally. He'd driven out to the house late Wednesday afternoon to see me.

I asked him to come in, but he suggested we chat in the back yard, if I didn't mind. We sat on an old picnic bench, both of us staring out into the woods, and didn't say anything for a few minutes.

Then Detective Martino stirred himself and spoke.

"I'm sorry about where things are," he said. "I was hoping that we'd have gotten some kind of a break in the case, and I'm still hoping for that, but it just hasn't happened yet."

"Yessir," I said.

"And I know this is frustrating for you, cause you're convinced about Jessup Rawlings, and I've pushed him as hard as I can, but he hasn't broken. He's got an alibi, and he's sticking to it."

"Yessir, I understand your predicament," I said, though I really didn't. In my mind, if there were any justice in the world, then somebody would listen to me. I was the witness they needed. I saw the whole thing, I heard Rawlings voice, I would swear to the fact that it was Rawlings on the highest stack of Bibles they could find. "But I still don't understand why not a single person will believe me."

"Fact is," said Martino, "lots of people do believe you. Including me.

Maybe me most of all. And what I want you to know, son, is that I'm not giving up. I won't quit on this case, I won't quit on your friend. Until we can nail the men who did this, this will be an open investigation. You have to trust me on that."

I turned my head, looked directly into Detective Martino's eyes.

For a brief few seconds, it was not a connection between a seasoned detective and a 16-year-old. It was a moment of understanding between two men who cared a lot about the very same thing.

"I trust you, Detective Martino," I said. "But I do not trust the Birmingham Police. I don't trust a city and I don't trust a country and I don't trust a world that knows the truth but won't act on it. And now my friend is dead, and all that will be left of his story is some stupid file that will get shoved to the back of some rusty file cabinet. And it'll say 'Deceased: Jackie Thomas and Assailant: Unknown.' And Jessup Rawlings will just go on living his stupid life without a worry in the world. And that'll be that."

I knew that I would have been in big trouble if my dad had heard those words coming from me. They were mean-spirited. And disrespectful. And full of hate.

Martino heard them, and I could tell they hurt, and I felt a little bit bad about that.

He looked at me for a few seconds without speaking, perhaps turning over in his mind exactly what he wanted to say. And then he spoke in a hushed voice, almost a whisper. "That will never happen," he said, "I promise you. I will keep the Thomas case on the top of my desk from now until we can prove the identities of the men who did this. I swear it."

I wanted to look Martino in the eye, but his voice and his manner were too intense. I glanced at my feet. "I think I need to go in now, sir," I said. "I need to help my mom with dinner."

"You go right ahead," Martino said as he stood up. "Thanks for taking a few minutes with me."

On Friday night—just before our last family dinner in our Lynn Acres house—I'd also managed to squeeze in a visit to Nammy.

I don't think she saw me coming. I found her sitting on her rocker on the porch, staring off into space. I could tell she was glad to see me, but she didn't get up, didn't make the traditional Nammy fuss. She just told me to come over to her and give her a hug. So I did.

I sat near her, on the steps, staring out into the front yard where Jackie and I had played so often. At one point, I tried to count up just how many times we'd gotten together out there, playing scrub or just having a catch, goofing off, talking about nothing, waiting until Nammy called out to us to come get some lemonade or cookies. I thought about the day I'd first met Nammy. Then, on a sudden impulse, I turned to her and asked who she thought might win the World Series this year. She told me she didn't rightly know.

After a while, I got up, went over to her, and gave her another big hug. "Moving to New Jersey tomorrow, " I said.

"I know you are, child," she answered. "You take care of yourself up there. Take care of your sister too. And that whole big family of yours."

"I will, Nammy. You take care of yourself too."

She didn't say anything to that, just gave me a weak smile. I nodded and headed for home.

My recollection about my visit with Nammy was interrupted by Dad and David coming through the door. "Let's go, McQuades," Dad said to the room. "The movers know what to do—and David will be here for any questions they might have. Time for us to hit the road—we're going to see Rock City and have a picnic lunch up there too!"

"But first," Mom said, "Line up and say good-bye to your brother."

All of us kids knew this moment was coming, but it didn't make things easy. We weren't sure when we'd see our brother again, maybe Christmas time. Maybe not until he graduated from high school.

It was tough on all of us kids. None of us liked the fact that David would not be with us on our adventure, and in our new home. For the first time ever, the McQuades would not all be living under the same roof.

But it was toughest on Mom. I could tell by the way she hugged him and whispered in his ear. I could tell by the way she wiped her eyes as we headed out to the cars.

It didn't take long to load us into the already packed station wagons. Mom and Sheila were in one with the little kids. Marti and Tom and I in the other car with Dad. It was a lot less crowded than when we took the one station wagon on our vacation to Sea Isle.

As we headed down Lynn Acres Drive, I looked to my right, toward the Rawlings' house. Their car was in the driveway—but no one was visible.

Marti caught my eye as I turned away from the window. We looked at each other. She'd been pleased to hear Detective Martino's promise when I'd told her about it, but she didn't much believe anything would come of it. "Evil men do evil things," she'd told me. "And sometimes, no matter how much you want justice, it just doesn't happen. And all you're left with is anger, and sadness, and hate." I'd nodded when she told me that. I knew all about the hate thing. I'd been living with it for a few weeks now.

The car accelerated down Lynn Acres Drive. Marti didn't speak, neither did I. But I'm pretty sure she knew and understood what was going on inside me. Just like I understood, pretty much, what was going on with her. That's the way it is with twins sometimes.

CHAPTER 42
AUGUST 28, 2000

I boarded my flight home to Boston on Monday morning feeling surprisingly content, like I'd accomplished something. I'd come back to Birmingham with one small but important task to perform. But it felt to me like I'd done a lot more.

The flight attendant was a smiling young woman with a nametag that read Bette Jane and a wonderful lilt to her southern accent. "Are y'all coming or going?" she asked me pleasantly, stopping in her walk up and down the aisles to greet her passengers.

"Heading home," I told her, in a voice that clearly sounded more Boston than Birmingham.

"Something about you," she said, "I was thinking you might not be from around here."

"I lived here in the 60s," I said, "long before you were born. Back in the day of Bull Connor."

"I don't know who that is," she said sweetly, "but I hope y'all had a nice visit. Can I get you a pillow, or anything to read?"

"I'm good," I replied. "I have a book with me that I should finish before we get to Atlanta. Hope so anyway—I've been meaning to read this thing ever since I was a kid."

Bette Jane smiled and moved down the aisle to greet another passenger.

I settled comfortably into my seat, pulled the book from my briefcase, but then immediately closed my eyes as I reflected on my last few days.

* * * *

Last Friday morning had arrived full of sticky, steamy Alabama humidity, the kind that turns your shirt collar damp in seconds. It reminded me of the oppressive mugginess the night Jackie was attacked, thirty-six years and two days ago.

My original morning plan was to find myself a little local café and order a huge Birmingham breakfast, with eggs, bacon, greasy potatoes if available, plus sausage gravy and biscuits—no grits, thank you very much. However, the soupiness of the day killed my appetite for anything so heavy. I decided instead to buy some ice-cold orange juice at the nearby supermarket and then eat later, after my visit with Detective Martino.

Sitting on a bench outside the store in the shadow of a large oak that provided shade but no relief from the moisture-laden air, I re-read the letter that I'd received a few weeks earlier from Martino's daughter.

Dear Mr. McQuade:

My father asked me to write to you and let you know that recent DNA tests, performed at the request of the Birmingham Police Department, have confirmed the presence of Mr. Jessup Rawlings in the August 23, 1964 hate-crime attack on Mr. Jackson Thomas of which you are familiar. He understands from contacts in the police department that the case files on the attack and the murder of Mr. Thomas will now be amended to name Mr. Rawlings as the principal assailant in the attack, though no further criminal action will be taken due to Mr. Rawlings' demise.

I hope that this letter finds you and your family in good health; my father sends his regards. Should you wish to contact him directly, he is now living in Hoover, Alabama at the Fairview Senior Residences, Parkinson's Disease Care Unit.

Sincerely,

Ms. Theresa Martino

As I sat there, I tried to recall each one of my decades old conversations with Detective Martino, and I re-felt the hopelessness and frustration that had consumed me every time we talked. I guess thirty-six years mellows a man; I no longer blamed Martino for the inability of the Birmingham Police to bring Rawlings to justice. And now I had to admit, however he'd accomplished it, Martino had kept his promise. Jackie's case had not been forgotten.

When I reached the Fairview facility around 11 a.m., I was escorted to a sitting room and asked to wait. A few minutes later, an attendant brought Detective Martino into the room in a wheelchair. Martino looked a little tired, and old—I was guessing his age at close to 80 though he looked much older. However, in spite of what might have been late-stage Parkinson's, he seemed clear-minded. He knew who I was.

"It's been a long, long time, son," he said. "You're looking well."

"We're both a little older," I said, "but we're still hanging in there, aren't we?"

Martino laughed. "Kind of, but that's life. Getting old with Parkinson's is not a game for sissies."

I nodded understanding. For a moment, I could not think of anything else to say to a man I really didn't know at all but who'd played such a huge role in my life.

"Sit awhile," Martino said, "and tell me about your big family. We can catch up on the Rawlings business in a bit."

I sat, and we chatted, though I did most of the talking. I gave Martino an update on my parents and each one of my brothers and sisters, capsule commentaries, who was doing what. He was most interested in Marti and her work as an assistant DA in New York. I bragged about her.

"I knew she was a tough kid," Martino said. "During those few weeks, she was a battered young woman, and you could tell she blamed herself, but she never broke. Never. Somehow she held herself together."

I nodded agreement, and for a while we both sat quietly, lost in memories that still had the power to wound. Martino broke the silence.

"DNA profiling is a miracle," he said. "I remember when they first started talking about it, back in the 80s. I thought the test results would never hold up in court. What'd I know?"

"Was the Rawlings test definitive?" I asked. "It's not something that some fancy lawyer could challenge, right? Although I'm not sure who would want to get involved in that. Maybe Rawlings' family, wherever they are."

"This is America," said Martino. "Anybody can challenge anything. But the results of the testing, from what I understand, were as definitive as DNA fingerprinting—that's what they call it down at the station—can get."

"You kept your promise," I said. "I don't know if anybody else in the world cares, except me and Marti, and I guess Jackie's family. Did someone get in touch with them?"

"Yes. They were notified officially."

"I flew down here to say thank-you in person, Detective Martino."

My statement seemed to bring on some sudden confusion, and I didn't know if it was what I said, or the Parkinson's acting up. "Flew down? From where? Really?"

I was ready to start explaining, but I decided not to. It wasn't important. The important stuff had already been accomplished. Somehow, even after his retirement, even after his disease and his confinement in this senior care facility, Martino had apparently been enough of a nudge to keep Jackie's case from being totally forgotten. Without him, I was convinced that the DNA profile on Jessup Rawlings would never have been run. And so, after thirty-six years, it seemed appropriate to come back and say thank you on behalf of my friend, Jackie Thomas, a baseball-loving colored kid that had never wronged a soul, but who had kissed my sister, and died for it.

"Time for me to go, Detective Martino," I said. Martino glanced at me, still appearing befuddled, and nodded. I put my hand on his shoulder for a brief few seconds, then left.

* * * * *

I spent much of Saturday visiting Davis Williams and his family of five. Davis and I had stayed in touch over the years, the only friend from my Birmingham days with whom I'd maintained any kind of communication. Davis was a history teacher and a track coach at Hoover High School. His teams were typically ranked in the top ten in the state and he was especially recognized for developing middle-distance runners, for the 400- and 800-meter races. Davis himself had been a pretty good 440-yard sprinter in high school and college.

I met his three kids and wife, Tina, who made Bar-B-Q pork for our midday meal. I told her it was just as good, maybe better, than the Bar-B-Q I remembered from Johnny Ray's. She liked that.

After our two o'clock dinner, with kids playing around us, Davis and I spent a couple of hours in his back yard reminiscing about the old days and catching up on the recent ones. I told him all about my brothers and sisters; he told me about his family as well as all the changes that had taken place in Birmingham. One of the biggest was that the steel mills, which had once dominated both the economy and the rhythms of the city, were all but gone.

On a separate note, I laughed when he told me what happened to each and every one of the Fabulous Four, none of whom he had ever managed to date in his years at John Carroll.

Davis turned to the subject of my twin sister.

"Married with two kids," he said, "and a New York City attorney. Wow."

"Prosecuting attorney," I reminded him. "She goes after the bad guys. And gets a lot of them. We're all very proud of her."

"Does she ever . . . I mean . . . prosecute . . ."

I guessed what Davis was driving at. "Yes, sometimes she has been involved in prosecuting hate crimes. Skinheads. Aryan Nation. There's still more of that going on than most people know."

"Good that she's doing that," Davis said. "Good. That's something, I guess."

"Sometimes they get away," I said. "Like Jessup Rawlings. Until they don't." I took a few minutes to tell Davis about my visit with Detective Martino.

"But . . . y'all know. . ." Davis asked, "y'all know what happened to Rawlings, right? Marti knows, right?"

I nodded. "We didn't hear right away, but then one of Marti's friends from Birmingham contacted her and said he was shot in some kind of a hold-up."

"Wrong place, wrong time," said Davis. "Innocent bystander. Goes into a liquor store on a Friday night for a bottle of something, winds up dead on the floor. I guess you didn't see the newspaper stories?"

"Never did," I said.

"Crazy situation," said Davis. "The first reports that came out said the robbers were two African Americans. Turns out it was a white guy and a black guy. And the white guy was the one that shot and killed Rawlings.

Karma?"

I shrugged my shoulders. There wasn't much else to say. I still hated Jessup Rawlings—and how he affected or destroyed the lives of so many people. But, for some reason, after two days in Birmingham, and my visit with Martino, I could feel the intensity of my hate beginning to wane. My therapist would be pleased.

Davis and I sat quietly for a moment. Then he stirred. "I think it's time for Tina's famous peach cobbler. What do y'all say to that?"

"Sounds great to me," I said. "Haven't had anything famous to eat for quite some time."

* * * * *

The next morning, I got up early, enjoyed a wonderful Sunday morning breakfast, then decided to treat myself to a solitary, nostalgic tour of the town. I cruised Highland Avenue on the Southside, where my high school used to be, then headed out to Lakeshore Parkway to see the new school. I drove by the city's well-known statue of Vulcan at one point, squinting into the August sunlight to see the world's largest cast iron sculpture, still wondering how a bare-bottomed statue was ever approved by Birmingham's conservative city council.

After that, I drove the old neighborhoods, past St. Barnabas, past our old house on 80th Place South. I got lost a couple of times, and marveled at the changes that had taken place. Throughout my drive, I kept wishing Marti was with me.

Eventually, my haphazard wanderings took me out past the Roebuck section of the city. I laughed out loud when I saw the sign that my mother loved so much, the one on Five Mile Road that read Five Mile Baptist Church, One Mile. It was the kind of oddity that delighted Mary McQuade—

and she'd always commented on the sign's wording whenever we'd driven past it.

I slowed, and took a deep breath, before turning off Killough Springs Highway and driving up the hill, past the house on Lynn Acres Drive. I could not help but look to my left to see what the Rawlings house looked like after all these years. The garage door was open—but it looked a lot different from what I remembered. Smaller somehow.

I turned back to look at our old house and, for a moment or two, considered knocking on the front door, and asking if I could see the house, and walk around the yard. But something kept me from it. The flood of memories I was experiencing was powerful and disturbing; I was not sure how much more I could handle.

Finally, with one last look at the house and carport, I headed back down the hill and drove to the cemetery where Jackie Thomas was buried. That Sunday, August 27, was the 36th anniversary of the day Jackie died, alone in a bed in the one hospital in the city that had allowed African Americans— the people we used to call "colored"—to practice medicine.

I located the cemetery more easily than expected, then stopped by the office to get directions to Jackie's gravesite from an elderly black man. He spoke half to himself as he squinted into a dim computer screen to review a dense spreadsheet. "Thomas, Thomas," he said. "Gloria Thomas, Henry Thomas, here it is . . . Jackson Thomas. Interred September 1, 1964. That right?" He turned his head toward me when he asked, looking over his eyeglasses, and I nodded yes. I wondered if he was curious as to why a middle-aged white man who clearly was from out of town wanted to visit the grave of a black teenager who'd died 36 years ago. If so, he didn't ask.

I parked a couple of hundred feet from where I thought Jackie's grave was located. No one else was around—it was quiet for a Sunday.

I walked across the well-cut grass—strangely still green despite the

Alabama summertime heat—and located Jackie's headstone. I'd heard it was purchased with donations from the community and Jackie's church. A nice gesture, since I did not recall Jackie or Nammy as regular churchgoers.

I stood in front of Jackie's grave, silent, staring at a piece of granite but looking into the past. And found myself immersed in both memories and feelings that I'd kept on the shelf for a long, long time.

I had no idea how long I stood there. My thoughts were not coherent: I examined them the way you go through a drawer of unmatched socks, pulling out one, then another, occasionally finding two that go together.

And then, with no particular notion serving as a catalyst to the moment, I knew it was time to go. I felt like expressing something to Jackie aloud, and was considering what I might say, when I was surprised by a voice that came from behind me.

"I'm sorry," I heard, "for intruding. Could I . . ."

I turned to look at the speaker, an attractive black woman, dressed in stylish slacks and a sleeveless summer top, holding a bouquet of flowers. She stepped past me, knelt down at Jackie's gravestone, pulled a few stray weeds from the ground in front, tossing them off to the side, then placed the flowers delicately on the ground. She stood up and turned back toward me.

"I didn't mean to surprise you," she said, "I waited awhile." She pointed toward a late-model car, parked behind mine, that I'd never even heard pull up.

"I'm sorry," I apologized. "I'm just leaving."

"Did you know my brother well?" she asked.

I put two and two together. "You're Carmella," I said. "Jackie's sister. From Tupelo."

She nodded.

I responded to her question. "I used to live near Jackie and Nammy. On Lynn Acres Drive. Jackie and I used to play together, baseball, football, you know."

I could see her mind processing what I told her. Understanding dawned. "You're Mickey," she said.

"That's me."

"But I thought you moved away," Carmella said. "To New York or Chicago or somewhere like that."

"Boston's where I live now. I'm just down for a visit. So I thought I'd stop by and pay my respects."

"I try to come up from Tupelo every year on the anniversary of Jackie's death," Carmella said. "Just to leave him some flowers. He didn't even like flowers especially. But," she shrugged her shoulders, "that's what I do."

We stood silent for a few moments, both lost in reflections, and not knowing exactly what else to say to each other. I could have asked her what life was like in Tupelo, and how her mother was doing, and maybe whatever happened to Nammy. But I didn't, and she did not ask me any of those small talk kinds of questions either.

As I stood there, though, I thought she might be feeling what I was feeling, that it was good to see someone else, at this place, thinking about Jackie, thirty-six years after his death.

We stood together a while longer, both staring at the gravestone and the bouquet of flowers.

"I think I'll go now," I said, breaking our individual reveries.

"It was good to see you, Mickey."

"It was good to see you, Carmella."

Then I turned and walked back to my car, leaving Jackie's sister standing by his grave.

I turned to look back just before opening the car door, and Carmella waved at me, and then yelled "Thanks, Mickey!"

I waved back, wondering for a brief moment what specifically she might be thanking me for, and realizing that it did not matter.

"Bye," I yelled before getting into the car.

* * * * *

The captain's voice came across the speakers in the plane, advising us that we had just touched down in Atlanta. I would catch an afternoon flight to Boston.

My timing was good. I'd finished my book, held it in one hand while I grabbed my small duffel bag from under the seat in front of me. I still held the book in one hand as I approached the plane's exit. The flight attendant who'd spoken to me earlier smiled again, then asked if I'd finished my reading.

"I did," I said. Then, impulsively, I gave the paperback to her. "Here, read it—you might like it."

Surprised, she took the book from me without even looking at the title.

"What kind of book is it?" she asked.

I thought for a moment. "Kind of like a history book," I said. "It was written way back in the fifties or sixties. It's called *Black Like Me*."

"Never heard of it," she said, "but thank you. Thank you very much."

"You're welcome, Bette Jane," I answered, then turned to head up the jetway. I still had another flight to go, and I couldn't wait to get home.

The End

ABOUT THE AUTHOR

Mike Diccicco graduated from La Salle College in Philadelphia with a degree in English and a burning desire to write award-winning radio commercials and TV spots. Today, after more than four decades in the advertising business, Mike has turned his energies toward the writing of fiction. *Beyond All Sense and Reason* is Mike's debut novel.

Using a character from the book, Mike wrote a short story entitled *The Bus Rider*, which was awarded fifth prize among 6700 entries in a national Writer's Digest competition.

In addition to short stories, two of which are published on his website, Mike is currently working on a second novel. Married since 1975 to his wife Fran, the couple splits their time between their home in Pennsylvania and their condo on the Jersey shore. They have a daughter, Mariliz, and a son, Michael.

mikedicciccowords.com